I0713729

ALSO BY M. MALONE

THE ALEXANDERS

One More Day
The Things I Do for You
All I Want is You
All I Need is You
Just One Thing
One More Chance

BLUE-COLLAR BILLIONAIRES

Tank
Finn
Gabe
Zack
Luke
Blue-Collar Christmas

MESS WITH ME

Beg Me
Ask Me
Need Me
Want Me

"I don't even like you."

He didn't have the decency to be offended by the mean words. Instead they made him smile.

"You don't have to. I can like you enough for the both of us."

I melted a little at that before grasping desperately for the last bit of resolve I had left. He didn't get to do this to me.

Wasn't there some rule that you weren't allowed to be evil your whole life and then turn around and say the most unexpectedly sweet things?

He kissed me again but lower this time, his lips against my cheek. "What about now? Getting warmer?"

"I still don't like you and we are not friends," I insisted but my voice was a little too breathy to be believable.

Hendrix clearly heard it because he gave me that cocky grin I loved and hated. "We don't have to be friends for me to make you scream, right?"

My mouth went dry. "I can't disagree."

"Good. Let me know if you still hate me in an hour."

youRUIN EVERYTHING

NYT & USA TODAY BESTSELLING AUTHOR

M|MALONE

contents

youRUIN
EVERY
THING

one

. . .

CHARLOTTE

When I was a little girl, my gran used to say that life was like cake because even the bad ones still had icing. Usually, she'd say this when life had dealt out another disappointment.

Sorry if we're out of ice cream, but that just means we have more room for pie!

Sorry if the boy next door won't play with you, but that means we have time to invite your best friend for a sleepover!

Over the years, as I got older, I realized that she was trying to teach me to roll with life's disappointments. Her motto was that a little bit of creativity and a positive attitude could transform even the worst situation into a blessing.

Small victories, she'd say. *Celebrate the small victories.*

I loved Gran more than just about anyone else in the world, but over the last month it had become abundantly clear that she'd lied to me.

Every cake didn't have icing.

There wasn't always a pot of gold at the end of the rainbow.

Sometimes things just sucked.

Like discovering my would-be haven needed its own rescue.

"It's a wreck!"

"What did you just say?"

I jumped at the sound of Retta's voice in my ear. She'd called a few minutes ago, but I'd instantly forgotten she was on the phone when I pulled into the driveway of my Gran's house. I was so distracted that I took my foot off the brake and the car lurched forward.

"Oh crap!" I quickly put the car in park.

Retta's voice boomed through my headphones. "Can we just back up for a second? Where are you?"

"My Gran Grace's house."

"The gran who died when you were in high school?"

"Yes."

Retta sounded thoroughly confused. "Didn't she live in the middle of bumfucksville?

"Virginia."

"Isn't that what I said?"

Despite the circumstances, that got a smile out of me. "Retta, someone was supposed to maintain the place, but the house is a mess."

"Charlie, what happened with Aaron?"

The mention of my ex was enough to distract me from the shambles of my grandmother's house. Aaron had seemed like the perfect boyfriend: successful, romantic, and supportive of my career. I hadn't realized until too late that his idea of happily-ever-after had not extended to supporting me when my family got bumped from A-list to D-list.

"You thought he was going to propose over lunch and then everything happened with the police. I know the last few days have been crazy."

I got out of the car and stood at the edge of the yard. My

eyes didn't know where to land. They moved from the house's dingy siding, to the cracked asphalt on the driveway to the unkempt yard. The Knock Out roses that had once been Gran's pride and joy were now an overgrown tangle of thorns and brush. Then I turned toward the house and threw my hands up.

"I mean, even the steps are rotting!"

Retta paused. "Everyone who showed up to work this morning got told to go back home. I started sending out resumes."

My stomach twisted, equal parts sympathy and shame. None of this was my fault, but I still felt responsible in some way. After all, my stepfather hadn't just screwed over investors: he'd betrayed hundreds of employees who relied on his company—our family's company—to provide a stable, honest job.

I kicked at a patch of weeds. "He was packing, Retta."

"*Packing?* Oh."

"Yeah. He said he thought I wouldn't be home for a while."

She groaned. "*Now* is it okay to say that I really don't like the guy?"

———

As I entered my grandmother's house, I switched on the lights and took in the full effect of years of neglect. The dim overhead lighting didn't do much to cut through the gloom. Even from a distance I could tell the rose-patterned wallpaper was peeling and the air smelled stale, like no one had been here for a very long time.

Suddenly I was seeing this room as it was in summers past: alive with the sound of Gran's laughter and my excitement, back when the floors were meticulously swept and the candy dish on the coffee table was always full.

I dropped my bag on the floor, instantly regretting that move when a small cloud of dust bloomed at my feet. The furniture was covered with white sheets at least but there was a thick layer of dust on every other surface, so much of it that it swirled in the air every time I moved.

After driving for six hours straight I'd hoped to be able to sit down and relax. Maybe even take a nap.

However, as I looked around the shrouded room, all hopes of that disappeared. If it looked this bad down here, it was unlikely the upstairs would be any better.

Gran's favorite picture of Billie Holiday still held pride of place in the entry hall. Like everything else it was covered in a thick layer of dust. I touched the picture with two fingers just the way Gran always had.

"Nice to see you again, Lady Day."

Exhaustion dogged my steps as I walked toward the kitchen. A cobweb brushed my cheek and I shuddered. This was supposed to be the easy part. When things had fallen apart in New York, I'd left thinking that at least here I could get my bearings.

It turned out that things were falling apart everywhere.

After brushing dust off one of the wooden bar stools, I sat down. The house was eerily quiet and was going to take a lot of work to clean up, but I was still grateful to be here. It had the most important thing I needed after all.

Solitude.

Everything in my life was a mess and handling it with an audience had just made it all so much worse. Not just the obvious things like watching my stepfather being escorted away in handcuffs or having to console my mother as she drank her way through breakfast, lunch, and dinner. But it was the little things that got to me.

Coming home to my own apartment and finding my boyfriend packing.

The loud silence of all the "friends" who had apparently blocked my number.

Discovering that my entire perfect life was a fraud.

"Home again," I said.

Saying the words out loud made it real. After ten years I was finally back in the only place I'd ever felt like I belonged.

Looking around at Gran's house, hundreds of memories rushed through my head. Singing in the kitchen while she whipped up pancakes. Sliding down the hallway in my socks. Cooking dinner side by side while she told me all the gossip going around town. Those summers with Gran were the best of my life and when my mom finally let me live in Violet Ridge year-round, I thought I'd had it made. Then Gran died and my perfect life went up in smoke.

I should have learned by now that perfect didn't last.

My (hasty) plan had been to spend the next month getting the house ready for my mom and sister to move in. But I'd envisioned some light cleaning and decorating, maybe purchasing new furniture for the bedrooms. Not a full-scale renovation.

No, there was no icing here.

I sighed and picked up my handbag. First, I needed to go back into town and get some cleaning supplies. Then I could tackle making the main rooms habitable.

The nap would have to wait.

———

Three hours later, the sun was shining directly through the windows I'd just cleaned, brightening the entire room. Once I'd gone back to town and managed to find not only cleaning supplies but coffee, my mood had improved considerably.

Violet Ridge was different now. The town even had a Facebook page! The house was a little more run-down than I'd expected but it was nothing I couldn't handle. If I'd learned anything over the past few days, it was that I was much stronger than I'd given myself credit for. Rolling with the punches was kind of my specialty.

At least this time I was on my own turf.

"Knock, knock."

I looked up at the sound. A woman poked her head around the door. She had pink-tipped hair that swirled wildly around her head and a grin so large it almost swallowed the rest of her face.

"Well, damn. It's a hot mess in here."

Santana Evers had never been one to mince words, and I was grateful to find that hadn't changed.

"Tana!"

The word was swallowed as she pulled me into a hug and just about squeezed the life out of me. The stress that had dogged me for the past three hundred miles melted away. She let out a squeak when I suddenly hugged her back, almost lifting her off the ground.

"Charlie Monroe, in the flesh. Girl, you look *good*." She fluffed the ends of my hair that I'd recently started wearing in its natural curly state.

"I'm just trying to keep up with you, Miss Instagram."

She preened. Tana had a beauty salon in town and had achieved some modest social media fame posting pictures of the rainbow highlights she'd done for her clients. We'd kept in contact over the years but trying to maintain a friendship long distance was a challenge. Video chats and watching the highlights of each other's lives online just wasn't the same.

"Are you really here for the whole summer?"

"And next year, too. I figured we could stay here until we get back on our feet. But I have to admit that I wasn't expecting...this."

Her eyes followed mine, taking in the dilapidated interior, the peeling wallpaper, the musty smell, and the general feeling of doom. My earlier unease returned full force as I thought of all the things I'd have to do to get the house ready before Mom and Billie arrived. It had been a shock when Gran left it to me instead of my mom but then again, she knew what this place had always meant to me. Not to mention that my mother wasn't exactly known for being good with money.

If she'd inherited the house, she would have sold it immediately and blown the money in a few years. That wasn't what Gran would have wanted.

She'd always hoped I could bring my own kids there someday. It had sounded like such a far-off thing back then but now that I was moving back to Violet Ridge, I had to admit how much I'd hoped for that, too.

"Well, I'll help you in any way that I can. Although I probably won't be much help since the only thing home improvement-ish I can handle is painting."

I glanced over at the hole in the wall next to Tana's shoulder. It was about the size of a fist. "Painting is the least of my worries for right now."

Since I'd inherited the house so young, my mom had hired a local management company to maintain it until I was older. But now that I saw their version of "maintenance," I wished I'd just done it myself.

Tana could probably guess at my thoughts if my face was

any indication. Whatever the case, she'd always been a pro at getting right to the point.

"What are your plans?"

"For starters, I need a roommate. Just for the summer."

If she was surprised, she did a good job concealing it. Not that I was under the illusion that people in The Ridge weren't aware of my family's troubles. This might not be a major city, but gossip was international, although they probably had no idea how bad things *really* were. The news reported my stepfather being arrested for fraud, but they hadn't mentioned that he'd stolen from family, too.

My mother had been inconsolable when she told me that Christian had taken all the money she'd inherited from Gran and the little trust fund established for my sister. She hadn't thought anything of asking him to help her with her investments. He was this big-time broker, a superstar of Wall Street, so who better to ask?

I'd always felt a little guilty that Gran had left the house to me, like I'd taken my mom's legacy or something. But as usual, Gran was the wisest of us all. Since it was solely in my name it was the only thing the stepjerk hadn't been able to take away from us.

I looked over at the hole in the wall again. This had to work. It was the only option left.

Tana must have sensed my thoughts. "It's all going to be okay. I'll tell my mom to spread the word, too. Between my customers at the salon and everyone that comes through the hardware store, we'll find someone. I wish I hadn't just renewed my lease because I could have stayed here."

"Hopefully I'll get some responses to my ad."

"Your ad?"

"Yeah, I put up an ad on the Violet Ridge Facebook page. I figured that would be faster than posting flyers."

"Charlie, that page is public. All kinds of weirdos might see that post!"

"Really? How many people are looking at the Violet Ridge Community Page on any given day?"

"You'd be surprised," she muttered under her breath. "Maybe one of my customers will know someone."

"Thanks, Tana. Even if they can only pay a couple hundred a month, it's something."

Her phone blasted a song. She withdrew it from her pocket with an apologetic smile.

"Sorry, I have to get back to the shop. But if we're lucky we'll find you someone decent before the weekend." She paused in the doorway. "I'm *really* glad you're back."

"Me too."

After another hug she was gone, leaving me standing in the middle of the room. When I turned around, I realized that I meant it. I was really glad to be here even if moving back wasn't going to be as simple as I thought.

The proof was all around me. After cleaning, I'd spent some time putting Gran's knickknacks and books away and I still wasn't done. Boxes were scattered around the living room, their wide cardboard flaps mocking me like gaping mouths. Anyone observing would see boxes waiting to go into storage so they wouldn't be damaged during the renovation. They couldn't know that each bubble-wrapped package represented a memory.

It might look like a hot mess, but it represented a new beginning. *My* new beginning.

I could only hope that I wouldn't screw it up.

two

. . .

HENDRIX

The wall was shaking.

I had never been a morning person so it took longer than it should have to pull the covers off my head. The guest room in my brother's apartment wasn't where I wanted to be, but it had seemed like the best option after I lost my own place. I knew he wouldn't say no. We were as different as brothers could be, but Van always came through for me.

He was the happy-go-lucky one, the perfect foil to my perpetually annoyed personality, so I'd figured living with him would beat living with my little sister or god forbid, my parents. However, when I'd made my calculations on the least offensive place to land after being made unexpectedly homeless, I hadn't known about one vital factor.

A vital factor that my older brother was head-over-heels for.

My sleep fog had finally cleared enough for me to figure out what the *bang, bang, bang* on the wall was about. The sound was muffled, but I couldn't escape the way my own bedframe shook from the vibrations.

Nothing like waking up to hearing your brother having sex in the other room.

After I was done gagging, I leaned over and pounded against the wall.

"Some of us are trying to sleep!"

It was quiet for a few seconds then I heard muffled laughter. A few minutes later the bedsprings started squeaking.

"I really need to move," I grumbled before yanking the covers back over my head.

I thought fondly of the garage apartment I used to share with my girlfriend in town. Ex-girlfriend, I reminded myself. I had gotten lucky when I found that place. It had been perfect. Cheap. Close to town. And most of all, *quiet*.

Well, unless you counted the sound of Janelle screaming at me whenever she didn't get her way.

After another round of laughter from the next room, I decided coffee had to be better than trying not to hear my brother and his girlfriend making up. Don't get me wrong. I was happy for Van. Before they got back together, he'd been a mess and miserable company at the shop. He was the friendly one who handled customers at our family hardware store while I did the inventory and anything that kept me away from people. But the way he'd been acting the last few months, most of the customers had given him a wide berth.

Anything that would cause people to ask for *my* help had to be bad.

I opened my bedroom door just in time to see my brother's naked ass going into the hall bathroom. His hips were bracketed by the pair of long, slim legs wrapped around his waist.

"My eyes!"

Beth squeaked in surprise and buried her face in Van's shoulder right before he slammed the door behind them.

I slapped my palms against my forehead as I contemplated my sins. Whatever I did in a past life was clearly catching up with me this year.

"I seriously have to move."

Fifteen minutes later, I was leaning against the fridge, watching the coffee pot desperately when Van made his next appearance. There were scratch marks all over his chest and his hair, a slightly darker brown than mine, was sticking out in every direction. I hung my head to hide my amusement.

"Morning, bro. A very good morning it seems."

He gave me the finger before grabbing a bottle of orange juice out of the fridge and drinking straight from the container.

"Dehydrated?"

"Exhausted. God, that woman is a wildcat."

I covered my ears playfully before turning back to the coffee pot.

Country Club Beth was definitely not what I would have envisioned for my brother, but he'd been completely wrapped around her stiletto since he met her at some business conference in DC a few years back. I was happy for him but a little worried about how quickly he'd fallen. Maybe I was just being overly cautious since my heart still bore footprints from my last girlfriend trampling all over it. It seemed to be an Evers family trait for the men to fall for women way out of our league.

Once Van was no longer dying of thirst, he fixed startling blue eyes on me. "How goes the apartment search?"

"Is that your not-subtle-at-all way of telling me to get out? Classy."

He rolled his eyes. "Do I want to bang in the morning without your ear plastered to the wall? Yes. But I'm not kicking you out. Yet."

"I appreciate the generosity. Nothing in town is affordable anymore. When did Violet Ridge get so expensive?"

"Ever since all these city folk started buying up all the real estate." He said the last part quietly since Beth's parents were part of the city folk in question.

"I guess I could go stay with mom and dad."

We both shuddered at the thought. If I was traumatized by the sight of Van's naked ass, the last thing I needed was to see my father's. Again.

Yes, you heard right. The last time I stayed at home I caught my parents going at it on the kitchen counter. At least Van kept it in his room. Mostly.

Plus, he didn't try to fix me up. I would rather walk around with a blindfold on than sit through another awkward dinner with my mom's nail technician's cousin's daughter.

"I'll get some earplugs."

Van's chest shook with laughter as he took another swig of orange juice. "Isn't your friend Carter a real estate agent?"

"He's either an agent or a broker. I can't remember which."

Carter had moved back to town recently to help his father recover from surgery. He'd been working remotely and driving back to Washington, DC, when necessary.

"Maybe he can help you find something outside of town. You'd have more room for all your stuff. Maybe even a studio where you could paint."

He didn't look at me as he said it, aware that it was a sensitive subject. The only reason Van knew I was still painting was because he'd seen my canvases when he helped me put some of my stuff in storage.

"Maybe. I'll ask him the next time I see him."

He shrugged. "There's no rush. I'd rather you hang a little longer so you can find the right place than end up in another bad situation."

"I thought the situation with Janelle was good. She seemed cool in the beginning."

"They always do. Then the next thing you know all your shit is on the front lawn." His eyes cut to the time on the microwave. "Hey, aren't you scheduled to be at the shop this morning?"

"Is that the time? Fucking hell."

I poured the coffee into a travel mug. The day was already a bust. I was late. I was hungry. And I still needed to shower. Then I thought about what had just happened in that shower.

Maybe I would shower at the gym later.

———

As soon as I cleared the door of Evers Hardware, my father looked up from behind the counter. His hair was naturally dirty blond and he had blue eyes, but other than that it was like looking at a middle-aged version of myself.

"You're late!"

"Don't ask!" I shouted as I headed for the back room where we had a small employee lounge.

Working for the family business wasn't what I'd thought my life would be at twenty-eight years old, but it wasn't a bad deal. I did the inventory for the hardware store and in exchange I could use the space to store the materials for my own business. Since I'd been working alongside my dad fixing things since I was a kid, it seemed like a natural fit to do odd jobs on the side. Before long I'd had so much work that it became a legitimate business.

A few minutes later, my dad pushed through the door and went to the coffee machine. He'd finally allowed me to upgrade it to a new one that didn't scorch the beans.

"Son, I've been meaning to ask if you have time to do some work for the neighbors."

"Of course. Which neighbors?"

"The Jeffries."

I smiled. His next-door neighbors had lived here even longer than my parents and were one of those funny older couples who'd been together an ice age despite fighting constantly.

"Pearl wants one of those she-sheds she saw on TV. You know Hal is too old to build anything like that."

"I'll stop by this weekend."

He nodded. "He almost called that company all the way over in Springfield until I told him you could do it. Give me some of those cards with your business name. I can pass them out at church."

I pulled out the fancy business cards Tana ordered for me. It was stupid to have business cards in a town as small as Violet Ridge, but she'd insisted it was part of my "branding." Whatever.

"Thanks, Dad."

"What are you thanking him for?" Mom asked. She was wearing one of the plaid shirts she always said made her feel "handy" and carrying a pool inflatable.

She had some unorthodox ideas about how to compete with the big-box stores popping up in nearby towns. Dad wasn't as adventurous when it came to our inventory, but she had a way of wearing him down. Ways I did not want to think about.

"I got him another job!" Dad crowed with delight. "He's going to build one of those she-sheds for Pearl."

"That's nice of you," Mom said before leaning down to kiss my cheek.

"It's no big deal. It's just business." I tried to keep the bitterness out of my voice. It wasn't their fault that I'd rather be painting canvases than fences. They didn't even know I was still painting. Van was the only one who knew. It was something I preferred to keep private. Not that the rest of my family wouldn't support me. The opposite, in fact.

They'd all be excited and interested which would only make it worse if it didn't work out. Especially my mom. She'd given up on her art degree when she got pregnant with my brother. It would make her so happy to think I was doing something with my art, and I wasn't sure I could deal with the weight of her dreams on top of my own.

"Have you guys heard of any rooms to rent in town?"

Dad looked amused. "I thought you were staying with your brother?"

"I am. I was just wondering."

He chuckled. "If the lovebirds are too much to handle you could just come home. Perfectly good room just sitting empty."

"Like you and Mom are any better?"

Dad looked affronted. "Maria, how did we raise such prudes?"

Mom laughed. "He has a point."

Still smiling at their predictable banter, I grabbed an extra Evers Hardware shirt and yanked it over my head. As they went back up front, I took a deep breath and tried to prepare myself mentally for another day of manning the register and answering questions in the event that my father was busy with another customer. After that, I'd go work on a side job repairing a fence before heading home. Then I'd watch some TV, eat whatever Van had in his refrigerator, and go to sleep. Just to do it again the next day.

There was nothing wrong with my life. It was a simple life but filled with good, honest work, friends, and family. Maybe it was getting dumped by my girlfriend or some sort of almost-thirty life crisis, but I couldn't help wondering if this was it.

Was this all I could expect out of life?

three

. . .

CHARLOTTE

A good night's sleep has a way of making everything look different. I woke up on Tuesday morning ready to work. Since I'd spent the prior day cleaning and organizing, I was able to remove the drop cloths from the living room furniture. Now I had room to pull out my laptop and get down to business. I was finally ready to tackle a renovation budget.

Numbers I could handle.

I cracked my knuckles before opening a blank spreadsheet. Dorky as it was, making a budget was one of my favorite things to do. When things were chaotic, having a list of what to spend and where made me feel better. Moving home and fixing up a house was overwhelming. Checking items off a list, that was doable.

First, I listed all the things I knew needed to be fixed. On the exterior, the steps were crumbling, and the siding was dingy. I listed:

(1) step repair

(2) exterior paint

Looking around the room, my eyes landed on the hole in

the wall I'd noticed earlier. I definitely couldn't fix that on my own. I would need a professional.

(3) drywall patch

(4) interior paint

As I continued noting things that needed to be fixed, anxiety tightened my stomach. Even though my mom's attorney didn't think she'd be kicked out of the penthouse right away, I was trying to be practical. Her assets were tied up with Christian so at some point, she was going to lose it all. This house was all we had left. Looking at the list I'd already accumulated, my savings weren't going to be enough to fix everything. I would need to be really smart about how I spent my money.

My cell phone dinged with a text message. I tapped it and then frowned. Some guy had sent a selfie. It must be a wrong number.

Then my phone rang. It was another unknown number. Normally I would have answered just in case it was my little sister calling from a friend's phone, but something told me to wait. A minute later, I had a new voicemail. When I played it, I heard muffled breathing and what sounded like whispers. By the time I realized what I was listening to, he was apparently reaching the finish line.

"What is wrong with people?"

Not that I was judging people who wanted to have phone sex, but who sent this sort of stuff without checking to make sure it was the right number first? Then another message came through.

UNKNOWN

I can pay you with this.

The next message was a dick pic.

"Gross." I hurriedly deleted it.

When my phone rang again, I started to panic. What was going on? There was no way multiple people were coincidentally dialing my number by accident. If I didn't know any better, I'd assume Aaron had leaked my number to the press. But he was the one who had left me. Truthfully, he hadn't cared enough about me when we were together to go to this much trouble. So that didn't make sense either.

I was scared to look at my phone again but maybe one of the messages would give me a clue as to why this was happening. After taking a deep breath, I flipped my phone over and winced at the number of red flags on the screen. I ignored the voicemails and scrolled through the text messages.

UNKNOWN

Is the house still available? I'm never sure if these Reddit posts are real.

Reddit? I didn't even have a Reddit account. Honestly, I was barely ever online at all. I'd been avoiding social media since Christian's arrest.

Then I remembered the message I'd left on the Violet Ridge Facebook page.

Oh no.

———

"No, I don't allow snakes!"

I hung up without waiting to hear whatever other questions the caller might have. So far there had been almost fifty phone calls about the room for rent and none of them were promising.

Apparently someone had reposted my original message on a Reddit thread about crazy low rents. Since my location on Facebook was still set to New York, everyone thought I was renting an entire house *in the city* for only five hundred dollars a month. Considering the cost of New York real estate, I could understand why it had gone a little viral.

The idea of renting *anything* in the city for five hundred dollars was insane. You couldn't even rent a shoebox for that price. I was getting calls from people all over the country asking if the house was still available.

The first woman wanted to know if there was a yard for "all" of her dogs. The second caller was a guy who wanted to know what the menu was. He'd seemed perplexed when I explained that the house was not a bed and breakfast but very helpfully told me that he'd seen a screenshot of my message posted on Instagram.

Then there were the scores of perverts asking what I was wearing, sending text messages with dick pics, and one guy who called several times in a row just to breathe heavily into my ear. I shuddered remembering.

Who knew there were this many weirdos looking for a place to live? Not only that but willing to call a random number they saw online to harass me.

Who had that kind of time?

The doorbell rang and I sighed with relief. Tana had texted earlier promising to stop by after work with a bottle of wine. After the day I'd had, I could really use a drink and a sympathetic shoulder to cry on. I pulled the door open and gasped at the sight of an unfamiliar man on the porch. He was wearing a battered hat and mud-splattered boots.

He looked me up and down before a shocked smile pulled at his lips. "My friend saw the post online and recognized the house. Are you the pretty lady looking for a renter?"

On pure instinct, I slammed the door in his face and then twisted the deadbolt.

"Is that a no?" His voice was muffled by the door.

"The room has been rented. Sorry!"

My breath still coming fast, I waited until I heard his ambling footsteps cross the porch. His shadow passed in front of the living room window and I twisted my fingers to resist the urge to peek through the curtains to make sure he'd really left.

Well, I would definitely have to give Tana the benefit of saying *I told you so.*

My phone rang and I crossed the room to where I'd tossed my handbag on the old couch. It was a busy flower design that was still covered in plastic. When I was a child, I was scared to sit on any of the furniture in this room. Now, like everything else in the house, it just looked sad. Neglected.

I could relate.

After I dug my phone out of my bag, I breathed a sigh of relief when I saw my mother's picture on the screen.

"Hey, Mom. How are you?"

"I'm hanging in there, honey. How do things look at the house?"

I looked around at the neglected interior. "Not great. Mom, I thought you said you had a management company taking care of the place? It looks pretty bad."

She was quiet for a moment. "Really?"

"Yeah. It doesn't look like anyone's been here in a long time. Also, there's a hole in the wall."

"A hole?"

"Like someone fell into it by accident."

"Well, that's strange."

"I know. What company did you hire?"

When she didn't respond right away, I sighed. Now that I was thinking clearly, I realized it would have been right around the time when we first moved to New York. She would have been pregnant with Billie and newly married.

"The stepj—uh, *Christian* handled all that, didn't he?"

"Yes. At the time it seemed so much easier to let him

handle everything. I was so exhausted then. Having a baby in your thirties is a very different experience than when you're younger. That's something you should keep in mind."

"Mom."

"I'm just saying. Have you spoken to Aaron at all?"

"*Mom.* He left me. It's kind of hard to speak to someone who moves out and blocks your number."

"Okay, honey. I think maybe this is all a misunderstanding. He's probably just overwhelmed. He and Christian were so close."

"Too close," I muttered under my breath.

With a little distance it was easier to see that the only reason Aaron had been interested in me was to gain a closer relationship with his idol. He probably saw the boss's stepdaughter as a shortcut to the executive floor. The worst part was that he wasn't wrong. In the time we were together, Aaron had been promoted twice. Dating him was the only thing I'd ever done that Christian had liked.

"Well, I'm going to find a contractor to handle everything. Hopefully it won't take long to get the place ready so you and Billie can move in. When do you think you'll be coming?"

"Her summer camp doesn't end until August. I'll need that long at least to get everything squared away here. Alan doesn't think they'll take the penthouse right away."

Alan Spencer had been a lawyer for the Delacourt family for years. Christian used to say Alan was the only one "who knew where all the bodies were buried." Considering everything that had happened, I could only hope that was a joke.

"I'll try to get it ready as fast as I can. Does Billie know what's happened yet?"

"No and hopefully it'll stay that way. The less people talking about this the better. What a disaster."

"Mom, I really think we should tell her."

"Let's let her have one last summer free of worry, hmm?"

"Okay but I'm—"

"Oh, that's Alan on the other line. I have to go. I love you, sweetheart. Bye!"

Frustrated, I dropped my phone back into my bag. Mom had a lot on her plate right now, but it would be nice to get a little more information about how things were going at home. Did she really think no one in her social circle was talking about this? Billie had just left for summer camp the day before Christian got arrested, but that didn't mean she was completely cut off from Manhattan gossip. I didn't want her to find out from someone else, but my mom seemed to think keeping her in the dark was for the best.

Maybe she hoped to have something positive to tell her before we dropped the bad news.

Exhaustion warred with my restless desire to be doing something. Taking a nap wasn't going to help me get the house ready any faster. But with the way I was feeling, I probably wasn't going to get much more done anyway.

I decided to compromise by taking a break for a hot bath. After all the cleaning I'd done yesterday, I should have showered before bed. Now I felt grungy.

Maybe after a little time to relax I could figure out a way to make my meager savings stretch to cover renovating an entire house. Especially since the roommate thing was looking like a bust. Out of all that, I hadn't found even one decent person. Dejected, I walked upstairs. There were only two bathrooms in the entire house, one downstairs and one in the upstairs hall. The first bathroom was pretty small with just a toilet and a sink. The upstairs bathroom hadn't changed since I was a kid, a relic from the seventies with pink tiles and an old-fashioned claw-foot bathtub. It was surrounded by a frilly shower curtain attached with metal rings to a rod in the ceiling. I tugged on the curtain gently. It seemed sturdy enough. That was a good sign.

After carefully pushing the curtain back, I turned on the tub faucet, praying for hot water. It took a few minutes but soon the water was piping hot. Success!

Ever since I was a little girl, I'd always used the small bedroom at the end of the hall. As I passed the closed door to Gran's room, a wave of sadness took me by surprise. Eventually I would have to go in there, but I honestly couldn't ever imagine sleeping in Gran Grace's room.

In my room, I gathered up a change of clothes and took them into the bathroom. The water was only halfway but the tub was deep so that was probably enough. I twisted the knob to turn the water off.

Nothing happened.

"Oh no." I frantically turned the knob back the other way with no results.

"No, don't do this to me!"

Unsure of what else to do, I pulled the plug, hoping it would drain fast enough to prevent the tub from overflowing. But as I watched, the water level kept rising.

four

. . .

HENDRIX

The gym had been my sanctuary again that morning, in more ways than one. Not only was I happy to take a shower somewhere my brother *hadn't* been having sex, but it also gave me the mental boost I needed to get through another day.

I loved my family and was proud of the business they'd built, but there were days when I wanted to scream from the monotony of it all.

That was when I came here.

To my secret lair.

I chuckled at the thought of calling a musty old shed a secret lair. But it was. Originally, I'd gotten it just to keep all the stuff I didn't want to bring to Van's place but then I realized I could paint there. Mr. Donald let me use it for free since I usually helped him out with fixing the fence line on his property. So I just propped the door open a bit and ran a fan while I worked.

I feathered my brush against the canvas, blending the colors into a gradient. Usually after an hour of working on my latest piece, I was in a much better mood. Painting gave me an outlet for all my destructive energy. I could explode on the canvas and rage with color. Then after expelling all my emotions, I could go to work and shelve paint and cabinet hardware.

But today it wasn't working. I was just as unsettled as when I got here.

Maybe it was all the uncertainty with my living situation but as I stared at the canvas, I wondered what the hell I was doing.

Frustrated, I dropped my brush on the edge of the easel. Maybe I was wasting my time. The walls of the unit were now lined with finished canvases but that didn't mean they were any good.

I sighed.

For years, I'd lived and worked with no further goals than to have a comfortable life and maybe build a house one day. Lately though, I'd felt this uncertainty about the future. A restless longing for something different.

For a while, I thought Janelle could fill that longing. We'd gotten along well enough, and she enjoyed the same simple life. She worked two towns over as a receptionist at a small law firm. She was content to come home after work and watch movies or hang out with family.

I'd dated city girls before and usually they were cool with small-town living until one day they suddenly...weren't. Janelle's parents were locals, so she had the same deep connection to Violet Ridge that I did. I never had to worry that one day she'd decide this town was too small for her and leave it behind.

Janelle had only wanted us to take the next steps. It was a logical thing after being together for almost a year and living together for the last six months. I mean really, where else did I think things between us were going? You dated, you got engaged, and then you got married. That was how things were done, especially in small towns.

She hadn't done anything wrong expecting our relationship to follow that same predictable pattern.

I was the one who was changing.

I was the one wondering what else might be out there if I was brave enough to go after it.

Lately, I'd been thinking about what I was doing with my art. Was it enough for me to do it in secret and never show it to anyone? Some people created art solely for their own enjoyment and that was fine. Everyone didn't have a driving need to be famous or even to make money from what they created.

But was that enough for me?

Not having the answer to that question bothered me more than I cared to admit.

Not that it really mattered since nothing I was working on was coming out the way I intended. Every piece I'd done in the last month started well and then devolved into an unfocused mess. Rage painting was great for dealing with my frustration, but it wasn't anything I could display.

When my phone rang, I was a little too eager to snatch it up. Santana's picture flashed across the screen.

"Hey, sis."

"Where are you? Are you at work?"

Of course, that would be the first thing she asked.

"No. I don't go in until this afternoon. Did you need something?"

"I just wanted to tell you I found you a place to live!"

Tana's voice told me she would have been doing jazz hands if she'd been standing in front of me. Despite her excitement, something about the way she'd said it made me pause.

"You found me an apartment? That's great. Where is it?"

"Um, I'll send you the directions."

I stared at the phone after she hung up. That was weird even for Tana. In a town as small as ours, directions were a bit of a joke. There weren't that many houses in town that you'd need directions. Usually we would just say "the other side of Main Street" or "the houses by the train tracks."

My phone dinged.

TANABANANA

I really think this might be perfect for you.

TANABANANA

Keep an open mind, okay?

TANABANANA

The house is adorable.

I called Tana but she didn't pick up. With a sigh, I put down my paintbrush. I might as well go ahead and clean up early. I needed to check this place out. Otherwise, the suspense was going to kill me.

I loved my little sister but her idea of adorable might not fit mine.

When my eyes landed on the muddy canvas in front of me again, I stood up. Maybe it was time that I came back down to planet earth and got my head out of the clouds. Painting was fun but maybe that was all it was meant to be.

I was Hendrix Evers, son of the best parents ever and brother to some of the biggest pains in the asses ever born.

That was all I needed to know.

———

By the time I cleaned my brushes, it was just a little after noon.

As I wiped the sweat from the side of my face, I realized that I was going to need another shower.

I'd been on the verge of calling Tana again when a text message had come through with directions. I hoped the owners of the place didn't mind me dropping in unexpectedly. Since Tana wasn't taking my calls, I couldn't even ask her to let them know I was coming. I definitely didn't feel like hearing my dad bitch about me being late again so I would just stop in quickly to see what was up.

Keep an open mind, okay?

If that wasn't a red flag, I didn't know what was. There was definitely something going on. I was picturing a little old lady with white lace doilies on all the chairs.

It was humid in the cab of my truck, so I rolled all the windows down. Hopefully whatever senior citizen I was going to meet up with wouldn't judge me too harshly for showing up sweaty and unshaven because I was far too curious to bother going home first to shower.

I stared down at the message again, my earlier hesitation coming back full force. The turn-by-turn directions were a dead giveaway that something was up. Otherwise, she would have just given me the address.

I hung my head. Lace doilies were definitely in my future.

Keeping one eye on the road and the other on the directions in Tana's text message, I carefully made my way through town.

From Main Street turn left on Sycamore Road.

Then keep going straight past the old mill.

Right on Oak Lane.

With each new turn, a strange sense of familiarity started buzzing in the back of my brain. Not that being familiar was unexpected; this was Violet Ridge, after all. But I had a sudden idea why Tana hadn't wanted me to know where I was going.

The last turn onto Cedar Avenue slammed the feeling

home. I pulled to a stop in front of a faded blue Victorian. I hadn't been here in years and the last time it had been painted white, but there was no doubt that this was the place. Which made no sense at all because Gran Grace had been dead for about ten years and no one had lived there since.

Unless the house had sold?

I called Tana but it went straight to voicemail. "Tana, I don't know what—"

Then I saw the car in the driveway. A sleek, black Audi sedan.

With New York plates.

five

. . .

CHARLOTTE

Have you ever watched a horror movie and thought to yourself, *No one is this dumb in real life?*

It's usually the blonde coed investigating the weird noise in the basement, or the jock who runs into the creepy woods to escape instead of toward town. Whatever the case, the solution seems so obvious and yet no one on screen sees what's right in front of their faces.

As I watched the water level in the bathtub continue to rise, I had the sobering thought that I might actually be the too-stupid-to-live heroine in this particular horror movie.

"What do I do?"

At this point I was full-on panicking. The knobs weren't working no matter which way I turned them, and the force of the water was so strong that the tub was filling faster than the water could drain.

After looking around the bathroom frantically I finally decided that bailing out the water manually might be my only option. Or at least it would buy me some time until I could think of something better.

I needed a bowl.

Cursing myself for not doing it sooner, I ran down to the kitchen and pulled open all the lower cabinets until I found a plastic bucket. I carried it back into the bathroom and started scooping water out of the tub and into the sink.

I heard something faintly but didn't have time to stop and find out what it was until another resounding boom went through the house.

Was that someone at the door?

With one last, pained look at the almost overflowing tub, I ran downstairs. If it was the weirdo from before, he'd get a bucket to the face but with any luck it would be one of the neighbors coming by. Hopefully someone who wasn't as clueless as I was about how to fix a broken faucet.

The perpetual nosiness of the neighbors was one of my mom's favorite things to complain about whenever she was forced to return to her hometown, but I had always thought it was nice.

Was it really the worst thing in the world to be surrounded by people who cared about you?

Instead, when I flung the door open, I realized that I hadn't been that lucky. No, I didn't get a visit from a kind neighbor who cared about me.

I got Hendrix Evers.

The one person in the world who'd hated me on sight.

"*You're* the one looking for a roommate?" He glared at me with barely concealed annoyance.

"I am going to kill Santana," I grumbled. I left him standing there as I ran back upstairs. The water level had risen considerably just in the thirty seconds I'd been gone so I resumed my frantic bucket diving, tossing the water in the bathroom sink.

"*Holy shit.* What the hell happened in here?"

I turned around to see Hendrix had followed me into the bathroom, his six-foot-something frame making the room seem even smaller. Had he always been this much taller than me? I didn't remember him being this big in high school other than his big, fat head.

"What does it look like happened? The tub is broken!"

He pushed me aside and started turning the knobs. I almost strained a muscle rolling my eyes. Did he seriously think I hadn't already tried that? Maybe he thought having a penis would make all the difference.

"I don't need your help. I have it under control."

He cupped his hands under the faucet and directed the stream of water upward to splash me right in the face. My shriek was short-lived as more water went into my mouth and streamed down the front of my shirt.

"Oh my god. Would you get out!"

He left and I was shocked that he actually listened to me. But I quickly got back to work bailing water into the sink again. My arms were already burning from the effort.

There was no way I could keep this up. Maybe I shouldn't have told Rix to leave.

He was the worst, but I assumed he could handle calling a plumber. Okay, maybe not. He'd probably think it was funny to watch me float away, but I could have told *him* to use the bucket while I called for help myself.

Maybe it was the exhaustion or the sudden appearance of my nemesis on the front porch, but tears flooded my eyes. This whole trip was one giant fail. After everything fell apart in New York, it had seemed like a lifeline to realize that we still had a place to live, a place that no one could touch.

Well, so far my plan was a complete bust. It was only my second day in town and I'd already ruined one room of the house.

After a few minutes the water suddenly slowed to a trickle and then stopped completely. Panting, I pushed soggy hair out of my face. I looked around in confusion. Hendrix appeared in the doorway again.

"You're still here?"

"Why didn't you just turn off the main water valve?" he asked finally.

My face flushed before I turned back to the tub. I didn't want to admit that I hadn't known to do that. No one told me about a water valve! I wasn't exactly Bob the Builder so why the hell would I know any of this?

"You never explained what you're doing here."

If he noticed my deflection, thankfully he didn't comment.

"Tana knows I've been looking for a place."

I was a little skeptical that Tana would send him here knowing how much we'd always hated each other. Rix was the last person I would *ever* want to live with.

Tana wouldn't have lived with him either if she'd had a choice growing up. Not only was Hendrix a pain in the ass, but he was also a complete slob. Think sporting equipment and free weights everywhere along with an eau de gym socks odor so strong it could be used as general anesthesia.

I doubted he'd improved much over the years. That was probably why he needed to find a new place. When I turned around again, his eyes quickly jumped upward. Was he staring at my butt? I narrowed my eyes suspiciously.

"What's wrong with your current place? Did you get kicked out?"

Suddenly he looked uncomfortable. "I'm living with my brother right now."

There was definitely more to the story. The way he was acting didn't add up, but I smiled at the thought of Van Halen.

His older brother was flirtatious and charming, basically everything the surly Hendrix was not.

"That's not working out?"

"It's great. Until he's having sex with his girlfriend in the next room." He made a face.

"Jealous?"

"Immensely. Which is why I really need to move out."

I laughed. "Good luck with that."

"Look, I know we haven't exactly been friends in a while—"

"Ever. We haven't been friends ever," I interrupted.

"—but surely we can coexist in the same place for a few months. Tana said it's just for the summer. That's perfect. It'll give me the time I need to find a place I want to buy."

"Nope."

As I walked out of the bathroom, I held my sopping wet shirt away from my skin. The last thing I wanted to do was keep wearing a gross shirt but there was no point in changing until I'd mopped up all the water from the bathroom. Gran Grace had always kept cleaning supplies in the small closet off the kitchen so I could only hope her old mop was still there. I opened the door.

Yes.

I grabbed the mop, thankful it was one of those old rag ones that lasted forever. If I got all the water up quickly, it wouldn't do permanent damage to the floors, right? Bathroom floors were made to get wet, after all.

Maybe this wouldn't be as big of a problem as I'd thought. I called on my PhD in HGTV to mentally calculate how much it would cost if I was wrong about the bathroom floor. Having to replace the subfloor would be expensive, adding thousands to my bathroom renovation budget.

"Why not? What's the big deal?"

Startled, I whirled around. I was so consumed by my

thoughts I hadn't realized Rix had followed right on my heels. I didn't like the idea of him sneaking around behind me. Despite being an adult (allegedly), I didn't trust him not to give me a wedgie or put something in my hair.

"What's the big deal? Seriously? *We hate each other.*"

"Hate is a strong word."

Rix shrank back when I whirled in his direction, the mop held in front of me like a sword.

"You stole my clothes while we were at the creek. Everybody saw my boobs!"

"I told you that was an accident! Your shirt was the same color as Carter's—"

As if he wasn't even talking, I poked him in the chest with the mop handle while listing his many sins. "You told your mom I dropped that pie at Christmas when *you* were the one who tripped me."

He snickered but then shrank back when I poked him with the mop handle again.

"Then you told everyone that I smelled like yogurt."

He winced at the reminder. "Well—"

"You ruined my prom!"

With that last, sobering fact, I walked back to the living room. At least he'd remembered to close the front door so I wouldn't have a house full of flies.

I stopped with my hand on the front doorknob. "Thanks for stopping by."

He sighed. "This is my only option. Otherwise, I'll end up sleeping in my car."

"Why would you sleep in your car?"

"Anything is better than seeing Van's naked ass cheeks again."

A laugh escaped before I could stop it, which only pissed me off more. I didn't want to laugh at his stupid jokes or notice how strong his jawline was, and I definitely shouldn't care about where he slept.

When I didn't say anything else, he finally got the hint. His shoulders slumped but when I opened the front door, he walked out.

It was tempting to slam the door behind him but then I remembered he'd saved my bathroom by turning off the water. As much as I hated the idea of owing Rix for anything, I couldn't deny that he'd been helpful for once. If the situation had been reversed, I might not have been so quick to end his misery.

"Thank you for turning the water off," I finally said.

He acknowledged that with a wave over his shoulder as he skipped down the steps. Right before he reached the driveway, he turned around.

"By the way, nice bra."

I looked down. Of course today I would be wearing a black lace bra beneath my white shirt. My *wet* white T-shirt.

Perfect.

———

Retta's face loomed large, taking up the majority of my laptop screen. I grabbed the bottle of wine Tana had brought with her.

"Why is your face so close to the camera?"

"I'm trying to see! This is so weird. I'm used to you sitting right next to me."

"I know. Everything is weird right now though."

Tana came from upstairs. "Danny is almost done. He said something about a washer."

"So I'll have a working bathroom tonight?"

"Yes. Thank god for ex-boyfriends who'll actually answer the phone when you call."

On the screen, I watched as Retta poured herself a glass of wine. "You have ex-boyfriends that are useful? And that you can talk to without wanting to gouge their eyes out? I'm definitely doing this dating thing wrong."

"It's inevitable in a town this small. Once you break up, you'll see them all the time so it's better to keep it friendly. But that's also why I usually don't date much."

Tana hopped up then as a lanky guy came down the stairs holding a toolbox. While they whispered to each other, Retta's face filled the screen again as she tried to look behind me. A few minutes later, he was gone and Tana came back to sit next to me. She picked up her wine glass and took a big gulp.

I turned to her slightly. "Um, so I feel bad not paying him. I know you said you were calling in a favor, but he came out here on such short notice and he's not getting anything."

Retta snorted. "Oh, he's getting something. Probably tonight after we drink all this wine!"

Tana laughed but raised her wineglass for a toast.

I tapped my glass against hers. "Thanks for taking one for the team."

"It's not a hardship, believe me. We may not have worked out, but Danny is the one I call for all my plumbing needs, if you know what I mean."

Retta's cackle could probably be heard on the next block. "I hear that!"

"Well, we're starting off on a good note. At least I got something accomplished today. I think it's us. Our combined power seems to help me get stuff done. We should do this weekly. We can have our own accountability group."

"As long as it's not another book club with books I'll never read," Tana grumbled.

"What book club are you in?" I asked.

Tana laughed. "It's my mom's so I couldn't say no. But that

was before I figured out she was just going to use it to try to set me up. The last time her friend's son was in town and *surprise*, wouldn't it be nice if I was the one who showed him around?"

Retta nodded knowingly. "Sorry to inform you ladies but it's only going to get worse. Try being thirty-nine with a Jamaican mother who thinks there's something wrong with me because I don't have a man."

"No book club. Just us, working through our problems."

"Wait, are we supposed to be doing something productive at these meetings?" Retta asked. "Because I thought this was an excuse to drink wine and bitch. That could be the name of our group: three bitches and bourbon!"

I spluttered over the sip I'd just taken. "Retta, that's not even wine!"

"What's a wine that starts with *b*?"

I held up a finger. "Bordeaux. The stepjerk was so proud of his wine collection. Although I guess the cops will take that too."

Suddenly it was quiet in the room. I could see the other two exchanging glances through the screen. I sighed.

"Okay let's do this once. Aaron is gone. I thought he was going to propose but then Christian got arrested. Then I came home to find him packing. My mom is distraught and still thinks this is some kind of mistake and my little sister has no idea what's happened because she's away at summer camp. Any questions?"

"Nope." Tana took another sip of wine.

"Not at this time. But I reserve the right to come back to this after you're drunk," Retta drawled.

It was a struggle to keep my stern demeanor, but I did call this meeting for a reason.

"What I need to do now is make a plan. I *thought* I had a plan. I figured I'd come here and fix the house up so we'd have a place once Mom finally realizes all the money is gone. But this is not what I expected. This place needs a lot of work."

Tana reached over and squeezed my hand. "You know we'll help however we can."

"Thanks. But I'm going to need to figure out how to get the money for this."

Retta eyed me knowingly through the screen. "You're regretting all those years you insisted on paying your own way now, huh?"

I gulped my wine. "Little bit. Because if I'd let Christian pay for everything, I'd have the money saved to fix this place up."

Maybe it was the wine but suddenly it all hit me at once. This was an impossible task, and I was in way over my head. The plan that I had concocted while still in shock suddenly seemed absolutely bonkers.

Sure, Charlie. Just jump in your car and drive three hundred miles on a whim because that seems easier than dealing with your empty apartment.

"I don't know what I was thinking. There's no way I can handle renovating this whole place. I can't expect Tana to find an ex-boyfriend to fix everything that goes wrong in here."

Tana patted my hand. "Today was bad luck. But I'm sure the rest of the repairs won't be that big of a deal. It's probably mostly cosmetic."

Retta hummed in agreement.

Somehow the two of them being so nice and supportive just made the panic clawing at my throat climb higher.

"Oh my god. I'm going to need money. A lot of it. I'm going to have to sell pictures of my feet! That's a thing. Did you know that?"

Retta leaned forward, her face huge in my laptop screen. "Um, Charlie. I have bad news for you. Your feet look like two trolls fighting under a bridge. Girl, nobody's paying for a picture of that!"

Tana snickered. "Okay, I think we can find a solution that doesn't involve anybody's toe cleavage."

I stood up to retrieve the other bottle of wine Tana had brought from the fridge. The label wasn't one I recognized, but it had a picture of a bunch of grapes on it so it would have to do. This was an emergency.

"Just because the roommate thing didn't work out so far doesn't mean you won't find someone. The perfect person might have tried to call, but they couldn't get past the weirdos," Tana pointed out.

That brought my panic level down a little bit. Today was a perfect storm of catastrophes. It didn't mean I was cursed. It just meant that I had to buckle down and really focus on what I was doing. It was the beginning of June and school started in September. I had a limited window of time to get this place decent so Mom and Billie could move in. There was no way I could do it all alone.

But maybe I could do it with a little help.

"Maybe I can do some of the work myself," I said hesitantly.

On the screen, Retta paused in the act of pouring herself another glass. "You can do what now?"

Even Tana looked skeptical. "Do you really think you can do this stuff?"

"Well, not all of it. Of course, I'll need to hire people for the big jobs. But the painting and the yard work, I can probably handle. Plus, I've watched so many of those decorating shows that I'm sure I can do a few of these projects on the weekend!"

"Whoa, slow it down." Retta pointed at me with one red, lacquered nail. "Let's not get ahead of ourselves. Maybe you should talk to a professional first. It might not be as expensive as you think."

"She's right," Tana said. "I can ask Hendrix—"

"We are not asking Hendrix for anything!" I said, obviously way too loudly if the way Retta winced on screen was any indication.

"Okay, well my dad knows lots of people. And Carter moved back to town. He's in real estate and knows lots of contractors. Maybe he can help." Tana shrugged.

"Sounds like you two have a plan. Meanwhile, I am going to focus on finishing this bottle of wine," Retta muttered. "After all, it's not like I have a job to go back to."

I looked glumly down into my empty wine glass. If that wasn't a good way to put things in perspective. Yes, things were pretty sucky but at least I had a place to live. If Retta couldn't find another job soon she wouldn't have any way to pay the rent. God, this was depressing.

Tana looked between us. "So anybody read any good books lately?"

six

. . .

CHARLOTTE

back in the day ...

Once again, the month of August was my enemy.

For everyone else, the last day of school was what they looked forward to, but my summer didn't really start until my parents dropped me off at Gran Grace's house at the end of June. The sight of that big, white Victorian lit up my heart more than any amusement park. The first day was a flurry of activity because Gran always made a big dinner for my parents, but the next day, after the car pulled out of the drive, she'd look over at me with that twinkle in her eye and say, "Now we can have fun."

Our brand of fun changed slightly every summer, but we always started with baking a cake. Sometimes it was her velvety pound cake with cream cheese icing or the red velvet cake I loved. One year, we experimented with turning her carrot cake recipe into huge cupcakes. The only thing Gran loved more than baking was people, so we'd then venture into town to deliver our goodies to friends.

Which meant I got to see my summer bestie.

It was a strange thing having a best friend that I only saw in the summer. A best friend is an important milestone in a girl's life. Best friend forever necklaces were all the rage in my elementary school, and I'd wished to have someone to split one with.

They even made necklaces with three equal pieces in case you had two best friends.

I couldn't imagine being lucky enough to have *two* best friends. But as I glanced over just as she effortlessly leaped over a fallen log, I had to admit that Santana Evers was worth more than two best friends put together.

"Where are we going?" I finally managed to gasp. It wasn't easy keeping up with Tana's long legs. She seemed to have sprouted a foot since last summer.

"To the barn," she yelled over her shoulder.

The old barn on the edge of Mr. Donald's property was our favorite place to play. It was about a million years old and still smelled like hay and manure, but no one ever bothered us here. Well, no one except...

"If you fall, I'm not carrying you back," Hendrix yelled as Tana leaped over a rock.

I blinked as sweat stung my eyes. It was August and the heat was like a wet blanket. If Hendrix hadn't been with us, I would have pulled up my shirt and wiped my face with it, but I wasn't going to give him a chance to poke me or give me a wedgie.

The summer was almost over and all I wanted was to spend every last minute with Tana. Too bad she usually came attached to one of her brothers. Mrs. Evers didn't like us "running wild" as she called it without one of the boys with us.

If someone had to babysit us why couldn't she send Van Halen? At least he was cute although I couldn't say that out loud because Tana got so mad the last time I did. Instead, we had to deal with Rix and his best friend, Carter. They were only a year older than we were but somehow managed to make us feel like babies.

"You don't have to come with us," I reminded him. I hoped he wouldn't.

Tana turned around. "You can leave. Carter can stay. We still need a groom."

I ran a hand over the lace veil I'd borrowed from Gran's room. It was so pretty, and I loved to put it on and imagine how I'd look when I got married someday. Everyone said I looked just like Gran Grace so I imagined I would look exactly like she did in her wedding photo.

Happy.

"Why do we have to play stupid wedding?" Rix whined. "Let's go to the creek."

Tana ignored him. "Okay, Carter, you go here. Charlie, you stand here."

We all moved around as Tana put us in position and pulled props out of the plastic bag she carried. I was always the bride, Carter was always the groom, and Tana had the loudest voice so she was always the preacher.

Rix was the person who objected before being kicked out. When I let him play, anyway.

"Who giveth this woman to be married to this man?" Tana yelled.

She'd turned her black bath robe backwards. It looked pretty impressive, almost like a judge's robe. The effect was only ruined by the sight of her ankles sticking out of the bottom since it was too short.

"I do!" Carter said in the deepest voice he could manage.

Since we were low on numbers, he had to play multiple roles. He was wearing an old top hat that Tana claimed belonged to a Halloween costume and she'd drawn a fake mustache on his face before we left home with some eyeliner she'd "borrowed" from her mom.

"If anyone has reason this woman should not be married to this man—" Tana paused to peer down at the paper crumpled in her palm —"speak now or forever hold your peace."

It was quiet. Then Carter sneezed.

"Sorry." He wiped his nose on the sleeve of his shirt.

Tana exhaled loudly. "Speak now or forever hold your peace!"

At the last part, she leaned down and picked up a stick before chucking it at her brother.

Rix startled. "*What?*"

"It's your turn," Tana whisper-yelled.

He groaned. "This is taking forever. Why do I have to be the guy who objects? Why can't I be the preacher?"

Annoyed that Rix was ruining things, *again*, I pulled Tana back in position.

Maybe if I was here all year, I wouldn't feel so desperate to take in every possible moment with my best friend. But the date when my parents would arrive to pick me up next week loomed larger than ever. That was the way of life for military families or at least that was what Mom said. You had to be ready to move on to a new place.

A new adventure.

All I really wanted was to have Tana all to myself. Instead, I was forced to spend time with Rix while the days flew by like they had wings and all I could do was watch them escape.

"You can't be the preacher. Gran Grace says you have the devil in you," I said.

Rix kicked the dirt with the tip of his sneaker. "Whatever. I don't want to go to your stupid wedding anyway."

When I turned back to face the front, something yanked at my hair. Hard.

"OUCH!"

When I turned, all I saw was my veil in the mud and the backs of Rix and Carter as they ran away laughing.

"Ugh. I hate you Hendrix Evers! You ruin everything!"

I didn't have many friends. There was no point making them when I'd just have to move again in a year or two. But my summers in Violet Ridge were forever. No matter where we were living, I always got to spend the summers in Virginia with my grandmother. Even though I technically had lived all over the world, this was my real home.

Now my last days with Tana were being ruined.

Tears welled as I picked up the veil carefully, biting my lip when I noticed the side was ripped.

"This was Gran Grace's veil when she married Pop. I'm going to get in so much trouble."

Tana slung her arm around my shoulders. "It's okay. Maybe we can fix it."

We both looked down at the muddy veil.

She covered it with her hand. "We'll tell her Rix did it. Let's keep playing on our own."

"We don't have a groom anymore."

Tana leaned down and grabbed the old top hat Carter had abandoned. "So what? We don't need boys. We're going to be best friends forever and that's better than a husband anyway."

seven

. . .

HENDRIX

The next day, I tentatively opened my eyes, fist at the ready in case there was another early morning party going on. After a few minutes of blissful quiet, I relaxed. The reprieve probably wouldn't last long but I would take it.

After coffee, I called Tana again. She hadn't answered any of my calls and texts the prior day, but the traitor could only avoid me for so long.

After the fifth call she finally picked up. "I was just trying to help," she said in lieu of hello.

"Fantastic way of helping. Sending me straight into the lion's den."

What the hell had she been thinking sending me over to Charlie's place with no warning? The two of us have never gotten along. Apparently in Santana's twisted mind lifelong hatred is a great qualification in a roommate.

"Most of my customers have families and they need to rent an apartment or an entire house. I asked everyone who came into the shop yesterday, but no one needed a single room."

"So your next thought was of me?"

"She needs a roommate. You need a room. It's only a problem if you make it one."

"Or if she kills me before I can rest my head on the pillow."

"She posted on freaking Facebook!"

As annoyed as I was, I had to admit to being worried about Charlie. We might hate each other, but at least she knew I wasn't a serial killer. What was she thinking advertising to live with a stranger?

"She's going through a lot. Just be nice to her," Tana threatened.

"I'm always nice," I muttered but I really wanted to ask what she meant by that.

What could Charlotte Monroe possibly be going through? Last I heard, she was living the life she'd always dreamed of as a Park Avenue Princess.

Was she traumatized because she couldn't get the *Hermès* bag she wanted?

Or maybe living though the extreme hardship of her day spa running out of her favorite moisturizer?

Give me a fucking break.

After reassuring Tana that I would be on my best behavior, I took a quick shower and shaved. I was halfway out the door before I remembered that I wasn't scheduled to work until late afternoon. Whatever. That would give me some time to start boxing up my stuff. The sooner I was gone the better. Van might not have minded me crashing but I minded. The apartments in town were expensive as hell but maybe it was worth it for us all to get some privacy.

The dishes were mainly Van's except for my favorite beer glass since I hadn't bothered to unpack my kitchen stuff when I moved in. After pulling out the main outfits I wore all the time, I grabbed armfuls of clothes and dropped them into my suitcase. Since I was on a roll, I got the vacuum and cleaned the carpet. Then I carried my dirty clothes into the hall to do laundry. By the time I was done, it was almost noon and I was starving.

There wasn't much in the refrigerator other than leftovers from Van's shitty cooking. Mine wasn't much better so I decided to swing by the diner. I pulled out my phone and texted Carter to see if he wanted to meet for lunch. When he hadn't responded ten minutes later, I decided I would order an extra meatball sub and bring it to him. If he'd already eaten, then I could save it for later.

When I walked in the diner, the chime over the door tinkled merrily and I returned a few friendly hellos. The owner, Dot, winked as she passed by with a full tray, but all of my attention was on the last table along the wall of windows. When Tana noticed me, she sat up in her seat and waved. I nodded at her but kept walking and took a seat at the counter. I didn't need a menu, but I picked it up anyway, careful not to crush it between my palms.

For five full minutes, I managed to stare straight ahead and even responded appropriately when Dot asked for my order. Eventually I couldn't take it anymore and looked over my shoulder.

Carter was still sitting so close to Charlie that he was practically in her lap. Her curly black hair surrounded her face like a halo, and she was wearing another one of those damn white T-shirts. At least it wasn't wet this time.

Tana caught my eye and tilted her head. I whipped around and grabbed blindly for the soda in front of me. No wonder Carter hadn't answered my texts: he was too busy crawling into Charlie's cleavage. Why were they having lunch? Had he just happened upon the girls out eating or had they invited him?

Had he invited *them*?

"Here's your order, pumpkin." Dot placed a loaded plate on the counter in front of me.

The heavenly smell of fries hit my nose first and I knew without looking that she'd given me extra. She always did.

"Thanks, Dot. You're a lifesaver. Tell your old man he better treat you right otherwise he might have some competition."

She snapped the towel she held in my general direction, but the high color in her cheeks betrayed her pleasure.

"You go on. Such a flirt. I swear you were making eyes at women even when you were in diapers. I'll wait to put in your meatball sub order so it'll be hot when you're ready to go."

The burger was delicious as always but as Charlie's laughter rang out across the room, it might as well have been paste. What the hell was so funny? Carter was a freaking real estate agent, not a comedian, and Tana definitely wasn't that funny.

I shoved the last of the fries in my mouth before taking another look over my shoulder. My teeth clinched when I noticed Charlie's hand on Carter's shoulder. They were awfully chummy considering she'd just gotten back in town. Carter hadn't been back in town that long, either. He'd moved home from DC when his father had a heart attack and had always said he would move out once his dad was back on his feet.

Wait...Was she asking *Carter* to move in?

I stuffed the last of my burger in my mouth and stood. I held up a finger so Dot would know I'd be right back. I waved to a few others as I made my way to their table.

Tana noticed me coming first and sat back in her chair with a knowing smile. Nobody else at the table had seen me yet, probably because Carter hadn't taken his eyes off Charlie the whole time. He pushed the rest of his milkshake in front of her.

"You want a sip? They just added this to the menu. We've been calling it the Oreo Orgasm."

Before she could respond, I leaned over. "That's the only way he knows how to give a woman an orgasm. But I don't mind if I do."

I grabbed the milkshake and drained half the contents of the glass in one pull.

Carter just blinked at me. "What the hell? Get your own, man!"

"Oh, not in a sharing mood anymore?"

He chuckled. "Such an ass."

"What are you guys over here whispering about?" I didn't miss the knowing look that passed between Tana and Charlie.

"*Nothing.* I have it under control," Charlie replied finally.

"Just like you had the water under control," I added just because I knew it would annoy her.

"What water?" Carter asked.

The face Charlie made at Tana clearly indicated that she didn't want to talk about it. Or more likely that she didn't want to talk about it in front of me.

Tana sat up straighter. "Why are you here? You usually get your food to go."

"Maybe I wanted to say hi."

"Unless you don't want to go home." She turned to the others with mirth in her eyes. "Rix is traumatized from catching Van having sex. And our parents."

"I'm disgusted by this conversation." I ignored their laughter. Let them catch their family members going at it like bunnies and see how well they reacted!

"You're like a good luck charm," Tana teased. "Swing by my apartment and maybe I'll find a boyfriend."

"I hate you."

"You love me."

Resolved to ignore her, I turned to Carter. "Think you can help me negotiate a good deal on one of the plots of land right outside of town? If you're not too busy heading up the town welcoming committee, that is."

Carter's lip quirked at the dig, but he nodded. "You want to buy?"

"I can build for cheaper than the places in town."

"Do you really think this thing with Janelle is permanent? What if you get back together?"

Even though I wasn't looking at her, I could suddenly feel the weight of Charlie's judgmental stare burning a hole in the side of my face.

"No chance of that," I said finally.

Carter smirked. "Yeah. You're not exactly the picket fence type."

There were so many things I could have said to that. Between his demanding career, constant travel, and dealing with his alcoholic father, he wasn't the poster child for stable relationships either. But instead, I bit my tongue.

"Whatever. I'll see you later."

I finished the rest of the milkshake as I walked back up to the counter. Behind me I could hear Charlie asking Carter to recommend some local contractors. Before I could even sit down, Dot deposited a paper bag stained with grease on the counter in front of me.

Charlie's laughter assaulted my ears all the way from across the room. Was it just me or was she deliberately being even louder than before? I slapped some money down on the counter and picked up the bag. If she wanted to use the overpriced contractors Carter knew, that wasn't my problem. Hell, she could live with the guy, too. I wasn't going to spend another second thinking about what Charlotte Monroe might or might not be doing.

I had better things to do.

Like eat a meatball sub.

———

I was halfway through my meatball sub, *which was fucking delicious by the way*, when I heard a little growl. Rolling down the truck's window, I surveyed the parking lot. Main Street was usually pretty dead this time of day so there was no one else around. The only reason I was still here was because I was hungry.

It wasn't like I was waiting to see how long Carter was going to hang around.

And I *definitely* wasn't hanging out eating another lunch because I wanted to make sure Charlie left alone.

Definitely not.

Another growl, this time right outside the door, drew my gaze down. There was something that looked like a demented squirrel glaring up at me.

"What the hell?"

I opened the door and climbed out slowly, trying not to startle it. Upon closer inspection, I decided he was probably a dog even though he looked more like a gremlin. I looked around. Plenty of people walked their dogs off leash but none this small. One wrong step and he would have been under my boot. He stood up on his hind legs and let out another pitiful whine-growl.

"Where did you come from?"

He blinked at me but didn't offer any information that was helpful.

The door to the diner opened and a young woman walked out. I was pretty sure she was a Murphy because she had red hair and a ton of freckles. She was wearing yoga pants with stains all over them.

"Is this your dog?"

She shook her head before looking around. "Sorry. Maybe Dot knows?"

After she climbed into her car, I waited to see if anyone else would come out. There was no one else in the parking lot so he had to belong to someone who was still inside otherwise that meant he'd wandered all the way down Main Street by himself. His legs were so short that I figured he couldn't have come that far. Based on size alone, he had to be a puppy still.

He stood on his hind legs again and pawed at my jeans. When I noticed his eyes fixed on my sub sandwich, I felt a little pang of sympathy. Poor little guy was probably hungry if he'd been wandering alone.

"Sorry, buddy, but I don't think dogs are supposed to eat meatball subs."

He barked once and then latched on to my pant leg.

"Ow! *Motherf—*"

I danced around trying to dislodge the pup's teeth from the fabric of my pants. Just when he let go, the door to the diner flew open and Charlie came out, flames of fury in her eyes with Tana following right behind her.

"Are you kicking that puppy?" Charlie demanded.

"I didn't kick him. *He bit me.* All because he wanted a meatball."

Tana shook her head. "Seriously, Rix? It's a dog, not a criminal mastermind."

"Really?" I pointed to the dog happily feasting on the meatball sub I'd finally dropped.

Although she still looked like she wanted to breathe fire, Charlie relaxed slightly at the evidence that I was not in fact a puppy-kicking monster.

She knelt next to the dog. "Aww, you like meatballs? You look like a little meatball."

The dog snuffled over to her and licked her fingers. She petted him on the back a few times before picking him up. The puppy cuddled right into the curve of her cleavage with a happy sigh.

"Pretty sure he likes melons as much as he likes meatballs," I muttered.

Charlie gave me a nasty look before she turned her attention back to the little thief burrowing against her breasts. "Don't be scared, cutie pie. I won't let the big old meanie get you."

"Reminder: he's not scared of me. He just tried to take a chunk out of my ankle!"

As if he could sense that he had the attention of the room, the puppy whimpered and put a dramatic paw over his eyes.

"You've got to be kidding," I muttered.

Charlie walked away, cooing at him the whole time. Tana shook her head at me again before she followed. I was left standing in the middle of the parking lot with nothing but the sad remains of my sandwich next to me.

Meanwhile, that little gremlin was leaving with a pretty girl to hold him and the rest of my meatball sub in his belly.

Not a criminal mastermind, my ass.

eight

. . .

CHARLOTTE

We watched as Hendrix climbed into his pickup truck. A bunch of people had come outside during the ruckus so this was definitely going to be the subject of every conversation I had over the next few days.

I glanced over at Tana. "Your brother is still a dick."

She laughed. "The doctor said the condition is chronic."

"This time tomorrow the word on the street will be that Hendrix saved me from a wild animal. What do you want to bet?"

Tana acknowledged the point with a rueful smile. "That's life in a small town. Welcome back."

The last thing I wanted was to be the subject of the town gossip mill. After the awkward milkshake moment, silence had settled over the diner, which meant everyone had noticed the contentious exchange. Just one more thing to add fuel to the fire.

I had actually been having fun until he showed up. I hadn't really wanted to come out when Tana called, but I'd only bought a few essentials at the grocery store when I arrived and I was already tired of scrambled eggs. She'd promised it would be a low-key lunch where we could pig out on diner burgers just like in high school.

When Carter had shown up ten minutes into our pig-out, he hadn't waited for an invitation but just planted himself at the table. Not that I minded. The last time I saw him he was a scrawny teenager with a chip on his shoulder. Now I could tell he was completely built beneath his cotton T-shirt.

"Are we going to talk about it now or just keep pretending you didn't send my mortal enemy as a potential roommate?"

Tana shrugged her shoulders. "He needs the room. I never said he wasn't a jerk. I just said he can afford the rent."

Carter had just walked up in time to overhear the last part of her sentence. He looked between the two of us. "Rix is going to be living with you?"

He wasn't exactly quiet and several people standing nearby glanced over with interest. I sighed. By this time tomorrow, everyone in town would be talking about me and Hendrix *living in sin*.

Meanwhile the only sinning between us would be when I finally murdered him and hid his body in the woods. But in a small town, the truth didn't matter nearly as much as what people wanted to believe.

"No, Tana just thinks he should. I'm renting a room to help pay for the repairs to Gran Grace's house. It's in pretty bad shape."

Carter reached over and squeezed my arm. "If you need any help, like a loan or something—"

"Oh no. I'm okay. I'm going to do some of the repairs myself to save money. But I might need both of your help when it's time to repaint. I'll pay you in pizza and beer."

"We'll be there," Tana promised. Her eyes flashed to the side. She'd noticed that Rix still hadn't left either.

God, that cocky bastard. What was he even doing? Hadn't he caused enough trouble? I tried to pay attention to what Carter was saying but my mind was stuck on Rix's face when he'd first approached our table. He'd already looked pissed off before he even walked up.

Did he just walk around perpetually annoyed and go out of his way to inflict his bad moods on me? Well, I wasn't going to let his mood swings influence how my day went. I'd had a plan, sort of, when I woke up this morning and I wasn't going to let anything derail it.

I glanced down at the puppy in my arms. Nothing other than a five-pound ball of fluff, anyway.

"I'm going to the store. I need to get some food for this little guy."

"Okay. Call me later?" Tana stroked the top of the puppy's head before she waved goodbye.

On impulse, I pulled out my phone and took a selfie making sure the puppy's sweet little face was visible. Billie loved dogs as much as I did so I figured she'd get a kick out of seeing him.

After a moment of hesitation, I sent it to my father as well.

Our communication over the years had gotten a little better but we still had a somewhat distant relationship. After the divorce, he'd kept up his visitation for the first year but after that his visits were increasingly sporadic.

To her credit, my mother hadn't bad-mouthed him at all. She'd explained that his deployments made it hard for him to maintain a consistent visitation schedule. However, once he'd retired from the Air Force and moved back to Louisiana, it was obvious that he considered us part of his past. A part that he'd clearly wanted to forget.

I sighed and stroked the puppy's soft fur. "It's just you and me for now, huh?"

The little dog snuggled closer into my neck. He'd been

lulled to sleep by all the activity and his chunky little body was a comforting weight on my shoulder. I was not going to get attached. His owner would probably show up looking for him soon and I'd have to give him back. But until then, I got to cuddle him.

Not a bad deal.

———

When I was little, having a dog wasn't practical since we moved so much. After the divorce, the timing never seemed right either since New York City apartments weren't exactly known for being spacious. My mother definitely hadn't wanted the fuss of cleaning up after an animal once she'd moved into Christian's pristine penthouse.

This was all to say that although I'd always wanted a dog, I had little practical experience with how much stuff dogs needed to be safe.

I'd meant to get just a few things, but the pet section at the general store was overwhelming. Food, beds, bowls, leashes, and an array of toys that would make any toddler jealous. Not to mention all the grooming products I needed to clean him up. My bank account was going to chastise me later, but when I looked down at Meatball sprawled comfortably in his little bed, I couldn't regret any of it.

It was a bad idea to name him, but I felt terrible just calling him *the puppy*. Plus, I got a laugh out of it every time I remembered him attacking Rix for his meatball sandwich. He had a home with me forever just for providing that little gem of blackmail material.

"What should we do first, huh? Bath or play?"

He huffed out an exhausted breath so I figured both options

were a no. I wasn't sure why he was so dang tired. I was the one who'd just given my credit card a workout.

I decided to make some found dog flyers first so I wouldn't have to feel guilty about absconding with someone's dog. Yes, I could have hung around the diner a little longer to see if his owner showed up but honestly, if they let him wander off so easily I wasn't thrilled with the idea of giving him back.

"But I have to at least try to find where you came from. So flyers it is. God knows I've learned my lesson about Facebook."

The flyers were simple, just a picture I snapped on my phone, and the location where he'd been found. Instead of putting my number, I created a new Gmail account and used that. I hadn't thought an innocuous little Facebook post would be seen by many people, but I hadn't taken into account how quickly it could be shared and reposted.

After the roommate fiasco, I was using an abundance of caution.

Since Meatball was still snoozing, I used the time to answer some emails and work a little bit more on my renovation budget.

Carter had given me the name of several contractors in the area so I left a message for each of them. Hopefully at least one of them would get back to me soon. After that, I spent some time researching average prices for each of the items on my renovation list.

The more I learned, the more confident I was that I could fix some of these items myself. As I inserted the estimates on my spreadsheet, I realized I was singing softly under my breath while I worked.

Gran's house still needed a ton of work, I was unemployed and definitely going to be broke soon, but at the end of it all, I was smiling. I'd been smiling for hours.

Small victories.

———

After about an hour, it was time for a break. I rolled my neck to relieve the tension of sitting hunched over my laptop for so long and then glanced down at Meatball. He was still fast asleep in his new bed with his little legs sticking straight up in the air.

It was the perfect opportunity to get started on my list.

I'd tried to be as comprehensive as possible, but I was sure there were things I'd missed. Either way, the more things I could do myself the better my chance of getting through this renovation without having to sell a kidney or something.

The porch was number one on my DIY list.

Tiptoeing upstairs so I wouldn't wake up my new little buddy, I made my way to my room to change into something I wouldn't mind getting dusty. The jeans I was wearing were my favorite pair and I definitely didn't want to mess them up. The porch needed to be power washed, but I could hammer in all the loose nails first. I figured that was a great place to start. How difficult was it to swing a hammer?

My mind drifted to Hendrix. If he could do it, obviously it wasn't that hard.

I didn't have many choices since I'd only brought one suitcase with me, but I did find an old T-shirt in the closet that I'd left here on a visit while in college. I rubbed the edge of the material between my fingers, remembering those early visits. I'd tried so hard at first, coming home at least twice a year. I'd hang out with Tana and just spend time here, thinking about Gran Grace.

But then at some point things had gotten busier and busier and it had been too hard to get away so often. My visits fell to once a year and then finally not at all. Then it seemed easier to just stay away. Or maybe I'd just gotten used to pretending I was fine. Pretending that it didn't break my heart every time I came home and then had to leave again.

I undressed quickly and pulled on the shirt. There was more in this closet than I thought. It was like a time capsule. I pulled out a pair of leggings that I used to wear to sleep in and put those on, too. Then on the top shelf I found a box filled with old accessories. I laughed as I pulled out a jumble of necklaces. I had always been hopeless at separating them once they got tangled. There was also a red bandana in the box. I shook it out. This would work to cover my hair. With my kinky curly texture, I preferred to only style once a week.

I definitely didn't need a head full of dust to wash out later.

When I went back downstairs, I moved through the kitchen to the utility closet. I'd seen a hammer in there when I was getting the mop out and I was pretty sure I'd seen a pair of gardening gloves, too. When I found them, I slipped them on. Hopefully that would protect me from splinters. I would need to go to town for supplies for the bigger projects, but at least I could get started.

As I walked through the living room, Meatball was still snoring softly, so I made sure to close the door behind me as quietly as possible. It was a beautiful day, and I was grateful that this part of Virginia didn't truly get hot until July. Right now, it was picture-perfect late spring weather with just enough breeze to carry the scent of the violetberry bushes from the side of the house. They were a particular subspecies of the American beautyberry that only grew in and around Violet Ridge and Gran had been very proud of them.

It was nearing the time when they would be ripe. Maybe I would make a pie in her memory.

I shook my head. I was already getting distracted. This porch was in dire need of some TLC.

I approached the first plank of wood and knelt to examine

it. It was only protruding a little, so I braced my hand about a foot away from the nail and then swung the hammer.

Crack.

It went in perfectly. I smiled. It was silly but it felt great to actually start on a home improvement project. Planning was my forte, but it was a little harder to actually execute. But this wasn't that hard at all. I moved down a little to the next protruding nail and brought the hammer down.

Crack.

For the next few minutes, I hammered in any nails that were loose. Then I sat back to survey my work. This side of the porch was looking pretty good!

Okay, it was still in desperate need of a good cleaning but that was probably something I could do myself, too. I wasn't sure where to buy one of those powerwash machines but maybe one of the neighbors already had one.

I looked over to the other side of the porch. The boards were much worse on that side. Some were actually lifting, and there were even a few spots where the wood had warped and you could see spaces in between. Maybe I couldn't fix all that so easily, but I could at least get the loose boards flat again. I picked up the hammer and then walked past the stairs. Then I took another step and one of the boards made a loud creaking sound.

"Okay, that doesn't sound too good," I muttered.

Then there was a terrible crash and the world disappeared. After a few seconds where I was pretty sure I was dead, I peeled one eye open and looked around warily.

Thankfully I wasn't dead, just waist deep in a hole. I had fallen through a weak section of the porch.

I looked around carefully taking stock of the situation. It had happened so fast I was lucky I'd managed to catch myself.

As it was, I'd let out an unholy scream they had probably heard all the way in the center of town.

Meatball was barking and I could hear his little paws scratching at the door. It was a good thing I'd left him inside. The thought of him falling into this hole was terrifying. At least I could get myself out.

I braced my arms on the side that seemed relatively sturdy and tried to hoist myself up. I thought I was in decent shape, but my arms burned from the effort. I'd fallen so far down that I couldn't get the leverage to lift myself up. With each attempt, I grew more exhausted.

Okay, maybe I *couldn't* get myself out.

What was I going to do? I hadn't brought my phone with me so I couldn't even call anyone for help.

Just then I heard a shaky voice say, "*What in the world was that?*"

The voice sounded vaguely familiar but at that point I would have welcomed a visit from the devil himself if it meant getting help.

"Hello? Is someone there?" I yelled.

The face that popped around the edge of the porch was such a relief that I could have cried. It was the next-door neighbor. She had lived next to Gran Grace since long before I was born.

"Miss Pauline! I'm so glad you're here. I need your help."

She lifted the glasses hanging on the chain around her neck and then squinted at me. "Charlie? Is that you?"

"Yes, ma'am. I was trying to fix the porch, and the boards must have been loose." I tried in vain to pull myself out again but this time a sharp pain shot up to my shoulder.

She came closer, clucking softly. "Maybe I can pull you up."

I paused. Miss Pauline had to be in her eighties by now.

There was no way she could pull me up without hurting herself.

"Maybe you can call someone for me? I'm not even sure who to call. Not the police. Oh, call Santana! Or maybe her dad."

Miss Pauline waved her hand dismissively. "No need for that. I'll call the fire department. Whenever my Eddie falls, they come and get him right up. They also got Agatha Kitty when she was stuck in a tree."

"Agatha Kitty?" I asked hesitantly.

"My cat, dear," she explained. "I'll just go call right now. Not to worry."

"Miss Pauline, you really don't need to bother the fire—" But she was already gone.

"Great. Just great."

So far, I was zero for two. After flooding the bathroom and now falling through the porch, I was starting to think this whole project was doomed. Now I was going to have to smile politely while a bunch of firefighters snickered behind my back.

I heard footsteps before Miss Pauline appeared again. "Don't worry, dear. They'll be here soon."

We chatted while I tried to see if there was anything below me I could use to push myself up. My foot felt like it was touching something, but I couldn't get a good foothold to try and jump out. After what felt like forever but was probably only another ten minutes, I heard a familiar voice.

The last voice I ever wanted to hear.

Rix's face appeared over the porch railing. "Well, what do we have here?"

I looked over at Miss Pauline. "I thought you called the fire department."

She nodded. "He is the fire department. He got Agatha Kitty right down. She didn't even scratch him."

"Yeah, I'll just bet all the kitties love him," I muttered.

Rix shook his head. "Ma'am, I'm actually not with the fire department anymore since I hurt my shoulder last year."

Poor Miss Pauline looked so confused. "Well, you come every time I call?"

"Of course I come. We're friends, aren't we?"

Miss Pauline beamed up at him. Rix looked over at me with a smug smile.

I rolled my eyes. "My leg is stuck. And my arms are really hurting from trying to hold myself up."

Rix knelt next to me and peered at the cracked wood. 'What were you doing, anyway?"

"Trying to fix the porch. I was hammering the loose nails."

He examined the area where I'd fallen through. "The wood may have been too weak to withstand it."

I glared at him. "You would just love to make it my fault, wouldn't you? Except I hadn't even started on this side when I fell in."

He grunted. "You know if I lived here, I could have gotten you out right away."

I glared at him. "You're trying to blackmail me into letting you move in?"

He frowned. "Of course not." Then he grasped me under my arms and with a grunt pulled me straight up. My foot snagged slightly on something, *something I didn't want to think about*, but with another tug I was free.

Hendrix deposited me gently a few feet away from the broken section of wood. "Are you okay?"

I really wasn't so sure, but I nodded anyway, hoping it would convince him to leave faster.

"Despite what you think of me, I don't want you getting hurt, Charlie."

Suddenly he raised his voice so Miss Pauline could hear.

"I'm just saying it's much safer to have a roommate, don't you think, ma'am? It's good for a woman to have a man about the house."

Miss Pauline clapped her hands. "Oh, you're going to be staying here. How wonderful."

I rubbed at the scratches on my thigh. When I'd fallen through, the rough wood had torn a hole through my leggings. "Miss Pauline, he's not staying here."

"In my day couples couldn't live together. But I suppose things are different now," she continued.

"We're not a couple," I interrupted.

"It's probably for the best. I *was* wondering how you'd get on in this big house all alone, Charlie." Miss Pauline rambled on as if she hadn't heard a word I'd said.

Rix smirked.

I sighed. What could I expect? Small towns were slow to change and people like Miss Pauline were from a different time. She didn't mean any harm but good lord, it was like being drop kicked back into the 1950s.

And of course, Rix would play right into that.

Miss Pauline finally noticed my ripped leggings. There were several scratches on the skin underneath that welled with blood. "I'd better get the first aid kit. We don't want those scratches to get infected."

"Yes, ma'am. Thank you."

While she bustled away, I examined the damage. Why hadn't I just worn my jeans? Then they'd be messed up instead of my skin. This home improvement thing was more dangerous than I'd anticipated. If I was going to be doing this kind of work, I would need to get appropriate clothing.

And buy life insurance.

Suddenly Meatball started barking again. He'd stopped eventually when no one had come to let him out but now he seemed to have gotten a second wind. Either that or he'd heard Fix's voice. I understood. The sound of that deep baritone made me want to scream my head off, too.

Rix glanced at the door warily. "You brought the dog home with you?"

"Where else was I supposed to take him?"

He shrugged. "I figured you were taking him to the vet."

I leaned back and hissed as the movement brought my attention to a whole new range of aches and pains. I would definitely be paying for this little adventure tonight.

"I will eventually. He can stay with me until I find his owner. All he does is sleep anyway."

Rix grunted. "If I lived here, I could get this patched up quickly. This isn't very safe. What if the dog had fallen in?"

"You are really laying it on thick, huh?"

In the distance, a door slammed, and we could hear Miss Pauline's voice. It sounded like she was fussing at someone. Probably her husband. Or maybe the cat.

Rix glanced over his shoulder at the sound. "I know you don't want to hear this but renovating a house can be complicated. When you get quotes, it would help to have someone look them over and make sure you aren't getting taken for a ride. If I moved in here, I could at least take care of some of these smaller projects for you and help you pick the best company to go with."

"I appreciate that but that doesn't mean you need to live here. We would kill each other inside of a week!"

"Look, I need a place to crash where I don't have to see any members of my immediate family naked or hear them having sex. It's just until I can find something else. I can pay above the market rate for rent. Hell, I'll pay anything just to get some peace and quiet in the mornings at this point."

"I don't know."

He must have sensed my weakness because he knelt until we were at eye level. "I can be an adult about this if you can. This is a good deal for both of us."

I hated to admit it, but he was right. So far everything I had touched had turned into a disaster. Rix might be a jerk, but he was a jerk who knew his way around a hammer. As much as I might hate the idea of him being around any more than necessary, maybe I needed to accept some help before the roof caved in.

"Fine."

Miss Pauline's voice suddenly seemed to get closer. Hendrix looked over in the direction of the noise.

"Fine. Does that mean we're doing this?" he asked.

I nodded. "We're doing this. God help us."

He ignored the last part. "I'll go get my stuff. We can figure out the rest tomorrow. Van will be happy to know he can bang in the morning with no witnesses."

Despite everything that made me smile.

I just hoped we weren't making a huge mistake.

nine

. . .

HENDRIX

The scent of coffee teased my nose. I blinked as the fog of my dreams slowly cleared and I remembered where I was. The walls were painted a sickly pink shade and there was nothing in the room except an old chest of drawers and a lamp I vaguely remembered turning off last night.

However, my entire body was covered in a patchwork quilt that looked like somebody's grandma made it which was the only clue I really needed to trigger my memory.

I was in Gran Grace's house.

Charlie's house.

At the thought, I jackknifed straight up in bed, intending to get up but didn't realize I was wrapped in the quilt. With a muffled groan, I rolled awkwardly off the bed and onto the floor.

"And things were going so well," I muttered.

Twisting until I could get my arms free of the quilt, I grabbed the clothes I'd left at the foot of the bed. With my luck, Charlie would come investigate the noise and find me naked as a newborn on the floor.

After I was dressed, I pulled the bedroom door open slowly. Clearly, I'd overestimated Charlie's interest in my welfare since she hadn't come to check on me. I hadn't wanted her to, of course, but couldn't help feeling grumpy about it. What if I'd actually needed help?

The battle lines were already drawn it seemed.

Still, anything was better than hearing Van's headboard banging against the wall. So I reached into the depths of my soul to summon the manners my mother claimed she'd raised me with.

"Morning."

Charlie looked up when I walked in the kitchen and waved, almost dropping the plastic spatula in her hand. Maybe she'd forgotten I was here too since she'd definitely not dressed for company. She had on a pair of pink pajama pants and a tiny top that once again had her nipples on display. Luckily, I was distracted from her full beam headlights by the monstrosity of a bun on top of her head. It was a jumble of curls with random pieces sticking out all over.

"Nice hair."

She made a face. "I was going to offer you a pancake but never mind."

I laughed as she flipped me the bird before stirring the pancake batter. There was a carton of orange juice on the counter, so I grabbed a glass from the cupboard. I was completely aware of Charlie moving behind me, humming under her breath as she moved to the sink to wash a carton of strawberries. There were several bags on the counter filled with food.

"You had time to go to the store?"

Before she could respond, I picked up a bag of salad and opened the refrigerator. There was a small compartment with space, so I stuffed it in there. Charlie shrugged so I went back to digging through the bags. After I pulled out a bundle of asparagus and then a bag of avocados, I looked around searching for the real food.

"Is that your plan, then? Starving me to death to get me to move out faster?"

She huffed. "These are healthy."

I held up a few sticks of asparagus. "These are gross."

"Bold of you to assume I'm sharing my food with you."

"You didn't seem opposed to sharing food the other day. Or is that enthusiasm just for orgasm shakes?"

"That enthusiasm is for gentlemen."

"Who says I'm not a gentleman?" I grabbed her hand and brushed a kiss across the back. "Is this good enough for her highness?"

She yanked her hand away and then stood on tiptoe as she reached above the refrigerator to stuff several boxes of crackers up there.

Why did she need so many of those?

Did she have a secret cracker fetish that I didn't know about?

When she noticed me looking, she quickly dropped back down, yanking her shirt lower at the same time. The movement pulled the thin fabric tighter across her chest and I couldn't help but notice that she'd filled out a lot since high school. Her breasts were a lot bigger and a lot rounder, facts that I probably could have politely ignored if her nipples weren't so hard and pointy and clearly visible through her shirt.

Was she walking around town like that?

"Did you think you'd see Carter while you were out? Is that why you're not wearing a bra?"

She gasped and dropped the bushel of weird lettuce she was holding on the counter. "I am wearing a bra, not that it's any of your business. It's not my fault you're a freaking perv. Stop looking at my nips!"

"I'm pretty sure *they* are staring at *me,*" I mumbled.

She shook her head. "Okay, we need to establish some ground rules."

The exasperated look she sent my way should have been annoying but instead had the effect of being scolded by my favorite teacher.

My hottest teacher.

I shifted uncomfortably.

"Rules? What kind of rules? I fix stuff. You don't try to make me eat asparagus."

I dug through another bag and laughed softly when I found a package of Oreos. That was more like it. I ripped them open leaving a trail of brown crumbs along the counter.

She pointed at the mess. "I am not your maid or your mother. We are roommates. You will need to purchase groceries half the time and we can decide on a cooking schedule later."

I walked over and sat on the living room couch. It groaned under my weight while the plastic on the cushions squealed at the sudden movement. Oh hell no. There was no way I was listening to that sound every time I sat down.

"Can we decide on a schedule to replace the furniture? I know Gran Grace loved this couch, but this is not going to work."

Her expression turned mulish. "We are not getting rid of my grandmother's things."

"Seriously? You plan on watching Netflix on this thing? It'll scream every time you move."

She ignored me. "Also, we need a cleaning schedule since there's only one full bathroom. You might be used to living in filth, but that's not how I roll."

"Why do you assume I lived in filth? Van's place was nice."

"It was nice, but you left so…"

"Did you not hear what I said about the naked ass cheeks?"

She rolled her eyes, but I could tell she was trying not to laugh as she went back to fussing with the groceries.

"Van is really happy. I wanted to give the lovebirds some space. They can't make it work with me underfoot."

Charlie just stared at me. I shifted uncomfortably, the plastic squeaking with every twitch. I hadn't meant to say all that out loud.

She walked over to the couch and put her hand against my forehead. I was so stunned it took a few seconds before I grabbed her wrist. Her touch felt good. Too good.

"What now?"

"You thought about someone other than yourself. Just checking that it's really you, Pinocchio. For a minute there, you almost sounded like a real boy."

I ducked away from her touch and followed her back to the kitchen. She'd plated her pancakes and added some sliced strawberries on the side. While I watched, she added two slices of bacon and drizzled maple syrup over the whole thing.

I'd bite my tongue before I admitted how much I wanted a pancake, so I took a gulp of juice and then pulled the bread from the pantry. Toast would have to do. When I turned around again, Charlie was gone.

———

After choking down the least satisfying breakfast ever, I grabbed a change of clothes and went into the bathroom. The door stuck slightly when I tried to close it. I leaned down to get a closer look at the latch. The frame must have warped slightly. It was common in older houses. That was something I could help with. Charlie might not want me here but having a handyman around would definitely be to her benefit. Plus, I could get a discount on the materials she would need to fix this place up.

Charlie said that she'd had a plumber come by already, but I still eyed the tub warily. There was no shower stall, just a shower curtain on rings around the tub. I turned on the water and was pleasantly surprised when it heated quickly.

After undressing, I ran a tentative hand over the scruff on my jaw. I usually tended to let my beard grow in a bit before I bothered shaving, but I found myself wondering whether Charlie was into facial hair. When I realized what I was doing, fantasizing about whether she'd run her hands over my face, I scowled and got into the shower. Maybe if I dunked my head enough times I could clear her out.

I let the hot water flow over my face but as soon as my eyes were closed there was nothing stopping me from imagining Charlie on her knees in front of me. My abs tightened as I ran a hand down to grab my cock, tugging roughly as I imagined how she would look up at me, with her tongue out and fire in her eyes.

Fuck, I wanted to see exactly what that smart mouth could do.

With every stroke, my imagination escalated the scene, as I pictured her lips wrapped around my dick as she moaned at the taste. I had a suspicion that she would be just as contrary while sucking me off as she was everywhere else, using her mouth to tease me until I was half mad with it. My hand flew faster, rubbing over the sensitive head as I imagined her reaching between her legs to rub herself while she had her way with me.

I groaned, the sound mixing with the steam in the room as I shuddered violently, the image of her getting herself off finally taking me over the edge. I opened my eyes and then cursed. I wasn't supposed to be imagining that she-devil when I was fucking my hand. It was like I couldn't even escape her when I was by myself.

Furious at my loss of control, I washed quickly using Charlie's girly body wash that smelled like peaches. With a flick of my wrist, I turned the water off and carefully pulled the curtain back.

Just then the door suddenly burst open, and Charlie paused in the doorframe.

At the sight of her my dick filled again, as if I hadn't just come like a train five seconds before. I groaned. If this was what I was in for every time we crossed paths, it was going to be a very long summer.

"Oh!" she said before looking down.

With the curtain pushed back there was nothing to shield me as her eyes dropped from my face down to my chest.

Then lower.

"Oh my god!" She blinked several times before her hand clenched on the doorknob.

Having her this close when the remnants of my fantasy were so fresh in my mind was torture. I couldn't have her in here staring at my dick when I could still see dream Charlotte on her knees with her tongue out. She needed to get gone. *Now.*

"This is the part where you close the door."

"Right. Of course." She nodded frantically. Her big brown eyes looked a little glassy and unfocused.

When she still didn't move, I couldn't resist messing with her a little.

"Unless you plan on joining me. In which case you should lose the clothes."

ten

. . .

CHARLOTTE

I pulled the door closed with a loud bang. For a moment I just stood in the hallway, my heart racing.

His bedroom door was closed so I had assumed he was in his room. And who takes a shower without closing the door all the way?

I groaned, remembering the smug look on his face when he caught me staring at his junk. Such a cocky asshole. How did he know I wasn't looking because it was crooked or something?

If only. But no, the universe wasn't that kind. Hendrix Evers had the face of an angel and a body made for sin. He'd filled out over the years in all the right places. That was the body of a man who did physical labor on a routine basis. The kind who would have rough hands. I shivered at the thought.

Then I shook my head.

No. No. No.

We are not thinking about stupid Hendrix or his stupid, rough man hands.

He was clearly just trying to embarrass me, and I wasn't going to give him the satisfaction.

When the bathroom door finally opened, Rix was thankfully dressed.

"*Maybe we need to be clearer about the rules,*" I yelled.

He scoffed. "What did I do? You're the one who just invaded my privacy, remember? Maybe I don't feel safe. Maybe *you're* trying to steal *my* virtue."

Oh my god.

I wanted to strangle him.

"You left the door open on purpose."

He gave me the cocky smirk that always made me want to scratch his eyes out. "I closed the door. I remember because I had to lean *hard* to get it to latch. It was definitely closed, Charlie."

I held up a hand and marched around him. The bathroom door was hanging open, so I pulled the knob and sure enough, it got stuck when I tried to pull it closed. Rix leaned on the wall next to me. I ignored him but it was impossible not to notice him cross his arms as he watched me wrestle with the door. Finally, I yanked hard and it closed with a bang.

"Just because it sticks doesn't prove your point. If anything, it works against you. If it's this hard to get it to close, then it would have been hard for me to open, too."

He clicked his tongue against his teeth. "I wasn't listening to how hard it was for you to open the door. I was a little busy being naked."

"Busy playing with your dick, you mean."

"What was that?" He leaned closer, bringing with him that fresh clean scent that would forever remind me of what he looked like dripping with water.

"Nothing. It doesn't matter. The door has a lock!"

Just then, the door popped open. Startled, we both looked down at the same time.

"Did that just–"

Rix ran his hand up the wood frame. "The door frame is warped. I figured that was why the door was sticking. Apparently, it's worse than I thought."

As his fingers traced over the wood, I swear I could almost feel those fingers tracing up my spine. "Uh huh."

"If I replace the frame that might fix it, but there's a chance I might need to move the hinges," he muttered to himself under his breath as he examined the door, seemingly no longer aware that I was even there.

Hopefully I nodded at the right places because in my mind all I could hear was white noise as my eyes followed the movement of his lips as he spoke. Then he looked at me suddenly, his brow furrowed as he noticed where I was staring.

I spun around. "I need to go."

He blinked. "Okay."

"Okay." Without another word, I crossed the hall to my room and closed the door.

I seriously needed to get out of the house.

After a brief debate I threw on a pair of jeans and a pretty flowered blouse. It was high time I visited Tana's salon. While she wasn't a formal person, she'd always had her own unique style. Instead of my usual pair of Chucks, I pulled out a fun pair of strappy sandals.

There. That was probably as good as it was going to get. Better than my usual jeans and white T-shirt, anyway.

At the last minute I grabbed a tote bag. Tana had curly hair too so she'd always carried a large selection of products geared to ethnic hair types. I might as well grab some more shampoo and conditioner while I was there.

When I emerged, the first thing I saw was Rix's back as he squatted next to a toolbox.

He turned around holding a drill in his hand. "This should

be done by the end of the day. Hopefully I won't scare you again."

"Who said I was scared?"

He just smiled and turned the drill on. I scowled before looping the tote bag over my shoulder. Maybe I should ask Tana if she had anything to wash the smell of a cocky but handsome man out of your hair.

Not that I could tell Tana about any of this. Despite their childhood history of annoying each other, the Evers siblings were solid as rock. If she ever found out I'd seen him naked, things could only go two ways.

She'd be excited about the possibility of us being together, which would only end in disappointment since Rix was hardly husband material.

Or she'd think it was weird and that would make things awkward between us.

Now that I was finally back in town and living the life I'd dreamed of, nothing was going to stand in my way. Still, I figured it was best if she found out about our new living situation directly. I didn't want her to think I was hiding anything.

Downstairs, I grabbed a towel and then quickly took Meatball out for a walk so he could empty his never-ending bladder before settling him into the passenger seat of my car. Normally I would just walk into town, but I figured it was smart to have a means of quick escape in case he wasn't in the mood to behave today.

"We're going to visit one of my favorite people, so I need you to be nice for a few hours. Don't bite anyone. Deal?"

Meatball grumbled which I took to mean, *I'm making no promises.* I made sure to tuck the edge of the towel around my car's seat just in case he got any ideas.

I'd had enough of men flashing their junk for one day.

———

Hair Me Out sat on the very end of First Avenue, one of the older sections of town. Most of the buildings here were in bad shape and quite a few of the spaces were empty. The shop's colorful awning stood out like a ray of sunshine in a storm. I grinned up at the sign I'd previously only seen on Instagram.

As children we'd shared our dreams in the completely guileless way you only can before the world breaks your heart. I knew what it meant to Tana to create a welcoming place for all that was a safe harbor for creativity. The only other salon in town was owned by an older lady named Irma who thought that highlights were scandalous.

As I entered the shop, I shifted Meatball to my other side, being sure to keep a good grip on his little belly. A bell chimed as I pushed the door open and multiple heads turned our way.

"Hi. I'm looking for Tana," I said to the woman behind the reception desk.

She had an angular black bob sharp enough to cut glass and when she tossed her head, the swing of her hair revealed that the underside was a bright magenta.

I instantly felt so plain in comparison.

Now that I was there, I realized I probably should have called first. This was almost *fancy*. Everything in the shop was white or black but all the display cases were neon pink. It had a retro 80s vibe that somehow felt completely modern but also expensive.

Looking around at the sleek interior of the shop, my heart filled with an inexplicable burst of pride.

Tana had created something really special.

"Do you have an appointment?" The woman leaned over the computer and started clicking with her mouse.

"Um, no. I probably should come back. You guys look really busy."

A squeal from the back of the shop had every head turning that direction. Tana stood in the back of the salon wearing all black covered with a neon pink apron. Her colorful hair was bundled up into a bun that looked sexy and cool with pink highlighted pieces pulled out and artfully framing her face.

"Charlie! You actually came?"

She made her way through the salon, stopping to make a comment to one of the stylists. When she reached the front, she pulled me into a side-hug since she was carrying a box in her other arm.

"I had to come see your empire of style. Tana, this is even better than it looks online. It's amazing."

"Thank you. I still can't believe this is real sometimes," she said softly.

"Do you need me to pinch you?"

"Please do." She held out her arm. "I'm afraid I'll wake up and still be doing helmet hair in Irma's house of horrors."

I followed her to the back of the salon, averting my eyes from the women in the chairs in various stages of being washed, prepped, foiled and who knew what else. Personally, I'd always hated being on display in the salon, especially when a cute delivery driver would come in.

"So what's been going on? I meant to come by yesterday, but things got so busy at the shop. I had a walk-in who needed color correction for the brassy highlights she got while on vacation. And I'm using the word 'highlights' loosely."

I followed her into a small office in the back. The room was painted the same pink as her apron and had sleek black furniture. A laptop was open on the desk.

"Funny you should ask. Your brother moved in yesterday."

She fumbled the box. "He did?"

"Just until he can find something else. Plus, he offered to help with a few repairs, too."

Tana watched me carefully for a moment. It took all my restraint not to fidget under her knowing gaze. It was completely foreign to edit my thoughts around Tana. For years, the hallmark of our unique friendship was complete and utter realness. We told each other everything, even things we probably shouldn't have. So it went against all of my natural instincts to keep a secret from her. I could feel the urge to confess rising in the back of my throat like vomit.

I saw your brother naked.

He's hung like a god.

I want to bang him despite hating his guts.

"My brother is living with you," she repeated, as if she needed to hear it again before she could believe it. "And he's still...*alive?*"

I chuckled at her bewilderment. "Hey, this was your idea. You're the one who sent him over."

"True, but even I didn't actually think either of you would go for it," she mused.

"Well, as it turns out having a handyman for a roommate is exactly what you need when you own a house that's falling apart."

She conceded the point with a nod. "I can see how that would be a point in his favor."

"Anyway, he's working on fixing some stuff today, so I figured I'd stay out of the way. I'd love to see the salon if you have time to show me around."

"Of course. Let me introduce you to everyone."

She gave me the five-dollar tour, showcasing the new ionic dryers that she bought earlier in the year that could set a style in half the time. I marveled over the wall of professional photographs of her clients and the incredible styles she'd created.

A stylist standing nearby waved when I mentioned them. Like Tana, her dark hair had highlights except she only had it on the tips, a different color for each layer. She looked like some kind of gorgeous unicorn.

Tana trotted to her side. "Meet my rising star. This is Piper Ross. Not only is she an amazing stylist but she's also a photographer. The shop's entire Instagram success has been because of her photos."

Piper took a little bow. "I do what I can."

"Your photos are stunning. Seriously, I could see these in a gallery in New York."

"Really? I'm hoping to do a big show one day. Probably not in a gallery but I'm thinking about going to this arts festival in the fall."

"You definitely should. You're really talented."

Tana pointed at the both of us. "While we're here, I've been meaning to organize a Girls' Night."

Piper perked up. "Ooh, another bonfire at the barn?"

I looked between the two of them. "The barn. Like, *The Barn?* No way. You guys still hang out there?"

"Yes, we still hang out there." Tana hip-checked me.

"I guess you're probably used to hanging out at really cool places in the city," Piper said, her tone of voice noticeably cooler.

"Oh no. I just realized how that sounded and that's not what I meant *at all*. I've been to some really exclusive bars and restaurants in New York, but do you want to know what usually happens there? The waitstaff silently judges your outfit before you even have a chance to sit down. A hot guy *will* buy you a drink, but then he'll proceed to talk about nothing but himself. Then if you don't want to go home with him, he leaves after calling you a bitch."

Piper laughed. "Wow, way to ruin the fantasy."

"Some of the best times I've ever had were at that barn. I just can't believe Mr. Donald hasn't figured out how to ban kids from his property yet."

Tana smiled. "Are you kidding? He loves it. Now that we're older, he's finally stopped pretending to be angry that we're there. He actually comes out and drinks with us sometimes now."

"Wait, what?"

"The first time it happened, I was sure we were in the end times. But I think he and his wife are kind of lonely out there by themselves. My parents have them over for dinner sometimes and I know Rix helps him maintain the property."

"He does?"

The thought of grumpy Hendrix going out of his way to help out two empty nesters softened my annoyance toward him considerably.

Damn him for being such an unexpectedly moral person. I guess that was a side effect of being an Evers though.

Luckily, Tana seemed oblivious to where my thoughts were. "He runs that huge mower and fixes stuff around the house. I know he doesn't charge him even half of what he should, but Mr. Donald gives him some moonshine in exchange, so I guess that's a fair deal."

Piper sighed. "I know you don't want to hear this boss lady, but your brother is ridiculously hot."

"Okay, I'm going back to work if you're going to be gross." Tana covered her ears playfully. "Actually, I need to get back to fighting with this stupid QuickBooks program. I accidentally deleted something, and I don't know what to do."

"You can put in a journal entry. That should fix it," I told her.

"A what?"

"I can show you if you want."

Meatball had perked up while we were talking and was now surveying the room with interest. When his little face popped over my shoulder, Piper held out her hands.

"I can hold him while you guys work."

"Are you sure? He can be a bit of a handful."

"Play with a puppy? You don't have to twist my arm." Piper took him and cuddled him close.

"Also, he pees randomly."

She chuckled. "Thanks for the warning."

For the next half hour, I helped Tana navigate her accounting software. She had a freelance bookkeeper who'd become increasingly unreliable and was trying to manage on her own until she could hire someone else.

Although I'd gotten my degree in Finance, I'd taken several accounting classes and was able to figure out how to do things pretty quickly. By the time we came back out, Meatball was being petted by one of the customers while Piper trimmed another client's hair.

"Good news. Charlie has fixed the accounting issues. Peace reigns in salon land!"

Cheers went up around the salon and I gave a little wave. I was silly but helping a friend with her small business was more fulfilling than any of the big corporate transactions I'd assisted with while working for Delacourt. Who cared if Fortune 500 company A merged with Fortune 500 company B?

Every project I'd worked on over the years had just been helping the rich get richer and I'd never felt like I was part of anything that really mattered.

But helping Tana meant helping a local business stay oper-

and profitable so she could hire other local women. It was a revelation to look back at the life I'd once been so proud of and see it was completely empty.

After Piper finished with her client, she spun the woman's chair around so she could admire her new look.

"Thank you for fixing the money. Because I, for one, enjoy getting paid," Piper said.

Her client fluffed the ends of her hair before turning to face us. "Do you know how Etsy works? I need someone to help me set up my shop. I make jewelry. I've been selling at craft fairs but I'm ready to try selling online."

"I've never done that before but I'm sure I can find some tutorials online."

She beamed as she handed Piper her credit card. "Let me give you my number. I could use some help organizing my receipts also. I tried to put them in a spreadsheet, but I'm not so good with that part."

I cracked my knuckles playfully. "Spreadsheets are kind of my jam."

After she left, Tana hugged me. "You're going to have a business of your own soon if you keep this up."

My heart sped up as she walked away. A business of my own? That wasn't what I'd expected when I'd moved out here. I'd assumed I'd find something in a nearby city or start working for a company remotely once I was done renovating the house. However, the more I thought about it, the more right it seemed.

I'd never started a business before and had absolutely no idea what I was doing but for the first time I thought that maybe that was okay.

eleven

• • •

HENDRIX

The next day I stood outside the hardware store wondering what to do next. I'd already finished all the errands I could come up with and I couldn't go grocery shopping until I was sure it was safe to go back home. Maybe I could buy all the nonperishables first? I rubbed my eyes in frustration.

At least my morning hadn't started with banging. No, this time I was treated to the visual delight of Charlie in sleep shorts so tiny they showed the curve of her ass.

Meanwhile she wouldn't look me in the eye. It would have been funny if it wasn't so stupid.

So she saw me naked? Big deal.

Although I had to admit that it would be a huge deal if I had seen *her* naked. Even though she hated me, and I found her stuck up and anal retentive, I couldn't help fantasizing about her in the shower again.

God, the thought of Charlotte Monroe on her knees in front of me was enough to short-circuit my brain every time. I couldn't even imagine pushing through those full lips while she looked up at me with those big dewy eyes.

Even her blowjobs were probably angry.

I groaned and pinched my nose in frustration. This wouldn't do. I couldn't go back there until I was sure I had these errant thoughts under control. I glanced at my phone to see the time. It was only a little after ten. Surely she was out of the house by now?

As I was standing in the middle of the sidewalk trying to decide if it was worth the risk to go home, I heard a familiar little growl.

"Would you come on?" a voice whispered from behind me.

When I turned around, Charlie was a few feet away tugging on the end of a retractable leash while her little dog friend sniffed my boot. It was obvious that she'd been hoping to sneak by without having to speak to me. Since I loved nothing more than scuttling her plans, I raised my voice as loud as I could when I spoke.

"Good morning, Charlie! Fine day, isn't it?"

"Well, I thought it was until now." She plastered the biggest fake smile on her face before turning to leave, but the dog resisted her effort with a pitiful little whine.

"He looks better. Did you give him a bath?" I wasn't sure why I was determined to engage her in conversation other than the fact that she so clearly didn't want to talk to me.

Annoying Charlotte Monroe was an evergreen joy, it seemed. I fully expected us to be puttering around town in our eighties still slinging insults and rolling our eyes at each other. The mental image of us as little old people took me off guard for a moment because I was struck with how much I actually hoped it would come true. It was a stupid thing to wish for since Charlie would likely have moved on to some other place to live long before then.

"Yes. He got a bath."

"As long as you didn't do it after midnight, we're safe."

"What?"

"Obviously he's a gremlin disguised as a dog." I was a little surprised she didn't get the reference after how many times we'd watched that old movie as kids.

She rolled her eyes before tugging on the leash again. The little dog paid her no mind as he growled playfully and tried to bite one of the laces on my boot.

I moved my foot away slightly. "Hey! If you want to bite me at least buy me dinner first."

He seemed to take that as a challenge as he hopped around, chasing my foot like it was a game. But at some point I must have done something he interpreted as aggressive because he suddenly went wild, barking furiously at my feet.

"What did you do to him?" Charlie accused.

I pointed down at the dog who was still barking madly like he was being attacked. "All I did was move my foot. Does he have a thing about boots? Did he get stepped on or something?"

She peered down at him curiously. "I don't know. Maybe he's just remembering the day he met you."

"Funny."

"I can relate. I feel uncontrollable rage when I see you, too."

Shaking my head, I looked back down at the little dog. It didn't look like he was going for my ankle this time so I took the risk of petting his back. His huge tongue lolled out of his mouth as he panted. When he pawed my leg, I picked him up.

"Wow, Meatball. Really? You have no loyalty." Charlie scowled at me, but she reached over to give the puppy a scratch behind the ears.

"Meatball? You're actually calling the dog *Meatball*?" I cracked up.

"Well, it's better than calling him *the dog*." She lowered her voice while she imitated me.

"At least it's accurate. The little bastard ate my food."

She scowled. "Don't call him that. He's just a baby."

"He's a homeless thief."

She leaned over to kiss Meatball's head before whispering, "If this is going to work, you cannot be nice to Rix. We do not like him. *Stranger Danger*."

When I heard the distinctive sound of water hitting the ground, I looked down to see that the dog had just peed all over my favorite boots. I scrambled to adjust my hold to keep it away from me until the stream finally stopped. Then just when I relaxed, he let out one last shot that hit me right on the thigh, leaving a huge wet spot on my jeans.

"Well, it seems the gremlin has unlocked his first weapon: the pee cannon. You've trained him well." I handed him back to Charlie carefully.

She gulped. "Okay now I actually feel kind of bad. I didn't expect that to happen. He just went to the bathroom on five different trees."

"I think he was saving that one for a good cause."

She leaned down to whisper in Meatball's ear. "Good boy. You get an extra treat today."

I shook my boots to get as much of the pee off as possible before making my way over to my truck. The last thing I wanted was for that smell to get into the interior.

I should have been annoyed that I needed to go home and change but honestly, it was kind of funny. From stealing my food to destroying my clothes, the dog was racking up points in our ongoing war.

I was going to have to step up my game.

———

As soon as I got in my truck, I decided to go ahead and get my groceries before I went home. Going home to change my shoes would waste way too much time and I was due at work soon. This was a small town, so everybody knew everybody's business. Going into the general store with dog pee on my boots definitely wasn't the worst thing that had ever happened.

I drove over to the general store, which was a charming old building on the corner of Main Street with a striped green and white awning. As far as I knew, the store had been here as long as the town had, and it had always been run by a Murphy.

When I walked in Mrs. Murphy, the elderly store owner, glanced up from the magazine she was reading. "Morning, Rix."

I waved back and grabbed a basket. "Morning, Mrs. Murphy."

My first stop was for snacks. I couldn't survive on the wheat grass and berries that Charlie seemed to love. I would die if I didn't get some real food.

Just the sight of all the potato chips lined up made my mouth water. I grabbed a salt and vinegar, a sour cream and onion, and two different types of Doritos. I looked down at the handheld basket I was carrying and then walked back up front to exchange it for one of the small push carts.

I loaded my cart with all the chips before moving on to the dairy section. I was a simple man and I wanted simple, old-fashioned ice cream. Vanilla. Chocolate. Butter pecan. Not those tiny cartons with the weird names.

As I reached the ice cream case, my heart sank. Mrs. Murphy had apparently rearranged everything again. All I could see was vegan, low-fat, non-fat...

"What the hell is the point of non-fat ice cream? Might as well just eat an ice cube."

"The vanilla is on the bottom shelf."

I stiffened. Then I turned around. Janelle had a handheld

basket hanging on her arm and looked like she was dressed for work. Maybe she was going in late today.

"Thanks." I knelt and grabbed a tub of the vanilla ice cream.

"You're welcome," she replied.

God, this was awkward. As I turned to leave, Janelle cleared her throat. "So how have you been?"

"Fine. How about you?" I tried to keep my voice steady.

She shrugged. "I got a promotion."

"That's great. Congratulations."

I moved down to the milk. I wanted the real stuff, not that almond garbage Charlie bought. Janelle followed a few feet behind. I could feel her eyes on me as I looked over the offerings. I grabbed a gallon of 2 percent and dropped it into my cart.

"My cousin Theresa is getting married," Janelle said finally. "She wants me to be one of her bridesmaids."

The word *bridesmaid* hung heavily in the air between us. Janelle had already been a bridesmaid in four weddings.

I swallowed. "Tell her I said congratulations."

As I was about to walk away again Janelle laughed. "That's all you can say? Congratulations?"

The store was empty, save for Mrs. Murphy at the front counter. Every so often she flipped a page in her magazine, but I could tell she was listening.

"What do you want me to say, Janelle?" I asked finally.

Her face fell. "I don't know. Maybe that we didn't waste a year of our lives. That we can start over. That you miss me."

That hit me right in the gut. I took a deep breath and walked back toward Janelle. "I wasn't trying to waste your time. I thought we were having fun. Maybe I was the only one having a good time."

We stood in silence, both pretending that we didn't notice

Mrs. Murphy hanging on our every word. She wasn't even pretending to read her magazine anymore.

She sniffled. "Sometimes I wonder what could have been if we'd tried a little harder."

"I think we tried. Both of us. We just wanted different things. It's okay. We've both moved on."

Her gaze turned speculative. "I heard you moved in with that girl. Tana's friend. What was her name?"

I sighed. Janelle could be catty as hell and the last thing I needed was her targeting Charlie.

"I had to find a room to rent after you kicked me out. You remember throwing all my shit in the grass, right?"

Her expression turned mulish. "I was upset, okay?"

"I get that. I was upset, too. Being screamed at will do that to you." I moved around her and started walking toward the front of the store. Maybe an audience would discourage further conversation. I should have known better. Janelle followed so closely that when I stopped, she crashed into my back.

"Did you ever love me, Rix? Even a little?"

I looked over my shoulder and the sheen of tears in her eyes was unmistakable. That was why I'd left.

Okay, technically she had thrown me out, but that look was why I'd stayed gone.

It was hell being with someone every day knowing you could never be what they needed. I hadn't intended to lead her on. Things between us had started more out of convenience than anything. I think we both had just gotten tired of the dating scene.

But somewhere along the way her feelings went somewhere that mine couldn't follow.

"I'm sorry, Janelle."

We both knew what I meant by that.

The sound of the cash register startled us both. Mrs.

Murphy looked at me with sympathy. "You ready to check out, hon?"

"Yes." I grabbed everything in the cart and started piling it on the counter. I couldn't wait to get out of there.

Behind me I could still hear Janelle sniffling. Mrs. Murphy glanced over at her in between scanning items. I groaned. It would be all over town by tonight that I'd broken Janelle's heart. Again.

"That'll be $18.73," Mrs. Murphy announced.

I shoved a twenty-dollar bill across the counter and grabbed the bags. "Keep the change."

Suddenly Janelle sniffed even louder. Then she sniffed again.

"Rix. Is that *you?*"

I looked at her. Her cheeks were still wet but now she was looking at me with disgust. She put her hand over her nose.

"What?"

"You smell like..."

Just then I remembered Meatball's pee attack. It startled a laugh out of me. Both Janelle and Mrs. Murphy looked at me like I was crazy.

"It's a long story. But anyway, I have to go. Congratulations again on the promotion. That's impressive. See, you're doing so much better without me."

I backed out of the store, still laughing to myself at the looks on their faces. But as I got into my truck, I couldn't help but wonder when things got so complicated.

———

Later that afternoon, I was still thinking about the pee attack while restocking the shelves. Leave it to Charlie to bond with a dog that had a vendetta against me. As much as I didn't want to admit it, the little gremlin was pretty funny. His aim was impeccable. I was never going to be able to wear those boots again without remembering that.

"What are you laughing about?" Dad asked once the customer he'd been helping finally left.

"Just thinking about attack dogs." At his curious look, I shook my head. "Nothing. You had to be there."

He came from behind the counter and pulled out his Swiss Army knife so he could open one of the boxes next to me. We worked in comfortable silence for a while before he glanced over again.

"I've been meaning to ask how Charlie is doing out there at the Everett house all alone."

My back stiffened. Had someone seen us talking in town this morning and told him? I hadn't been surprised that Janelle knew since she and Tana had friends in common, but I'd hoped I had a little longer before the gossip trickled over to my parents' age group.

I wasn't planning to lie. But it wouldn't take much for my parents to get the idea that something was going on. Despite our hatred for each other, my parents adored Charlie and always had. If I showed even the slightest bit of interest in her then my mom would start "forgetting" that she'd invited Charlie over on the same day I usually visited or any number of other ridiculously obvious setups.

"Fine, I guess." Hopefully that sounded appropriately noncommittal.

Dad continued chatting as he opened another box. "The place has gotten really run-down over the years. That's a lot of work for one person to handle. But I'm sure you already offered to help. You'll give her a way better deal than anyone else she could hire."

"You're sure, huh?" I watched him from the corner of my

eye. My mom was usually the one matchmaking, but that didn't mean my father was immune.

"Of course, I'm sure. You're my son and I raised you right. Although I fully admit that was ninety percent your mother's doing."

I laughed. "You might have had a little more impact than that."

"Son, you would never let a family friend get taken for a ride by those fancy city contractors. They charge twice the price they need to. Those scammers wanted twenty thousand to redo a bathroom. Twenty thousand!"

"*Dad.*"

I needed to redirect his attention before he went on a complete tangent. He had a tendency to get riled up when talking about money.

"I'll take a look at any estimates she gets to make sure they're fair. She's not going to get scammed."

"I'm sure she'll appreciate it. It's good she's back after that New York business. People around here take care of each other. We always have."

He turned away when the bell over the door chimed but not before I spied the satisfied smirk on his face. I sighed. It was a good thing I'd already decided to help Charlie out since my dad had just taken me from zero to sixty in less than five minutes.

I had been played by a master.

"Nice guilt trip, Dad."

He shrugged. "I said it was ninety percent your mother. I have to do my ten."

As he wandered off to help a customer, I thought back to how Charlie had looked yesterday after I'd pulled her out of that hole in the porch. She'd looked so...defeated. Home improvement shows made everyone think they could renovate over the course of a weekend, but the reality was rarely so simple. Not to mention that it could be dangerous, something she had already found out the hard way.

What if Miss Pauline hadn't been home?

How many hours would she have been stuck there before anybody thought to check on her?

We might not be friends but that didn't mean I liked the idea of her getting hurt. Now that I was living there, I could at least make sure there weren't any other major disasters waiting to pop out.

As much as she hated it, she was going to have to get used to my help.

twelve

. . .

HENDRIX

back in the day ...

The sound of the rain against the windows was hard enough to make me jump. The storm ensured that we were stuck inside for the afternoon. I sighed and looked over at Charlie. She sat on the shaggy living room carpet next to me, listlessly holding one of her dolls.

Usually playing Barbies with Tana made her happy but today it wasn't working. Not when we could all hear my mom on the phone, despite her attempts to whisper.

"The poor thing. I don't think she understands what's happened."

Tana winced before shoving her doll next to Charlie's. "Let's play beauty shop!"

It was their favorite game even though they got into trouble every time they cut their doll's hair. Last time Mom had taken Tana's dolls away for a whole week. I sneaked a glance over my shoulder to where Mom sat in the kitchen.

Somehow, I knew they wouldn't get in trouble this time.

"Lena is just broken up, of course. What is she going to do now? Raising a child is hard enough but to do it alone?"

Charlie closed her eyes.

She'd shown up out of the blue a few hours ago clutching her mother's hand with a haunted look on her face. Her mom had dark circles around her eyes like a raccoon and had disappeared into the kitchen to whisper with my mother. Eventually she'd left after kissing Charlie on the head.

Charlie hadn't said a single word, not even to Tana.

Tana bit her lip. She'd been at a loss trying to play with a silent friend. They'd already played two rounds of Candyland and some version of poker that she'd claimed Van had taught her.

"Um, I'll get the leftover Halloween candy from the bottom drawer in Mom's room. She won't even notice." Tana got up and ran down the hall toward the bedrooms.

I watched as she left before my eyes returned to Charlie. She squeezed her eyes shut. She'd been doing that a lot since she got here. Mom told us before she arrived to be extra nice to Charlie today because her daddy was going to be working in another state for a while.

I sat next to her on the floor. She looked over briefly before pulling her Barbie closer. It made me smile. The last time she'd come over, I'd popped the head off and it was one of the only ones left with long hair. Tana had yelled at me until I muscled the head back on.

"When Carter's dad left, he got a new bike."

Charlie didn't give any indication that she heard me other than a soft sniffle. But she didn't tell me to go away either. That was something.

She rested her head on her knees.

"Anyway, now Carter gets two Christmases. That's not so

bad. Maybe you'll get two Christmases. Then you can ask for more Barbies."

She still didn't say anything else, but I could hear her breathing. On any other day I would have told her to go breathe somewhere else but not today.

Today it was okay.

"He didn't even say goodbye," she whispered.

I bumped her shoulder. "He didn't say bye because he knows he'll see you later."

She looked at me with big, liquid eyes. "Do you think he's mad at me?"

The idea of someone being mad at her was so stupid I almost laughed. Charlie was nice to everyone. Well, everyone except me. Plus, she always smelled like strawberries. She was a girl and girls were annoying but at least she smelled good.

"He's not mad at you."

"Are you sure?"

"I'm sure. You'll see him later. And you'll definitely get two Barbies."

When she smiled at me, it felt like flying.

"One day I'm going to live in Gran Grace's house with my kids. And we'll get to stay there all the time and I'll never have to leave." She wrapped her arms around her knees again but this time, she didn't look as sad.

I looked over my shoulder at the window. "The rain has stopped. Maybe we can go outside now."

Tana flopped down on the floor between us, pushing me out of the way. "Which one do you want, Starburst or Skittles?"

I rolled my eyes. Of course, she hadn't brought me any. Besides, everyone knew Skittles were Charlie's favorite.

"Skittles," Charlie whispered.

Tana reached out but before she could drop them in her hand, I snatched them and took off running for the back door.

I could hear them yelling behind me as I cleared the back steps. The rain had stopped but the ground was slippery. They would never reach me before I made it to the treehouse and neither of them could climb up once I pulled up the ladder.

Safely in my aerial hideaway, I watched with delight as they threw rocks at me. Charlie stood with hands on hips. When our eyes met, I stuck out my tongue.

I felt a little bad for eating her candy, but at least she wasn't crying anymore.

thirteen

. . .

CHARLOTTE

Meatball settled down after peeing on Rix. I'd felt terrible in the moment, but once he was gone, I couldn't deny I'd given Meatball extra kisses. For his valiant work, I'd taken him to the park and let him roll around in the dirt a bit. While he played, I checked my messages. I had received calls back from three different contractors. All the feelers I'd put out over the past few days had paid off.

Two of them couldn't start work until the fall but the third had been available for a same day appointment. I called him back and he agreed to come by at 4 p.m. that afternoon to give me an estimate.

"Things are finally happening, Meatball. We are going to whip this place into shape and then you'll get to meet Billie. Would you like that? She's going to love you."

He danced around in circles at the sound of my voice. But when I stood and tugged on his leash, he dug in his heels.

"Come on. We have a lunch date with Tana."

At the word "lunch" he gave a single, joyful bark.

"Yeah, I know the way to your heart."

This time when I held out my arms, he launched himself forward almost knocking me off my feet.

Of course, that was the very moment my phone started to ring. Luckily, I still had my Bluetooth headphones in from when I was talking to the contractor. I tapped my right ear while I tried to keep a good hold on Meatball. He had short legs and we'd been walking for a while already. I could tell he was tired.

"Hello?"

"There you are!" Retta's face appeared on the screen. "This is the third time I've called. I'm feeling a little neglected."

I winced. "I'm so sorry. Things have been crazy here."

"I got your message about falling through some hole? What is that about?"

I couldn't help but laugh. Hearing it coming from Retta made it sound even more absurd. "You were right. I should have waited for the contractor. I tried to fix some of the loose boards on the porch and ended up falling through. I guess the boards were weak in that section."

"Oh, geez. Are you okay?"

"Fine. My scratched-up thigh might not agree, but yeah. The neighbor came by and then called for help."

Retta's snicker was unmistakable. "She called the police to come drag you out? I know you must have loved that."

I coughed. "Worse. Not the police. She called Hendrix."

Retta paused. "Interesting."

"Why is that interesting?"

"Nothing." Her faux innocent tone only made it sound even worse.

"Retta. Spit it out."

She finally cracked. "Just that it's funny how whenever you need something, Hendrix seems to show up. Sounds like a good man to have around."

I bit my lip, not believing what I was about to say. "I agreed to let him move in."

"Uh-huh." Two simple words but they dripped with innuendo.

"It's no big deal. I told Tana that it just makes sense because he can fix some of the immediate issues while I'm waiting to find a contractor."

"Did she believe that crap?"

I decided to ignore that. "Anyway, I'm already regretting it. He's disgusting, he's eating all my food, and he doesn't even close the door when he's in the bathroom."

There was a noticeable delay before Retta asked, "What are you not telling me?"

"Nothing," I insisted. "Just that I may have, potentially, accidentally seen him...kind of...naked."

I heard Retta choke on whatever she was drinking. "That's moving pretty fast for you. You didn't even kiss Aaron until after he'd passed a background check and provided three references."

"I didn't see him naked on purpose! He's just a Neanderthal who leaves the door open while he's showering."

As I turned the corner, Tana's shop came into view. I'd promised to stop by again and take another look at her books. Just then Tana walked out onto the sidewalk. When she spotted me coming, she raised her arm overhead. I waved back.

"Okay, I'm about to see Tana so that thing that we just talked about *never happened*. Got it?"

Retta's husky chuckle was not reassuring.

"Loretta Thompson," I hissed in warning. "Promise me."

"Okay, okay. No need to pull out the government name," she grumbled. "Besides, what is there to tell, right?"

"Right! It's no big deal. And Tana doesn't want to hear about how annoying her older brother is."

"Uh huh. Or about how big his dick is."

"Retta! Would you—"

She howled. "Girl, you can fool yourself, but you can't fool me. Because if it wasn't big, you would have said that first."

It felt like my face was on fire. Luckily my skin tone was deep enough to disguise it and if my cheeks were suspiciously rosy, hopefully Tana would just think I'd piled on the blush that morning.

"We are not talking about that. Okay, Tana's walking up. Behave," I warned her.

"I'll behave. You're no fun. But Charlie, just for research purposes I think you should *accidentally* see him naked again. Because I need details. Lots of details. Not just size but shape. Girth. Maybe you can do a taste test—"

I hung up just as Tana walked up. "Hey!"

She scratched Meatball on the top of his head. "Hey. It's such a nice day that I figured I'd walk down and meet you."

"It's beautiful. We just got back from the park so hopefully this little guy will sleep while we get some work done." I followed her back down the sidewalk.

"Who was that you were talking to?"

"What?"

She gestured to my earbuds. "It looked like you were arguing with someone."

"Oh. I was just, um, talking to the contractor. He's coming this afternoon."

Tana grinned. "That's good news, right?"

"It's great news. At least until I see how much he's going to charge."

She nodded. "I hear that. Another day another dollar, as they say."

Something about the way she said it made me think she wasn't just commiserating.

"Is everything okay with you?"

She perked up at that. "Everything's fine. It's just our lease is up at the shop. We have to negotiate a new one with the landlord. Hopefully the rent won't go up too much."

"I hope not. I know how hard you've worked to get this place open. It would stink to have to move so soon."

"Exactly. Which is why I need your help to look at our expenses. I'm trying to save as much money as I can."

"Well, I can definitely help with that part."

She hooked her arm through mine. "I really am glad you're back. This is just the way I always imagined things would be when we grew up. Getting to see each other every day. Remember when we decided we were going to start our own ice cream shop together?"

I laughed at the memory. "That seemed like the perfect job at the time. Oh, for life to be so simple that free ice cream is all you can dream of."

The shop wasn't as busy as the last time I came by but there were still a few customers inside. I waved at Piper as we walked back to Tana's office.

"Sorry it's so messy in here." Tana pushed a few boxes to the side. Her laptop was pushed to the side of the desk and there were pens and paperclips strewn across the surface. She hurriedly started stuffing them back into the holder.

My spidey senses started tingling. I looked around curiously and then over to Tana. Looking at her directly, I noticed a few things I hadn't before. Her hair was in her usual high bun but this was...sloppy. Tana didn't do sloppy. Even her messy buns were artfully done. Her T-shirt was wrinkled and looked like it had been crumpled up into a ball before she put it on.

There was no other way to say it. She looked like she'd just had sex.

"Um, am I interrupting anything?"

She spun around. "What? Why would you think that?"

"Nothing. I just...could come back if you need time to sneak your secret boyfriend out of the supply closet."

She fumbled the pens again. My mouth fell open. I had been just joking around but her reaction told the true story.

"I was just joking around. There actually is a guy? Anyone I know?"

"No one. There's no one. It's nothing."

I switched Meatball to the other arm when he started wriggling. "Uh huh. Did Mr. Nothing give you that epic case of bed head?"

With a huge sigh, she flopped down in her desk chair. She looked so defeated that I immediately regretted teasing her.

"You don't have to talk about it."

Tana glanced over. "I'm just not ready to talk about it yet. Talking about it makes it real. And also I'm probably stupid for trusting him again."

"I am the last person to cast judgement. Believe me."

She pulled a spare chair over so I could sit next to her. "Okay let's get going so you can get out of here before your appointment. Here are last year's expenses. I'll order our lunch while you take a look."

After she hit a button, columns of numbers populated the screen. She winced. "Ugh, sorry. Next time I invite you out it'll be for fun stuff. Not sandwiches and torture by numbers."

I handed her Meatball so I could type freely. "Are you kidding? This is the fun stuff!"

———

By the time we finished I had just enough time to get back to the house to meet the contractor. The numbers for the shop actually looked pretty good which made me wonder why Tana seemed so worried. She was trying to hide it, but I knew her too well for that to fool me. Something was going on with her. I could only hope that trimming expenses in the few areas I'd identified would help alleviate that bit of panic I'd glimpsed on her face a few times while we were working.

Meatball had been more than happy entertaining everyone in the salon so Tana volunteered to keep him so I could concentrate on the appointment. That was a relief. I didn't know how he'd react to a strange man being near me.

As sweet as he was to all the ladies in the salon, I couldn't forget how he'd taken an immediate dislike to Hendrix that day in front of the diner. The last thing I needed was for him to take a bite out of whoever showed up to give the estimate.

When I finally got home, the contractor was just getting out of his truck. He looked slightly familiar.

"Hi. Sorry I'm late."

He turned at the sound of my voice and tipped his worn baseball cap in my direction. "It's no problem. I just got here. I'm not sure if you remember me. I was a few years ahead of you in school."

As soon as he smiled, I recognized him. "Dusty Evans. Of course I remember you! You used to cut the grass every week when I was here in the summer."

His cheeks flushed. "I did. Got out of the lawn cutting business as you can see. I work for a contractor in Fairfax now."

"Thanks for coming on such short notice. Let me show you what I need fixed."

For the next hour, I pointed out all the things I wanted done while Dusty made note of a few other things that needed work as well. No one could accuse him of not being thorough because he'd inspected every inch of the place, even going up into the attic to check things out. Now he was scribbling on his clipboard with a tense expression on his face.

"So, do you think we can get everything done in three months? I'm hoping my mom and sister can move in here before school starts in September."

He took his hat off. "Let's sit down. Then we can go over everything."

I perched on a barstool next to him and followed as he pointed to each line on his estimate to explain what it was. With every word, my stomach sank lower and lower. I could only hope that I responded appropriately to what Dusty was saying because all I was hearing was *money, money, money*.

Namely, money that I didn't have.

I thanked him for his time and then spent the obligatory ten minutes chatting about how my mom was doing and accepted condolences about my grandma. He was halfway through some story about when Gran Grace caught him stealing a rose from one of her bushes as a kid when my phone rang.

I gestured to my phone and waved to Dusty as he let himself out. By the time I answered the phone I almost sounded normal.

"Hey, bug. How is summer camp going?"

"Ugh, I want to come home. Stupid Angie Wyler is here too."

"Stupid Angie who made fun of your hair?" I wrinkled my nose.

Little kids weren't the most sensitive and Billie had come home in tears last year when one of the girls in her class had made fun of her hair. Being biracial in her exclusive private school was a bit of a nightmare and my mom's *turn-the-other cheek* approach certainly hadn't helped.

"Do I need to call your counselor?"

"No! Don't do that. It's fine. Summer camp is for babies anyway. Can I come home early?" Billie grumbled.

"I don't think Mom is going to go for that."

"Maybe she will if you ask her. Please?"

I hesitated. I doubted my mom had changed her mind and decided to tell Billie about what was going on. It was unlikely that she'd want my younger sister to come home while she was in the middle of dealing with everything. It would be virtually impossible to keep the truth from Billie once she was back in Manhattan.

"Have you talked to her today?" I asked.

"No. She's probably on vacation. That's the only reason she still sends me to camp. So Dad can take her on vacation without me."

My shoulders slumped. As much as I wanted to, I couldn't refute that statement. We would both know it was a lie.

"You'll be home before you know it. Now tell me what else you've been doing at camp."

I gave her my full attention as she told me about the full schedule of activities slated for the coming week. It sounded more like a boot camp than a summer camp. It was probably billed as some sort of skills building opportunity for the future leaders of America, but at least Billie sounded like she was enjoying it. That was all that mattered.

After we hung up, I went to the kitchen and got a glass of water. I took a sip as I stared at the hole in the wall. Her call had come at the perfect time. As frustrating as this renovation project would be, it was one of the most important things I'd ever done. Maybe it wasn't a big deal to some people, but I remembered what it felt like to lose everything you knew and loved.

At least my mom seemed to be thinking about Billie's

feelings for once. It was important that we made her feel safe since everything she knew was about to change.

Funny that my mom hadn't been nearly as concerned about ruining my life way back when.

The next thing I knew the glass in my hand was shattering against the wall. The huge gaping hole should have been alarming, but instead the sight just fueled my rage. I grabbed the napkin ring on the table and threw that before spinning in a circle, frantically looking for something else to take the weight of my pain. Both of my shoes flew before I picked up an umbrella that I had never been able to open. I threw that at the wall, too.

Chest heaving, I stood there and surveyed my handiwork. Now that my adrenaline had subsided a little, I couldn't believe I'd just thrown all that stuff at the wall.

When I turned around, Rix stood near the door watching quietly. All the anger drained away, leaving me exhausted.

And embarrassed.

"Oh hey."

He didn't move but his eyes followed my movements as I slumped against the counter.

"I saw Dusty's truck outside. I figured it might not hurt to stop in. Sometimes contractors jack up the prices for women. It's bullshit but it happens."

It was an unexpectedly sweet gesture. Especially since he had no reason to care if I got ripped off. I wasn't sure what to make of it.

"You didn't have to do that. Dusty doesn't seem like the type to cheat anyone."

"No, he's good people. But I figured you might be getting some bad news."

With a sigh, I looked back down at the torn-off sheet Dusty had left me with. It was just a rough estimate. He'd said he would email me the official quote in a few days after he priced everything out, but I was looking at almost twenty thousand dollars' worth of repairs between the drywall, the porch, getting the kitchen and bathroom up to code and the unexpected mold damage he'd found in the laundry room.

"Yeah." I couldn't think of anything else to say.

What was I supposed to do, tell him all about how screwed up my life was? Complain about getting ghosted by a boyfriend who'd obviously never cared about me? Vent about my sweet little sister who was about to have her entire way of life blown up?

Why would he care?

No, I was on my own with this just like I was with everything else.

I raised my head and looked him directly in the eyes. "I'm fine. Unless you needed an umbrella, in which case, I can't help you."

It was so quiet that the heavy tread of his boots ricocheted through the room like thunder. Hopefully he was leaving because I really wanted to be alone. Losing control in front of anyone was humiliating but especially Rix. If he made a joke right then I might actually kill him.

"It's okay to be upset," he said softly.

That almost broke me. Somehow him being nice about my little breakdown made everything so much worse. I didn't want him to be nice to me right now. Not when my emotions were so raw.

I knew I should just be happy that Mom had changed enough to consider what was best for Billie, but a tiny selfish part of me couldn't help wondering why I wasn't deserving of protection? Why she hadn't cared about taking me away from everything I loved?

Now history was about to repeat itself so what had it all been for?

The rage rose in my chest again and Rix must have sensed it because he grabbed my wrists. I struggled against his hold, wanting to throw something. To hit something.

He placed my hands on his chest. "Hit me."

The sound that came out of my throat was like a wounded animal. I pushed him away, but his hands were still wrapped loosely around mine, keeping me close. My fingers curled into fists and I deliberately dug my nails into his chest, wanting him to feel some of my pain. He grunted softly at the pressure but didn't move away.

"That's it," he grumbled.

I pounded against his chest, over and over until my arms began to tire. Through it all, Hendrix stood firm, taking the blows and absorbing the full force of all my anger and frustration. He whispered to me the whole time, things that didn't even make sense, but the steady rumble of his voice was what finally got through to me. Slowly I became aware of the weight of his arms around me and the solid feel of his chest under my hands.

"Go ahead, baby. Let it out."

The softly whispered words carried the last bit of my anger away. My hands were still resting on his chest and I could feel the flex of his chest muscles beneath my hands.

Then his lips were on mine.

I had no idea who reached out first, although later I would swear that he kissed me, but in the moment all I felt was relief. It was like the first lick of ice cream on a hot day and everything inside me melted into perfect stillness.

His lips were firm but soft, so much softer than I could have imagined, and they tickled as he feathered kisses over my mouth. It should have been ridiculous. He was kissing me with these quick, soft pecks like he was trying to calm me down, but every time his lips made contact it started a new burn. A different burn.

Frustrated, I grabbed his face and held him still, biting his bottom lip gently. The sound that rumbled from his chest sent a spear of satisfaction arrowing straight between my legs.

Even as I continued to devour his face there was a little warning sound in the back of my mind.

Danger.

Danger.

You are kissing Rix.

THIS IS NOT A DRILL.

Abruptly, I pulled back and the room swam as I tried to get my bearings. His fingers flexed around my waist and I almost whimpered at how good it felt. I wanted those fingers to dig in and squeeze me other places. But as usual the sight of Rix's face was enough to bring me firmly back to reality. The bastard was smiling that cocky grin he always wore when he'd just bested me in some way. Only this time it wasn't because he'd stolen my candy or hidden my clothes.

No, this was so much worse.

"I have to go get Meatball," I blurted finally.

"Right now?" he asked.

His cocky grin faltered slightly. Probably because he'd thought I would fall to the ground and worship at the altar of Hendrix like the rest of his bimbos. But the first lesson I'd learned about dealing with Rix was to never let him see when he'd actually gotten to me.

"Yes. Right now."

I purposefully avoided looking at the mess I'd made or the hole in the wall. My face flushed as I thought about my little temper tantrum, but I pushed it down as I gathered up my things.

Rix was still standing in the middle of the room looking confused. Probably trying to figure out how he'd lost a live one. Meanwhile I had to figure out where I was going to get twenty thousand dollars.

fourteen

. . .

I waited. Made myself a sandwich and then watched some TV. Once I figured out that she wasn't coming back anytime soon I decided I might as well make myself useful by fixing the wall.

As I left, I pulled the door behind me, leaving it unlocked. As I drove through town, I couldn't help but wonder what Charlie saw when she drove these streets. Violet Ridge was as far away from New York City as you could get. I passed Dot's Diner as I cruised down Main Street and briefly wondered if I should stop for some pie. A slice of her apple crumble would probably do more to get me back in Charlie's good graces than anything else I could do.

Finally, I pulled up in front of the hardware store. From outside I could see my mom talking to a customer. I waited until she followed them down one of the aisles before I slipped inside. I would just gather the things I needed to fix the drywall and settle up with my father later. He wouldn't care.

It was hardly the first time an Evers needed emergency supplies to patch something. Van trashed his bedroom after

Beth left him the first time and many of the holes in the walls of my parents' house were there because of me.

Mom would want to know where I was going, and she had an uncanny ability to tell when I was hiding something. If her Mom-dar caught wind that something was wrong with Charlie, the whole family might show up on her doorstep.

I definitely couldn't claim to be a Charlie expert, but I didn't think that was what she needed right then. There was way more going on than just an unexpected repair bill.

Surrounded by the familiar smell of lumber and paint, I quickly made my way to the stock room. The shelves were lined with everything from duct tape to power tools. I knew this room by heart so I made my way down the aisles, grabbing the things I would need.

I picked up a four-by-four sheet of drywall. There was a putty knife in my toolbox, but I would need joint compound and another sanding block.

Mom suddenly appeared at the entrance to the room, the light from the store casting a glow around her. "Hey, what are you doing here?"

"Just grabbing a few things." I shifted the drywall to the side, hoping she wouldn't pay too much attention to what I was buying.

She walked into the room and started organizing the shelf next to me. "Okay but just make sure you leave a list."

"Will do."

"I feel like I've barely seen you lately." She was trying to be casual but there was an element of hurt in there.

I leaned down and kissed her forehead. "I was running late today so I missed you."

She gave me a quick hug. "Sorry to be so needy. I just worry about you. That's all."

"I know but you don't need to. Everything is fine. Actually,

Carter is going to help me find some land to buy so I can work on building my own place."

Mom smiled. "That's nice of him."

Her gaze dropped to the drywall sheet at my side. "Your new roommate have you punching walls already?"

Busted.

"Actually, I'm just fixing a few things."

Mom crossed her arms. "Uh huh. And when were you planning on telling us about your new living situation?"

Sometime after never.

"You know, whenever. I've been so busy with everything."

"And you didn't want us butting in. I get in."

I scowled. "It just happened. I was going to tell you. But I also didn't want you to get the wrong idea."

"The wrong idea?" One eyebrow lifted.

"You know, assuming that something is going on just because we're living together. Men and women can be just friends, you know?"

"Is that right?"

"Yes."

She crooked a finger at me. I moved closer. She shook her head and motioned for me to come even closer. When I bent my head down, she swiped at something right below my bottom lip.

Then held up her finger to showcase the reddish lipstick on her thumb.

"Mom–"

She turned on her heel and walked away, carrying one of the boxes with her. "Don't forget to leave a list!"

I hurriedly swiped at my mouth, groaning when I saw another swipe of red on my hand.

So much for keeping things low-key.

Well, it was too late to keep things under wraps at this

point. So I just grabbed everything I needed and then went up front so Mom could ring me out. When I was done, I gave her a wave, ignoring her smug smile.

I was definitely getting the third degree at Sunday dinner after this.

When I got back, the driveway was empty, so I knew Charlie wasn't back yet. I was measuring the hole in the wall when she came in. She didn't look at me, just sailed past with the puppy on her shoulder. When he saw me, he gave a little growl-bark.

I made a face at him.

Whatever. She could ignore me, but she'd have to come down eventually to walk him. We both knew the little gremlin couldn't hold his bladder.

———

There was no sound downstairs except the soft scrape as I smoothed over the seams of the newly replaced drywall. It was now close to eight o'clock and she still hadn't come down. The repetitive motion was exactly what I needed to help me forget what I'd seen.

Not the bitch fit. Hell, she could trash the whole place if it made her feel better. That I could understand.

It was the look on her face. The complete loss of control and the utter devastation.

The Charlotte Monroe I knew was always in control. Whether it was something good or bad or unexpected, Charlie just accepted it with a smile and a laugh. I used to wonder if she ever felt the way I did, tumultuous and vulnerable.

I used to wonder if she really cared about anything at all.

The woman I saw tonight was not in control and she definitely wasn't handling things well. It was the only time I'd ever seen her display a raw reaction instead of the perfect façade she usually showed the world and like the beast I was, I wanted to see it again.

Although I wanted to understand what caused it more. I looked at the stairs behind me. She wasn't going to tell me which only left me one choice.

I pulled out my phone and called Tana.

"Why did Charlie come back?"

She was quiet. "She owns the house."

"Don't play games with me, sis. Because I just watched her wage war on all the loose valuables in the room. I either need to understand what's going on or I'm going to have to stock up on drywall."

"Is she okay? What happened?"

"Not really sure. I think the contractor gave her bad news. But I need to know what I'm dealing with here."

"It's too long for me to even explain it other than to say it's the stepjerk's fault. Just google Christian Delacourt and you'll understand."

After assuring Tana that things were fine and that she absolutely did not need to come over, I started my web search. Ten minutes and what felt like a million CNN articles later, I wanted to throw something at the wall, too. I knew nothing about finance but even I understood that the words "SEC" and "insider trading" were serious and Charlie had been living smack-dab in the middle of all that.

After high school, I'd just assumed that Charlie was off living the life she'd always deserved. She'd gone to some Ivy League school for her degree so I figured it wouldn't be long before she'd settle down with a Wall Street Ken doll just like her mom had. She might look back on her time in Violet Ridge with fondness, but she could never truly be happy in a place like this, with one diner, two beauty salons (one courtesy of my sister), and a whole lot of nothing else.

I wanted to go up there but what would I even say? It wasn't like she'd want comfort from me anyway. I wasn't good with words. Never had been. So I'd just do what I knew how to do. Fix what was broken.

I just wished I could patch up what was hurting Charlie inside as easily as the wall.

Hadn't I already promised to do that? I'd told my father I would look over her estimates, but there was nothing stopping me from actually doing the renovation myself in exchange for free rent. My eyes darted to the estimate on the kitchen counter. I'd looked over Dusty's list and the only things I couldn't handle were the electrical issues and the potential mold. I could probably call in a few favors and get my brother or Carter to help when I needed an extra set of hands.

If I helped her, she would be getting all the labor for free. Then she could afford to renovate the house at cost and get it done faster than any of those big contractors who wouldn't be able to fit her in right away anyway. Plus it would mean that I had a place to stay while saving up to build a house. It was perfect.

Now I just had to convince Charlie.

I chuckled. Getting her to let me move in temporarily was one thing. But convincing her that we could live *and* work together without bloodshed wouldn't be easy. You would think that scorching hot kiss would help my point, but if anything, that was going to work against me. She probably hated having to admit that she didn't find me completely repugnant. Maybe pretending that hadn't happened was the right way to go.

I would just focus on the benefits and ignore the fact that I'd been minutes away from having my hand in her panties during that kiss.

fifteen

. . .

CHARLOTTE

At the soft knock, I buried my face in my pillow, hoping he'd think I was asleep. His shocked face was burned into my mind and I would have laughed if I wasn't so mentally fried. I doubted I was the first woman in his life to throw stuff around, but he was probably used to the items coming toward his head.

When he knocked again, I turned the other direction toward the window. Rix had always been nosy so he was probably listening at the door. I didn't want him to hear me crying. Not that it should have mattered. He'd already seen me chuck an umbrella at the wall so crying should be no big deal, but I didn't want to give him the satisfaction of hearing me fall apart.

It would probably make his day.

Eventually he'd get the picture and go away. The door was locked so he wouldn't have much of a choice unless he wanted to talk through the door.

Then I heard the door open. Shocked, I rolled over to see Rix standing awkwardly in the doorway.

"I thought I locked that."

"You did." He held up the entire doorknob.

We stared at each other until the corners of his lips turned up. Soon we were both chuckling. I laughed so hard tears came to my eyes and then before I knew it, I was crying all over again.

Meatball hopped up and pranced over to the side of the bed. I ruffled the wild hair on top of his head before whispering to him softly. Satisfied that I was okay, he lumbered back to his pillow and collapsed.

Being so adorable must be exhausting.

Rix still stood in the doorway looking uncertain. "I'm sorry, Charlie. I'll fix the door."

"It's not the door. I mean, it's not *only* that. It's everything." Suddenly it felt like the weight of the past month came crashing down right on top of me.

What was I going to do?

"Do you want me to call your mom?" he asked finally.

"She'll just say not to worry and that it'll all work out. She's not even ready to admit that everything is gone. It's like she thinks this is all some big mistake and once it gets straightened out, Christian will come back home and things will be fine."

He didn't say anything, but I could tell by the look on his face that he'd seen the news. People always acted differently once they heard the details.

"It's okay. You can say it. We were stupid to trust him."

He grunted. "That is not what I was going to say. He took advantage. This is on him."

I know he meant it in a good way, but it only made me feel worse. Once again I was poor, sad Charlie who got left behind. The one who had to pick up the pieces and start over, only this time, I wasn't sure I had the strength to do it again. This time I felt like I'd crack if I even tried.

"Everything is falling apart."

He sat on the bed next to me and then reclined until his head rested on the pillow next to mine. It should have been weird, but it felt so natural to lie there with nothing but frustration between us.

"I'm twenty-seven and unemployed. My boyfriend left the day Christian got arrested. It's like I blinked and my whole life was gone."

"Coward," Rix muttered.

"I'm not even sure I blame him. Aaron worked for Delacourt, too. He probably wanted to get another job before everyone found out what happened. Maybe I should have done that."

"You were more concerned with making sure your family was okay. Like a human being."

"But they're not okay. My little sister doesn't even know her dad was arrested, and my mom is acting like we're coming back to Violet Ridge for a short vacation instead of as a last resort."

He didn't say anything, and I appreciated that he didn't try to tell me everything would be all right.

"We could help each other out, you know?" He glanced over at me warily.

Instantly suspicious, I pushed up onto my elbow. "I swear if you pull out your dick right now—"

"Whoa! That wasn't what I meant at all." He grabbed his chest as he laughed so hard he almost fell off the bed.

Unable to resist the temptation I decided to help him along with a strategic shove. He tumbled over the edge landing on the hardwood with a solid thump.

Rix popped up from the floor wearing his trademark scowl. My eyes were drawn to his lips and I suddenly wanted to lean over and bite him. I should have been pissed at him for having the nerve to kiss me the way he did earlier.

Did he kiss me?

Or did I kiss him?

I wasn't exactly sure because all I remembered was how incredibly hot it was, channeling all my anger into pure, unfiltered desire. But he was the last person I wanted to have that effect on me so it was better that we weren't talking about it. In fact, it was probably best if we had a silent agreement to pretend it hadn't happened.

"Okay, I was trying to be nice and propose an arrangement that would help us both."

With his usual grumpysauce expression, he looked more like the Hendrix I was used to, the pain in the ass, not the sensitive soul that was listening to my problems. He seemed so earnest that I actually felt a little bad.

"Sorry. But don't pretend you wouldn't have done the same."

"Fair enough." He flopped back down. "All I was going to say is that I can handle most of the work you need done. You could save a lot of money if you used a handyman instead of one of those big contractors."

The thought of all the items on that list downstairs made me tired just thinking about them. I glanced over at Hendrix. He had been helping his father fix stuff since we were kids so I knew he wasn't boasting when he said he could handle the work. Plus, he was right here, and it would save me not only money but *time* if he could start work right away.

"What's the catch?" I narrowed my eyes at him.

"No catch. Just let me stay here rent-free for the summer so I can save money to build my house. You'll pay for the materials, but you'll get my labor at night and on the weekends for free."

I nibbled on my bottom lip. Now that I knew just how much it would cost to renovate everything, the money I'd get from a summer roommate seemed like a drop in the bucket. I'd save a lot more letting Rix stay here for free and work on the house at night.

Honestly, I wasn't sure why he wanted to do this. I was getting way more out of the deal than he was. Most of the Victorians in this part of town were built in the early twentieth century and had the small rooms characteristic of the time period. Not to mention that he would have to share a bathroom with iffy plumbing.

"The guest room was fine when I thought it would only be a couple of weeks but why would you want to stay in that tiny room all summer? Especially when you have other options. I know your parents would let you move back in."

"I'm not moving in with my parents. If I don't want to see Van's butt cheek, I definitely don't want to see my father's." Hendrix threw his head back and laughed.

The sight was almost enough to make me forget what I'd asked him. It wasn't often that he lost his grumpysauce expression. It was probably for the best because he had a smile that could make smart women do stupid things.

"How are they? I meant to go see them yesterday. They were like a second home during the summers."

The thought of the Evers made me smile.

They were the cool family growing up. They had this funky van that Mrs. Evers painted herself and Mr. Evers always told stories about his days playing with his rock band. They encouraged their kids to express their creativity, and no matter what trouble they got into, they just loved them.

I secretly wished to be one of their kids. I actually spent the night with Tana once and then didn't call Gran the next morning to come pick me up, hoping they wouldn't notice.

They took me back home eventually, but only after a chocolate chip pancake breakfast.

"My parents are doing just fine. Still as gross as ever. The last time I crashed with them, I saw things I can *never* unsee." He gave me a look and then mimed poking his finger down his throat.

It made me laugh again, but honestly, I couldn't imagine having parents who liked each other enough to be caught making out. I couldn't even remember the last time my parents had eaten a meal together, even before the divorce.

Our eyes met and it was as if we both realized we were having fun at the same time. Hendrix stood up and brushed off his pants. I rolled my eyes. Like lying next to me had contaminated him?

"I'll go get some more supplies from the shop to fix the door. I need to go pick up the rest of my stuff anyway."

Just before he reached the door, I called his name. He stopped and looked over his shoulder.

"Why are you really doing this? Moving out of your brother's place and into my tiny spare bedroom doesn't make sense."

Suddenly he wouldn't meet my eyes. "My brother just got his girlfriend back and I'm sure they want some time alone. They need it. Someone deserves a chance at a love like my parents."

He opened his mouth like he was going to say something else then shook his head.

"Why did you fix the wall downstairs?" I whispered.

His eyes flew up to meet mine. "Because *you* needed it."

Without another word he turned and left. I listened as his heavy tread crossed the living room downstairs. Then a few seconds later, the front door closed.

Meatball growled again but he didn't bother to get up, so I figured I'd take his input with a grain of salt.

———

Rix got back about an hour later. He nodded as he passed by with a big cardboard box balanced on his shoulder. At least he didn't have that much stuff. Not much would fit in that room for sure.

I busied myself in the kitchen making a sandwich, ignoring the sounds of his footsteps clomping upstairs. The sound of him banging around wasn't distracting at all, and I *for sure* wasn't thinking about the fact that he was upstairs getting ready for bed. Undressing.

Naked.

The banging stopped. Then a door opened. A few seconds later, another door closed.

After gathering everything I needed for my quick dinner, I put some potato chips in a bag, cut up an apple and poured myself a drink. There was no way to carry it all at once, so I tucked the chips in the crook of my elbow while holding the apple and a napkin. I carried them into my room and set them carefully on the nightstand.

My hands stilled when there was a loud bump on the other side of the wall. What was Rix doing over there? Then an image popped unbidden into my mind of the kinds of things men did under the covers at night.

This was going to be a very long summer indeed.

Living together was going to be even more difficult than I'd imagined. I could only hope this initial weirdness would pass quickly because I couldn't hide in my room every night just to avoid him. He'd been so different earlier. He'd actually listened and cared about what I was going through without giving me the usual empty platitudes people offered when they didn't know what else to say.

Maybe things would be different between us now. Our conversation earlier felt like a breakthrough. We were no longer the silly children who'd fought over nonsense. We were adults now. For the first time, I wondered if the two of us might actually become friends.

It was already so hot in the room, so I sent up a small prayer that Gran's ancient air conditioning unit didn't give out on me. I stripped off the T-shirt and jeans I was wearing and replaced them with a thin camisole and sleep shorts. After throwing my hair up in a messy bun, I ventured back downstairs to get the rest of my food. I'd left my sandwich on a napkin in the middle of the counter next to my glass of water.

The water glass was full.

The napkin was empty.

I put my hands on my hips and looked over my shoulder, half expecting to see Rix standing there laughing. Then I calmly took out the lunch meat and bread and started fixing another sandwich.

sixteen

. . .

HENDRIX

You would think it would be impossible for two people to live in the same house without crossing paths. But somehow Charlie had done the impossible.

For the past week, I had only seen her in passing. She had to be waiting until I got up and left the house each morning before she came out. The only time I ever saw her was when I came home unexpectedly during the day. She was even eating her meals in her room.

That part probably was my fault.

Stealing her sandwich had been funny but if we were going to live together, I needed to learn to curb my instincts for destruction where Charlie was concerned.

It was probably going to hurt but I was going to have to learn to be nice to her.

Not too nice, I thought.

I shoved a box of nails into a free space on the shelf. That was the real problem, wasn't it? Every time I tried to interact with Charlie, I was derailed by how inconveniently sexy she was.

Whether she was making pancakes in her pajamas or working on her laptop on the couch, she managed to make the most mundane things arousing. I could barely string together a sentence around her because my mind was filled with images of all the things I wanted to do to her. Like pull those miniscule sleep shorts down and bite her right on the curve of that delectable ass. Or bury my face in the abundant cleavage that threatened to spill out of every top she wore. Or lay my head in her lap so she could stroke my hair.

To have her attention when she wasn't mad at me for once.

This sudden attraction was completely inconvenient. It was like my dick had suddenly developed temporary amnesia about anything or anyone else I'd ever been attracted to. And I had tried to think of other people, running through my usual spank bank collection of Hollywood actresses, old girlfriends, and even one of my high school teachers.

Nothing.

Nada.

Apparently, it was Charlie or bust. I was suddenly only attracted to a woman who wouldn't even talk to me.

As if my thoughts had sent out a beacon, the door to the hardware store opened and Charlie stepped inside. Tana followed a few seconds later holding a tray of coffee.

"Hello, family," Tana crowed. "I've brought sustenance."

Mom came from behind the register to hug them both. "We have one of those new coffee machines, but I do love a good latte. It's so good to see you girls. Charlie, welcome back."

"Thanks, Mrs. Evers. I'm glad to finally be back."

"Let me know when Lena comes into town. I'd love to have her over for dinner and catch up."

I tried to tune out their voices, but it was easier said than done. The shop wasn't that big and the only place I could hide was the stock room. I'd have to pass them to get there. Since they seemed to be staying near the front of the store, I walked to the aisle furthest from the door.

I skidded to a stop when I turned the corner and almost bumped into Charlie. "Oh. Hey."

"Hi. I was just looking for a hammer." She dipped her head and the top of her cheeks flushed slightly. "Not a hammer. I don't know why I said that."

It was my first time seeing her today. This morning she'd either snuck out early or deliberately slept in so she didn't have to talk to me. She'd pulled her curls back into two long braids that trailed over her shoulders. The style reminded me of something she would have worn in high school. Maybe that was why I suddenly felt like a tongue-tied teenager trying to think of something to say to her.

Tana appeared at the end of the aisle. "There you are. What are you guys doing?"

Charlie gestured at one of the blocks of sandpaper hanging next to her. "Oh, you know. Just picking up a few things." Her hand accidentally hit one of the blocks and sent it flying.

I caught it before it hit the ground. "You don't need to buy any of this stuff. Anything you need you can take from my toolbox."

"I'm not touching your *toolbox*." She swallowed. "You're right. I don't need anything. Tana, I'll wait for you outside."

She practically sprinted down the aisle. I shoved the sandpaper block back on the shelf and walked to the stock room. Just as I was opening a box, Tana pushed through the door.

"Well. I was going to ask how things were going, but I guess I don't have to." She climbed on the table next to where I was working.

She held out a cup of coffee and I took it gratefully. At least she'd brought a peace offering. It was the least she could do really since she was technically responsible for this whole mess.

"That woman is crazy," I muttered.

Tana's shoulders shook with silent laughter. "It's funny because you both say the same things. Somebody has to be lying. Although it's not like her to just flounce off."

"She's pissed at me."

"It's barely been a week. What could she be pissed at you for already?"

"Breathing."

"Okay, what is up with you guys? You're being all squirrelly and she was so weird just now."

"Nothing is up. It's a temporary situation and we both need time to adjust to living together."

But even as I said the words an image flashed through my mind of when Charlie walked in on me naked. My face must have given away something because Tana gasped.

"Oh my god. You *like* her? Also, please never make that face again."

"I don't *like* her. This isn't grade school."

"Are you sure? Because you looked like you were two seconds away from pulling her pigtails earlier."

When I didn't say anything, just attacked another box, she shifted. I looked up to find her watching me intently.

"It's not the worst thing ever if you like her. Unless you screw things up. I really don't want her to leave again."

The vulnerability in Tana's voice tugged at my deepest insecurities. We weren't so different, after all. We both knew what it felt like to be in Charlie's rearview when she moved on to bigger and brighter things.

What could I really offer a woman like Charlie?

"Don't worry, I'm not going to scare your friend away. We just need to adjust to sharing space, I guess."

Tana took a noisy slurp of her coffee. "I told her we were having a bonfire tonight. You should give her some moonshine. That might help your cause."

"Is there a reason that you're here?"

"You mean besides spreading joy to my dear sibling? I'm feeling distinctly unappreciated around here."

I nudged her aside so I could have more room to open boxes. She finally got the hint and hopped down.

"Fine. I'll go. But if you ever need advice, I'm here. Despite being gross you're somehow an amazing guy."

The unexpected approval meant more than I could say so I just nodded. "Thanks, Tana."

She grinned wickedly. "Plus, you might actually have a chance. Charlie is used to an absent father, a criminal stepfather, and a boyfriend who ghosted her. Her expectations of men are not that high. If you like her you should go for it. You're not *completely* hideous."

Mom was coming in just as she said it. "Santana, be nice to your brother!"

"*What?* That was nice."

As the sounds of their arguing followed them from the room, Tana's words rolled through my brain. She thought I had a chance, but I wasn't so sure. That was assuming Charlie didn't shove me out the door just for suggesting it.

I smiled imagining her reaction. That might be reason enough to try it.

Angry Charlie was endlessly amusing.

However, my common sense finally kicked in and told me to leave well enough alone. I finally had a place to stay and definitely didn't want to start the great apartment hunt all over again. Starting something with my roommate would be the dumbest move ever when we had to live together for the next three months. Plus, this random attraction was likely to disappear as fast as it had arrived.

But despite all of those excellent reasons, I couldn't stop thinking about it.

———

An hour later I was checking an order of Phillips head screwdrivers when I looked up to see Mom watching me with a strange look in her eye. Usually that look meant I'd broken something, cursed where she could hear me, or eaten something she was saving for dinner.

"Van did it."

"What?" Her brow crinkled.

"Nothing. That's just my go-to line if I think I'm in trouble. It's usually true."

"You're not in trouble."

"Then why are you looking at me like that? Is there something on my face?"

"Yes. A smile." She grinned as she said it.

Oh god.

If I'd tripped the Mom-dar and she thought there was something going on with me, I would get no peace until she'd asked a million questions. After the breakup with Janelle, she'd been relentless in her quest to get me to talk about my feelings and *unburden myself*.

"It's a nice day."

She waved that off. "I was thinking. You should bring Charlie to dinner on Sunday. We've barely seen her since she came back."

"Why would I bring her to dinner? She's probably got plans."

"Maybe I want to spend a little time with the woman who has my son smiling. I've waited a long time to see you sweet on someone."

"Mom, we're just friends. Not even friends. Roommates. I'm not *sweet* on her just because we're living together."

"I don't think you're sweet on her because you're living together."

"You don't?"

"No."

She waited, her smile growing bigger by the second, knowing I couldn't resist asking. Ever since I was a child my curiosity had always gotten me into trouble. I was the kid peeking in closets trying to find my Christmas gifts and the quickest way to drive me crazy was to hint that you had a secret. You'd think I would have conquered that by now.

Apparently not.

"Okay, tell me. Why do you think that?"

"Because of the way you moon after her whenever she walks by." She whistled as she left the stockroom.

I hung my head. Even as a grown man I could still be outmaneuvered by my mother. Because I'd definitely set myself up for that one.

I wasn't mooning after Charlie, was I? My face recoiled instantly at the thought of being like Van who followed his girlfriend around like a dog after a bone. I wasn't some junkyard canine begging for scraps.

That would make me pathetic.

That would make me desperate.

That would make me...Meatball.

Oh, *hell* no. I was not panting after her like that ungrateful little pug.

"Rix!" My mom stuck her head in the room, breaking me

out of that unfortunate train of thought. "Can you bring some more paper bags up?"

After I found the recycled paper bags Mom had insisted we switch to, I brought some up front. She gave me a grateful smile before pulling one out and bagging items for Mr. Donald.

The older man loved starting home improvement projects but hated finishing them. He'd hired me to finish many of the items on his wife's honey-do list and always tried to haggle me down on my prices. I usually cut him a deal just because I could tell the negotiating gave him a bit of a thrill. He lived with his wife but all their children had moved away as soon as they grew up so I got the feeling he wanted the conversation just as much as the deal.

I was barely paying attention to what they were saying until something stuck in my head.

"What's that about a dog?"

Mr. Donald shifted the flowers he held under one arm. "One of my pups went missing. I'm putting up flyers."

He held it up and I cursed softly. It was a picture of a pug mom and a bunch of babies.

"That was the only picture I had of them. They're still quite young."

If I didn't say anything there was a chance no one would know Charlie's dog came from that litter. Once Meatball got a little bigger, everyone might think she'd brought him with her from New York. But as usual my conscience got the final say. Charlie would never want to steal someone's dog. As a matter of fact, she was usually the person going out of her way to make sure everyone else was happy. Often that meant that her feelings got ignored in the process.

Who was looking out for her?

Charlie liked to pretend that nothing got to her but if she had to give that puppy back it would break her heart.

"So I've been staying out at the Everett place," I mentioned.

"I heard about that. It's a damn shame what's happened to it. Beautiful house. Grace took a lot of pride in it. I noticed the steps were rotting."

"Don't worry, I'm working on it. Anyway, it's owned by Grace's granddaughter now."

His face lit up. "I remember little Charlie! She used to help Grace with her roses every summer."

"That's right. Well, she found that missing pup. At least I think it's the same one."

"Is that right?" His expression didn't change.

I had to be impressed. The wily old codger really didn't give anything away.

"You've been married a long time haven't you, Mr. Donald?"

"It'll be forty years this September."

"An expert, then. Maybe you can give me some advice. The thing is, Charlie's taken a bit of a shine to that little greml—uh, puppy. I thought I could get him for her as a gift. Think you can give me a deal on the pup? Maybe that'll win me some points."

He scratched his beard. "Well now, those pugs are expensive. The mother is purebred. We've even got her papers."

I scowled. He expected me to believe that little meatball-stealing gremlin was some kind of show dog? Plus, he didn't even look like a purebred pug. His body was too long. Not to mention the wild fluff on his ears.

"*Purebred?*"

"Well, the mother anyway."

"And the father?"

"Can't be too sure about that," he hedged. After I gave him

another look, he admitted, "Probably the cocker spaniel two doors down."

"A cocker spaniel."

"Yessir."

"So he's a *cocker* pug."

I laughed. This was too good.

You couldn't even make this shit up.

"Well, I'm not sure what the market value is for *cocker pugs—*"

"Those dogs fetch a good price! I looked it up. On the internet." Mr. Donald held up his phone in triumph as if I might have thought he meant something else.

I decided to try a different tack.

"Look, I'll cut you a sweet deal on that deck you've been meaning to build if you let us keep him."

"Done." He looked down at the flowers in his arms. "Maybe you should take these, too. You need them more than I do."

After he collected his bag of purchases, he whistled softly as he left. My mom looked over at me.

I sighed.

"So can we expect you for dinner?" she asked finally.

"We're not a couple. Sorry to disappoint you, Mom. I just said that because I figured he'd be more likely to let Charlie keep the dog."

She nodded along as if everything I said made sense. "Right. Not a couple."

"Definitely not. Charlie really loves that dog and I know she'd be sad to give him back."

"Mm-hmm."

Her knowing stare felt like it was burning holes in the side of my face so I picked up an item from behind the counter and took it back into the stockroom. Once the door closed behind me, my shoulders dropped. After that little performance it was going to be harder than ever to convince my nosy family that there was nothing going on between me and Charlie.

However, most alarming was that I wasn't entirely sure I'd fought so hard to keep the dog just for Charlie's sake.

seventeen

. . .

CHARLOTTE

Friday night as we walked through the open field leading to the bonfire, I suppressed the first bout of nerves.

Years ago, this had been a part of a farm but when the owners decided to sell, they subdivided the land. Mr. Donald had the property on the westernmost end and as kids we'd considered it the best since it included the massive barn that had become our favorite place to hang out.

"Oh good. People are already here." Tana huffed a little as she dragged a rolling cooler filled with wine and ice while I lugged a bag she'd filled with cups, paper towels and you guessed it, more wine.

I looked up to see that she was right. Several small groups of women were already gathered around the small fire. Behind them a group of guys tossed around a football.

Instantly I felt like I was teleported back to high school.

After years of being the new kid, I'd never really felt comfortable at parties. The only reason I'd had friends in high school was because Tana, social butterfly that she was, knew everyone.

Someone had brought a folding table and there was a keg on it already. Tana set the cooler on the ground and then immediately opened it to take out a bottle of wine.

"I don't know about you but I really need this," she said and twisted the cap off.

I reached into the bag I carried and pulled out two plastic cups. She poured a generous serving in both.

"Cheers. Here's to us."

I took a small sip of mine before looking around. "How many people have lost their virginity in that barn, do you think?"

Tana shrugged. "Not me. I'm too classy. I was more of a *lower the tailgate on your truck* kind of girl."

We were still snickering when we walked up to the small group of people already gathered around the fire. Piper saw us and waved her hands in the air. There were several other women sitting with her around a picnic table. Two of the blondes were waving, trying to get Tana's attention.

"You guys have a picnic table now? Fancy. To think we used to sit on the ground and drink beer we stole from your dad."

Tana laughed. "Rix made it from some spare lumber after he fixed the fence."

Of course he did.

I looked across the field to the fence in the distance. Logically I knew it must be there to separate the land from someone else's property, but I honestly wasn't sure why Mr. Donald bothered. There were so many trees there it was a natural barrier. Plus, as kids we'd always scaled that fence so we could play in the woods anyway.

But it must have meant something to Mr. Donald if he kept it. And of course, Rix would fix it. Because it was clearly too much for me to hope for one night without thinking about him.

I took a deep breath, determined not to let the ghost of naked Rix haunt me all night. Not wanting to tip Tana off to my interest, I'd deliberately not asked if he was coming. This was my chance to get a little room to breathe.

Everywhere I turned at home, he was there.

Eating shirtless in the kitchen, lounging his big muscular body all over my gran's furniture and staring at me like he could see straight through my clothes.

I sent up a wish for some cute guys to show up. There weren't that many single guys in town according to Tana, but I would settle for some distracting eye candy. Anyone who wasn't tall with dark hair and hazel eyes.

Anyone.

"Charlie, do you remember the Taylor sisters? This is Cassidy and Cora." Tana pointed out the two blondes. Both seemed friendly enough and I relaxed a little.

"I'm not sure if you've met Beth yet," she said, pointing out a woman with wavy, dark hair. "She's super sweet but obviously has very bad taste since she's banging my brother."

I choked. The small sip of wine I'd just taken burned as it went up my nose.

"*Van Halen,*" Tana emphasized, her dark eyes narrowing as she observed my reaction. "She's dating Van."

"Right. Of course." I swiped some of the wine off my chin, avoiding her eyes.

Beth laughed. "It isn't like you don't have a million brothers, Tana."

"Two of them are practically infants so they don't count," she sniffed.

The Evers had unexpectedly had two more kids when we were in our early teens, much to Tana's disgust. Campbell and Beck were almost teenagers now but to us, they would always be the first reminders that "old" people had sex.

I grinned. "I'm sure they love that you still call them infants."

"At least they're potty trained now." Tana smiled.

"Anyway, it's nice to meet you, Beth."

"Nice to meet you, too. Now that you guys are here, we can get this party started. Despite what Tana thinks, I do more than just her brother. I also brought the tunes!" She held up a little portable speaker.

"Yes. Let's get this party started!" Tana whooped.

Soon Dua Lipa was on the air and everyone was swaying to the music. Tana shimmied her shoulders playfully before dancing around Piper. Someone tapped me on the shoulder. I turned around and a genuine smile crossed my face when Carter hugged me.

"Hey. You made it. We weren't sure you'd be back in town."

He ran a tired hand over his face. "Yeah. Tana's message came right as I was leaving DC. Going back and forth is taking its toll. I might have to make some hard decisions soon."

"Sorry to hear about your dad."

He accepted a beer that someone thrust in his hand. "He's getting better, just not as fast as his doctors hoped. But enough about that. How are things going with the house?"

I was in the middle of telling him my dream plan for renovating the kitchen when Rix suddenly appeared next to the beer table. He didn't look over, but I could feel his judgment hitting me like a wave.

What the hell was his problem? I'd left the house to get away from him and still couldn't escape his grumpy glares. And why was he staring daggers at Carter? Weren't they friends?

I hadn't had enough wine to even try to figure out what was going on in Hendrix's brain. But I wasn't leaving just because he'd put his boxers on the wrong way. He could glare at my back all night long if he wanted.

I focused all of my attention on Carter. "Do you want to dance?"

Carter looked a little startled at the complete change of subject, but he shrugged so we moved closer to the fire. Over the last hour, darkness had fallen and more people had shown up, some I recognized, some I didn't. Things had gotten rowdier now that everyone was a few beers in and soon Tana was yelling back and forth over the fire to a guy on the other side that I vaguely remembered being a little older than us.

"Everybody remember the time Greg got so drunk he ran through the fire?" Tana yelled.

Greg made a face. "Are we going down memory lane? Because I remember you decided it was too hot and took your top off that same night!"

Tana smirked. "Did I scare you away? Or was that your first time seeing a woman hot and bothered?"

The group erupted into laughter. I laughed politely even though I had no idea what they were talking about. The events in question must have happened during senior year or afterward.

Everyone else here was bound by a lifetime of memories while I was only working with puzzle pieces. No matter how much I tried, I would always be the one who couldn't relate to all the stories or who might or might not remember some funny thing that happened.

It was so strange to be back here ten years later, jumping back into the life I could have had if things had been different.

If Gran had lived.

Suddenly I felt very alone.

There was only a little bit of wine left in my cup so I tipped my head back and gulped it all. I didn't want to think about what-ifs and all the things that had gone wrong. For once I just wanted to exist in the moment.

I wanted to feel free.

I wanted to feel everything.

Carter held his cup in one hand and put his other arm around my waist. The music had changed to a slower country song and as I closed my eyes, it was so easy to pretend that life was simple.

Gran's house was already renovated.

My mom and Billie were safe and happy.

The shoulder I leaned on belonged to a man who loved me and I never had to wonder how much.

Halfway through the song I opened my eyes. A few feet away Hendrix stood on the edge of the dancing throng watching us. In his eyes I could see a promise of all the same things I'd just imagined and a burning desire for the arms holding me to be his.

I wasn't sure how long we stared at each other, but our standoff was only broken when someone stepped between us. The young woman was pretty with long brown hair styled in one of those elaborate waterfall braids I thought only existed on Pinterest.

She put her hands on Rix's chest like she had every right to touch him so intimately. Apparently, she thought they were alone since her hands didn't stop at his chest, roaming down like she was about to grab his dick in front of everyone.

He caught her hand, but his lips quirked in that stupid half smile that looked so good on him. He whispered something, hopefully instructions on how to keep her hands to herself, but must not have been since she didn't look upset. No, she looked quite happy with herself and why wouldn't she? Any woman would be thrilled to be where she was standing.

Including me. In the rapidly fading light with the heat of the bonfire raging behind me, I could admit that she had what I wanted.

What I wanted but couldn't have.

Rix clearly didn't mind her pawing all over him because he didn't push her away. His arm was draped loosely around her waist as he talked to her and he looked happy enough. Maybe she was what he wanted. His eyes met mine. Then my heart banged against my chest when he leaned down to kiss her.

"Charlie. Are you okay?" Carter's arm tightened around my waist when I swayed.

I shook my head, suddenly dizzy from the combination of the heat from the fire and the wine. "I think I need to sit for a while."

"Of course."

He helped me over to the picnic table. Someone scooted over so I could perch on the end. I rested my head on my arms and the dizziness subsided.

"What's the matter with her?" Tana's voice sounded like it was far away.

"I think she had too much wine." Carter's hand was still on my arm and I wanted to shrug it off, but I was too tired.

Without raising my head, I said, "I'm okay. I didn't even have that much wine but I think I stood too close to the fire."

A deep voice grumbled right behind me. "I'll take her home."

I sat up slowly and glared at Rix. The girl who'd been climbing him like a tree was still over by the fire. Her eyes followed his every move as he knelt next to me.

"That's not necessary. I don't want to make you leave your friends."

Now that I was away from the heat, I felt much better but I was still a little dizzy. Going home and curling up in bed sounded heavenly but that didn't mean I wanted to leave with Rix.

Carter leaned over. "I can take her home—"

"We're going to the same place anyway," Rix interrupted. He took my arm and helped me stand.

Tana gave me a hug goodbye. "I'll call you tomorrow."

I nodded. Rix led me back toward the long driveway where we'd all parked our cars.

"I didn't mean to end your night early."

He shrugged. "It's fine. You've been to one bonfire, you've been to them all."

The further we got away from the fire, the darker it was. I tripped slightly over a rock and Rix grabbed my arm to steady me.

"Thanks. I'm just saying I feel bad for ruining your night. You can drop me off really quickly and then come back."

He stepped in front of me so I was forced to look at him. "Charlie, I'm *exactly* where I want to be. Okay?"

"Okay."

When we reached his pickup truck, he opened the door and helped me up into the cab. I sucked in a surprised breath when he leaned over me to fasten the seatbelt. On any other day I would have slapped his hands away or told him I could do it myself but instead I didn't say anything. For once it didn't feel like he was being pushy or high-handed but like he was taking care of me.

How long had it been since anyone had tried to do that?

When the metal belt snapped into place, the sound was loud in the quiet cab of the truck. The only other sound was the faint voices in the distance and the soft hush of our breathing. In that moment I felt more peace than I had in weeks.

Because I was exactly where I wanted to be, too.

————

The quiet between us lasted all the way home. Hendrix did his usual strong and silent thing, and I didn't feel compelled to fill the space between us with conversation. Once we pulled up to the house, I tensed. Maybe it was because we were going back into our usual environment, but I suddenly felt really odd about being alone with him.

He unlocked the front door and motioned for me to precede him. I leaned down to greet Meatball, ignoring Rix hovering over my shoulder.

"Were you good while I was gone?"

My eyes swept over the floor tentatively just in case he'd left any presents in the few hours I'd been gone. I didn't like leaving him alone at such a young age so I fully expected him to have shown his displeasure with a puddle or two.

After a quick walk so Meatball could visit his favorite trees, we came back inside. I'd expected Rix to be gone but he was still standing in the living room, like he was waiting for us. I took Meatball's leash off and he immediately attacked one of his squeaky toys.

When I stood up, Rix was still watching me.

"Did you have fun tonight?"

The words were simple enough on the surface. Maybe it was the brooding look on his face or an undercurrent in his rumbling voice but there was something dangerous about the question that sent a shiver down my spine.

"I had a great time tonight hanging out with my best friend. It was perfect."

There was only a small tick in his jaw that betrayed his agitation. "That's your idea of a good time? Getting drunk and making yourself sick? What the hell was Carter doing letting you have that much wine?"

"Letting me? No one lets me do anything. Newsflash: I can take care of myself. And what is your obsession with Carter? You glared at him all night."

"How would you know what I was doing unless you were watching me?"

"It was a little hard not to notice your girlfriend trying to grab your dick in front of everyone."

"Ex-girlfriend," he stated quietly as he moved closer.

"You kiss your ex-girlfriend?"

He chuckled. "I kissed her on the cheek. I'm trying to keep it civil. Breaking up doesn't mean you have to be enemies."

Swallowing, I took a step back but bumped up against the wall. He kept coming, using his big body to crowd me. But instead of feeling threatened, my blood rushed, every nerve ending tingling at the prospect of being close to him.

Not wanting him to know just how off-balance he made me feel, I raised my chin defiantly, staring him right in the eyes.

"She seems a little obsessed with you, Rix. You probably shouldn't lead her on."

He looked away and for a brief moment I wondered if what I'd said had hit a nerve. Then he glanced back with his usual smirk in place and the moment was gone.

"I'm sure that surprises you. You may not like me, but that doesn't mean no else does."

"Whatever. I don't care. You can date anybody you want."

"That's not true."

He leaned over and now I could feel the brush of his breath over my hair. Why was he so close?

"W-Why not?"

"Because the one I want hates me."

At his words, my eyes flew up to meet his. What was he talking about? I was caught off guard by the vulnerable expression on his face. I wasn't used to serious Rix. He had to be teasing me.

"You shouldn't say things you don't mean."

"I never do," he whispered.

We stared at each other for what felt like hours. It was like seeing him for the first time. His hair was still slightly too long and flopped over eyes that weren't sure if they wanted to be green or brown. The nose I'd once wished one of his brothers would punch was covered in a light dusting of freckles I'd never noticed before but found unexpectedly charming.

"Why are you telling me this?" I finally asked.

"The same reason you didn't like seeing me with Janelle. The same reason I wanted to rip Carter's arms off. Because I want you and you want me."

His blatant words were thrilling but also made me panic. I couldn't even fathom admitting I felt the same way only to find out this was another one of his sick jokes.

"I don't even like you."

He didn't have the decency to be offended by the mean words. Instead they made him smile.

"You don't have to. I can like you enough for the both of us."

I melted a little at that before grasping desperately for the last bit of resolve I had left. He didn't get to do this to me.

Wasn't there some rule that you weren't allowed to be evil your whole life and then turn around and say the most unexpectedly sweet things?

But then he did something I could never have expected. He took my face between his hands and pressed a gentle kiss to my forehead. Somehow it was more affecting than a steamy kiss could have been.

This was more than just *I want you.*

This was *I care for you.*

I cherish you.

"You still don't like me?" he whispered.

"Nope."

He kissed me again but lower this time, his lips against my cheek. "What about now? Getting warmer?"

"I still don't like you and we are not friends," I insisted but my voice was a little too breathy to be believable.

Hendrix clearly heard it because he gave me that cocky grin I loved and hated. "We don't have to be friends for me to make you scream, right?"

My mouth went dry. "I can't disagree."

"Good. Let me know if you still hate me in an hour."

eighteen

· · ·

HENDRIX

Over the years I'd imagined what it would be like to seduce Charlotte Monroe many times. It was always a clash of teeth and hands and being buried alive under an avalanche of passion. I imagined that we'd fuck the same way we did everything else, with intensity and hatred, each of us trying to best the other.

The reality was beyond anything I could have ever dreamed. Charlie wasn't fighting or grabbing me the way I'd assumed she would. No, she melted into my embrace.

Melted.

One minute her eyes were hot with defiance and then with one little kiss she liquefied like butter in a hot pan.

Her hands slid through my hair gently, her nails scraping over my scalp in a way that made me shudder. Whatever magical switch I'd flipped had taken her from mad as a wet hen to licking my neck like a kitten. She jumped into my arms and my hands landed on her ass instinctively to catch her. There was no way in hell I was putting her down to walk so I just headed for the stairs with her tongue on my neck and my hands filled with her abundant curves.

Maybe a different man could pause and think about the consequences when the woman he'd lusted after for years was in his arms, but I wasn't that guy.

As we passed through the living room Charlie took one of my earlobes between her teeth and bit down gently.

"Oh fuck—"

Distracted, I stubbed my toe on a side table as we passed through the living room and cursed as we listed to the side, the wall the only thing that saved us from going down. Her soft, husky laughter in my ear made me forget the pain as her mouth continued its exploration down my neck. I stumbled again near the stairs when her tongue darted over my collarbone.

"You'd better not drop me," she whispered before her hands snaked between us to yank at the tail end of my shirt.

"Never. Just let me get up the stairs before you bite anything else."

"Can't handle it?" she teased.

"Not even slightly."

She must have enjoyed my admission of weakness because her hand paused before coming back up to wrap behind my neck. I took the reprieve and darted up the stairs. The amount of racket my boots made on the staircase would have inspired a comment any other time but apparently even Charlie didn't care about noise right now.

As soon as we fell through the door into her room all bets were off, and suddenly she seemed to have a million hands, each running over a different part of my body.

"Why do you have these abs?" she moaned as her hands snuck under my shirt, her nails scraping over my skin.

I hissed at the sharp sensation. Her eyes narrowed at the sound before she did it again. Deliberately.

"Watch the claws, brat."

"Don't tell me what to do." Her eyes glittered as she leaned forward and bit my lip.

"I think I know exactly how to shut you up."

Moving closer to the bed, I tossed her none too gently on top of the covers. Her hair flopped all around her face and she scowled at me. I laughed before climbing on the bed with her. She watched as I climbed over her, her legs instinctively coming up to wrap around my hips. I took my time, enjoying the tease as we connected and my weight pressed her into the bed. The sensation of her under me was one I didn't want to forget, especially since it was unlikely I'd ever feel this again, once she came to her senses and remembered that she hated me.

For a brief moment, time suspended as I stared into her eyes. Color was high on her cheeks, a rosy hue that made her golden-brown skin glow. Then again Charlie always looked luminous to me, like she carried some extra light inside that no one else had. But seeing her all lit up with excitement and anticipation *for me* made the moment surreal, like I'd temporarily stepped into one of the many fantasies I'd had over the years.

But this was no fantasy. Charlie was here, warm, and right beneath me, looking into my eyes like I was all she wanted.

Until she opened her mouth, that is.

"You are so much hotter when you aren't talking." Charlie's hands ran over my shoulders and down my back only stopping to squeeze my ass.

The movement made me rock my hips and she whimpered slightly at the movement. She rolled her hips and the way she moved let me know exactly how hot things were about to get. She moved like a woman who knew what she wanted. And right now what she wanted was me.

"Never thought I'd see the day I had Charlie Monroe begging for it."

Her hands tightened on my ass. "That's assuming it'll be any good."

"Oh you know it'll be good," I muttered against her neck as I licked my way down her neck, taking in her peaches scent.

Why did she have to smell so good? What magical pheromones was she putting out that all I could imagine lately was filling that smart mouth with my cock?

Charlie slid her hands into my hair pulling me back up for another scorching kiss.

"Talking this much means you don't know how else to use your big mouth. I'll probably be begging you to stop soon."

"The fuck you will."

I reached down to unzip her jeans and she lifted her hips to make it easier. As she inched her jeans down her legs, my mind blanked when I got a flash of black panties and plush thighs. The next thing to go was her shirt, revealing a black cotton bra.

"Take this off," she whispered before tugging at my shirt.

Her hands stayed with me as I yanked it over my head, running over the skin revealed. The flush on her cheeks increased and her eyes went glassy as she stared at my bare chest.

I started to unbutton my jeans then paused. "Are you sure?"

"Nothing makes sense lately. Up is down and right is left. But the only thing that hasn't changed is the fact that I want you. I'm tired of pretending I don't."

Her hands rested on top of mine. Then with slow deliberation she unbuttoned my jeans and tugged the zipper down, the metallic sound almost as loud as my heartbeat in the quiet room.

My breath whooshed out all at once when she reached into my underwear and gripped my cock in her hot little hand. I was aware that she was waiting for me to respond and that this was the time to have the mature conversations about expectations and birth control. But then she slid her fist down my length, squeezing hard just the way I loved it and conversation was no longer possible.

"Thank god," I finally choked out before pushing my jeans and underwear the rest of the way down.

Briefly I was annoyed with myself for rushing because the movement caused Charlie to release her grip. Luckily she used the time to unhook her bra and tug her black panties down her legs. She threw them on the floor beside the bed. Under any other circumstances it would have made me laugh or I would have at least teased her about being so impatient. However, I was just grateful that she felt the same urgency I did, something inside pushing me to hurry before she came to her senses and realized she could do so much better than me.

There was a brief hiccup when I realized she didn't have any protection in her room. I ran naked to get the box of condoms in mine, followed by the husky sound of her laughter. When I got back she was laying on her side, her head propped up on one arm.

She whistled softly. "What a view."

The way I blushed took me by surprise. Of all the things she'd ever said it was ridiculous that *this* would embarrass me. But maybe it was because I'd never been butterball ass naked when she was teasing me before.

After rolling the condom on, I climbed back on the bed. The sound she made as I settled between her legs would be forever imprinted in my mind. Her little sigh made my blood burn and I took a deep breath trying to regain some control. But as I entered her slowly, I realized that was an illusion.

There was no way to have control when my cock felt like it had just entered heaven.

Charlie shuddered beneath me, her hand clenching around my forearm. I paused giving her a moment to adjust and taking one for myself. I opened my eyes and was stunned to find her watching me.

"Don't you dare stop now. I'll kill you if you do."

Then she smiled so tenderly like we shared a secret, one that only we would ever know. Her affection was intoxicating, the full force of it made me dizzy.

Was this why I loved arguing with her so much? Because her anger was the closest I could get to having her undivided attention?

"Rix? You can move. I'm okay now."

Her smile was meant to be reassuring but it only made the dizziness worse. She might be okay but I wasn't. Her hand rubbed my chest. Slowly. Comfortingly. My eyes closed against the pull of wanting to bury myself in her and never come out. I knew then that I'd made a mistake.

After knowing her like this how would I ever let her go?

Suddenly I was overcome with the urge to have her, all of her, while I could. My thrust took us both by surprise and her hand on my chest flexed, her nails dragging over my skin. I gritted my teeth at the bite of pain.

"Sorry. That was–"

Her hand touched my lips, stopping whatever I was about to say. She simply nodded and tightened her muscles around me.

"Yes. Just like that," she whispered.

Soon we were moving together like a wave, her hips rising to meet my every thrust. Her legs curled around my waist and the new angle made her cry out. The shock of pleasure that arced down my spine threatened to take me under so I frantically tried to recall the most unsexy things I could think of, gym socks, the roster of my favorite baseball team and in a moment of final desperation started counting in Spanish.

———

I listened intently. Charlie's breathing was slow and even. She must be asleep. I moved slowly, pulling my arm from beneath her head. She stirred and looked over her shoulder at me.

"Sorry," I whispered. "I was trying not to wake you."

"Where are you going?" Her eyes dropped to somewhere in the middle of my chest.

"To get snacks. Um, I'm hungry."

That seemed to mollify her so I climbed out of bed. My jeans were on the floor but I didn't feel like putting them back on so I just walked downstairs naked. Before I attempted to make any food, I walked over to the freezer and stuck my head inside. It didn't help as much as I thought it would but at least I didn't feel like my face was on fire anymore.

Why was this so hard?

Talking to Charlie shouldn't make me feel like my tongue was three sizes too big for my mouth. But suddenly, I was second-guessing everything and as nervous as a virgin in Vegas. It was just Charlie. She'd seen me naked before I had anything anybody wanted to see.

I was starving but there was no time to make anything complicated so I slapped some turkey on the nasty whole wheat bread she liked so we could have sandwiches. There was a half a bag of chips left so I took that before folding a dishtowel over my arm so she didn't have to yell at me for getting her bed dirty. At the last minute I went back to the pantry and grabbed the bag of Skittles on the top shelf.

When I came back, she was sitting up in bed with the sheet

yanked all the way up to cover her chest. I arranged my bounty on the dishtowel. Charlie raised her eyebrows.

"Not bad." Then she noticed the bag of candy and her face softened. "Careful, Rix. If you keep being so nice, I might actually think you like me."

I took a big bite of the sandwich and made an effort not to grimace at the taste of the whole wheat bread. She noticed anyway and laughed.

"You'll get used to it. It's better for you."

I grabbed some chips and stuffed them in my mouth. Anything could taste decent if you covered it with nacho cheese flavor. As we ate, we settled into a comfortable kind of silence. Charlie seemed completely content to scarf her sandwich down before diving directly into the bag of candy. Things were so easy that it was scary. Things were never this easy.

"I always liked you," I mumbled.

Charlie looked up in surprise. "What?"

My face flamed. Now why the hell had I just blurted that out? Well, it was out there now. I could either pretend it hadn't happened or just go with it. As much as I hated to admit it, I didn't like this idea she had that I had been deliberately trying to fuck things up for her over the years. I liked to tease her, yes. But that didn't mean I'd ever wanted her to actually be hurt.

"I always liked you. Even when I was playing pranks on you," I finally admitted.

She didn't look at me but her hand drifted closer to where mine rested on top of the covers. "You couldn't have convinced me of that."

Her fingers trailed over the back of my knuckles. Just that simple touch made my skin feel electrified. Unfortunately, my dick noticed too and immediately lifted. She smirked.

I snatched the covers from her and slid beneath. She sighed

and rested her head on my chest. Her fingers trailed from my neck down to my belly button before coming back up. Over and over.

"I didn't want you to know," I admitted finally.

Her hand was still rubbing circles on my chest. I picked it up and kissed the back of it. Her answering smile made my heart turn over. Beneath her tough exterior she was so fucking sweet.

Whatever this was, it was unexpected but in some ways inevitable.

"I bet you never thought you'd be lying here with me when you came back. A country boy."

She moved back slightly and frowned. "What's wrong with country boys?"

"I'm not exactly your type. Your last guy probably wore a suit every day."

"He did. And had a stick up his ass the rest of the time."

I didn't respond. The thought of her with some Wall Street douche made my chest tight.

"Rix, I don't think a guy is better because he wears a suit to work. I think a guy is better when he fixes the doorknob or when he helps a neighbor with his fence. Or when he remembers that I love Skittles."

"I knew it was the Skittles," I whispered before leaning down to capture her mouth in a kiss.

All I wanted was to sink into her and forget all the reasons this thing between us would never work. With my eyes closed it was easier to pretend this was real and not just two people scratching an itch they couldn't reach for far too long. But Charlie stopped me with a hand to my chest, her dark eyes roaming over my face. She always had seen far too much.

"Hendrix Evers, you are annoying, irritating, gorgeous, and sexy. You are everything that drives me crazy but I have never thought you weren't good enough for me. I just thought you were a pain in the ass."

My lips quirked. "Sexy, huh?"

"Figures that's the only part you heard. I also said *annoying*."

"But sexy."

She sighed and settled her head back on my chest. "Very sexy."

nineteen

. . .

CHARLOTTE

Morning afters were always awkward.

Usually, you just had that weird stretch of time where you weren't sure if you were supposed to sneak out or stick around and make small talk. But I'd never dealt with a morning after in my own house. Especially since he'd snuck out instead of sleeping with me. What was I supposed to say to Rix?

Morning!

Would you like pancakes or more sex?

It wasn't as if there were that many other options. Hendrix Evers was not the settling down type. He was blunt and grumpy and definitely not Mr. Right. Yet somehow, despite being everything I thought I didn't want, I'd been happier living with him than I ever was with Aaron.

I opened the door and peered into the hallway. Rix's door was still closed so I tiptoed past to the stairs. Downstairs, everything looked the same as when I left it last night except the wall in the living room was bright white and there was a can of paint sitting on the floor.

He'd had time to paint?

When I turned around and bumped into a firm chest, I let out a screech.

"Whoa! It's just me!"

I clamped my lips shut to stop the noise and put a hand over my pounding heart. Rix was wearing a pair of black track pants but no shirt and his hair was slightly damp like he'd just showered.

"You were gone so...I thought you were in your room," I said when my heart had finally climbed out of my throat.

He shrugged. "I couldn't sleep. I figured I'd get some painting done today."

Heat rose to my face. So basically, he'd given me the best orgasm of my life and still had energy to get up and do home improvement projects. Meanwhile I'd slept in like a lazybones.

"You didn't have to do that."

"I wanted to. It's no big deal, Charlie."

Unsure what to do with my hands, I crossed my arms. Maybe that looked a little defensive? I uncrossed my arms and then put my hands on my hips.

Rix watched my fidgeting with amusement. "What's going on with you this morning?"

"Nothing."

He suddenly grinned and grabbed me around the waist. "Are you nervous? It's just me."

I shoved him slightly so I wouldn't have to look him in the face. "I know it's just you."

"Do you? Because you're already acting weird. Is this about last night?"

Why was this so hard to talk about? I hadn't been expecting him to actually bring it up directly. Not when dancing around it was so much easier. Maybe it was because my interactions with Rix were usually a combination of annoyance and teasing but I wasn't sure how to have an earnest conversation with him.

Things had to be different now though, right?

After the bonfire something vital had changed between us. I'd never been a jealous person but seeing his ex-girlfriend running her hands all over him had awakened a green-eyed beast that I wasn't sure I could control. He seemed to have that same feeling whenever Carter was anywhere near me. It shouldn't give me such satisfaction, but I definitely loved that he didn't want another man near me.

What did that mean exactly? I wasn't sure and I doubted Rix really knew either. Last night we'd admitted our intense attraction but what did that mean beyond one night?

I wasn't sure I was ready to have that conversation yet.

Or ever.

He winked. "I usually didn't stick around for morning afters, so you'll have to tell me the protocol."

As usual he could make me laugh. "Suddenly I'm the expert on the walk of shame?"

"I'm definitely no relationship expert," he said. "Otherwise, my girlfriend wouldn't have decided we were getting married without telling me."

"Neither am I. Otherwise my boyfriend wouldn't have bailed with no explanation."

His expression darkened and he opened his mouth like he was about to say something. I put a finger over his lips. I didn't really want to talk about Aaron at all. So I walked to the kitchen and turned the coffee pot on.

"I'm not sure about the usual walk of shame protocol but I vote for no walking and no shame," I said.

There were no more coffee mugs in the cabinet so I leaned over to get a clean one from the dishwasher. When I stood up, Rix was right behind me. He groaned as my hips brushed against his.

"Can I help you, sir?"

His arm snaked around my waist. Whatever else I was about to say stalled in my throat as he kissed behind my ear. He was hard already and I rubbed my ass against him, loving the soft grumbling sound he made.

"I vote we establish our own rituals. Number one, coffee comes first." My voice was shaky as he continued to explore the skin on my neck.

He reached over and took the mug from my hands, tossing it none too gently on the counter.

"Number one, *you* come first."

———

It was almost lunchtime before we came up for air. My head was resting on Rix's shoulder as he trailed his finger down my arm, sending tingles of sensation all over my body.

"We can't just stay in bed all day," I moaned.

He raised an eyebrow. "Can't we?"

"I'm pretty sure there's a rule against it somewhere. The too-much-fun rule."

"Since I've never paid much attention to rules, I'll have to take your word for it. But what happens if we break it? Are you going to spank me?"

He laughed when I rolled on top of him, raising his hips suggestively. His smile changed to a frown when I kept rolling and landed on the floor.

"You're actually getting up?"

I thought about it for a second. "Maybe. I feel like we need to schedule in a food break, at least."

The sound of my phone ringing interrupted his reply. Hendrix leaned over to retrieve it from the nightstand and smiled before turning it to face me. The screen displayed a picture of my sister from two Halloweens ago wearing a ladybug costume and a huge gap-toothed smile.

He leaned over and kissed me on the forehead. "I'll take a shower while you talk to your sister."

I watched his naked ass disappear out the door as I answered. "Hey, Billie Bug. How are things going?"

"Charlie, what's going on? Someone at camp said that Dad was arrested?"

I closed my eyes. This was exactly what I feared would happen. If Mom had just told her the truth it would have been a million times better than hearing it unexpectedly.

"I'm sorry, Billie. Mom thought it would be better not to tell you until the end of camp."

"She probably just didn't want to deal with me. She knows I would have asked to come home."

I couldn't dispute that. Billie had never been shy about calling our Mom out when she was being self-centered. She might be the little sister, but she was also a little badass.

"Right now, I'm in Violet Ridge getting the house ready so we have a place to stay. I know it's not ideal but it's all going to work out."

Billie was quiet. "We're going to live in Grandma Grace's house?"

"That's the plan. I'm fixing it up and it should be ready soon. Try not to worry too much, okay?"

"Okay. I wish I could come home now."

My shoulders slumped. Billie sounded miserable but there wasn't much I could do since I didn't have the authority to withdraw her from camp. It had to be terrible to know that the adults in her life were keeping secrets from her while surrounded by a bunch of kids she didn't even like that much.

"I know things are hard right now but just remember that you'll be here in August."

"Okay. Love you, sis."

"Love you too, bug."

After hanging up, I immediately called my mother. She answered on the first ring sounding stressed.

"Hi, honey. I can't talk now. I have a meeting—"

"Billie just called me. Someone at camp told her what happened."

"Fantastic. This is just what we need. You can say I told you so."

I wasn't even going to respond to that bait. My mother had a tendency toward the dramatic and we didn't have time for that right now.

"What are we going to do about Billie? She sounded really upset. Can you take her out of camp early? I really think she just wants to come home."

"I'm not sure that's a good idea. Every day there are people in and out of here and I have all these meetings with the lawyers."

Even though I knew it was an excuse, I couldn't pretend being at home would really be much better. With everything going on, Billie would probably spend most of her time in the penthouse alone. I closed my eyes. Maybe I should have waited before coming back to Violet Ridge. If I had, I could have been there with her.

"I wish the house was in better shape. I could have taken her for the summer. Let's just hope the kids there get bored with this news quickly and move on to the next scandal."

"That's what I'm hoping. I have a meeting with Alan today so we can discuss options. Let's just hope all of this is over soon."

She didn't ask any questions about the renovations, but I assured her that things were still on track. I figured it would be good for her to hear that at least something was going according to plan but I don't think it helped. By the time we hung up I felt as stressed as she sounded.

I sighed. Every time I thought the dust had settled, the rug was pulled out from under us again. It was exhausting.

Meanwhile, instead of working on the house I'd been rolling around naked with Rix. He loved to flirt and have a good time but that was all it was. I couldn't get used to his help or attention. The repairs on the house had to be my first priority. I was still on my own and all those promises I'd made to Billie weren't going to come true unless I stopped playing around and got focused.

Fast.

twenty

. . .

CHARLOTTE

back in the day ...

Turning from side to side, I eyed the fluffy lavender dress that Tana claimed made me look like a fairy princess with a critical eye. Maybe I should have worn the dress my mom brought back from New York. Prom was a big deal so I wasn't sure going for a cocktail length dress had been the right choice.

If only I was a little taller, then I could pull off a dramatic gown like the one Tana had decided on. Going dress shopping was half the fun of prom so I probably still would have worn this one. Watching Tana try on and make fun of a bunch of dresses was worth more than an outfit from some exclusive boutique in the city.

Voices floated up the stairs and I smiled at the sound of Mrs. Evers prompting Tana to "say cheese" again as she posed for the millionth photo in front of the fireplace. It drove her crazy that her mom wanted to take pictures of everything but I thought it was sweet.

What I wouldn't give to still have someone who cared so much about documenting the moments of my life.

Especially since this was my last year with them.

Not that anyone knew that yet. I hadn't told Tana. She would cry and want to go talk to my mom. In her world, if you begged and cried someone gave in. I didn't have the heart to tell her those tactics only worked if someone cared about your tears.

As always, thoughts of my grandmother's death took my breath away. She'd died right after the new year, almost like she was holding on just so she wouldn't miss one last holiday season. Then as soon as the new year came in, she was gone and I'd cried buckets of tears since. The tears hadn't brought her back and they hadn't made me feel better either.

All it had done was remind me that the only person who'd cared when I wept was gone. I had no tears left.

No, crying wouldn't get me another year in Violet Ridge. When Gran was alive there was someone else to reason with Mom. Now that she was gone, I was going to have to do my senior year at some snooty school in Manhattan.

It was just one year, I reminded myself. After that I was coming right back. I was already hiding money to pay for my train ticket. Once I was eighteen, I could make my own decisions.

A shadow passed over the doorway.

"Would you stop lurking already," I finally said.

There was silence and then Rix appeared in the doorway. "Why aren't you downstairs taking pictures with Tana?"

"Your mom wants pictures of her daughter. I don't want to get in the way."

"My mom already considers you one of us. She would probably trade me out for you in a heartbeat."

"That's not true. Your parents love each of their kids. Even when you get in trouble."

He stepped into the room, keeping half of his body in the hallway almost like he wasn't sure if he was really welcome. "Why are you crying?"

"I'm not." I swiped at my cheeks, horrified to find them wet.

Luckily, he didn't bother to call me out for the obvious lie. His eyes traveled over the chaos in the room, all the makeup Tana had pulled out before deciding what she wanted to use and the boxes of shoes all over the floor. The strappy lavender sandals I'd found to match my dress were kicked off in the corner because they were already making my feet hurt. I'd spent an hour straightening my hair and actually put on more than just mascara for once. I would have felt beautiful if I wasn't so heartbroken.

"Are you going to the prom?"

He shrugged. "Not really my scene."

I wasn't sure why I asked since I couldn't even imagine a world where Hendrix Evers willingly wore a tuxedo.

"Good. Maybe we'll actually be able to have fun for once." I raised my eyebrows before sending him a sweet smile, the kind I knew annoyed him.

"We? You and your date?" He chuckled to himself, like the idea of me having a date was so ludicrous.

"Yes. I have a date." Technically I had a pity date since I was pretty sure Kenny had only asked me because his best friend Steve was going with Tana. But Rix didn't need to know that.

"I heard. You're actually going out with Kenny Baker."

"He's nice," I insisted.

"I guess if that's your type." Rix didn't look impressed.

"What does that mean?"

"That's the type of guy who is just looking to cop a feel. Are you going to let him kiss you?"

Annoyed, I threw the makeup brush I wasn't even using down on Tana's desk. "That is none of your business."

"It would be disappointing anyway."

"How would you know? Maybe he's a good kisser. Maybe he'll kiss me under the stars and it'll be perfect just like in the movies."

Hendrix smiled in that cocky way that always made me want to punch him. "A perfect kiss? That's what you want?"

"Yes. It'll be soft and sweet and romantic. Not that you would know anything about that."

He moved closer. "Maybe he'll tell you that you look beautiful in your dress, like something out of a dream."

His voice was so soft and the way he was looking at me when he said it made my chest hurt. He always smelled like wood chips from the work he did with his father. It should have been annoying, but the scent wrapped around me making my head spin.

"Yes. I guess so," I whispered, wishing that he would hurry up and leave.

"Then he'll take your hand. He'll feel lucky that he gets to be that close to you."

I sucked in a breath as he took my hand. His eyes stayed on mine for a long moment before his fingers curled around my wrist, lifting my hand to rest against his chest.

Something in the back of my mind was telling me to move away or scream or laugh in his face. To do anything other than lean into him, enjoying the heat of his body.

"He'll look down at you and remember all the times he wished he could kiss you before," Rix whispered.

When I looked up at him, his lips passed over my forehead. I went still and he looked at me, waiting. When I nodded, he dipped his head and kissed my lips softly, brushing back and forth in a soft, ticklish sensation. I smiled and felt the curve of his lips turn up when he smiled, too. Then his hand slid behind my head and held me in place as he slanted his head, taking the kiss deeper. His tongue slid against mine and I sighed into his mouth. The hand that was still resting on his chest went higher to tangle in the hair that was curling over his collar. When he finally pulled back, my head was spinning and my lips felt swollen.

For a moment he looked down at me and I could have sworn it was like looking at a different person. There was something in his eyes that I'd never seen before, but then he blinked again and it was gone.

"So was it perfect?" Rix's voice jolted me out of the hazy, dreamlike state I'd fallen into like a face full of ice water.

"What?"

He smirked. "My kiss technique. It's perfect, right?"

I snatched my hand away from his chest like it was contaminated. What was that? Had I seriously just sucked face with my nemesis? And what if Tana had come up here and seen us?

"Why did you do that?"

"What do you mean?" He stuck his hands in his pockets and rocked back on his heels, looking for all the world like he had no idea what I was talking about.

"You just kissed me!"

"Oh that? That was to make up for the crappy kiss you'll get from your date later. At least one part of your night won't be a disappointment."

I pushed him toward the door, ignoring his laughter. He was so much bigger than me that my shove barely moved him but finally he held up his hands and walked out of the room.

My heart was still pounding so I sat on the small bench in

front of Tana's makeup table. When I looked in the mirror, I winced at the shiny lip gloss smeared across my cheek and the section of hair that was tangled in the back of my head. I used a tissue to wipe my cheek, but my hands were shaking so I figured I'd better wait before I reapplied.

Then I dropped my head into my hands.

What had I been thinking?

It was time I got over this stupid crush that had persisted for years. But every time I thought it was over, he did something that drew me back in. That was the thing about Rix. He was so awful most of the time but then he'd have an unexpected moment of sweetness. I couldn't let myself forget that it was all a game to him.

And I was never, *ever* going to tell him that he'd been my very first kiss.

twenty-one

. . .

HENDRIX

If there were a contest for keeping it casual, Charlie would be winning. Over the past few weeks, she hadn't treated me any differently.

When we passed in the hall, she didn't avert her eyes. She still teased me and pretended to be annoyed when I ate her food or used her body wash. But she also wouldn't let me sleep in her room anymore, claiming I snored. She would hug me, but she wouldn't cuddle.

Men everywhere would probably think I was crazy, but I didn't want a casual thing with Charlie. The sex was out of this world, but I found myself wanting more. I wanted her to look at me the way she did that first night, like she saw something more in me than just a good time. Instead, she seemed to be doing everything possible to take us back to day one: two roommates who could barely tolerate each other's company.

After dealing with Janelle's constant demands and clinginess, you would think a non-clingy woman would be right up my alley. It wasn't.

I hated it.

I hated everything.

Sunday afternoon, I pulled to a stop at the end of my parents' driveway. My brother's car was already here and no doubt Tana would arrive thirty minutes late, as usual. I blew out a breath. Sunday dinner was non-negotiable unless you wanted my mom to appear at your door the next day, so I always pulled my shit together enough to show up.

When I'd left the house, Charlie was curled up on the couch watching something on her laptop. She'd finally agreed to take that awful plastic off and had covered the couch with about a million throw blankets. It still wasn't exactly comfortable, but I would have given anything to dive under one of those blankets with her.

I opened the front door and was immediately hit with the sound of voices. Van and Beth sat on the couch in the living room watching TV.

"Is that Hendrix?" Mom called from the kitchen.

"Yes. He just got here," Van yelled back, smirking at me.

Mom came into the room, wiping her hands on a dishtowel. "Hey, sweetie. Can you help me get this bowl down in the kitchen? Your father is out back."

I looked over at Van. There was no point in asking why she hadn't asked him to do it. Now that he was her best chance for grandchildren before the next century, he had officially hit favorite child status.

"Of course, Mom." I followed her into the kitchen and inhaled the delicious smell wafting in from the open window behind the sink. "Is Dad grilling?"

She grinned. "He made his famous baby back ribs."

The prospect of having one of my favorite meals immediately lifted my mood.

Just as I was getting the bowl down, I heard a loud voice coming from the living room.

"Sounds like Tana's here," I commented needlessly.

When I walked out into the living room, I paused in the doorway. Van and Beth had moved to the recliner in the corner and Tana and Charlie were on the couch.

My mom had apparently taken things into her own hands and invited Charlie for dinner directly. So now I'd have to spend my Sunday eating across the table from a woman who'd ride me like a pony but wouldn't hold my hand.

The situation was so bizarre, but of course I couldn't talk about it with anyone. What would I even say?

The sex is amazing, but I want her to like me for more than that?

My friends would laugh their asses off if they could hear my thoughts. I was living every single guy's dream but somehow it didn't feel right.

Not with Charlie.

Luckily my Dad came in then with a tray of ribs. As usual, I set the table while Tana got the drinks and Van went to call the kids. A few minutes later Beck and Campbell came running into the room, carrying the scent of sweat and grass with them.

"Wash your hands!" Mom yelled over the chaos as she handed a bowl of coleslaw to Tana before bringing out a platter of grilled corn.

After we all filled our plates, we settled around the scarred oak table that had been in our family since before I was born. Without having to be told, we all linked hands. Right before I bowed my head, my eyes snagged with Charlie's. She quickly shut her eyes. After my mom said the blessing, we all dug in.

"Thank you for inviting me, Mrs. Evers," Charlie said. "Everything looks so good."

"You have a standing invitation, Charlie. You know that." Mom grinned.

Charlie took a bite of her corn and hummed in

appreciation. Butter ran down her hand and she quickly licked her finger. A flashback from the prior night of her licking something else almost made me moan out loud. I tucked my head and took another bite of ribs, relishing the heat in the sauce. At least if I started sweating everyone would think it was from the food.

When I looked up Tana was watching me. She narrowed her eyes. "Rix. Guess who I saw at the store today? *Janelle.*"

Mom sighed. "She was such a nice girl. I know you don't want to talk about it—"

"I don't."

"But if you ever need to talk about it, you can," she continued, unfazed.

"I won't."

She smiled sweetly. "No need to be so grumpy."

Van snickered. "Yeah, little bro. You're even worse than usual. When was the last time you got laid?"

I choked as a clump of barbecue went straight down my throat before my eyes instinctively flew up to meet Charlie's. Her eyes widened before she stuffed a rib in her mouth.

"Van!" Mom scolded, but we could all hear the amusement in her voice.

"Leave the boy alone," Dad interjected, his voice stern. "Janelle wasn't the one for him. If she was, he would have known. There would have been a sign. A soul tie."

Charlie looked up then. "A soul tie? What's that?"

A collective groan filled the room. Everyone knew that once Dad started talking about this, there was no stopping him.

He ignored us. "My grandfather always told us growing up that souls recognize old friends. He truly believed that loved ones from our former lives would find us again in this one."

"I wish I could have known him," Tana said. She'd only been a baby when our great-grandparents had passed away.

Even though we have pictures of me sitting on their laps, I don't really remember them.

"I wish you could have, too. When he met Grandma, she was going by her middle name of Rose. It wasn't until they were much older that he found out she had the same first name as his sister."

Charlie smiled at that. "He fell in love just like that?"

"Oh no. It's not that easy. It's just a way for the universe to let you know you're on the right track." Dad blotted his mouth with his napkin before continuing. "When I met Maria, I was a twenty-three-year-old punk who had no idea what I was doing with my life. Then I met an angel at a Van Halen concert who happened to have parents from Mexico. The same place that I was born."

"You were born in Mexico?"

He laughed. "I was. My parents were on vacation when my mother went into labor unexpectedly. I was born premature."

"So it was destiny?" Charlie asked, hanging on to his every word.

"Exactly," Dad said, pointing at her with a rib. "And when it happens, you'll know. Everything will just fall into place. Of course, at the time I didn't know whether I'd ever see her again. She was like a silent breeze."

Van whispered. "When he starts quoting song lyrics, you know he's serious."

Tana snickered. Charlie covered her hand with her mouth to hide her laughter.

"*Anyway,*" Dad shot Van an annoyed look, "that wasn't what made me fall for Maria. It was all *her*, her personality, her sense of fun, and of course that incredible heart."

Mom covered his hand with hers and gave it a little squeeze. "He promised me forever. And we've been together ever since."

Dad leaned over and kissed her right there at the table. "Forever Evers."

Tana raised her wine glass. "As gross as they are, that deserves a toast."

Beth rested her head on Van's shoulder. "I agree. To your parents."

I met Charlie's eyes before I raised my glass. "Forever Evers."

———

I was elbow deep in sudsy water when I realized that things were suspiciously quiet. Everyone was either sprawled on the couch or still in the dining room talking. Charlie, however, was conspicuously missing.

"Hey Santana, have you seen Charlie?" I asked my sister when she came into the kitchen with a stack of dirty plates.

"Nope. Maybe she's getting some fresh air?"

I dried my hands on a dish towel before going to the back door. As I stepped outside, my gaze swept across the backyard. I looked past where Campbell and Beck were kicking a soccer ball around to where the yard dipped before it connected to the neighbor on the other side. Nothing.

Then my gaze stopped on the old treehouse.

On a hunch, I ambled over and began to climb. There, in a nest of old blankets, sat Charlie.

"Wow. You're brave."

She tilted her head. "What do you mean?"

"Touching those blankets. Who knows how long they've been up here. In fact I'm shocked this thing is still standing."

Charlie rolled her eyes. "Always a critic. Can you ever just enjoy anything?"

I pulled my body up the rest of the way and then sat with my back to the opposite wall.

"I'm not trying to be critical. It's just...I'm a fixer. If I can't identify what's wrong with something, then I can't fix it."

She watched me with a strange expression. It made me a little uncomfortable so I let my gaze wander over the carved names and scribbles on the wooden walls.

"It's strange to be up here as an adult. I used to spend so much time here when I was a kid wishing I could be anywhere else."

"You did?"

"The world seemed a lot smaller then."

She blew out a breath as she looked around. "I was so jealous of this treehouse."

"Really? Why?"

"I just always dreamed of having a treehouse in my backyard. But I knew it would never happen." She sighed. "You only got one of these if you lived somewhere a long time."

I was hit with a sudden, inexplicable urge to pull her into my arms. But that wasn't what we were, was it? We weren't together and she didn't expect or need comfort from me.

No, she only needed one thing from me.

But I couldn't take it, seeing that longing on her face. I would have done almost anything in that moment to take that pain away.

"Well, consider this your honorary home," I said, gesturing around the treehouse.

She chuckled. "Gee, thanks. I don't know what to say."

We sat in silence for a while, the quiet only broken by the occasional yell from one of the kids in the distance. I peeked out the door of the treehouse. No one had figured out we were up here yet. Hopefully it would stay that way.

When I turned around, Charlie was watching me.

"Do you know how lucky you are to have a childhood home to come back to?"

I turned to her. "Didn't you have that with Gran Grace?"

She sighed. "For a little while. It's the only place I've ever lived that felt like home. But what made it home was being with her. Now it's a disappointment every time I look to her chair at the kitchen table and it's empty."

"I guess we always want what we don't have. I was jealous that you got to travel all over the world."

She made a face. "All the traveling definitely wasn't my choice."

Since she didn't seem bothered by me being up here, I took a chance and moved a little closer.

"Every summer you would come back with the coolest stories about the places you'd been. I figured we were just country hicks to you."

She shoved my shoulder. "I never said that!"

"I know. That was just how I felt, I guess. We were the kids with the parents who drove the junky old bus and were too poor to take vacations." I laughed. "I still haven't gone anywhere."

Her gaze softened. "All I saw was a family with two parents who loved each other and their kids like crazy. I would have given up vacations to have that instead. To have a real family. To belong somewhere."

"Don't be fooled by my dad's little kismet story in there. He left out a lot. My great-grandpa might have been a romantic, but that didn't extend to the rest of the family. Dad's parents disowned him when they found out he was marrying a Hispanic woman."

"Really?" She drew her knees up to her chest. "So you don't know his parents at all?"

"Not very well. Ironically, my mom is the one who always

urged him to stay in contact with them. She never wanted him to have to choose. His older brother Adam lives nearby in Violet Falls. We have a bunch of cousins that we barely know. Uncle David was always closer to Dad, so as soon as he was eighteen, he moved in with us."

"I never knew that."

"My dad has always said that it was worth it. He says he lost relations, but he gained family."

She toyed with the end of the blanket. "I guess there really is no such thing as a perfect happy ending, is there?"

"Maybe not but I'm okay with an imperfect kind of happy. Our family is crazy and loud and drives me up the wall half the time, but we love each other. What more do I need?"

"You're right," Charlie whispered.

I nudged her. "You're part of this family too, you know? You and Tana have been thick as thieves since you were in diapers. The question is, do you *want* to belong here?"

She looked at me, and she looked so sad that I instinctively put an arm around her. I expected her to pull away but to my surprise, she settled into the embrace and rested her head against my shoulder.

"I want to make this work. I'm just not sure how. Even if I finish renovating the house, I'll need a job. And it's not like I have the kind of skills that are useful in a small town."

It was wild to me that she couldn't see her own potential. "Charlie, you have plenty of skills. You can find a job here."

She gave me a skeptical look. "I'm not fishing for compliments, Rix. I'm smart. I worked hard for that finance degree. But unless there are some big companies headquartered in The Ridge that I don't know about, it'll be kind of hard to get a job with that. Maybe I could brush up on bookkeeping. That's more useful for most small businesses."

"You're the most organized person I know."

She smiled. "If only organizing could be my business. I could whip people's messes into shape."

My chest tightened. If only she could see herself through my eyes. "You can. Bet I can prove it."

She didn't say anything to that, but I could tell she didn't believe me. That was okay. Charlie didn't really understand the power of being an Evers in this town. Not only did my parents know everyone but they were owed favors by everyone. If Charlie wanted a job, we would find her one. I already had a few ideas.

I sat up. "Come on. I know exactly what you need."

To my surprise, Charlie didn't let go when I tried to get up. Instead, her arms wrapped around my waist, holding on tightly. I put my arm back around her shoulders and at the touch, she buried her face in my shirt and let out a satisfied little sigh. When I looked down, the sight of her snuggled so contentedly in my arms made my heart turn over.

"Rix?" she whispered.

"Yeah?"

"Can we stay here for a little longer?"

I settled back against the wall. "As long as you want."

twenty-two

· · ·

CHARLOTTE

After a few more precious moments in the quiet of the treehouse, we climbed down and went back inside the house. I mentally prepared myself for the chaos. Being an only child for so long, the energy of a large family could sometimes be a bit much for me to handle. As much as I loved it, I also needed a little space. I snickered to myself at the thought of needing a time-out.

It was funny how the things that used to be a punishment when you were a child were your salvation as an adult.

We stepped through the back door into the living room. To my surprise, it was quiet. I could hear the soft chatter of voices from the other room, but the frenetic energy from earlier was gone.

Rix glanced over at me with a smirk. "Even the Evers aren't loud all the time."

When we walked into the living room, Tana looked up. "There you are. I was just coming to find you."

"Oh, I was just checking out the tree house. Sorry if I held you up."

She nodded but wasn't meeting my eyes. I instantly felt bad. When she'd come over to drag me out of the house, I'm sure she was thinking that we'd get to spend some time together. Instead, I disappeared right after dinner and hid like a child.

But then I looked at her again. Tana's eyes were suspiciously bright and there was a bright red mark on her neck. She'd been wearing an oversized shirt when we came but must have taken it off when she was helping her mom clean up after dinner.

I pointed at her. *"You've been keeping secrets."*

She grabbed my arm and dragged me into the corner. "Shh. It's nothing."

"Nothing, huh? It's definitely something if you have to hide a hickey from your parents." I laughed as her hand flew up to her shoulder. "You forgot it was there, didn't you?"

Tana grabbed her shirt from the back of the couch and yanked it over her head. "Not a word."

"Oh come on. It's so obvious. I could see it the night of the bonfire."

Her eyes swung to mine, looking unexpectedly vulnerable. "You could?"

I leaned closer so Rix couldn't hear us. "Everyone could tell. You and Greg were yelling back and forth over the fire all night. He's cute. I don't know why you don't just ask him out."

She laughed weakly. "Greg. Right. The situation is kind of complicated—"

"Hey, man! I didn't know you were here." Rix's voice broke into our conversation.

I turned to see Carter stepping into the room. He had a bottle of wine tucked under his arm. His eyes swept over me and Tana in the corner before he raised his hand in a wave. "Sorry I'm late."

He handed the bottle of wine to Rix before they did some sort of complicated handshake that turned into a hug.

Rix looked at the bottle of wine with amusement. "You know you didn't have to bring anything."

"I wanted to. Your mom told me to come and get plates for me and my dad. Believe me, I appreciate not having to cook. Also, an excuse to get out of the house."

"Well, Mom is going to love this," Rix replied.

When they disappeared into the kitchen, Tana turned back to me. Her eyes narrowed. "Is everything okay? You were gone a long time."

My face heated. "I just needed to get some air. I'm amazed that tree house is still standing."

She hummed in agreement, but I could feel her eyes on the side of my face, assessing.

Luckily, Rix chose that moment to come back. "So I figured I'd give Charlie a ride home, since we're going to the same place. We're starting a new project today."

Tana shrugged. "That works. I need to stop by the shop before I go home anyway."

After a quick hug, she grabbed her bag and headed for the front door. Before we could follow, a blur ran from the other room and tackled Rix. He laughed before picking up the bundle of giggling eleven-year-old.

"Hold on, Charlie. I just need to take the trash out." He tossed Beck over his shoulder and made a show of stomping toward the back door.

Beck screeched with laughter. "No! I'm not trash. Put me down." His hair was lighter but he looked so much like Rix did at the same age it was uncanny.

Rix paused and then tilted his head as if confused. "Did you hear something?"

I shrugged and looked up to the ceiling. "Nope. I didn't hear anything."

"Me either. But this bag of trash sure is smelly. I'd better put it right in the can."

Beck flailed helplessly before Rix finally turned him over and dropped him gently on the couch. His legs were so long one of his feet almost caught Rix in the face.

"What have they been feeding you, kid? You look like a Daddy Longlegs."

Beck grinned up at him, exposing a gaping space on the side of his mouth where he was missing a tooth. "Chicken. And Lucky Charms."

Rix snorted out a laugh. "Well, that'll do it. Where's Cam?"

Beck shrugged. "He's texting his *girlfriend*."

Rix knelt down and whispered something to him that made Beck smile. It was so illuminating to see Rix like this. As grumpy as he usually was, he had such an endless well of patience and love for his family. As I watched, I tried so hard to keep my mind from going places it shouldn't but it was impossible. Because this was exactly what I imagined Rix would be like with his own kids. Playful and fun but always there to listen when needed.

Picturing Rix as a father was the last thing I should be doing but the mental image came so easily, almost like I was remembering instead of daydreaming. I could see him standing with his hand on a child's shoulder while cradling an infant in the other arm. He'd handle the stress of parenting the same way he did everything else, with a grumpy expression but a secret smile when he thought no one was looking.

He'd be the father that was always there to play catch or teach his kids how to build something but also there with a firm word when they needed correction.

There. That was the operative word. He would be there. Always.

If I knew anything with certainty it was that nothing short of death would keep Hendrix Evers away from his kids.

"You ready to go?"

I looked up to realize Rix was talking to me. I nodded but caught the faint look of disappointment on Beck's face.

Rix must have seen it too because he ruffled the boy's hair. "I'll see you at your baseball game in a few days, right?"

Beck brightened. "Yeah."

Rix pulled out his phone. He typed something and then looked down at Beck. "Also I just sent you some game bucks."

Beck whooped. "Yes. Thank you!" He gave Rix another hug before racing off.

Rix yelled after him, "Say bye to Charlie at least!"

Beck poked his head out of his room. "Bye, Charlie!"

I laughed. "Bye, Beck!"

Rix shook his head. "Sorry. Let's get out of here while we still can."

As we passed by the kitchen, Rix stuck his head in. "We're leaving guys."

Mrs. Evers came out and pulled him into a hug before turning to me. I melted into the embrace gratefully. Maybe my emotions were still raw from the unexpected heart-to-heart in the treehouse but something about being welcomed so warmly really cracked me right open.

"Thank you so much for dinner," I murmured.

Mrs. Evers squeezed me gently before patting my cheek. "Of course, sweetie. We'll see you next Sunday."

"Is that Charlie?"

The voice coming from the kitchen was familiar, but it wasn't until Maria stepped aside that I caught sight of the familiar face.

"Uncle David!"

He wrapped me up in a bear hug so tight my feet lifted off the ground. I laughed, instantly transported back to childhood.

Tana's uncle had been a young teenager when her parents got married, so he had always been more like a really cool older brother to their kids. He was a central fixture in my summer memories, always full of fun stories and game to break the rules with us. He was a mechanic and he'd been the one to teach me and Tana how to drive a stick shift. He'd also insisted we both learn to change a tire (just in case). This was my first time seeing him since I'd gotten back to town.

"Charlie! I heard you were back. Feels just like old times." He tweaked my nose, just like he used to when I was a kid. "How have you been?"

"I've been good." I stumbled over the obvious lie. Surely he'd heard the real reason I was back in town just like everyone else. "Uh, how about you? How's Tammy?"

His smile faltered. "Oh. Yeah that didn't work out. She's engaged to someone else now, actually."

I squeezed his arm. "Sorry to hear that."

"It was for the best. She's really happy now. I don't think marriage is in the cards for me. I'll be the crazy uncle to all the kids you guys have."

"You sound like my friend Retta. I'm pretty sure she has already sworn a vow to buy my kids the loudest and messiest toys she can find."

He huffed out a laugh at that. "Looks like I'll have some competition."

Rix appeared at my elbow then. He gave his uncle a hug before tugging gently on my arm. "The only way to exit is to just make a run for it. Otherwise we might as well pull out the sleeping bags."

Laughing, we snuck out the front door without saying goodbye to anyone else.

———

After riding for a few minutes in silence, I perked up when Rix turned onto an unmarked road. His truck swayed from side to side as we drove onto a dirt road that was a combination of rocks and gravel. He had told Tana we were starting a new project today but wouldn't tell me anything when I asked. What kind of project could "we" be starting? Rix had already seen the extent of my home improvement experience. I was still mildly traumatized from being attacked by the porch.

"Where did you say we were going again?"

Rix lifted an eyebrow. "I didn't say. That didn't work the first three times you asked, so why would it work now?"

It was a struggle not to laugh. "Just checking. I never know when I'll catch you slipping."

He rolled his eyes. "And I thought I was bad with surprises."

"Maybe I just want to make sure you aren't taking me off into the creepy woods alone to hide my body."

He finally pulled the truck to a stop in front of an old shed. "If I wanted to hide your body, I'm not sure that would be possible anywhere in The Ridge. This may look remote but there are probably multiple nosy neighbors staring at us right now. Which is why we need to move quickly before Mrs. Donald realizes we're out here and invites us in for tea or something."

"Mrs. Donald?"

He pointed over his shoulder. When I looked, I recognized the barn in the distance. Of course. We were on the other side of the land we usually used for bonfires.

"The Donalds live right there. When I needed a place to store my stuff, Mr. Donald said I could use this old shed."

There was a padlock on the doors of the shed which he unlocked with a key from his ring. Then he turned to me with a grin. "I brought you here so we could pick up some tools."

He disappeared inside and against my better judgment, I followed. It was a fairly large space but there wasn't much walking room because everywhere I looked was stacked with boxes. The air was stale and smelled like paint and dust.

"Is this all your stuff?"

Rix shook his head. "No. Mr. Donald has some stuff in here and I think his kids left some stuff behind also. This is me over here."

I followed him to the back corner where there was a folding table with a circular saw on it and a bunch of boxes stacked underneath. He started pulling things out of one of the boxes and setting them aside.

"I just need to find...here it is."

I raised my eyebrows. "A sledgehammer?"

Rix stood. "I know just how to cheer you up. We're going to start a new project today.

"We? I thought the whole point of this was that *you* were going to be doing all the work. Sounds like you're trying to get your rent for free."

Rix laughed heartily. "Grab that tile cutter over there."

I walked over to what I thought he was talking about. "This thing?"

When I leaned down to pick it up, my foot hit one of the boxes that was covered in a drop cloth. It slipped off to reveal a canvas leaning up against the box underneath.

I knelt down to get a closer look at the painting. It was a landscape but unlike any I'd ever seen before. The colors in the sky were more like explosions than the typical colors of a sunset. It was like looking at a picture of the world on fire.

"Wow. Where did you get this?"

Rix hurried over and draped the drop cloth back over the canvas. "That's nothing."

"Wait—"

"We need to go if we're going to start this today. I don't have time to waste fucking around."

Stung by his sudden brusque demeanor, I stood up. That was when I saw a set of brushes on the ground under the folding table. I put a hand over my heart. Now that I was looking there were other clues that my eyes had skipped right over. The can of paint thinner on the table. The stained drop cloths wadded up in the corner covered in paint. Most notably the uncomfortable look on Rix's face.

"Rix, did you paint that?"

He shrugged. He still wouldn't look at me. I wasn't sure why he was being so weird but I was so shocked that I was speaking before I could really think.

"I had no idea you could paint like that. I guess I should have figured at least one of you would inherit your mom's talent. How come I've never seen this before?"

He grabbed an empty box and started loading the tools he'd pulled out into it. "I don't know."

"The colors were amazing. It looked so real. You should be selling those. That was better than some of the art I've seen in galleries in New York. I bet you'd make a ton of money if you had a show."

Rix slammed the box down on the table. "Making money isn't everybody's goal, Charlie. Some of us are perfectly happy with what we have."

Shocked by his nasty tone of voice, I took a step back. "I didn't mean that–"

"Or do you think art is only worth something if it has a price tag on it? Everything doesn't need a Wall Street valuation. I would think you had learned that money isn' everything by now."

The words hit me like a slap in the face.

By the expression on Rix's face, I could tell he felt the impact just as surely as I did.

I turned and walked out, not stopping until I reached the tailgate of his truck. The sun was perched low in the sky and since there was barely any breeze it felt like a furnace. But I sure as hell wasn't going back in that stupid shed to ask Rix to turn on the air conditioning in the truck. I'd walk back to town first. Maybe I'd end up passing out from heat stroke, but at least I wouldn't have anyone throwing my mistakes in my face.

If that was what I'd wanted, I could have stayed in Manhattan.

What was that all about anyway? I was trying to give him a compliment. That was the thing with Rix, he was like a wounded animal, liable to lash out and bite you even when you were just trying to help him. Maybe it was time for me to acknowledge that he didn't want my help, and who was I to think I had help to offer anyway? I was the one with all the problems. I was the one with the fractured family and the ramshackle house that seemed determined to maim me.

Who was I to try to help anyone?

The sound of boots crunching on the grass was my only warning before Rix leaned up against the side of the truck next to me.

"I'm sorry," he said finally.

For a few tense moments, we just stood in silence listening to the sounds of the land, the random calls of birds in the surrounding trees and the chirp of crickets in the grass. I wasn't even sure what to say, especially since his apology was about as nonspecific as it could get. What exactly was he sorry for?

Sorry that I liked his painting?

Sorry for insinuating I was a materialistic bitch?

Sorry for being an asshole?

There were so many choices I could probably just take my pick. Either way I wasn't sure I really wanted to forgive him. Maybe we should just go home and forget this whole stupid thing.

"Come on, I said I was sorry."

I turned to him. "Talking to you is like walking on eggshells. I don't even get why you would be mad at me for... what? Liking your painting?"

He kicked at the dirt with the toe of his boot. "My art is something that I don't really talk about. To anyone."

I still didn't get how that translated to blowing up because I liked it. It wasn't like I was being nosy and invaded his privacy. He was the one who'd brought me here in the first place.

"Okay. We don't have to talk about it. I just don't get why being good at something would be some big secret."

He pulled down the tailgate to his truck. "I'm a handyman, Charlie. People hire me to paint fences, not murals."

I watched as he disappeared back into the shed and then came out a few seconds later with a brown box. He put it on the ground briefly so he could lock the shed again. The whole time I couldn't get his words out of my head.

What did that even mean? Did that mean he wanted to paint murals and felt like he couldn't?

I thought about all the things Rix did to help others in town, like helping Mr. Donald maintain his property and rescuing cats from trees despite not even being with the fire department anymore. He did all these things for others but it sounded like he didn't have much time to do things he wanted to do for himself.

It was unsettling how much I related to that feeling. I loved my family so much and I would never describe my feelings for them as an obligation. But could I really deny that my life would look very different if I wasn't always trying to do what I thought was best for them?

I would have never moved to New York.

My degree would definitely *not* be in finance.

But the most worrisome thing was that I wasn't exactly sure what I wanted my life to look like. I just knew it wouldn't be the life I'd lived the past ten years.

When Rix was about to close the tailgate, I put my hand over his. His eyes jumped to mine. I was struck by how vulnerable he seemed. This wasn't a side I was used to seeing of him. He was always so confident and seemed like he didn't care about what anyone thought. But it occurred to me that maybe he was doing the same thing I was, putting one foot in front of the other because he didn't know what else to do.

"I understand why you don't tell people. When something is personal, it's not easy to talk about."

I could tell he was uncomfortable with the direction our conversation had taken, so I decided to switch gears.

Pointing at the tile cutter, I said, "Just FYI, I'm not carrying any of this stuff inside. I've already got a scar on my leg from when the porch tried to kill me; the last thing I need is to drop one of these tools on my foot."

Rix's face broke into a smile. "Fine. But only because I know you're about to put in some work when we get home."

After he closed the tailgate, we climbed inside the truck. As soon as he turned it on the air conditioning came blasting out. I sighed in relief.

"Hey, Rix?"

He glanced over at me.

"People would hire you to paint murals if they knew you could do *that*."

He swallowed hard. "That was one painting. My others are different. What if they're not good enough?"

"I guess we'll never know," I replied softly.

———

When we arrived at the house, Miss Pauline waved from her yard.

Rix leaned over. "We have to move fast otherwise we'll get pulled into another conversation about Agatha Kitty or which relatives haven't been to visit lately."

Sure enough, I could see Miss Pauline peering over at us as we got out of the car.

"It's a nice day, isn't it?" Rix called out as he picked up the box of tools from the back of the truck.

Miss Pauline put down the shears she was carrying.

Rix glanced over at me. "She's about to come over. *Move your ass, Monroe.*"

I grabbed my bag from the floor and then hopped out. Rix didn't wait for me so he was already on the porch about to open the front door. Miss Pauline peered at us in confusion, probably wondering why we both looked like we were running from the devil himself.

"Nice to see you, Miss Pauline!" I waved over my shoulder before racing across the lawn.

As soon as I cleared the threshold, Rix closed the door behind me.

"I feel kind of bad. Maybe we should go visit tomorrow."

Miss Pauline probably didn't have many people to talk to. It sounded like her husband wasn't doing that well and her only other company was her cat.

Rix dropped the box on the kitchen counter. "I visited her yesterday. Before it was all over, I'd changed three light bulbs, dug up the weeds in her side yard, and checked in her attic because she *heard a noise.*"

I covered my mouth with my hand. "You're a good Samaritan."

He scowled. "I'm a sucker. I finally got the hell out of there before she decided to ask me to unclog a toilet or something. Or worse, invited her friends over."

The mental image of Rix being ordered around by all the town's octogenarians was too much and I finally succumbed to laughter.

"Yeah, keep laughing and I won't let you do the fun part."

I bit my lip. "What's the fun part?"

He handed me the sledgehammer and then a pair of safety glasses before walking toward the stairs. I followed him upstairs to the bathroom. He put on his safety glasses so I did too. Then he held up another sledgehammer.

"How many of these do you have—"

Before I could finish my sentence, he lifted it over his head and swung it down to the floor. Tiles went flying like confetti. I shrieked in surprise and jumped back.

"Rix! What the hell?"

He burst into laughter. Even though my heart was still racing, I started laughing too.

"You're absolutely insane!" I finally managed to say through my laughter. "You can't just start smashing stuff!"

"Why not? You hate this bathroom."

I blinked. "Well, yeah."

He pointed at the tiled counter. "You don't need to use as much force on these but it's still fun. Try it."

Tentatively, I picked up my sledgehammer and brought it down on the tiles near the edge. They didn't fly in every direction, but they split with a satisfying crack.

Rix pointed at the rest. "Just be careful around the sink area. I'm going to save as much of the cabinet and fixtures as possible."

With that, he went back to work. For the next few minutes, the only sound was the satisfying crack of tiles and the weird little grunt Rix made every time he swung his sledgehammer. About halfway through, he left and came back with another tool that he used to lift and pry away the broken tiles.

I had finished about half of the counter, leaving the part around the sink for last.

We were both covered in dust and sweating like pigs but by the time we finished, I was no longer thinking about New York, mistakes, or the treehouses I'd never had.

"Okay, time for a break." Rix abandoned the tool in his hands and sat on the floor.

I looked around at our progress. Without the tiles, the room looked so naked.

Considering how dusty I was already, I figured sitting on the floor could only do so much harm at this point. I plopped down on a bare section.

"I can't believe we just did that."

"But you feel better, right?" He leaned back against the wall.

"Yeah. I do." I wiped sweat from my brow.

"Then my work here is done." Rix leaned his head back against the wall and closed his eyes.

I looked around the destroyed bathroom. Although I'd

broken up the tiles on the counter, they still needed to be pulled off. Most of the tiles on the floor were gone but there was still a section near the toilet and tub that hadn't been touched.

It was what Retta would call a flaming hot mess.

I glanced over at Rix. "I'm sorry I disappeared like that at dinner. I hope your parents don't think I was rude."

He kicked at a piece of tile that was near his foot. "Nah, it was fine. Everyone kind of just hangs out doing whatever after dinner is over."

"I was surprised to see that treehouse was still there. But I shouldn't have been. Your dad built that to last."

Rix chuckled. "He rebuilt part of it when Campbell was born. I'm sure he'll rebuild it again now that Van and Beth have given them some hope of seeing grandkids soon. They know they probably aren't getting any from me or Santana. We're the heathens."

I shook my head. "You would be a good dad. I was thinking that earlier."

His foot stilled and his eyes lifted to meet mine. "No, you weren't."

"You were really good with Beck. It's obvious how much he looks up to you. I was thinking that you'd be just as great with your own kids."

Rix looked away then but his pleasure at the statement was obvious in the flush that appeared on his cheeks. "I don't know about that. I'd be defeated the first time they asked for help with their homework."

"Well, maybe your wife is good with homework. You would teach them how to fix stuff, how to make blanket forts, and how to roast s'mores. You'd carry them on your shoulders—you know that thing dads do? But you'd be there. Every single day."

His eyes were intense now as he looked at me directly. "Why were you really hiding out up there? And don't say it was the noise. You've been right in the middle of Evers family chaos since you were a kid."

I closed my eyes. I couldn't talk to him while he was looking at me like that.

"Everyone was so happy. Van and Beth. Your parents. Even Santana is giddy over this secret guy she's seeing. And I'm just the bitter friend who can't stand being around all that happiness."

When he didn't say anything, I peeked through one eye. He was still staring straight at me, but I couldn't figure out what message his eyes were sending.

"With everything going on, it just kind of hit me today that my family is never going to be the same. And let's face it: my mom definitely has a type. A French accent is her kryptonite. My dad is from a prominent Creole family in Louisiana."

"New Orleans?" he asked.

"Yup. *Laissez les bon temps rouler.*"

His eyebrows shot up. "You speak French?"

"Just well enough to know that I did not fit in there. Then there's husband number two. Billie's dad is the son of French ex-pats who spend their time attending five thousand dollar per plate galas and looking down their noses at everyone. With my luck, my next sibling will be across the border and I'll never even see them. I feel like I should warn the men of Montreal."

Rix cracked up. "Don't forget about Quebec."

I thunked my head against the wall. "How could I forget? Why am I even talking about this? I need to stop worrying about what might happen. I wish I could be more like you."

He snorted. "Why? Because I don't give a fuck about anything, right?"

"Yeah. I could use a little more of that."

"I care more than you think," he muttered.

As if the sudden weight of the conversation got too heavy,

he stood and surveyed the room. "Well, I guess that's enough for today."

I stood too. "What, just leave it like this?"

"Yeah. I can finish it up tomorrow. Unless you want to keep going?" He gave me a long look. "Maybe we should. You know, you have a lot of rage in you."

"You bring out the worst in me." I smiled sweetly.

He moved closer and tipped his head down before kissing the tip of my nose. "It's a gift."

He paused then and I could see the question in his eyes. My heart tripped a beat.

What was he doing?

But as he stared into my eyes, I nodded slowly. His head dipped again and his lips brushed over mine. Just once before he rested his forehead against mine.

By mutual unspoken agreement, we'd been operating like roommates by day and only acknowledged our new agreement to be lovers at night. We weren't kissing in the kitchen or holding hands as we walked down the street.

But this, this was different. Everything about today had been different. And I wasn't sure what to make of that.

I plastered a big, fake smile on. "I'd better go take the dog out again."

He watched me with knowing eyes before he nodded.

"I'll clean up a little in here so we can still use the bathroom without stepping on broken tiles."

"Okay."

I didn't dare look at him as I left the room.

By the time he came downstairs, I was just coming back in. I unclipped Meatball's leash and he barreled over to Rix to sniff his ankles.

He leaned down to give the dog a few scratches behind the ear before he stood back up. "So, are you busy right now?"

I arched an eyebrow. "Why? Because if you need more help with bathroom demo, then yes I am very busy."

"No more bathroom demo. There's something I want to show you."

"Okay."

He walked outside leaving me standing in the middle of the room. I went over to the front window and watched as he approached the bed of his truck. He rummaged for a bit before he stood back up holding his toolbox.

When he turned around, I scampered back so he wouldn't see me in the window. I sat on the floor and gave Meatball some kisses when he climbed in my lap. The door opened and Rix appeared.

"Here we go," he said before dropping the toolbox on the floor next to me with a thump.

I gasped when he took out the top layer of the toolbox to reveal the compartment underneath. It was stuffed with paper.

No, not paper. *Receipts.*

"What in the world..."

Tentatively, I reached out and picked up a random receipt. It was faded and crumpled like it had been through the washing machine. Or run over by a truck.

Or both.

"Rix, what is this?" I asked, even though I already had a pretty good suspicion.

He wouldn't meet my eyes. "My filing system."

I put a hand to my chest. "I was afraid you were going to say that."

"I told you I needed help."

"You did. And you definitely weren't exaggerating."

He squatted down next to me. "I wasn't exaggerating about any of it. Not about you being a part of our family or about how much this town needs you. The question is what do you want? If you imagine your ideal future, what do you see?"

"When I was a little girl, I used to have this recurring dream about when I'd live here with my own family."

I hugged Meatball tighter. He licked my chin like he could sense my discomfort.

"The same dream every time?" Rix asked gently.

"Not at first. In the beginning, I was just reacting to the things Gran Grace said. She'd say 'one day you'll have a husband and kids of your own' or 'one day when I'm gone you'll live here with your family'. After a while, I started having these dreams about the life I'd have."

He smiled. "And what kind of life did childhood Charlie dream of?"

"Nothing big. My kids are running around the backyard and the wind is blowing the scent of the honeysuckle all around me. What I remember most is just being happy."

"You can have that dream, Charlie. You have a place in Violet Ridge if you want it. I think that's the real reason your Gran left you this house."

"You think?"

His words touched me more than I could express. The idea that ending up here wasn't some horrible accident but where I was supposed to be was a comforting thought. Like maybe I wasn't completely screwing everything up.

Rix smirked, like he could tell that I wanted to run. The smug bastard had always known exactly how to push my buttons, except this time he was punching me right in the heart.

"You have roots here that run deep. This town, these

people, this mess of a house—this is your legacy. Gran Grace knew where you belonged."

My eyes welled up with tears. He didn't even know it, but he was giving me a puzzle piece I'd spent my whole life searching for. This was my Gran's house. But it was *my home.*

I turned my head and because we were so close, his lips brushed over my forehead. When he didn't pull back, I looked up. His eyes were wary. Hopeful.

"I finally know where I belong too."

twenty-three

. . .

HENDRIX

I closed the cabinet door and then opened it again to make sure it wasn't too tight. Mrs. Jeffries had hired me to do a few things while we waited for the wood to come in for her shed renovation. So far I had fixed a drawer that was off-track, replaced the kitchen faucet, and tightened a few loose cabinet drawers.

She'd scheduled me to come back on a day when Mr. Jeffries wasn't home. Apparently she'd gotten tired of waiting for him to get to all the items on her honey-do list.

"Thank you so much for coming by." Mrs. Jeffries patted my shoulder as she walked by. "When you get older, it's hard to keep up with all these things."

"Of course. I'll let you know when the wood is in so I can start building your shed out back."

As I packed up the last of my tools, it struck me how different the past few weeks had been. After our day of demolition therapy, I had started working full-scale on Charlie's renovation.

Since I'd already patched and painted one section of

drywall downstairs, I'd finished painting the main living area before moving on to repairing the porch and the steps. The upstairs bathroom was now almost done with a clean white subway tile that updated the look of the room while still working with the existing tub and fixtures. We'd fallen into an easy routine: going about our days separately and then working on various projects together at night.

Okay, Charlie's version of helping was more like chatting while I worked and keeping me company, but I wasn't complaining. I was getting free rent after all and this was the most fun I'd ever had on a renovation project. After working on the house, we'd cook dinner together and watch episodes of one of the many reality shows she was obsessed with.

In short, we just *lived*.

It was easy.

Almost too easy.

As I left the Jeffries house, I thought about how simple things were with Charlie. For the first time, I wasn't stressed about what the future held at all. I wasn't worried that the woman I was with was secretly plotting to get me down the aisle or trying to change me into her idea of husband material.

I almost laughed out loud at the thought. Charlie definitely wasn't trying to get me down any aisle. She was the only person who never expected me to be someone else. Apparently all those summers had taught her to accept that I was going to annoy the hell out of her.

But lately I didn't feel like I was annoying her at all. We had reached a level of comfort where we didn't even have to talk and it wasn't awkward. Sometimes we just existed in the same space: me working on something or eating and Charlie playing with the dog or reading.

Even the most boring things were fun with her.

All of which made me feel even worse when I remembered

how I'd reacted when she saw my painting. One of the main reasons I preferred to keep my art private was because people always pushed me to sell it. Why did it have to be about selling? Couldn't something just be done for the love of it?

But Charlie had always been the cheerleader type. When Tana had been debating whether she was ready to start her own salon, Charlie had been one of the main people who had told her that she should do it.

With the benefit of hindsight, I could see that she had genuinely been excited to find out something new about me. I had misjudged her enthusiasm to be about the money when really, she had been trying to find ways that I could share my art with others.

And instead of taking the compliment, I had thrown it back in her face and accused her of being a sellout.

I winced.

Even though she'd accepted my apology afterward, I still wanted to make it up to her. The thing was, this was Charlie. None of the usual things I would do for a woman to apologize felt right. Flowers were too generic. We already had dinner together every night and it wasn't like I could really take her out. The closest nice restaurant would take an hour to drive to and we definitely couldn't go to the diner without being interrupted by everyone in town.

I pulled out of the Jeffries driveway and glanced over at my parents' house. The drive was empty so they were probably both working at the store. I headed back to town still mulling things over.

The only thing Charlie cared about lately was getting this renovation done. As the weeks passed, we got closer to the date when she expected her mom and sister to move in. Someone was coming in a few days to deal with the mold damage in the laundry room and I'd called in a favor from an electrician friend to give her a good deal on updating the outlets in the kitchen and the bathroom so they were up to code.

As long as everything stayed on track, the house should be ready for her family by the middle of August. But she'd had to scale back the projects on her list to the bare essentials once she'd seen how much needed to be done. For example, she'd originally wanted to update the small bathroom on the main floor. That was something I could handle easily.

I grinned as the idea took root. It probably wouldn't even be that expensive since I could build a cabinet to replace the chipped pedestal sink in there myself.

As I parked in front of the hardware store, I pulled out my phone and made a quick list of the things I would need. It would be tricky to pull this off without Charlie figuring out what I was up to but it was doable. There was no way to hide that I was repainting but I could say it was extra paint from the living room. Then I could build a vanity cabinet for the sink off-site until I was ready to install it.

All I would need was a solid three hours when she was out of the house to install the new toilet and bring in the new vanity. Maybe I would ask for Tana's help. She could find new towels and bring over some of those girly soaps she liked.

As soon as I had the thought, I scrapped it. Tana would just blow it up into some big thing.

Better to keep it low-key.

———

It took a few days for all the things I ordered to come in. I was just leaving the diner when I got a message from Van that my order had arrived. I paused. The stuff I'd ordered for Charlie had come in at the same time as the wood I needed for another job. On a whim, I decided to see if Carter was around to help.

It was weird. He was now living in town and I felt like I saw him less than when he was living in DC.

HENDRIX

Hey, are you busy?

CARTER

No. What's up?

HENDRIX

I got a large order at the hardware store. I could use some help loading the truck.

CARTER

Wrong number.

HENDRIX

I'll buy you a beer after.

CARTER

Unsubscribe.

HENDRIX

:laugh emoji

CARTER

Since when do you need my help with an order? Back trouble already, old man?

HENDRIX

Better your back than mine. Meet you at the store.

CARTER

Be there in five.

———

As I entered the hardware store, my brother looked up from behind the register. "Hey! You got here fast."

"I was already in town when I got your message."

Van disappeared into the back and then came back out wheeling a big box on a dolly. He paused in front of me and then looked at the box with a smirk. "A new toilet. Very romantic."

I shoved him aside. "There should have been a mirror, too. Make yourself useful and find it."

While he was looking for the mirror, I wheeled the dolly outside. Van came out just as I was lifting the toilet into the bed of the truck. He carefully placed the mirror beside it. The mirror's box was pretty thin so I grabbed the bungee cord I always kept in the back to secure it so it wouldn't slide all over the place while I was driving.

"How is the renovation going?" Van asked.

"Main bathroom is finished. We just had the electrical work done. This is for the downstairs powder room. I want to surprise her."

Van raised one eyebrow. "You're redoing her bathroom? That's quite a gift."

I didn't meet his eyes. "It's no big deal."

Before he could respond, someone called my name. We both turned to see Mr. Donald parked a few spaces over.

Van raised his hand in greeting. "You're here for the weed whacker attachment, right?"

While Van disappeared inside to find his order, Mr. Donald wandered over to look into the back of my truck.

"Ah, fixing up the bathroom. I heard you worked quite a deal with Charlie in exchange for a room."

I smiled, unsure where he was going with that. He knew I was working on her house since I'd told him myself. But who the hell was going around town talking about my financial situation?

"Well, I'm not sure if you know that I just bought a house over on Magnolia Avenue. One of my daughters just moved in with her boyfriend and well, let's just say I give it six months or less."

"Oh, I'm sorry to hear that."

He scowled. "That boyfriend of hers is a real piece of work. Anyway, I thought it would be nice if I had a place for her if we can convince her to move back home. Just in case. The place needs a lot done. I thought after you're finished fixing up the Everett place, you might do the same for me."

I must have just been staring at him blankly because he waved his hand.

"You know, live on site and fix it up in exchange for free rent."

"Right. Well, I'm not sure when I'll be free, but I'll let you know."

Luckily Van came out then. Mr. Donald tipped his hat and walked over to take his order. Just as he was driving off, Carter pulled into the space right next to me. He got out, peering down the road after Mr. Donald's retreating vehicle.

Van greeted him with a handshake that turned into a hug. "What's up, man? Haven't seen much of you since you got back in town."

Carter ran a hand over his hair. "Yeah. Dealing with my dad has been a full-time job. I found a bottle hidden behind the couch cushions the other day."

Van winced. "He's still drinking?"

"Apparently." From the tone of his voice, it was obvious this was an ongoing problem. Considering his father's track record with sobriety, I knew he was fighting an uphill battle.

Van pointed at the store. "Well, I have to get back inside. I'm the only one on-shift today. But Rix, the rest of the wood you ordered is in the stockroom."

After he walked back inside, Carter turned to me. "What

was going on when I drove up? You looked even more pissed off than usual."

"Nothing. Mr. Donald just bought a house over on Magnolia that's in bad shape. He was wondering if I could fix it up the same way I'm doing for Charlie. You know, labor in exchange for free rent."

"Are you going to do it?" Carter asked.

I shrugged. "I don't know."

"Because that sounds like exactly what you've been looking for. More time for you to save your down payment."

"I know. I just..."

For a moment, I tried to imagine packing my bags and moving out of Charlie's place. The thought of not seeing her every day hit me like a truck. But that was the plan, right? To fix the place up and then move on? But for some reason, I suddenly couldn't picture it. The house, the lazy evenings, even the poop presents Meatball left in my boots randomly— I couldn't imagine that not being my life.

I didn't *want* to imagine it.

My life had been perfectly fine before, or so I'd thought. I hadn't even realized how much happier I'd been over the past month until I thought of moving out. But when I contrasted my current life with what had come before, it was no contest.

When I looked up Carter was watching me with a knowing look on his face. "Does she know?"

My brain was still stuck in the wasteland of imagining a Charlie-less world. "Know what?"

"That you're in love with her."

Even though it was in line with what I'd been thinking, hearing it out loud was so jarring that I actually took a step back.

Carter laughed. "Did *you* know? Maybe we should start there."

"I'm not in love with her," I muttered.

"Keep telling yourself that."

I peered at him. "You seem pretty chill about this."

"Why wouldn't I be?"

"Look, I knew you had a thing for her in high school."

He sighed and rested his hands on the back of his head. "It's not like that with Charlie and me. It never has been."

He's still not looking me in the eye which only makes it more obvious that we need to talk. This is a conversation that should have happened years ago, but back then it felt like the kind of thing that didn't have to be said. We were two teenage punks, both in love with a girl who was out of both of our leagues. Then Charlie left town and it had been just one of those things we never talked about.

But now we had to talk about it. No matter what else happened, Carter was my oldest friend. We couldn't keep avoiding each other in town. Violet Ridge wasn't big enough for us to keep this up forever.

"You've been avoiding me ever since the bonfire," I said finally.

He sighed. "I've been busy. It's not just dealing with my dad. It's my job. It's everything."

"Carter. This is me, man. You can't bullshit me. I saw how you were looking at her that night."

He laughed suddenly. "I adore Charlie. We understand each other. She knows what it feels like to be an outsider in this town."

"How are you an outsider? You've lived here your whole life."

"Yeah. As the son of the town drunk. As the kid who had to take odd jobs to get by since my dad would drink away his whole paycheck instead of buying groceries."

"Carter—"

He held up a hand before I could even finish. "I know it wasn't my fault. I know people would have helped if they'd known. *I know.* But I didn't want to be the kid who needed other people's parents to buy him new shoes. I didn't want to be the kid who was so fucking grateful your parents let me sleep over so much because they knew I was going home to an empty house otherwise."

Stunned, I leaned against the side of my truck and watched as he paced around the parking lot. It wasn't like what he was saying was a revelation. I knew the shit his father had put him through growing up. But he'd always seemed so calm. Like he was just biding his time until he could leave town anyway. I never would have known how isolated he felt, despite being right in the middle of everything with us.

He finally stopped moving. "Look, it may not make sense but when Charlie looked at me, it was like she understood how separate I felt from everyone else. And despite having money, she carried that same isolation inside of her too."

I shook my head. "It was supposed to be a casual thing. Just fun, you know?"

He closed the tailgate to my truck. "Casual, huh? And how is that working out?"

Frustrated, I pushed my hands through my hair. "I've fucked this up, huh? But I know Charlie. If I suddenly say I want more, she'll get spooked and run."

He laughed. "So don't tell her you want more. Show her."

"I don't know how."

"You *know* her. What does she want? Better yet, what is something that she's always wanted but doesn't think she can have?"

"All she's ever wanted is to belong here. To feel at home in Violet Ridge."

Carter nodded. "Exactly. So what's something that she

never got to do much since she was usually only here in the summers? Something that is conveniently only a week away?"

When it finally dawned on me what he was suggesting, I flipped him the bird. "Oh fuck you."

He shrugged. "She would love it and you know it. Now let's get this wood loaded. I need to get back to work."

———

It was a struggle to keep things quiet over the next week. Everywhere I went in town, people stopped me to chat about our plans.

All the attention just reminded me why I usually went into hiding on this day but when I imagined Charlie's reaction, I decided being civil was worth it.

Even if it felt like the fake smile on my face was frozen after the seventeenth conversation.

When I finally pulled up in front of the house after a long day, I rested my head on the steering wheel. It was time to shake this funk off because I was going to be forced into seventeen more conversations over the next few hours. I groaned.

Charlie looked up when I came in. Her laptop was open on her lap and Meatball was dozing in his little bed by her feet. He'd taken to dragging his bed closer to wherever we were. If we were cooking, then he'd sit by the entrance to the kitchen and watch. While we were watching TV, he was right by the couch. And of course, he slept in Charlie's room every night. I still wasn't entirely comfortable having him around while we were naked but if we put him in another room he howled like his heart was breaking.

The little cock block just liked to watch.

Pervert.

"Hey! You're home early." Charlie closed the lid on her laptop and stretched.

"Are you done for the day?"

"I am now. You know, I thought you were bad but Earl doesn't even have one place to keep his receipts."

I snickered. Earl was the barber in town and known for two things: being cranky as hell and his crush on Dot down at the diner.

"My toolbox isn't looking so bad now, huh?"

She leaned over and held up a loose receipt. "This one was in the cash box. He had others in the back seat of his truck. Then there were the ones he couldn't find but just sort of remembered the amounts."

"Well, if you're done I want to show you something. But you have to change clothes first. Wear something you don't mind getting dirty."

She narrowed her eyes. "Change my clothes. Why?"

"No questions. Oh, and put your hair up."

"Okay, this is getting weird. We're not going camping right?"

I gave her a look. "You hate camping."

She peppered me with questions all the way upstairs. I held fast and didn't say anything as she changed out of her sweatpants and into some old shorts and a ratty T-shirt. As she gathered her hair up into one of her usual messy buns, she bounced on her heels.

"Okay, I'm ready. Where are we going?"

Without a word I walked back downstairs. I was already wearing shorts and an old shirt since I hadn't wanted to bother with changing clothes. I got the small teething bone I'd bought for Meatball from the pantry and tossed it into his bed. That should keep him occupied while we were gone. All the while Charlie hovered on my heels bouncing excitedly.

Once we were outside and in my truck, she finally broke.

"Come on! Give me one hint."

I sighed. "Okay, I'll give you a hint. What is today?"

She sat quietly as she thought about it. "The only thing I can think of is that it's your birthday."

Shocked, I looked over at her. "You know today is my birthday?"

She rolled her eyes. "Of course. But you never do anything for your birthday. Are we meeting Tana?"

When I shook my head, she sighed. "I hate surprises."

"No, you don't. You just haven't been surprised enough by the right people."

While she continued to think, I drove the familiar route until we turned onto the newly paved road leading to the water. As we got closer, Charlie sat up straighter.

"This is the way to the creek," she said.

As we turned into the dirt lot where several other cars were parked, she finally noticed the group down by the water. A second later, a shriek carried through the air.

"Why are we at the creek? You hate the creek." Her voice shook slightly. Then she grinned. *Birthday dunk?*"

I groaned in acknowledgement. "Birthday dunk."

Suddenly she squealed and threw her arms around my neck. Even though the next hour was going to be nothing short of torture, I found myself laughing right along with her. She put a hand on my cheek and grinned at me and I swore my heart flipped over.

"Come on. I'll race you to the water!" She kissed me softly before opening her door. She was gone before I even got my seatbelt off.

"Cheater!"

twenty-four

By the time Rix got down to the water, I'd already waded in up to my waist. When we were teenagers, we would strip down to our underwear and jump in, but I was glad to see everyone was happy to leave that part of the tradition behind.

Piper was wearing jean shorts and a bikini top but Cassidy, one of the women I'd met at the bonfire, was wearing leggings and an oversized T-shirt. Greg was sitting on the ground drawing something with a stick.

"Charlie!" Tana bounded over. She was dressed similarly, but her old T-shirt had shredded sides and looked much cooler than mine.

She pulled me into a quick hug.

"Hey! Did you know about this?" I asked, gesturing around at the group.

Before she could answer, Carter grabbed her from behind and ran straight into the water. She shrieked as they were both instantly drenched.

"It's not my birthday, asshole!"

I covered my mouth with my hands to contain my laughter.

It was completely juvenile, but I'd always loved a good birthday dunk. I hadn't gotten to do that many of them since the only person whose birthday fell in the summer was Rix. We'd hung out at the creek, sure, but it wasn't the same.

Tana climbed out of the water and then held up her hands in excitement when she finally saw Rix. "Hey, big brother! Happy Birthday!"

Rix just stared at her.

"Is somebody in a bad mood? You know what will fix that? A birthday dunk. *Birthday dunk. Birthday dunk.*" Tana chanted and before long everyone else joined in.

Rix glanced over at me and even though he didn't say anything, it felt like he was whispering right in my ear. Something grumpy like *look what I'm doing for you* or *the things I put up with.* But despite his obvious annoyance there was a thread of amusement there also.

He was having fun whether he could admit it or not.

In true Rix fashion, he couldn't do anything simply. He reached over his head with one hand and yanked his shirt off. I huffed out a soft breath.

Why was that so hot when men pulled their shirt off in one motion like that?

But I didn't have too much time to appreciate his truly stellar six-pack before he took a running leap into the creek, splashing all of us in the process.

A cheer went up and then we all raced in. I took two hands and splashed Tana before swimming away. The water wasn't very deep so even though I wasn't a strong swimmer, I felt completely safe venturing closer to the middle of the creek. The sun was low in the sky and the light dappled through the trees painting everything with gold. The cool water was a welcome relief from the muggy summer heat and I almost wished we were swimming in our underwear.

Rix floated lazily by. His eyes were closed and his hair was slicked back which made the sharp lines of his jaw even more prominent. Seeing him like this, I realized that it was the first time in a long time that I'd seen him truly relaxed.

"Are you enjoying yourself?" He didn't open his eyes.

"I am. I was just thinking that maybe we should all strip down like we used to."

His eyes popped open. "Not a chance."

"Just kidding. Although when did you turn into a prude? The only reason you weren't skinny dipping back in the day was because your sister was there."

"That was then. And I sure as hell didn't want you skinny dipping."

He rolled over and pulled me into his arms. Alarmed, I glanced around looking for Tana. I didn't see her but then we'd moved slightly farther downstream from everyone else.

"What are you doing? Someone might see."

He didn't move. "You should have known that I didn't mean to steal your shirt that day. I didn't want anyone seeing you naked."

There was something in his voice that made me shiver. "Is that right?"

Voices got closer all of a sudden and his fingers tightened around my waist. For a second, I thought that he wasn't going to let go but then he turned around.

Greg swam by, splashing a ridiculous amount considering how slow he was moving. Rix glanced over and we both dissolved into laughter.

"Come on. Let's go before Michael Phelps comes back."

———

By the time we swam back to the group, someone had already started a small campfire. I looked around curiously. Tana had disappeared. As I was looking, Carter emerged from the edge of the woods. A few seconds later, Tana appeared right behind him holding some sticks.

She stopped when she saw me. "Oh hey! Where did you disappear to?"

My face heated but I kept my voice as normal as possible as I answered. "I swam a little further upstream. I forgot how beautiful it is back here."

"Yeah, it is. I got some more firewood. Piper is grilling some hot dogs, but I thought we could roast marshmallows, too."

She deposited the sticks on the ground and started arranging some rocks around the perimeter. While she was busy, I looked over at Rix. He had pulled his shirt back on and was sitting on the ground nearby. I went over and sat beside him.

"So was your birthday dunk everything you wanted it to be?"

His scathing look brought me so much joy.

"Why did you do this when you hate the creek?"

He didn't answer at first, just stared out at the water. Then he shrugged. "I hate the creek. But you don't."

That was it. When he was being his usual grumpy self, I had at least some defense against him. Yes, he had the kind of bedroom eyes that could make you agree to almost anything and an ass that was damn near impossible to ignore, but at least he was kind of a jerk most of the time. But this version of Rix, the one who seemed to know me even better than I knew myself, was a problem.

How was I supposed to resist falling in love with him when he kept doing these ridiculously sweet things?

"What happened with that guy in New York?" he asked suddenly.

The sudden change in conversation left me reeling. It was also a shock to realize that I hadn't thought about Aaron in the six weeks since I'd been here.

Well, you've been busy, I thought. But deep down, I knew that wasn't the real reason why.

It was because I didn't miss him. Not even a little bit. It should have been a relief that I wasn't that attached to the guy who had been so quick to discard me at the first sign of trouble. But what did it say about me that I'd stayed with him so long in the first place? Maybe I wasn't quite ready to think about that.

"Why are you asking about him?" I stalled.

Rix shrugged. "Just curious."

I thought about the girl who'd been about to hump his leg at the bonfire. "What happened with *your* ex?"

"I'll show you mine if you show me yours."

I made a face. "That didn't work even when we were kids."

"It was worth a shot."

We watched the group that was now roasting marshmallows over the fire. Tana was sitting right next to Greg and she was giving him the fake smile she only used when flirting.

"It has to be him," I whispered. If Tana was trying to keep her fling with Greg a secret, she was doing a terrible job.

"What's that?" Rix asked.

"Nothing. I'm just hungry. Those marshmallows look good."

He hopped up. "I'll get you one."

As he walked over to the group, I watched Tana and Greg more closely. They were talking so much at the bonfire that I should have seen it then. Although I wasn't sure why she would be so secretive about it with me? I could totally understand not wanting everyone else to know. Their moms would immediately start planning a wedding and knitting blankets for their future grandchildren. But she knew I would understand the need for discretion. The gossip mill in this town was relentless.

As far as I knew, Tana hadn't dated anyone local in a few years. She'd dated a chef about six months ago that she'd met online. But once they'd broken up, she'd channeled one hundred percent of her focus into her business.

Rix came back then with a still-smoking marshmallow on a stick and a handful of graham crackers. I held it while he placed a few squares of chocolate on one cracker and then carefully used the other to slide the marshmallow off the stick. It smooshed into ooey gooey chocolate perfection.

"That is a work of art."

He waggled his eyebrows. "You like how I did that, right?"

I took the s'more and bit the edge. Sweetness exploded on my tongue and I moaned.

"Don't make that sound," Rix grumbled. "I can't walk around with a hard dick in front of all these people."

Chuckling, I held out the s'more to him so he could bite the other side. Chocolate oozed out onto his lower lip.

"Fuck, that's good."

"Exactly." I didn't bother to hide my moans and groans as we finished the treat.

Rix folded his hands behind his head and gazed up at the stars just starting to appear in the sky. It was that magical time just past dusk when the sky looked smoky and endless.

"Janelle wanted me to be something different," he said suddenly.

Shocked that he was actually talking to me about this, I moved slowly as I lay down next to him. Rix didn't open up easily and I didn't want to move too fast or ask too many questions.

"Different how?" I finally said when he didn't seem like he planned to elaborate.

"First, it was moving in together. Because that's what people do when they've been dating almost a year, right? Then suddenly she wanted to know when I planned to get a real job. Because why was I doing these odd jobs instead of working for my parents? Then it was why aren't we engaged?"

He closed his eyes. "Everyone wants me to be someone I'm not. Like my life isn't enough unless I'm making a certain amount of money. Why can't 'Hendrix small town handyman' be enough?"

My stomach sank with every word. Was that how I'd made him feel when I told him he could sell his art in New York? That hadn't been my intention but it was hard not to see the parallels. No wonder he'd snapped at me that day.

I had been just one more person making him feel like he wasn't good enough.

"Rix, I think that you should do what makes you happy."

He looked over. But just then Tana flopped down on his other side.

"How did you convince this one to celebrate his birthday this year?" She elbowed Rix and he grunted in response.

"I didn't do anything. I didn't even know where we were going when we started driving."

Tana shrugged. "Well, we need to hang out without the deadweight. There's only one bar outside of town but that's good enough. We need to get you laid."

Rix sat up immediately. "Really? I am *right* here."

Tana stuck out her tongue before she got up. "You can't hog Charlie. I need some bestie time. And a wingwoman."

Two days later, my phone chimed again. Rix looked over and scowled. "Tana again?"

I picked up my phone. "She's not going to give up."

Tana had gotten it into her head that we needed a real Girl's Night. I looked back down at the text chain that had been going on since Wednesday at the creek.

TANA

We're getting drunk tonight.

CHARLIE

Good morning to you, too <3

TANA

Sorry. I really need to get out. This has been the week from hell. And this bar is slightly outside of town so we have a chance to meet some guys that we haven't known since kindergarten.

CHARLIE

I'm just not sure I'm ready to meet someone new.

TANA

It's not just for you. Piper hasn't dated since her loser ex cheated on her. She needs this night out, too.

CHARLIE

Fine but you're buying. I'm broke now, remember?

TANA

Girl, neither of us are paying. The jeans I plan to wear will be buying our drinks tonight.

CHARLIE

:laugh emoji:

TANA

Come on. I'll pick you up. I promise I'll be a
complete gentleman all night.

"Looks like I'm going out. Your sister is determined we're
all getting laid tonight."

He growled something under his breath.

"What was that?" I made a show of cupping my hand to
my ear.

Rix grabbed the phone and threw it on the couch next to
us. "I said, my sister is trying to kill me. You're going to be at the
bar drinking while every man under sixty in the county is
trying to hit on you."

"Jealous?"

He leaned over and gave me a quick kiss, stealing my
breath. "Maybe I am. You know things would be different if we
just told her."

My stomach tightened. The idea of telling Tana I was
sleeping with her brother filled me with dread. I wasn't even
sure why exactly. Tana had never been catty with her brother's
girlfriends. That just wasn't her style. She would be happy for
us and it would definitely stop her from trying to hook me up
with someone else.

But all I could think about was what would happen once it
was over. No matter what we said, the Evers would make
assumptions if they knew we were together. Assumptions about
the future that I wasn't ready to deal with.

I'd done the whole serious relationship thing and it
changed the way people viewed you. Tana would start
making jokes about us being sisters-in-law and her parents
would start including me in family events like I belonged
there.

It hurt to even imagine being welcomed so warmly only to

have it all snatched away when things between me and Rix inevitably cooled off down the road.

Besides, I didn't want Tana to think I was using her brother or treating him casually.

"Are you ready for your mom to start wedding planning?" I raised an eyebrow pointedly. "Because you know that's next if everyone knows."

"Good point." He kissed me again. "Maybe I'll call Carter and see what he's got going on tonight."

"How is his dad doing?"

I had seen Carter in town earlier that day and he looked like he was growing more tired by the day. I only knew a little bit about what was going on from Tana, but I felt so bad for him. He'd been dealing with his father's drinking since we were kids.

"Not great," Rix answered simply. "I'm sure he could use a night out. Maybe I need to get *him* laid."

I snorted out a laugh. "When you invite him out, make sure you use those exact words."

That night, I set my phone up on the nightstand and set the timer to take a picture. There were no full-length mirrors in the house so I would have to hope this outfit looked decent. I was wearing a pair of black jeans and an old band T-shirt knotted at the waist. To make up for the simple style of the outfit, I'd added some jewelry and styled my hair more carefully than usual. Tana claimed it was a casual vibe so it should be fine.

It would have to be since this was the best I could do on short notice.

The doorbell rang and I grabbed my phone before running downstairs. Rix had left to meet up with Carter an hour ago. They were grabbing dinner at the diner and going bowling with Van. I was glad he wasn't here actually. The last thing I wanted was him hanging around in the background while Tana talked about us hooking up with someone.

I pulled open the door and then paused. "Wow. You weren't kidding about the jeans."

Tana sashayed by, swinging her hips. She was wearing a T-shirt too, but it had been hacked off into a crop top. All the better to show off her tiny waist and the jeans which looked like they'd been painted on. Tana had been lamenting her small boobs since we were teenagers but the one thing the girl had was booty for days.

"Between your girls and these jeans, we're covering all bases. T & A all day!"

I cracked up at that. "Let's get out of here. Is Piper meeting us there?"

Tana nodded. "She's probably already there. It's closer to her apartment."

After giving Meatball a pat, Tana waited outside while I locked up. Rix promised to stop by after dinner to check on the little guy so he wouldn't be alone for too long.

I had been worried Meatball would feel abandoned if we were both gone, but he was remarkably good at keeping himself occupied. He'd spent half an hour chasing a piece of lint floating in the air that morning and then slept for three hours afterward like he was exhausted.

Tana grinned once we were in her car. "Finally. It feels like we've waited so long to be living in the same place again. Did I mention how glad I am that you're here?"

I laughed. "I've missed you too, crazy."

She pulled out of the driveway and turned the music up. "We're hot. We're single. This is going to be so much fun!"

———

Tana took having fun seriously.

From the moment we'd arrived, she'd gone into hyper sultry mode. She found us a spot at the bar, cocked her hip, and immediately some guy appeared offering to *"buy you ladies drinks."*

And so it went.

For the next hour, I'd watched in amusement as Tana flirted with every man who approached. Somehow she seemed to know everyone and they were all greeted with a sweet smile and a kiss on the cheek. One of the men looked so befuddled by the attention that he practically just threw his wallet at her.

I shook my head. I wasn't sure what had gotten into her tonight, but her energy was electric and impossible to resist.

As soon as her latest admirer turned around, I bumped Tana's shoulder. "You weren't kidding about not paying for any drinks."

She hummed. "This booty needs to be good for something. Otherwise it's just knocking stuff off shelves and making it hard to find pants that fit."

Just then Greg appeared. His eyes scanned over Tana appreciatively before he yanked his eyes away. "Hey, guys."

Tana grinned. "Hey, Greg."

When she turned to face the bar and he caught sight of her ass in those jeans, he turned slightly red in the face.

"Uh, can I buy you another ring? I mean another *round*," he stammered.

It felt voyeuristic to watch their blatant flirting, so I shifted on my wooden stool and looked around the place. The bar was called The Brew House and seemed to be a weird mix of a dive bar and a family restaurant. Tana had explained that during the day it served breakfast and lunch before morphing into a typical pub atmosphere at night. Apparently there weren't many options for nightlife unless you wanted to drive a half hour over to Harrisonville.

"Let's dance," Tana yelled over the music. "The bar has been invaded." She gestured over her shoulder.

Greg was nowhere to be seen but a few seats over sat none other than Carter. Which meant...

"Having fun?" a voice growled from my other side.

I turned to my left and glared at Rix. "Funny seeing you here."

He shrugged but his lips twitched like he was holding back a smile. "After dinner we decided to come have a beer."

"On the same night that you knew I would be here?" I crossed my arms.

"You know how it is in a small town. There aren't many options."

Tana nudged my arm. "Ignore them. They aren't going to ruin our night. We can get a booth instead."

I followed her over to a booth where Greg was sitting with two other guys. There was only one empty seat but there was no time to wonder if I should take it because Tana promptly planted herself on Greg's knee. He looked stunned but his hand immediately curved around her waist to steady her.

With a strained smile, I slid into the other seat. The guys all introduced themselves, but it was so loud that I just smiled politely. When I looked back over my shoulder, Rix was watching. Carter was too. With a sinking suspicion, I looked over my shoulder to where Tana was laughing at something Greg said.

When they got up to dance, Carter's eyes followed them. The sadness in his gaze tugged at my heartstrings. I had suspected he felt something for Tana back when we were teenagers. We'd both had crushes on him at some point. It was practically tradition to have a crush on your older brother's best friend in high school. Or just an older bad boy in general.

Tana had always known he wouldn't touch her. Hendrix had been his best friend for way too long and he sure as hell wasn't going to risk that.

But things were different now. He was a respected real estate broker. He graduated college and owned a house in Washington DC. He had his life together.

It wasn't lost on me that his situation had some eerie parallels to my own with Rix. Was I willing to risk my oldest friendship on a relationship that probably wouldn't last past the summer?

Tana appeared in front of me and grabbed my hands. "Piper just got here. Let's dance!"

Piper was in the middle of the dance floor rolling her hips to the music. She waved.

"I promised to be your date tonight," Tana yelled.

Putting Carter and forbidden crushes out of my mind, I figured what the hell. I joined her on the dance floor and laughed as Tana twirled me several times. I'd come here to dance and have a good time with my best friend. The rest could wait.

———

An hour later, Piper grabbed my arm and pulled me away from the bar. "We have a problem."

I stumbled slightly before planting my hands on her shoulders. "What's wrong?"

She pointed behind me. "That is the problem."

I turned to see Tana swinging her hair around as she danced next to the bar. I blinked. After dancing for a while, she'd insisted we get a round of shots to celebrate me moving back to town. But then someone had sent another round and she'd said it was rude not to take them. I'd tried to hand them out to everyone around us but Tana had swiped several from the tray before I could.

"She's drunk," Piper hissed. "And she keeps hitting on everyone. I'm afraid she's going to try to leave with someone we don't know. I don't know what to do!"

That made me stand up straight. There was a guy sitting right next to Tana who looked like he wanted to take a bite out of her and she was dancing in her own world, completely unaware.

"Let's get her out of here."

Piper chewed her lip. "I already tried that. She wouldn't come."

Hearing that made me more sure that we needed to leave. Tana wasn't a lightweight but she had definitely gone way past her limit. She could be a bit belligerent when she was drunk so you had to know how to talk her down. Carefully, I made my way over to the bar.

As I walked up I could hear the guy sitting next to her saying, "Let's get out of here."

When she swung her hair again, I grabbed her hand and pulled her against me. She fell into my side giggling.

"Charlie. We're celebrating!"

"We are! And now we're going to celebrate at my house."

I wrapped my arms around her waist like we were hugging. That seemed to work because she leaned into it instead of pulling away. The guy didn't look too happy that I was there though.

He glowered at me. "Actually, we were just leaving."

"No, *we* were just leaving. Because I'm not letting my drunk friend go home with somebody she doesn't even know. Do you know him?" I asked Tana.

She frowned. "Do I know who?"

"Exactly. It's time to go."

The guy stood up. "Who asked you, bitch?"

The aggressive tone made me take a step back but before I knew it, my view was blocked by a pair of shoulders.

"*Watch your fucking tone with my girl.*" Rix put one hand behind him, like he was making sure I was there.

"Your girl needs to mind her own business. And so do you." The guy shoved him as he stood up. He wasn't as tall as Rix but had him by a good thirty pounds.

I gasped and grabbed Tana to pull her out of the way.

Rix just laughed. "You want to start some shit? *Please* give me a reason."

Just then Carter came to stand next to Rix. Greg appeared on his other side.

The guy looked around before he muttered something and then walked out. I didn't let out a breath until after the door swung shut behind him.

Rix turned around. "Baby, you okay?"

I nodded, still feeling like my heart was in my throat. "This is not how I expected the night to go. But I'm really glad you were here."

He slid a hand around my neck and pulled me into a kiss. My eyes fluttered shut and I temporarily forgot where I was. Then slowly the sounds of chatter and glasses clinking filtered through. I opened my eyes to see Carter and the other guys watching us.

"So much for keeping things quiet," I whispered.

Rix's hand flexed on the back of my neck. "Yeah, well. Evers don't do quiet well."

"You just kissed Charlie," Tana muttered from behind us.

I spun around. Apparently Rix really had kissed me stupid because I had forgotten she was back there. As in *right* behind me. Tana leaned against the wall holding her hands to her head. She closed her eyes several times like she was seeing things.

She pointed at Rix. "You can't do that. You can't just kiss her!"

Oh boy. If I didn't get her out of here, there was about to be another fight. And this was a fight that Rix wouldn't win. Tana fought dirty.

"I think it's time to go home. Tana, give me your keys."

Tana shook her head and then groaned before sliding down the wall to sit on the floor. Clearly she was already paying for all the shots. She had to be pretty drunk if she didn't care about sitting on the floor considering how gross it looked.

Piper walked over. "I'll drive her home. I can stay with her tonight to make sure she's okay."

"Are you sure?"

"Yeah, I don't have anything else to do." She looked between me and Rix and then lowered her voice. "But you have something *way* better to do. On behalf of all women everywhere, please do *all the things*. Then ride that man like the Pony Express."

I must have been tipsier than I thought because I cackled at that. Tana looked between us in confusion before Piper looped her arm around Tana's waist to help her up.

"Come on, boss lady. Time for a sleepover."

Once they were gone, I turned back to Rix. He couldn't hear what we'd said, so he just raised a brow in silent question. I shook my head and then waved him over. I'd had more than enough dancing and I was ready to go home.

Like Piper said, I had something *way* better to do.

twenty-five

. . .

HENDRIX

As I pulled into the driveway, I glanced over at Charlie. She was leaning against the window staring out at the sky.

She hadn't said anything since I kissed her in the bar. I couldn't tell if she was pissed or just lost in thought. Had it been the best idea to kiss her in front of everyone? Probably not. But I was tired of pretending. We weren't kids and we shouldn't have to sneak around. But that didn't mean Charlie didn't have valid reason to be upset since she'd made it clear that she wasn't ready to go public yet.

Just rip the Band-Aid off, I thought miserably.

"Charlie, about tonight—"

"Were you seriously going to fight that guy?" She looked over at me.

I wasn't sure how to answer. Going with the truth usually didn't win me any favors. "Violence is always the last resort."

She chuckled. "Try that with someone who doesn't know you, Hendrix Evers. As if you didn't punch my prom date in the face."

My grin finally broke free. "Okay, you got me. He looked

251

like the type that has a glass jaw. Talks a lot of shit but will run home crying if you even tap him. I have three brothers. Four, if you count Carter. I can take a punch."

"So arrogant," she whispered but the way her eyes glittered in the low light told me that she wasn't upset at all.

In fact the way she was looking at me made my dick stand up and take notice. She looked like she wanted to bite me.

I could definitely get on board with that plan.

"Did Tana say anything? She was drinking a lot tonight. I haven't seen her like that before."

She looked away. "Something is going on with her. She was flirting a lot tonight. I think maybe things aren't going well with the guy she's seeing."

"You know who it is, don't you?"

Her face scrunched up. "That doesn't mean I can tell you. Girl code. She'll talk about it when she's ready."

"Did she say anything about *the other thing?*"

She tapped her bottom lip. "You mean her brother kissing her best friend right in front of her? Nope. But I'm sure I'll wake up to a million text messages tomorrow."

"Sorry. I really didn't mean to do that."

I got out and rounded the cab to open her door. She took my hand and hopped down. When she landed, she brushed right up against me and hummed. The sound went straight to my dick.

"Maybe it's wrong to admit it but it was hot the way you just stepped in."

All the blood in my body was still busy going south so I just nodded.

Charlie smirked as she walked off. I followed closely behind, watching her hips sway as she went up the steps. After she unlocked the door, she grabbed Meatball to take him outside while I toed off my boots. When she came back in, she picked up his bed and carried it with them upstairs without looking back.

Confused, I got a glass of water before following. By the time I got upstairs, she had the dog settled in the corner and was in the bathroom brushing her teeth.

So we were just going to bed then. Okay.

I went into the bathroom and grabbed my toothbrush. She finished at the sink before moving out of the way so I could use it. There was something so wonderfully domestic about sharing space this way. I brushed while watching her in the mirror but paused when she tugged her shirt over her head. Her hair got caught in it briefly before she tugged and then the wild curls spilled out over her shoulders.

"What are you doing?"

"Getting the bar smell off me. I think Tana spilled vodka on this shirt." She shimmied out of her jeans and left them on the floor.

Our eyes met in the mirror as she reached behind her to unhook her bra. I almost whimpered when she finally tugged it off and let it drop, her breasts bouncing with the movement. I licked my lips.

The nipples that loved to torment me through her tops were tight aching points that I wanted to bite. With a satisfied smile, she walked out of the bathroom in nothing but a black thong.

Hurriedly, I rinsed my mouth and followed. When I got to the bedroom, she was curled up on her side of the bed under the covers. I quickly undressed down to my boxers and slid in next to her.

She moved closer until she was half draped over me. She trailed a finger down the front of my chest. "Piper said I should ride you like the Pony Express."

"I knew I liked her."

Her husky laugh only made my boxers even tighter. She swirled her hips, settling herself right over my cock. Her mouth fell open so I knew that she was getting herself off and the thought of her shamelessly using my dick like her toy made me so hot I almost came right then.

"Charlie. Are you teasing me, baby?"

She bit her lip. "I think I'm teasing myself. Because it feels too good to stop."

I flipped us over and tugged her thong down in one motion. They were damp and I caught her eye as I brought the skimpy fabric to my nose.

Her lids lowered slightly. "*Oh my god.* Why is that so dirty?"

I grasped her under the thighs and yanked her closer so she was lying flat and her legs were draped over my shoulders. Fuck, she was so open like this, her little clit pouting for my attention. I licked her, groaning at the taste and her hands slid into my hair holding me in place. The noises she was making made me crazy, and I reached up with one hand to cup the swell of her breast, squeezing and pinching her perfect little nipple.

She shrieked as she came and I grinned against her skin, the sound of her losing it making me feral. There was something about Charlie, the scent of her skin, the way she loved to give me shit, the look of vulnerability in her eyes when she came for me, that had me completely gone over her.

I was fucking *lost.*

As I moved up, I sucked at the delicate skin between her hip and thigh before leaving a gentle kiss on her belly button. She giggled softly at that and then sighed when I moved up to her breasts, drawing the tip of one through my lips slowly.

Her hands that were gently stroking through my hair suddenly grasped tight. "Rix!"

She pulled so hard that I was forced to stop. With surprising strength she shoved me over so I landed flat on my back. Then she scooted down. My mouth instantly went dry as she pulled my boxers down.

All the times I'd imagined Charlie on her knees for me rushed through my mind. She was a fantasy come to life, leaning over me with her curls swirling around her face as she took me firmly in her grip. Her stroke was surprisingly strong, no tentative moves for my Charlie.

My head fell back on a groan as her palm skimmed over the head, picking up the drops on the tip. She stuck her tongue out to taste and I wrapped a hand behind her neck.

"That's it. Take it all in."

She looked up at me defiantly before sucking me down until I hit the back of her throat. When she swallowed, her throat muscles worked me over and I gritted my teeth, trying desperately not to come. My dick stretched the edges of her mouth and I knew her lips would be bruised tomorrow, the sight giving me a dark satisfaction.

"I thought about this, you know?" I admitted. "Alone in bed at night. Every time you wore those fucking tiny shorts in the kitchen. In the shower."

She pulled back and my dick slid out of her mouth with a pop. "You thought about me in the shower?"

"Fuck, the things I've done to you in that shower. If the walls could talk."

Her hand stroked me lazily before she licked the tip. "Tell me."

It was getting increasingly hard to think as she took me back in, moaning like my dick was her candy.

"That sound. I imagined that sound. You moaning for me while you fingered your little clit."

Her eyes glittered and then she adjusted slightly. I leaned

up to see that she had one hand between her legs. She was following my directions. My fantasy come to life.

"You put two fingers in. You're riding them while I ride your mouth."

She whimpered and I imagined the sight of her fingers sliding in her slick little pussy, her muscles stretching to take it. She was always so deliciously tight for me. My hand tightened around her neck and her eyes met mine.

She groaned and started bouncing on her fingers and I closed my eyes.

"I can't take this. I have to get inside you."

Suddenly she stopped. When I tried to sit up, she climbed astride. "You aren't taking away my chance to ride you like a pony."

I laughed but then groaned as she sank down on my cock in one smooth motion. Immediately her pussy started contracting, gripping me so tightly that I was already fighting for control. We'd had the birth control conversation already so we'd ditched the condoms recently. I still wasn't used to the insane feeling of being inside her bare.

As she rocked her hips, I placed both thumbs between us, giving her as much friction on her clit as possible. She cried out and clenched even tighter, which I didn't think was possible. Her head fell back as her orgasm rolled through her, her hips going wild as she slammed down on me one final time.

"Look how beautiful you are when you come for me." I pulled her down for a kiss.

My own orgasm was bearing down on me and I wanted to be connected to her in every way. Everything went white as pleasure arced down my spine. And the only thing I could think about was that moment in the bar when I thought she was in trouble.

The idea of her being threatened or scared had pushed me to face what I'd been running from this whole time.

Fuck. I'm in love with her.

———

A few days later, I stepped back to survey my work. The Jeffries backyard was not as big as my parents', but had more than enough room for the 10' x 12' she-shed I'd built for Miss Pearl. She'd wanted space for a comfortable chair, a writing desk, and a bookshelf. I'd added large windows so there would be plenty of light and installed beautiful glass French doors on the front.

It had come out even better than I expected.

"Can I come out now?" Miss Pearl called from the back door.

She'd tried to come out three times already and I'd had to promise that it would be worth the wait. Her excitement made me smile but also made me nervous. I really hoped she'd liked what I'd done since I'd taken a few liberties inside.

"You can come out now!"

I waved her over. She'd been so excited when I told her I'd be finished today, but I'd asked her not to peek inside since I had a surprise for her.

She made her way carefully across the yard with her walking stick. Behind her cat-eye glasses her blue eyes flashed with excitement. "I can't wait to see it."

"You are now the proud owner of the best she-shed in Violet Ridge."

She beamed up at me. "The French doors are just beautiful!"

"I thought they were a nice touch. But now for the surprise." With a flourish, I opened both doors so she could walk inside. "I'm not sure if you remember but when we first started you mentioned wishing you could have a window box."

"Oh yes. But I'm not much of a gardener. Every time I try, the poor flowers are dead as a doornail in a few weeks."

I laughed softly. "Well, I hope these will last a little longer than that."

Miss Pearl turned to look at the window and put a shaky hand over her mouth. She walked forward and touched the mural of wildflowers I'd painted right below the windowsill. My mom had told me that Miss Pearl was always complimenting her petunias so I'd made sure to include those along with marigolds, begonias and a few other types of flowers that were common in window boxes.

"Oh my word. Hendrix Evers. You painted that?" Miss Pearl demanded.

"Yes, ma'am. I thought you might like some flowers even if you don't have a garden."

Her eyes softened. "Oh, how thoughtful. I would have never even thought of something like that. Now I have flowers that will never die."

She shuffled forward and pulled me into a surprisingly strong hug. Her head barely reached my chest so I leaned over a little to make it easier. She sniffed a few times before turning around to exclaim over the matching mural on the other side.

"Oh and it's under both windows!"

I gestured to the armchair I'd brought out the prior day. "Why don't you have a seat and see how you like it?"

As she sat, she gazed around in delight, taking in the furniture I'd set up. Her bookshelves were still empty but I'd brought out a vase from her living room to put on her side table and placed a copy of a magazine there, too.

She then leaned back into the cushions with a satisfied sigh. "I can't believe this is all for me."

While she sat and gazed out the window, I gathered the rest of my tools and made sure I hadn't left any trash behind on the site. I told her not to get up and that I would let myself out. I had a feeling she would be sitting in that chair until her husband got home.

I decided to pop into my parents' house since I was here. The door was unlocked, as usual. My father looked up when I walked in. He was in his usual spot on the couch watching TV.

"Rix? This is a nice surprise."

I walked over and flopped down beside him before he could get up. "Hey, Dad. I was just next door finishing up Miss Pearl's shed."

"How'd she like it?"

"She loved it." I hesitated. "I painted some wildflowers below the windows since she said she's not good with keeping real ones alive."

He looked over. "That was nice of you. I bet she was thrilled."

"Yeah, she was."

Even though I wasn't looking at him, I could feel his stare on the side of my face.

"So if it's not work, then what's wrong?"

I glanced over in alarm. "What makes you think something is wrong?"

He didn't answer just continued watching me patiently.

The baseball game he was watching went to commercial and then a dancing bear appeared on-screen. I fiddled with a loose thread on the edge of my T-shirt.

"How did you know that you were in love with Mom? For real. Not that whole *soul tie fate* stuff, either."

He picked up the remote and muted the TV. "I wondered when you'd be ready to talk about it."

I shook my head. "Has everybody in town been talking about my love life?"

"Not everybody. *Most* everybody."

"Fantastic."

He chuckled. "You've never been the type who was bothered by what people said before."

When I'd started dating Janelle, people in town had made a lot of these same comments. Asking questions and just generally being nosy but it had never bothered me. I had been more than content to let them speculate and all the gossip just rolled off my back. But I didn't like the idea of people gossiping about Charlie. They didn't need to be making comments or saying things that might make her uncomfortable.

The difference in how I'd reacted to the two situations made me feel a pang of guilt for how I'd brushed off Janelle's concerns. We weren't right for each other, but she'd been the one getting the brunt of the town gossip. I just hadn't cared back then.

"This is different."

"It is. Everything is different when you find someone who matters."

"But how do I know these feelings are *really* love?"

He sat back to ponder the question. "Van Halen described it as looking into a crowd and waiting for someone's face to come into focus."

I looked over at him. My father loved to be cryptic but I needed real advice.

He laughed at my skepticism. "I'm not just quoting the song. That was *exactly* what it felt like. Falling in love with your mom felt like that moment when you turn around and see a familiar face in a crowd. It was like a part of me recognized her immediately. But that's not what you're really asking, is it?"

"It's just such a big thing and getting it wrong can hurt a lot of people. How can anyone make that kind of commitment without knowing whether it will last?"

I thought about the last two months with Charlie and how she'd become such an important part of my life. Somewhere along the way, protecting her and making her happy had become the key to whether or not I was happy. Her pain was my pain. Her laughter made my heart smile.

But those were just feelings, right? How did I know that I could trust them? And how did I know that she'd want me in her life long-term anyway?

"I don't want to hurt her," I said finally.

"That's a good sign that you're putting her first. When you truly love someone, you want what's best for them. Sometimes that means putting what you want on the back burner. And they will do the same for you. It's a joint effort."

"Is it supposed to be this hard?"

He chuckled. "Let me let you in on a little secret. Love requires effort, but it's not hard. There's nothing hard about coming home to your favorite person every day."

"I'm worried about life getting in the way."

"Life is going to get in the way sometimes. But it's the easiest thing in the world to be with someone you think is amazing. Even when you have no money. Even when you're stressed. I'd rather be with your mom in our little house than with someone else in a mansion."

My mind flashed through all the moments Charlie and I had shared. Every day the house was filled with both laughter and bickering, but somehow with her even the most mundane things were fun. With her, I felt more at home than any place I'd been since I'd left my parents' house.

I had a feeling that any place Charlie went would feel like home.

"You know, you and Mom have something amazing. I'm not sure everybody gets to have that."

"I definitely don't think everybody gets to have it. This world is unfair and a lot of people aren't lucky enough to meet someone they can't live without. The question is, have you?"

Confused, I just stared at him. "Have I what?"

"Have you met someone you can't live without?"

Caught, I looked back at the TV. The Nationals were up by two. To my father's dismay, I had never been much of a baseball fan. The only time I cared was when Beck was playing Little League.

"She's so much bigger than this town," I said finally.

Dad gave me a knowing look. "Maybe so but that doesn't mean she doesn't want to be here. Also, I know you don't want to hear about 'that fate stuff' but I wouldn't discount it. Have you ever asked Charlie about her name?"

"Her *name?*"

Just then my mom walked in carrying a basket of laundry. "Rix, I didn't know you were here." She leaned over the arm of the couch to kiss my cheek.

"I just finished up next door."

"Pearl has been talking my ear off all week about that. She is so excited to read next month's book club selection in her new she-shed." She patted my arm. "I'm glad you were able to make time to take that on, honey."

I decided to take that as my cue to go. If I stayed any longer she'd ask what we were talking about and I definitely didn't want to rehash everything again.

"Well, I need to go."

Mom kissed my cheek again. "You're coming to Beck's game, right?"

"Wouldn't miss it."

She picked up her basket and walked down the hallway

toward the bedrooms. I looked over at my father. He made like he was going to get up.

"You don't have to get up Dad. I'll let myself out. And thanks for the advice." I wasn't sure I really knew any more than when I arrived but his words had given me a lot to think about.

"Anytime," he replied. "I know things seem confusing now, but love isn't a bunch of things you can check off a list. If you feel strongly enough to even be asking these questions, then trust your gut. When the time comes, you'll know what you have to do."

twenty-six

. . .

As I walked down Main Street, I paused so Meatball could smell a lamppost. It was a beautiful day and plenty of people were out just enjoying the sunshine. I pulled out my phone to check the time. David was expecting me at his shop in ten minutes so I needed to hustle.

"This would go a lot faster if you didn't need to smell *every* patch of weeds."

Meatball gave me a dismissive sniff before resuming his usual investigative work. I swore he acted like he was on the trail of something amazing every time we left the house. But I hated leaving him behind. Bringing him with me everywhere was one of the unexpected perks of being an accidental business owner.

Charlie's Accounting Service had been booming over the past few days. I had a sneaking suspicion that Rix was the secret culprit behind it since he had a tendency to mention that I did bookkeeping to everyone when we were in town, even when it was out of context.

For example, I really didn't think that Mrs. Murphy at the

grocery needed a bookkeeper but yet he'd mentioned it while we were checking out buying milk and bread a few days ago. The same thing when we were in the post office.

But as embarrassing as it was, it was also really sweet. He could be so grumpy sometimes but since he'd moved in I'd noticed that he tended to do so many little acts of kindness for various people around town. Of course, if you mentioned it he would just scowl. I'd never met anyone who got annoyed at being outed for kindness.

But that was Rix for you, the ultimate contradiction.

As we finally turned the corner near the mechanic shop, I scooped up Meatball and tucked him under my arm. The door swung open easily and I was immediately assaulted by the scent of motor oil and rubber. The interior of the shop was very clean and sported generic blue chairs and a table with an ancient coffee pot. I approached the small reception desk. There was nobody sitting there and I could hear in the background the clanking sound of metal and a horribly loud grinding noise.

"Hello?" I called out once the noise stopped.

There was a door with a glass window on the other side of the room. I walked over and peered through. I could see a car up on a lift but I didn't see any people. Maybe I'd gotten the time wrong? I was just about to pull out my phone and check my calendar when I heard my name.

"Charlie! Have you been waiting long?" David stood behind the reception desk wiping his hands on a cloth.

"No, I just got here."

"Come on back. My office is much quieter."

We walked down a short hallway passing a small employee break room on one side. We finally stopped at the end of the hall.

David went to open the door and then grimaced. "Apologies in advance for what you're about to witness."

I laughed. "Don't worry about it. If I can handle Rix's office, a.k.a *the bottom of his toolbox*, then how bad can it be?"

When he finally opened the door, I looked around in shock. Papers were stacked on not just the desk but several chairs in haphazard piles and there were boxes everywhere. One of them was open and I could see they were filled with file folders. In between the papers there were clothes strewn about almost like someone had gotten dressed (or undressed) in a hurry. On the desk there were several empty coffee cups and the trash can was overflowing.

He winced when he saw my expression. "Sorry. It's my office but I practically sleep here sometimes. I really need an assistant."

"I was going to suggest an exorcist."

David slapped a hand to his forehead. "I deserved that. But us Evers men definitely aren't known for neatness. Rix is lucky to have you keeping him in line."

I wasn't touching that comment so instead I just got Meatball set up with his favorite squeaky toy and the blanket he loved to drag around.

After we cleared the desk, I had him log in to his accounting software so I could see what we were working with. Over the next hour, I cleaned up his chart of accounts and did what felt like two years' worth of bank reconciliations. David gave me permission to enable remote access, so I set that up as well. Now I could work on his books from the comfort of home, which would be a relief on days when I wasn't up for a trip into town.

I finally stood up and stretched. My back ached a bit from hunching over the desk. I glanced at the clock on the wall and realized it was later than I thought.

"Oh, shoot! I need to take Meatball out."

"This was a great start," David said warmly. "I can't thank you enough for this, Charlie. Seriously."

"It was my pleasure." After a quick tug of war, Meatball relinquished his toy and I packed it up with his blanket in the huge tote bag I carried. "I'll call you next week. Once you get into a routine, it will never get this bad again."

I waved goodbye and headed back out into the shop. As soon as I stepped into the hallway, I heard the grinding noise again. I realized his office must be soundproofed. Luckily Meatball didn't seem bothered by noise, just grumpy men wearing work boots.

As I passed the front desk, I saw Dot standing in the waiting area. Her hair was nicely curled and she was wearing a pretty blue sundress. It was strange to see her out of context. I'd only ever seen her at the diner. She put a piece of paper up on the bulletin board and secured it with a push pin. When she turned and saw me she waved.

"Charlie, have you seen this?" She handed me one of the colorful flyers.

I skimmed over it quickly. *The Violet County Fall Fair.* I remembered the fair since Gran had won several ribbons for her violetberry jam when I was a kid. By the time I'd moved here for high school, I had been way more interested in hanging out with Tana at the fair to ogle the farmhands coming in from Harrisonville.

The flyer mentioned games, a pie contest, and *booths.* There was a section for artisans to sell their wares and it specifically mentioned artwork. An idea clicked in my head.

"Dot, do you know if there are any booths still available?" I asked.

"I think so, hon. Would you like to reserve one?" She smiled warmly.

Rix had mentioned doing a small mural for his parents' neighbor. I hadn't wanted to make a big deal out of it since my ego was still smarting from the last time we'd talked about his painting. But maybe that was a sign he was ready to start showing the world what he could do. If I waited all the booths would be gone. It couldn't hurt to reserve one now, just in case.

"Yes! I would," I blurted before I could change my mind.

She pointed at the flyer. "Just fill out the form online. My daughter set us up with a fancy website."

"I'll do that. Thank you."

After taking a few flyers and promising to hand them out, I stepped outside. As I strolled down the street a kid on the other side waved frantically.

"Hi, Meatball!" His excited screech cut off as his mother scooped him up.

Laughing, his mom waved before they disappeared inside one of the small shops. I didn't recognize her but she was probably one of the many people I'd met at the diner or at Tana's shop.

I looked down at the dog trotting beside me. "Looks like you've got yourself a fan club, buddy."

Then it dawned on me, Meatball wasn't the only one with friends here.

Owning a home was only part of the puzzle. Being part of a community was about more than just property lines. People in town were getting to know me, and I was getting to know them back. That was the real gift that Gran Grace had left me. A warmth spread through my chest.

If I really wanted to belong here, then I needed to act like it. It was time to get the rest of my stuff from my old apartment. I needed to stop waiting for something to go wrong and start putting down some real roots.

Most of all, I needed to have a talk with Rix about his plans for the fall. Things were complicated because my mom and sister were coming soon. He had been planning to get another place. Maybe I could go with him and leave the house for Mom and Billie? I didn't know but we could figure it out if we really wanted to. Because I didn't just want to stay in Violet Ridge.

I wanted to stay with *him*.

———

As I made my way home, I decided to stop at the store. Maybe I would even surprise Rix with some onion rings since he loved them so much. Food was a good buffer for a potentially awkward conversation, right?

There was just one wild card in the plan.

I scooped up Meatball and placed him in my bag. "Okay, buddy. I'm not *entirely* sure if you're allowed in the grocery store so this needs to be a covert mission. No barking. Stealth mode, got it?"

Meatball looked up at me with his big brown eyes, and I could swear he was in on the plan. I leaned down to kiss his fluffy little head.

"Let's go."

When I entered the store, Mrs. Murphy looked up from behind the counter.

"How are you doing today, Mrs. Murphy?" I'd learned it was best to get the pleasantries out of the way early.

She turned a page in her magazine. "Can't complain. Wouldn't do no good if I did."

When my bag started moving I hurriedly grabbed a push cart. Once we were out of sight, I put my bag in the cart and made sure the top was as open as possible.

"Would you calm down in there?" I muttered.

Meatball popped his head out and looked around. So much for stealth mode.

I wandered over to the produce and picked up a bag of onions. Were onion rings usually made with yellow onions or white? After a quick search on my phone I decided these were good enough. Placing the bag in the cart, I thought of all the specialty grocery stores in the city where I could have found five different varieties of onions. Now, I was just happy with whatever I could find.

The thing was, it didn't bother me as much as I thought it would. The simplicity was kind of refreshing.

"Do you need help finding anything?" Mrs. Murphy inquired as I rounded the corner.

"No, I've got it. Just making some onion rings," I replied with a smile before picking up a bag of flour.

Mrs. Murphy gave me a knowing look. "Oh, Rix does love his onion rings. Smart girl." She winked.

My face flushed. I still wasn't used to how people in town not only knew all your business but had no problem commenting on it.

Just as I was about to go down the next aisle, I had this weird feeling. I turned and saw a woman standing a few feet away watching me rather intently.

"Hello."

She didn't respond.

Okay then. I pushed my cart faster. But when I turned to the next aisle, she was already there.

She looked into my cart. "Let me guess. Onion rings? Rix always did love those."

I took a closer look at her. It took a second but recognition finally clicked. Her hair was different but there was no doubt this was Rix's ex-girlfriend. "You must be Janelle."

She looked pleased. "He talks about me?"

"No. I just remembered seeing you at the bonfire."

Her smile wilted slightly. "You're the one he's living with then?"

I wasn't sure how to respond to that. "Well, renovations are a lot of work."

"Renovations?"

I angled my cart around her and headed for the front of the store. "Yes. I hired Rix to renovate my Gran's house."

She arched an eyebrow. "Hired, huh?"

Inside, my mind was racing. I didn't want any drama, especially not in Mrs. Murphy's store. But I also didn't want to be pushed around. Meatball, still hidden in my bag, gave a soft whine.

"Yes. Hired."

Mrs. Murphy smiled as I approached. I started putting things on the counter. In between I snuck glances at Janelle. She really was beautiful. Her hair fell in perfect waves, and her makeup looked flawless.

Meanwhile, I was usually either dusty or sweaty and hadn't worn makeup since I arrived in town.

If this was Rix's type, then what the hell were we doing?

As if she had read my thoughts, Janelle suddenly laughed. It was a sharp, mean-spirited sound that caught me off guard.

"Don't look so worried, sweetie. I'm not here to break you two up," she said with a smirk. "I don't have to."

"Look, I have things to do. Why don't you just say whatever it is that you're so desperate to say."

The direct delivery seemed to shake her a bit but finally she leaned closer.

"Rix has a hero complex. He loves playing the savior. But once he doesn't feel needed anymore, he's done. It feels really good to be needed by him. Trust me, I know. But don't get used to it. Just enjoy it while it lasts."

She unfolded the sunglasses hanging on her shirt and slid them on with a flourish. I think she was going for drama but since it was pretty dark inside the grocery it honestly just looked ridiculous. Either way, Meatball chose that moment to lose his damn mind.

I wasn't sure if it was her sudden movement or the shades themselves but apparently he didn't just have a problem with men's boots.

Add sunglasses to the list of things that triggered his rage.

"Oh my god, what is that?" Janelle screamed while I frantically tried to stop Meatball from throwing himself out of the cart.

Mrs. Murphy leaned over the counter. "Charlie, *what in the world?* Is that a dog?"

"Yes, ma'am. Sorry. He's normally pretty quiet."

I couldn't even finish the lie as Meatball climbed up my chest, using the higher vantage point to bark madly at them both. It was clear he was cursing somebody out in dog language.

Janelle turned and ran out. The bell over the door jangled loudly which only seemed to reignite Meatball's fury.

Mrs. Murphy hurriedly finished scanning my final items and I tossed two twenties over the counter before grabbing my bags and getting out of there. As soon as we emerged into the bright sunshine, Meatball stopped barking.

"Seriously?"

He looked back at me innocently as if to say, *you needed an extraction. You're welcome.*

It would be difficult to walk holding him and the bags so I set him down on the ground. Hopefully he could hold it together long enough for us to get home. Clearly we needed to have a talk about his anger issues.

As I walked, I thought about that scene back in the store.

Janelle was hardly an unbiased source so it would be foolish to take anything she said seriously. After all, if there were any truth to her words she wouldn't be so desperate to get Rix back.

But as I walked home, I couldn't deny that she was right about one thing.

It did feel really good to be needed by him.

What was going to happen when I wasn't?

———

By the time I got back home, my mood had plummeted. Despite knowing that she was likely just a bitter, jealous ex, I still found myself with very little enthusiasm to actually talk to Rix about the fall.

Maybe this was a sign that I was moving too fast? Our enemies-with-benefits arrangement aside, we were fundamentally roommates. Transitioning to dating was an entirely different thing.

This whole thing was moving at light speed and I was starting to feel like my head was spinning.

Once Meatball was happily snuggled in his bed, I washed my hands and started peeling the onions. Even if I didn't talk to Rix, eating something deep-fried would likely make me feel better. My eyes burned as I sliced into another onion.

Ugh. I was reminded of why I normally didn't cook. My mom was a vegan and basically only ate lettuce and working in a busy finance department, everyone there pretty much existed on takeout. But I'd baked so many different things with Gran. It couldn't be that different, could it?

I pulled up the recipe I'd found for onion rings. It said I needed to heat the oil, so I did that first and then started mixing the flour, cornmeal, and spices.

As I stood there waiting for the oil to heat, I felt the

overwhelming urge to talk to someone. I grabbed my phone and dialed Retta. She picked up on the second ring, her face way too close to the camera as usual.

"Who is this? It kind of looks like my girl Charlie, but I'm pretty sure she's been abducted by a mountain man." Retta's voice instantly lifted my mood.

"I know. I meant to call but I've been so busy. Did I tell you that I'm apparently the official Violet Ridge bookkeeper now?"

"How did that happen?"

"Not exactly sure but I think it has something to do with Hendrix and his *very* big mouth. Also the fact that I'm the only person in town who actually likes spreadsheets."

She laughed. "That sounds about right."

"I miss you so much! How's everything in the city?"

"Oh, you know, the usual chaos. How is Mr. Handyman? Have you two finally admitted you're sucking face yet?" Retta was never one to beat around the bush.

"We kind of didn't have a choice. He kissed me and everybody saw it." I hesitated. "Tana was super drunk but there's no way she doesn't remember that. But we're not talking about it. I mean, I know she knows. And *she knows* that *I know* that *she knows.*"

Retta squinted at the screen. "Girl, what?"

"You know what I mean."

While we were talking, I'd whisked together the milk and eggs and dipped each ring before rolling it in the flour. Carefully I used a pair of tongs to drop a few into the oil. It popped and sizzled so much I jumped back. A few drops landed on my forearm.

"Ouch!"

"Are you okay? What are you doing?" Retta asked.

"Making onion rings."

She blinked dramatically. "You have never fried anything a

day in your bougie life. What kind of magical dick is that boy slinging to have you standing over hot grease?"

Frustrated, I added another few slices of onion to the pan, being careful to do it more slowly this time.

"I just wanted to do something nice for him. Retta, he does all these amazing things for people in town and never even tells anyone about it. I'm talking like 'helping old ladies cross the street' type of stuff."

"Well, you knew he was a good guy underneath it all. He's Tana's brother and you've known him forever."

"Yeah, but it's not just that. He's different than I thought."

She put a hand to her head. "Oh boy. You're really in deep."

I huffed because, well, she wasn't wrong. "Then today his ex-girlfriend starts stalking me around the grocery store saying all this stuff about how he's going to get bored and leave soon. I mean, he was with her for almost a year so what do I know? Maybe that is his thing? He lives with women for a while and then leaves when things get intense."

Things were quiet for a moment as she watched me scoop the onion rings out of the pan. They were golden brown and the crust looked like it had held up. I slowly added the second batch of onion slices to the pan.

"Listen," Retta said in a serious tone, which was rare for her. "Don't you dare let some jealous ex mess with your head. She doesn't know anything about you or what's going on between you and Hendrix. Hell, the two of you don't even know what's going on between you."

"True," I admitted.

"But if you're really worried about what she said, just talk to him."

"You think so?"

"I think talking to him is way better than listening to whatever bullshit she's telling you."

She waited as I extracted the second batch of onion rings and arranged them on a tray lined with a paper towel. After they cooled, I could try one to make sure they tasted okay.

Just then I heard the distinctive beep on the line that meant I was getting another call. Billie's picture flashed on the screen.

"I have to go. Billie's calling from camp."

"Well, just leave me hanging, why don't you?" Retta grumbled. "Fine. Go talk to kiddo but you better call me back!"

"I will. Thanks for letting me vent."

"Anytime, girl."

I switched over to take Billie's call. "Hey, bug."

"Hey." She sounded glum.

"What's wrong? Is everything okay at camp?"

"Mémé said that I might be coming to live with them," Billie said.

I put a hand over my suddenly pounding heart. "She said that? When was this?"

Christian's parents lived in Manhattan but we usually only saw them at their Hamptons house for Memorial Day or at Christmas.

"Last night. She said that after camp is over, I might be coming to stay with her for a while. Charlie, I don't want to live in their apartment! It's like a museum. Not a fun one, either."

Despite the circumstances, I smiled. I'd only visited the Delacourts Park Avenue penthouse once and it made Christian's penthouse look cheap. Filled with priceless paintings and various sculptures they'd collected on their travels around the world, I'd been scared to move for fear of knocking over some rare artifact or something.

"I hear you on that. Let me find out what's going on but I

don't think you need to worry. She probably just meant they want to see you before school starts."

"Maybe."

I switched the camera around and walked over to where Meatball was sleeping with his feet sticking up in the air. Billie laughed.

"He's so cute. I can't wait to meet him."

I turned the camera back around. "You'll be here before you know it. Try not to worry, okay. I'll take care of it."

She waved before hanging up.

I immediately dialed my mother. When she didn't answer I hung up and called back again. As I paced in the kitchen, my elbow clipped the bowl with the egg mixture and it fell to the ground, splashing the remains all over the bottom of my jeans. I groaned but quickly wiped up the floor.

My mom still wasn't answering so I walked upstairs and into my room. I stripped out of the soiled jeans and threw them in the hamper. Quickly, I ducked into the bathroom and turned the shower on. There was some egg stuck to my left foot so I washed it off and then patted my leg dry with the towel. Once I didn't feel so gross, I went back to my room.

I wasn't planning to go anywhere else, so I just pulled on a pair of pajama pants. Then I picked up my phone and dialed my mom's number again. With every ring, my heart started beating faster.

"Hello? Charlie, I can't talk now—"

"Mom, what's going on with the Delacourts? Are they trying to take custody of Billie?"

twenty-seven

. . .

HENDRIX

As I opened the door of Charlie's house with my key, I was looking forward to putting my feet up. Today had been a long day and I'd spent most of it working directly in the hot sun. I could use a kiss, a shower, and a beer, preferably in that order.

"Charlie?" I called out. I poked my head into the kitchen, but she wasn't there. "Charlie, you home?"

She wasn't there, but there was a tray of onion rings on the counter along with a mess of flour and what looked like every spice from the cabinet. Tentatively, I picked up an onion ring and took a small bite.

"Not bad." I shoved the rest in my mouth as I wandered back into the living room. Meatball was in his usual position, playing possum in his dog bed.

Then I heard a voice above me. Charlie must be in her room. As I walked up the stairs, her voice got louder.

"Billie said her grandmother thinks she's going to be staying with them soon. Please tell me that isn't what it sounds like."

I paused outside of Charlie's bedroom, not wanting to intrude. But I couldn't help overhearing what she was saying.

"Are they really suing you? Can they even do that?"

The floor squeaked under my boots and I froze in place. The door wasn't closed all the way but Charlie didn't even look up.

"This is ridiculous. It's not like you're taking her to another country. Virginia isn't that far from New York. Couldn't they just visit?"

The other voice was muffled but it was obviously her mother.

"Let's try not to panic until Alan has a chance to talk to them. Maybe they'll be reasonable once they realize how much this is going to hurt Billie."

What would happen if this lawsuit prevented her mother and sister from moving? Could they even afford to stay in New York? Charlie had made it seem like they were on the brink of losing everything.

"I don't know what to do, Mom," Charlie's voice broke. "I don't want to sell the house. It's all I have left of Gran..."

I was torn between wanting to barge in and offer my help and respecting her privacy. But this was a private conversation. I shouldn't have been eavesdropping.

Carefully I made my way back downstairs, skipping the second stair from the bottom that always squeaked.

A million questions raced through my head. What if she did have to sell the house? If she had to sell, she would definitely leave town. Without a place to come back to, would I ever see her again?

My chest ached. The mere thought of not seeing her every day hit me like a ton of bricks.

This was what Dad meant, I realized. I didn't want to say goodbye.

Of course, Charlie had proven time and time again that family was her top priority. And it should be, shouldn't it? The very thought of making her choose between her family and me was unbearable. I couldn't, and wouldn't, be the cause of more pain for her.

As if he could sense that something major was happening, Meatball pawed at my leg.

I knelt down to scratch behind his ears. "We got off to a rough start, but I think we understand each other. You'll take care of her, right?"

When I heard noise on the stairs, I opened the front door and then slammed it shut, as if I was just getting home. A few seconds later, Charlie entered the room with reddened eyes, and a forced smile on her face. It was clear she had been crying.

"Hey. Did you just get back?" she asked.

"Yeah. How has your day been?" I replied, trying to keep my own voice steady.

"It was okay. I was with David at the shop for most of the afternoon. His office was a mess and so were his books. But I whipped him into shape." Her voice trembled slightly.

It took everything within me not to pick her up and cuddle her. It was hard to see her like this, looking so defeated but she didn't need me to break down with her. She needed someone who would put her first for once.

This wonderful, strong, beautiful woman had become the center of my world. All I wanted was to do what was best for her, even if it tore my heart out in the process.

I cleared my throat and looked at Charlie. "So, I got some good news today."

"Oh?" She looked over curiously as she walked into the kitchen. She skidded to a stop when she saw the mess on the counter and the tray of onion rings, like she'd forgotten she made them.

"Mr. Donald offered me a place in exchange for fixing it up, same arrangement as here. So, I can move out." My heart was racing, and I snagged another onion ring so I didn't have to look directly at her. "These are pretty good, by the way."

"Wait a minute." Charlie held up her hands. "You're leaving? What about our renovation?"

"We're almost done at this point. I can finish the rest easily," I said, trying to assure her. "Besides, you'll be happy to have your privacy back. You don't need me hanging around anymore."

There was a long silence, and then Meatball whined at my feet. It was as if he was trying to tell me this was a terrible idea.

I looked at Charlie, whose face was a mix of confusion and sadness. I wanted to take her in my arms and tell her everything I felt, but instead, I turned around.

"I should start packing."

As I walked upstairs, the heavy sensation in my chest increased. My mind knew this was the right thing to do, for her sake, but my heart felt like it was shattering into a million pieces.

I grabbed my duffel bag from the closet and started to throw my clothes into it haphazardly. Just then Charlie appeared in the doorway.

"Why are you acting like this?" she demanded.

I closed my eyes briefly before grabbing another bundle of clothes from the dresser. "Like what?"

She crossed her arms. "Like it's no big deal that you're leaving. Like we," she gestured between us, "didn't happen?"

"What do you want from me, Charlie? You said we were keeping things casual and that's what I'm doing. Did you expect me to fall in love and beg you to stay with me forever?"

The harsh words felt like knives even as I said them. She winced. "I didn't say that."

"You and me, it was never going to work anyway. It's better

to get out while things are good instead of waiting until you've lost everything."

Charlie came closer. "What are you talking about? Who have you ever lost? You've never been moved from country to country. From school to school. You have your parents, your brothers and your sister. Your friends from *freaking kindergarten*. What do you know about loss?" Her voice broke at the end.

I couldn't stand it anymore. I walked over and pulled her into my arms. She tried to turn away but I slid one hand behind her neck and rested my forehead against hers. Her ragged breathing slowed slightly until we stood there just breathing together.

"What do I know about loss?" I whispered into the space between us. "I know the girl I love has done nothing but leave me over and over again. So why did I think this summer would be any different?"

Charlie looked up at me with shocked eyes and the force of it tore through me. I cursed at what I'd just admitted.

"I have to go."

She didn't say anything else as I walked back over to the bed and zipped up the duffel bag. I couldn't get distracted. Charlie needed to be with her family right now and that meant going back to New York. I was willing to deal with her being mad at me for a while if it made it easier for her to do what she needed to do.

That was what love was about, wasn't it? Putting her happiness above my own.

When I looked up, the room was empty.

She was gone.

Fuck this. I'd get the rest of my stuff later. It wasn't like we wouldn't see each other around as I finished up the final projects on the house. But we'd spent the last two months living, working, and fighting together so it left me with a sick feeling to walk out without so much as a goodbye.

As I grabbed my duffel and threw it over my shoulder, I thought about that last conversation with my dad. He had said it was the easiest thing in the world to come home to your favorite person.

I wish he'd told me how hard it was to walk away.

twenty-eight

. . .

The next morning, I woke to the soft morning light filtering through the curtains. For the first few blissful moments, I listened for the sound of Rix shuffling around downstairs since he was usually up first. Then I remembered.

He was gone.

After he'd left the prior night, I'd tried to carry on. I hadn't wanted to waste the onion rings so I'd eaten a few before my stomach finally rebelled. There was no way Meatball could have really known what was going on but he'd followed me around as if he could sense that I was unsettled.

"I need to stop being such a baby," I muttered as I climbed out of bed.

This was how things originally were supposed to be, wasn't it? Rix was never meant to be my roommate; he had just stumbled into my life. But I had gotten used to him being there making noise and annoying the hell out of me. Now the house felt so big, and the silence seemed so loud.

After a quick shower, I padded downstairs to the kitchen and started making breakfast. A quick glance at my calendar showed that I didn't have any appointments today which I was grateful for. I could curl up on the couch and work on my laptop without having to see anyone.

Meatball followed me over to the table as I sat down with a plate of scrambled eggs. Usually he perched right by my side hoping to catch anything that fell but today, he stopped by the chair on the other side of the table.

The one where Rix usually sat.

"He's not here, buddy." I whistled softly and waited until he came to sit by my side. I scratched behind his ears. "It's just you and me in this big old house now."

Meatball looked over at the other chair again and whined.

I glanced at my phone, wishing there was someone I could call. I could use a friend right now, but for obvious reasons I couldn't call Tana. The main reason I'd wanted to keep things quiet was because of how awkward it would be for her to be in the middle of us. She shouldn't be forced to pick sides.

Retta would say to chase after Rix and bring him back. A part of me wanted to, but there was so much going on in my head.

Maybe he was right and it was better to stop things while we could. With this lawsuit hanging over my family like a dark cloud, I was in no place to make plans for the future.

My heart ached thinking about my little sister possibly having to live with her stuffy grandparents. The thought of her being taken away, after all I had done to keep our family together, made me feel sick.

After I finished breakfast, I cleaned up the kitchen. Last night, I hadn't been thinking clearly and had left it a bit of a mess. Now I took out my frustration with a sponge, scrubbing everything down, even the cabinets.

Once I was done, I went back upstairs to get my phone. Even though my mom said she was handling things, I needed to do some research of my own. I hadn't even known that 'grandparents' rights' were a real thing but I needed a crash course on whatever law that was and fast. Billie was counting on me to fix things and I couldn't afford to drop the ball now.

Then I walked in my bedroom and was hit with a memory of Rix lying spread out in the middle of the bed so I was forced to climb all over him. For such a grump, he was quite a cuddlebug. So many mornings I had woken up half draped over his chest, clinging to him like a starfish. I had loved that.

I had loved him.

I sat down right in the middle of the floor and sobbed. Meatball whimpered and forcefully pushed his way under my arm. I gathered him into my lap and cuddled him close. He licked my cheek, his entire body trembling as he tried to get closer.

"I'm okay." I wiped my eyes and took a deep breath as I tried to get myself under control.

My laugh turned into hiccups as I sat there missing Rix so hard it was a physical ache. The man had said he'd been in love with me since we were kids and I hadn't said *anything*. This was not the most convenient time to realize I had let the love of my life walk away, but then again, I had always had impeccable timing.

Why did it seem like everything was always falling apart at once? I couldn't even deal with how badly I'd screwed things up with Rix because of everything else going on.

There was something seriously wrong with people as rich as the Delacourts coming after someone like my mother who was already in the middle of a legal battle because of *their* son. I might not know them well, but I knew their type.

They probably didn't even want Billie to live with them full-time. This was more about their image than anything else.

So maybe I needed to remind them I had no problem

singing like a canary to whatever reporter would listen. I'm sure *someone* would be interested to know how little time they'd spent with their granddaughter before this.

I wiped my tears and pulled up Alan's number. No more waiting around; it was time we went on the offensive. I wasn't going to let anybody take Billie away and I definitely wasn't going to let anyone push me into selling my home to defend against this ridiculous lawsuit. I'd apply for custody before I'd let that happen. Billie had a family and a home here in Violet Ridge and that had to hold more weight than people who only saw her twice a year.

It was overwhelming to think about all the things that were against us right now, but I'd never been one to back down from a fight.

The funny thing was that Rix was the main one who'd tell me to give everybody hell. He was the one who'd reminded me this town, *this home*, was my legacy and that I needed to fight for it.

He didn't know it yet, but I was going to fight for him, too.

———

Two days later, I felt like I had spent years on the phone with lawyers. Alan had assured me the Delacourts' suit had no merit, but I had called a few other lawyers just to get a second and third opinion. Everyone had pretty much said the same thing. It was apparently pretty difficult to take a child away from their mother, so most thought we didn't have too much to worry about.

That made me feel a little better but I knew I wouldn't truly relax until the suit was withdrawn.

In all this time, I hadn't seen Rix once. After my little breakdown on my bedroom floor, I had decided not to message him right away. It wasn't fair to talk about the future when things were still so unsettled. But that was when I assumed he'd be coming back to finish the few outstanding projects upstairs. He had started replacing the windowsills in the guest room that would be Billie's. Also the small bathroom downstairs had only one wall painted so I'd figured he'd be back to finish that, at least.

Nothing.

I exchanged texts with Tana, Carter, and even went so far as to text Van to see if anyone knew where he was.

Nothing.

Then a little before lunch my phone rang. When I saw who was calling, I almost fumbled my laptop reaching to answer it.

"Hey, Van. Thanks for calling me back. I'm sorry to bother you."

"You're not bothering me. I just saw your message. Rix told me he'd be working late on a rush job for a client."

Even though what he said sounded perfectly fine, there was something in his voice that sounded *off*. It was like he was reciting something from memory or reading items off a list. Which meant he was simply repeating what Hendrix had told him to say.

"Okay, thanks for letting me know." I hung up before I embarrassed myself by crying on the phone.

How was I supposed to fix things when he wouldn't even talk to me? This was why I hadn't wanted to get involved. Sleeping alone and keeping things casual would have kept me safe from feeling like this. But I'd gotten sloppy by letting him sleep in my bed and falling in love with the big lug.

Now that the renovation was mainly over, he apparently had no problem moving on.

I hated that Janelle had turned out to be right, after all. Once I no longer needed him, he was gone.

Joke was on him though because I needed him now more than ever.

———

"Oh, Charlotte, honey. Thank god you finally picked up!"

Groggy, I sat up and looked around in confusion. I had meant to take a quick nap right after lunchtime and ended up sleeping for almost three hours.

"Hey, Mom. What's going on?"

"It's Billie. She got hurt at camp. They just called me."

I jackknifed straight up on the couch. "Is she okay?"

There was a rustling sound and my mom's voice was huffy like she was running. "They said she broke her wrist. I'm going up there to get her right now."

"Okay, I'll follow after I get someone to watch the dog."

"Are you okay, honey?"

Now she wanted to pay attention to my moods? Normally she wouldn't notice if I was out of sorts. If it wasn't so typical, I would have laughed.

"I'm just worried about Billie."

That must have satisfied her because after promising to call as soon as she knew more, she hung up. I sent Tana a text and then went upstairs to pack. Since I didn't know how long I would be gone, I just grabbed all the clothes in the top drawer of my dresser and dumped them in my suitcase. Meatball appeared in the doorway to the room, whimpering. I scooped him up.

"You can tell something's going on, huh buddy?"

He snuggled in to my chest and I scratched him between the ears. His weight was a comforting bundle in my arms so I carried him with me downstairs even though it meant I had to haul the suitcase with one hand. I was still holding him when Tana came to the door twenty minutes later.

"Hey, I got your text and came straight over."

"Thank you. Mom already went to pick Billie up but I told her I'd come as soon as I got Meatball settled."

Tana leaned over to take the dog. "We'll be just fine. I hope Billie's okay."

"Have you heard from Rix today? I texted him but I don't know if he saw it yet."

It was embarrassing to have to ask but I didn't want to just leave without letting him know. What if he tried to come by the house to talk and I was already gone?

Tana didn't look over, just kept scratching Meatball underneath the chin. His leg started kicking in time with her fingers.

"He isn't at work?"

"Van said he was working on some rush job. But it's not like him to not answer his phone."

"Hmm. It's also not like him to take a rush job. You know Rix. He would tell someone to shove it before taking a job that meant he was working around the clock."

Looking worried, she pulled her phone out of her pocket. While Tana was busy, I packed a bag for Meatball with his food and his favorite treats.

Tana appeared in the doorway, Meatball circling her ankles. The look on her face did not help my anxiety.

"What is it?"

She shook her head. "I just talked to Van. He said Rix was busy doing inventory."

Neither of us said anything for a minute but it was clear we were thinking the same thing. Why would Van tell me one thing and Tana another? Unless he was covering for Rix.

Covering for him because he didn't want to talk to me.

"I'm almost scared to ask what's going on," Tana admitted. She still wouldn't look at me.

"I'm in love with your brother."

Her eyes whipped up to meet mine. "You are?"

"Yes. Tana, I know you remember everything that went down at the bar that night but you never said anything."

"You never said anything either!"

"Because it's weird! And I thought that maybe you were mad at me."

"Charlie, I'm not mad at you." She let out a big sigh. "I thought you still had a thing for Carter. I knew Rix liked you, but I was so scared he was going to end up getting hurt. You loved Carter for years and I wasn't sure if Rix had a chance going up against that kind of history."

I winced. "Confession time. Tana, I've never had a thing for Carter. All those times you thought I was talking about my feelings for Carter, I was talking about Rix. You assumed and I let you because it was easier than admitting how I felt about a boy who hated me."

Tana laughed. "Wow. This changes how I remember some things. Actually, this changes everything."

"I'm sorry."

"No, I'm sorry. Because I was upset with you for keeping secrets, but I've been doing the same thing. Everything isn't okay. The shop is in trouble and I'm terrified I'm going to lose everything I've worked for."

I blew out a breath. "It seems like we've both been holding back trying to protect each other. We never used to do that. Why did we start?"

She pulled me into a hug. "I don't know but we need to quit it. No matter where you end up living, you're still my best friend."

Meatball let out a bark that startled us both before shoving his face between us.

I leaned over to kiss the top of his head. "Be good for Tana, huh? I'll be back when I can."

Tana squeezed my arm. "I don't know what's going on with my brother but don't worry about things here. Just make sure Billie is okay."

I grabbed my suitcase and rolled it to the door. The eyes on the picture of Billie Holiday seemed to follow me accusingly as I walked by.

"I'll be back." I said the words aloud, as if hearing them would give them more weight.

Suddenly it seemed like everything was happening so fast. I still didn't feel right about leaving without saying goodbye to Rix. I rubbed the center of my chest which was suddenly aching.

It shouldn't be a huge deal. It wasn't like he wouldn't understand. Billie was hurt. If he'd been there, he would have told me to go.

But I had a terrible feeling that walking out that door was saying goodbye to my life in Violet Ridge forever.

twenty-nine

. . .

HENDRIX

The slick of paint on canvas was the only sound in the room. I wiped my forehead with the bottom of my shirt. It was hot as hell in here. But I'd rather sweat it out than go back home to an empty house. A Charlie-less house.

There was also the little fact that I hated knowing she was mad at me. Charlie hated being ignored, had been that way since we were kids. But I wasn't ready to talk to her yet.

Call me superficial but my ego wasn't bulletproof. The idea that she was going to move on without me was necessary but the reality of it had thrown me for a loop. Funny how my Dad had never said that doing what was best for someone else could hurt this bad.

The door to the shed flew open, hitting the wall with a crash. I spun around at the loud noise. Tana stood in the doorway with fire in her eyes and an armful of Meatball.

"What the hell?"

She marched inside as if she had every right to be there, giving the canvases leaning against the walls only a cursory glance before stopping right in front of me. Meatball growled when they got close. I made a face at him.

"Stop making faces at the dog!" Tana yelled. "You don't get to play with the dog when it's your fault his mother is gone!"

I scowled. "Um, I'm pretty sure his mother left him to roam the streets begging for food from strangers so…"

"*Charlie*, you jackass! She left. And she probably thought I couldn't tell but she had been crying before that. So what did you do?"

I yanked my phone out of my back pocket and cursed when I saw the five new text messages and three calls. Ignoring her had seemed like a better option than starting a fight earlier, but I hadn't thought she would just leave town.

"What exactly did she say?"

Tana sighed, looking like she was on the verge of tears herself. "Her message said that she had to go back to New York and could I watch Meatball until she could send for him? So I just went and picked him up. But I don't even think she realizes she wrote that. *Send. For. Him.* That means she isn't coming back."

"Fuck."

"I repeat, *what the hell did you do?*"

The panic I felt at hearing she'd actually left mixed with the brutal awareness that I should have expected this.

"Why are you assuming I did something? This is what Charlie does: she blows through town and gets everybody all riled up and then she bails. Just when we've all gotten used to the idea that she might like us enough to actually stick around."

Tana shook her head. "No. She was happy here. Something changed. What changed?"

"Her mom called. Something about Billie. Her family needs her."

Tana waved her hand impatiently. Meatball tried to lick it

and then grumbled when he wasn't fast enough. "No, Billie's going to be fine. She just got hurt at summer camp. That's why Charlie left today, to go check on her."

Relief bloomed quick and bright. "That's why she left. Why are you panicking?" I placed a hand over my heart.

God, Tana was going to give me a heart attack.

She closed her eyes briefly as if I was just so stupid she couldn't bear it. "Billie is why she left. You are the reason she might not come back."

"Her mom said they needed to sell the house for the money. It's not like they were going to be here forever anyway. The only reason she came back was because she didn't have anywhere else to go. She was never going to stay here."

Tana held Meatball up like a weapon. "Pee, Meatball. *Pee on him!*"

I backed away almost tripping on the leg of the easel. "What the fuck? Why are you so weird?"

"You deserve it for being a dick. No wonder she left."

"So Charlie ditches us and somehow I'm the bad guy?"

Unbelievable. Even when I was trying to do the right thing I was still seen as the problem?

"If you believe for even one second that Charlie would ever want to sell Gran Grace's house, then you don't deserve her." Tana turned around and walked away.

"I heard her on the phone, Tana. Something about a lawsuit. They need the money."

"Well, I don't know what you heard but I know that Charlie would mortgage everything she owned before she would sell Gran Grace's house. And I would, too."

That made me pause. "I don't think it's that simple. There's a lot going on and it's not like she asked for my help. I'm not even supposed to know about it. She felt bad about leaving me in the lurch so I told her I already had a new place. I was trying to do the right thing and make it easier for her."

Tana wiped under her eyes. "I don't even blame her if she stays gone. What's here for her other than reminders of the life she never got to have and a boyfriend who doesn't believe in her enough to wait? She deserves people who will fight for her. If I could go back in time, I would have never let our Rescue Charlie plan go. I should have fought for her. So this is not just on you. It's on me, too."

It wasn't often I saw Tana looking so defeated. Even when we were kids, she was this bossy little ball of energy that kept us all on our toes.

"Rescue Charlie plan? Why would you think she needed to be rescued? I thought living in New York was her dream?"

Tana gave me a dirty look. Meatball's wasn't much better. "Charlie never wanted to live in New York."

My face was probably telegraphing my disbelief but I shook my head just to be clear. "It was all she talked about. How she was going to live in a penthouse and go to all those fancy shops you two always talked about. She was all too happy to leave us behind."

"Men seriously do hear what they want to hear. Charlie wanted to *visit* New York. She figured after high school her mom would be happily remarried to the step-jerk and Charlie would still be living here with Gran. She'd go visit but then she'd come back home. To Violet Ridge. To us."

Was it possible that I'd gotten it wrong all those years ago? I'd always assumed that Charlie had been happy to leave and go live in her stepfather's swanky new penthouse in the sky. It wasn't like there was much for her here.

What, did I think that she'd actually be attracted to the local handyman who barely graduated high school? The guy who could never give her all those fancy things she talked about?

"She didn't want to leave?"

"No. Living with Gran was what she wanted. But then Gran died and everything changed. Overnight Charlie went from happy and carefree to carrying the weight of the world on her shoulders. That house was her safe place but it was only safe because of Gran Grace. After that, she had to finish her senior year at that snooty school in Manhattan."

"She could have come back after high school. So what happened?"

Tana smiled. "Billie happened."

In that moment, I understood. Charlie had always wanted a sibling. She'd told Tana many times how lucky she was to have brothers. I'm sure she was talking about Van more so than me but still, if Billie had come along right after she finished high school there was no way she'd leave a baby sibling behind.

"She stayed to help her mom with Billie and also to make sure she was a part of her little sister's life. But I'm sure she would have come back to Violet Ridge more if a certain person hadn't made her life hell!"

There was nothing I could say to that because she was right. Over the years, annoying Charlie had seemed so much easier than facing how much it hurt every time she would leave. Not that it had helped at all. Pretending I didn't care hadn't changed the hollow feeling inside every time she left town.

"Tell me what to do here, Tana. I want this to work and I want to make her happy. Whenever I try it falls apart."

Tana let out a huge sigh. "I don't know. I just know that you have to fix it. Or this time we'll have lost her for good."

She turned to go, Meatball perched high on her shoulder. Even the dog looked defeated as he watched me accusingly.

Yeah, it's my fault. I feel like shit already.

"Despite what you think I always wanted her to stay," I said just as Tana reached the door.

She looked over her shoulder at me. "I know. I just wish it was enough."

———

Trying to paint after that had seemed pointless. After cleaning my brushes, I had gone back to the house on Magnolia but couldn't stop staring at the blank walls. Swinging a hammer in that mood hadn't seemed like the best idea.

Hell, going out drinking probably hadn't been the best idea either

"Another round." I slapped a twenty on the bar.

The bartender wasn't anyone I recognized which was a relief. The whole point of coming to a bar outside of town was because I didn't feel like talking.

The faint scent of stale beer and cigarette smoke hung in the air, a perfect complement to my sour mood. The place was a dive, but I had to give it points for being clean at least. The glasses were clear and someone was clearly wiping down the wood regularly. It was scarred in several places but it was polished to a high shine.

"Here." The bartender slid a fresh glass toward me. "On the house. Hendrix, right?" he asked.

"Who's asking?" I looked at him closely.

Fuck. He was probably one of my cousins. The thought made my head hurt.

"I'm Jimmy. I went to school with your Uncle David."

"Great. So this will be all over town by tomorrow morning."

He chuckled. "I'm a bartender. We know how to keep our mouths shut. A man should be able to drink away his woman troubles in peace."

I threw back the drink, the warmth of the scotch spreading through my chest like fire. It wasn't enough to make me forget Charlie was gone but it was a decent start.

"How did you know I had woman troubles?" I muttered, staring at my reflection in the mirror behind the rows of liquor bottles.

He shrugged. "Who doesn't?"

I figured this was the part where he expected me to spill my guts but instead he moved down the bar to help another customer. Clearly he didn't give a fuck about my problems. That made me laugh.

This might be my new favorite place.

I didn't need a therapist just some time to figure out what the hell I was doing. Leaving was supposed to make things easier on Charlie, but if what Tana said was true, then everything I'd thought about her was wrong.

Maybe going back to New York wasn't what was best for Charlie.

Which meant that I had well and truly fucked this up.

I wasn't sure how long I was there before the place started to fill up. Someone bumped my arm and I moved over slightly. Ice clinked against the glass as I took the last gulp of scotch. After the first few, the bartender had starting bringing them without me even having to ask. The burn wasn't going to ease my frustration, but it dulled the pain a little. Maybe if I had enough of these I could forget the shock in Charlie's eyes when I'd told her I was in love with her while I was leaving.

I dropped my head down on the scarred wood. I'd used my feelings for her like some kind of trump card, a gotcha to twist the knife before I left her behind.

"You're going at it a little hard, nephew." David stood next to me but when I blinked, suddenly there were two of him.

"Uncle David?" I mumbled, attempting to sit up straight but almost falling off the stool.

Just then Jimmy appeared. "Thanks for coming."

My brain felt like it was encased in quicksand, but I finally put together that he must have called him.

"Hey, you told my uncle on me?" I could hear my words slurring a little.

"Sorry, Rix." Jimmy almost sounded like he meant it. "I had to, man. You're in no condition to drive."

Even as drunk as I was, I had enough sense to feel ashamed. I wasn't going to drive drunk but I was in the next town over, with no way to get home. I hadn't even thought about it until now.

"Thanks, Jimmy." David clapped me on the shoulder. "I've got him."

"Sorry about this, Uncle D," I muttered, my pride stinging at the thought of needing someone to see me home.

But deep down, I knew they were right. I was in no state to be driving, or making any decisions for that matter.

"No need to be sorry. We've all been there. I was probably sitting on that same stool drinking away some brain cells when Tammy left me."

When I stumbled getting up, he grabbed my arm and waited until I had my balance.

"I was just trying to protect her. I thought I was doing the right thing," I mumbled.

"I'm sure you did," David said patiently.

It seemed like it took a million years but we finally reached his truck. In the time I'd been there, the parking lot had filled up so he was at the edge of the lot next to the road.

"Wait, Rix. Let me pull out a bit so it's easier to get in. There's a ditch–"

Maybe he didn't say it loud enough or maybe I just wasn't

listening but the next thing I knew I was on my back staring up at the stars.

"Okay, never mind," David chuckled.

"This is rock bottom, isn't it?" I groaned as the ache in my back registered. I wasn't sure what I'd landed on but this ditch felt like it was filled with rocks.

"It could be worse," David reminded me. "He could have called your father."

"She's gone, Uncle D. I shouldn't have let her go."

He sighed. "Probably not. But sometimes we don't have a choice."

"I should go after her. I'm going after her." I struggled to sit up.

"Maybe let's get the dog shit off your clothes first. How's that sound?"

It was so dark I could barely see but there was no mistaking that smell. "Uncle D? Let's keep this between us, yeah?"

He hoisted me up. "I've been keeping your secrets for years, kid. Not planning to stop now."

thirty

· · ·

HENDRIX

back in the day...

I wasn't supposed to be here.

Carter leaned on the back of my Firebird. I'd spent all of the past summer working on it with my dad.

"We should get out of here before Tana spots us," he mumbled. He threw the cigarette he'd recently started smoking to be cool on the ground before stomping on it.

"How is Tana going to spot us? Everyone is inside."

He shrugged. "Your sister has radar. Didn't you and Van already threaten her date earlier? I'm pretty sure the dude is going to be too traumatized to even get it up later."

I punched him in the arm. "Stop talking about my sister having sex!"

"I wasn't! I was talking about her not having sex." He moved away before I could punch him again, rubbing his arm. "Dude, you have got to calm down. I'm glad I don't have any sisters."

My eyes roved over the mostly empty parking lot. We were

both seniors so we could have gone to the prom if we'd wanted to, but Tana had already warned me to stay away if I wanted to keep my dick intact. It wasn't like I cared about prom shit anyway, which she knew. I hadn't cared at all about going until recently.

Until I heard that Charlie was going.

With Kenny Baker.

That little prick.

"No one is even out here. What are we waiting for?"

"Just checking things out." I avoided his eyes.

I couldn't tell him that I wasn't sure exactly what I was waiting for but that I would know it when I saw it.

A group of guys came out of the school, laughing and clapping each other on the back. Things were so quiet it was easy to hear everything they were saying.

"You aren't getting anywhere with Saint Santana. I heard she wouldn't even dance with you without a foot of space between you. Enough room for the Holy Ghost."

Laughter rang out. I straightened from where I'd been leaning against the car.

Carter groaned. "Fuck. They're being dicks, but if you start a fight Tana is going to kill you."

Kenny's voice carried toward us again. "Me on the other hand, I am about to have my hands all over Charlie Monroe's fine ass. While you're dancing with the Holy Ghost, I'm going to take Charlie behind the bleachers and show her what heaven is really like."

They were so busy laughing I was almost on them before one of Kenny's friends noticed me.

"Oh shit." He broke away from the group and ran back to the gymnasium door.

At least one of them had some sense.

Kenny yelled after him. "Where are you going?"

I tapped him on the shoulder. The others backed away slowly.

"He probably went to tell everybody about the fight."

Kenny looked at me warily. "What fight?"

I punched him in the face.

His friends erupted into a loud chorus of ohs, ahhs, and did you see that's? None of them bothered to help him up, I noticed.

"What the hell man? What is your problem?" Kenny rolled away and struggled to get up.

"Not such a big man now, huh? Talking shit about what you plan to do behind the bleachers."

His eyes rounded. "Whoa. I don't know what you heard but I didn't say anything about Santana. We're just friends."

"You think I'm only mad about what you said about my sister? So it's okay for you to talk shit about Charlie because she doesn't have a brother to beat your ass?"

He jumped up and rushed at me. I shoved him off me. He grabbed a rock from the ground and flung it in my direction. I laughed.

"Fight! Fight! Fight!"

I glanced around at all the people screaming. The crowd had grown considerably in the last few minutes. Like sharks scenting blood in the water, they wanted to see something happen. They were hungry for it.

"What the hell is your problem? It's not like Charlie's your girl or something?" Kenny narrowed his eyes. "Or is that your problem? You want her and you know she's going home with me tonight."

"She's not going anywhere with you."

His friends were chanting his name now, asking him what he was going to do. His eyes darted around, aware that everyone was watching.

"You sure about that?"

I punched him right in the mouth.

The crowd erupted as the guys around us went crazy, screaming and chanting. Suddenly someone pushed through the wall of people.

Santana glared at me.

Shit.

Wherever Tana went...

Charlie appeared right next to her, her eyes on the guy on the ground. "Oh my god. Kenny?"

The idiot was playing it up, too, moaning like he was dying. Already he had the beginning of a beautiful shiner on his left eye. He wiped the edge of his bleeding lip with the sleeve of his tuxedo.

I smiled. Yeah, there was no way he was getting his deposit back.

Charlie knelt next to him on the asphalt and reached out to help him up. He pushed her hands away and stood on his own.

"All this for some pussy. Not even worth it," he mumbled.

Her face fell.

If I could have punched him in the mouth again for that comment, I would have.

Charlie spun around to face me. "Rix, what the hell are you doing here?"

"I was in the neighborhood."

"And your first order of business was to beat up my prom date? For no reason?"

"Why don't you ask your boyfriend why I punched him?" I raised my voice loud enough to make sure Kenny could hear me.

He didn't look back.

Coward.

The crowd had mostly dispersed now that the fun part was over.

Charlie threw her hands in the air. "It's not enough that you annoy the hell out of me every other day but you had to ruin my prom, too. Great work."

My heart turned over in my chest. Even angry, Charlie was beautiful with her dark eyes flashing and a flush to her golden-brown skin. Maybe that was why I loved to annoy her so much.

I would take any of her attention I could get.

But that wasn't what was best for her, was it? She was bright and shiny and had a future to match. This time next year she'd be in New York City just like she'd always talked about, living the life of her dreams. Why was I still poking at her, desperate for her to notice me when I knew that she was destined for greater things?

I called myself protecting her but maybe the best way to protect her was to leave her alone.

"Then I guess my work here is done."

I turned to walk away.

Tana pulled her into a hug. "I'm sorry everything got so messed up. I don't know what Hendrix was doing. He wasn't even supposed to be here."

Charlie sniffed. "Doing what he always does. Ruining everything."

thirty-one

. . .

CHARLOTTE

The drive back to New York had seemed even longer than I remembered. By the time I got in town, my mom had taken Billie home. She was sporting a splint on her wrist that she was already tired of wearing.

The penthouse still looked the same. I don't know why I thought it would look different. Maybe because it seemed like so much had changed over the past two months that I expected everyone and everything else to have changed, too. But it was the same architectural marvel filled with expensive, uncomfortable furniture and decorated with the anemic color scheme my mom loved. I called it the *everything beige special*.

"I'm bored. There's nothing to do here." Billie had been especially whiny since Mom left to pick up ice cream.

Not that I blamed her. It had to stink to be escorted to the hospital by camp counselors in front of her friends. Did they even have camp counselors at this bougie camp? I wasn't sure. They probably didn't call them that anyway. I'm sure they were *activity specialists* or *leisure facilitators*.

Give me s'mores and campfire tales any day.

"I'm just glad you're okay, kid."

"I'm not okay. *I'm so bored.*"

She slumped over in bed, her face twisted in mock agony. Apparently boredom was a fate worse than death for a nine-year-old. Geez, and people thought teenagers were dramatic.

"You're supposed to be bored. That's what taking it easy means. Being nice and calm and not moving your wrist. Luckily it was just a sprain."

She pouted. "I liked parkour. Now I'm going to miss *everything.*"

"I still can't believe they were letting you all do that. Aren't they supposed to be supervising so you don't get hurt? Unless you were doing something you weren't *supposed* to be doing?"

Suddenly Billie wouldn't meet my eyes. "Where's Meatball? I want to meet him."

"I wasn't sure what was going on so I left him with my friend. But you'll meet him soon."

I felt a literal pang at the thought of my little guy. Not that I needed to worry. He was probably living in Santana's lap being spoiled beyond belief.

"I can't wait. I don't really remember Gran Grace's house. What's it like there?"

"You were really young the last time we visited. It's this great big old Victorian with a cool attic room you can play in and a huge backyard."

"I wish I could have met her," she said.

Being angry at death was stupid and futile but it was infuriating that a heart attack could change the course of so many lives. Obviously I was devastated to lose the most important person in my life, but it made me unspeakably sad to think of all the love Billie had missed out on just because she hadn't been born earlier.

"She would have absolutely loved you," I whispered.

Billie picked at a loose thread on her blanket. "I won't know anyone there."

"That's okay. My friend Tana knows everyone and she's going to host a party with all her family and friends so we can meet some new people. A lot of them have kids around your age."

"Do you think they'll like me?" she asked in a small voice.

"They're going to love you. How many kids there can claim a battle wound from jumping off a roof?"

She giggled. "It wasn't a roof. It was just a fence."

"Either way it's way more adventurous than anything I've done. I trip over my own feet."

She was quiet again. Billie could be like that. She was so strong and assertive but had these unexpected moments of uncertainty that always hit me right in the gut.

"What's the matter? I know this is all a lot to take in."

Billie sighed. "I miss my dad."

I closed my eyes. "I know. I'm sorry."

She sniffed. "Mom said that he's out on bail and he's going to come see me soon. But that there were some people yelling outside so they decided it was better for him to stay away."

"Since you're home from camp early, I'm sure you'll see him a lot. They're just being careful." I definitely didn't know how to talk to her about the protestors. Alan had mentioned it, but it hadn't really sunk in that it meant my sister was seeing people with picket signs calling her father the devil. My heart hurt for her.

Her eyes were bright with tears. "My summer independent project was going to be about the Axolotl. He was helping me. He even got me a shirt that said 'You Axolotl Questions'. It was so corny."

She leaned into my shoulder and I pulled her into a hug.

She was so mature for her age that sometimes it was easy to forget that she was just a kid.

"And if we move, I'm going to miss my friends. My friend Keri signed up for French classes next year so we can take it together. I was going to tutor her."

"Nothing about this is fair, I know."

After a long sigh, she wiped her eyes. "I just don't understand how we're going to live in Gran's house when Mom said that we might be living on a yacht next year. That we could travel around the world."

"She said what? Who has a yacht?"

Billie shrugged. "I don't know. But she seemed really excited about it. You know how she gets."

I had a sinking feeling in my stomach. My mother loved the idea of an adventure and usually didn't stop to ask whether it was really the best thing long-term.

Or the best thing for a child.

Or best for anyone other than herself.

"I know exactly how she can get." I patted Billie's hand before leaving to get her another ice pack.

When Mom came back with the ice cream, I took the opportunity to retreat to the guest room. Billie had been through enough and didn't need to see us fight.

I decided to bide my time and really think through what I wanted to say. But if my mother was doing what I suspected then we needed to have a serious talk.

Because after living through her idea of an adventure before, I wasn't going to let her do that to my little sister.

It was after midnight before my mom was able to coax Billie to sleep. When she came back downstairs, I was sitting at the kitchen counter waiting.

"Honey, I didn't know you were still up. You must be tired after driving straight here."

She pulled a bottle of wine from the custom rack built into the cabinetry. Exhaustion was all over her face, making the lines around her eyes, the ones I knew she hated, stand out in stark relief against the honey hue of her skin.

It was hard to stare at a face so similar to my own and realize I didn't know the person beneath.

"I wanted to talk to you."

She poured herself a glass of wine before holding it up, asking if I wanted some. I shook my head.

"Billie is going to be fine, honey. The doctor said it was just a sprain. The silly girl was already asking if she could go back to camp to see her friends!"

"I know. She'll be fine for now but what about next month? She mentioned something about a yacht? What is going on? I thought you guys were getting ready to move to Violet Ridge with me?"

She shifted uncomfortably. "We are, baby. But that's just a temporary fix. We can't stay there forever."

"Why not? I've worked so hard fixing the house up. It's a safe town. The perfect place for Billie to grow up."

"Oh Charlie." The words sounded like a weight. "With this lawsuit going on, I thought it might be wise to get away for a bit. I assume you heard about the protestors."

"Yeah, Billie told me. But that doesn't mean you can just sail away and never look back. Billie needs to be in school."

"It wouldn't be forever. I have a friend who has this amazing place in Greece. She invited us to stay while all these protests are going on."

Understanding dawned. "This is why the Delacourts are

suing, isn't it? They found out you're trying to take Billie out of the country."

She looked uncomfortable but didn't deny it. "We're going on vacation. All of this has gotten blown way out of proportion."

"A vacation that is going to take Billie away from her school and her friends. Did you think about that part?"

She waved that away. "She makes friends so easily. She'll be fine."

"Like I was fine? I wasn't fine, Mom. I've missed the friends I left behind every day since. Friends aren't interchangeable."

"I'm sorry, Charlie. I know I wasn't the perfect mother. I never thought I was."

"I didn't need you to be perfect. I just needed you to think about what I needed. You know, I really thought you'd changed but you still don't get it and now I have to watch you do the same thing to Billie. Did you ever intend to stay in Violet Ridge at all? Or was that a lie from the very beginning?"

She crossed her arms. "Watch your tone young lady. I am still your mother."

"Were you ever planning to stay?" I repeated.

"I figured we would stay there until you sold the house. Then we could come back to New York. Back home."

"*This is not home.* Violet Ridge is home. You were born there!"

"And left as soon as I could. I've never understood your attachment to the place. You only lived there for a few years and that was only because Mom wouldn't stop bugging me about it."

"Gran Grace did that for me. To protect me. I didn't want to live in the city, moving from apartment to apartment. How many new schools did I go to? How many friends did I have to leave behind before I figured out that there was no point making them?"

Mom threw up her hands. "I don't know what you want me to say. I'm sorry for wanting more for you than a small life in that backwoods town! I wanted you to have the choices I didn't have. I didn't want you to have to settle. I wanted you to have adventures."

"I want the small-town life. That's *my* adventure."

I stood up. I needed to get away before I said something I couldn't take back. My bag was resting against the side of the couch. I'd dropped it there when I first came in. I walked over and picked it up.

"Where are you going?" Mom asked.

"To my apartment. While I'm here I'm going to clean it out and box up the things I want to bring back with me."

She sighed. "Okay. What should I tell Billie? I'm sure she'll be asking for you in the morning."

"Tell her I'll be back for breakfast. I'm not leaving. I wouldn't do that to her." I paused at the front door with my hand on the doorknob.

"Please just think about what's best for Billie before you make any decisions. Because I know what it's like to be uprooted and I'm not going to let you do that to her."

The walls felt like they were closing in on me as I made my way to my apartment, which was only a few floors down. Christian owned all the apartments on that floor and most were used as corporate housing for visiting executives.

When I got off the elevator, I pulled out my keys and found the right one. My hands shook as I inserted the key, feeling the familiar click of the lock disengaging.

The moment I stepped inside, memories flooded my mind. Working late on accounts for a boss that wouldn't notice my hard work anyway. Countless nights sitting on the couch watching TV while Aaron was on his phone. Walking in on him packing. As I looked around, it all felt so foreign, like I was trespassing in someone else's life.

My phone vibrated and I pulled it out. Hopefully it wasn't my mom asking me to come back tonight. I thought it was best for us to have some space before we spoke again.

RETTA

I got your message. How is Billie?

CHARLIE

She's fine. The crazy girl was already bored and asking for ice cream.

RETTA

That's great. I'm so glad she's okay. How are YOU?

CHARLIE

Currently staring at all the stuff I need to clean out of this apartment.

RETTA

I'm coming over. I'll bring wine and we can burn Aaron's shit together.

CHARLIE

You're the best.

I wiped my eyes and took a deep breath. With Retta there to help me, going through everything wouldn't be so bad. It was impossible to be depressed in her presence. Although I should probably try to clean up a little before she got there.

As I walked back up front, it was obvious that Aaron had come back while I was gone at least once. The throw blanket that was usually carefully placed on the back of the couch was haphazardly thrown on the floor. There were a few dishes in the sink and there was a sour smell coming from the trash can.

He couldn't even be bothered to clean up his mess before he left. Typical.

As I loaded the dishwasher, I looked around the beautiful, state-of-the-art kitchen. Everything was brand new and high-end. Then I thought of my ancient kitchen at Gran Grace's with the scarred oak cabinets and the uneven counters. It might be old but everything in that house was attached to a memory. I didn't have any memories attached to this gorgeously cold apartment.

And I had never felt at home here.

The doorbell rang, and I raced over to answer it. When I swung the door open, Retta stood there, grinning like a kid on Christmas morning.

"Let's get this party started!" She was armed with bottles of wine, a box of chocolates, and a huge tote bag.

I gave her a hug before stepping aside to let her pass. "I can't tell you how glad I am to see you."

"Same here, girl," Retta replied, bustling into the living room and depositing her load on the coffee table.

While she uncorked one of the wine bottles, I brought over glasses. She poured both of us generous servings before settling in on the couch.

"All right. We might as well get to the good stuff right away. What's going on with your hot handyman?"

It didn't take much for me to spill the whole tale. Retta listened attentively, nodding at all the right places and asking questions. But as I spoke, I could tell she was holding something back.

"Retta." I narrowed my eyes at her. "Why do I get the feeling there's something you aren't saying?"

"Who me?" she asked innocently, taking another sip of her wine. "I'm just listening."

"No," I insisted, setting my glass down on the table. "There's something you want to say, I can tell. So just say it."

"Fine. But promise you won't get mad, okay?"

"There really is something? Tell me!" I demanded.

"All right, all right," she said, raising her hands in surrender. "I was just going to say that I can see why Rix might have done what he did. He's used to you leaving. And let's face it, you're not the best at keeping in touch."

Her words stung, but I knew she was right. I had a habit of putting things out of my mind that I didn't want to deal with. Not running away, exactly, but avoidance for sure.

"I don't mean to."

She reached over and squeezed my hand. "I know. You've been hurt so many times that it probably seemed easier to just forget people instead of having to miss them. I get it. But maybe he doesn't?"

I stared into my half-empty wine glass. Retta watched me nervously.

"Hey," she said softly, reaching for my hand. "Don't listen to me, okay? You've got enough on your plate with your mom and sister."

But I couldn't shake what she'd said. All my life, I'd been trying to make everyone else happy—my mom, my sister, even Aaron. And yet, it had never seemed like enough.

"Ever since Christian got arrested, I feel like I've been running in circles trying to make things okay for us."

Retta sighed. "Maybe it's not your job to make everything okay."

"If I don't try, who will? I've been trying so hard to keep Billie from being uprooted the way I was. And now it might all have been for nothing."

"Sweetie, Billie was going to be uprooted no matter what. Even if she'd moved to Violet Ridge with you."

I blinked as that sank in. Billie had told me herself how much she was going to miss her friends and the classes she'd signed up for next year. This whole time I had been operating under the assumption that I was saving her but the truth was that I was uprooting her, too. Fighting for her should mean helping her get to stay where she wanted to be. Violet Ridge was my home but it wasn't hers.

"I'm doing the same thing to her that my mom did to me. How did I miss that?" I rested my head against the back of the couch.

Retta looked sympathetic. "You were doing the best you could. I don't think there's a handbook for when your sister's father gets arrested for fraud."

I snorted a laugh at that. "No. There isn't." I glanced over at Retta. "It's going to get worse before it gets better, isn't it?"

"Probably." She refilled our glasses, emptying out the bottle. "Hey, how long are you going to be here?"

I looked around the room. "Well, I need to box up everything I want to keep. So probably a few days at least. Why?"

"Because I don't have another temp job lined up until the end of the week. I'm living with my mother and she's driving me crazy. So how about I stay with you and help you get this place cleaned out?"

"Really?"

"Absolutely." Retta nodded. "And tomorrow morning, we'll throw all Aaron's shit in the trash."

"Deal." We clinked our glasses. "Although throwing everything out might be a little cold-blooded."

"Fine, we'll recycle," Retta amended, rolling her eyes.

thirty-two

. . .

HENDRIX

I woke up with my face buried in a pillow that wasn't mine. I blinked, trying to piece together where I was.

Then the door opened.

"Morning," David said, placing a glass of orange juice and a bottle of Tylenol on the bedside table. The faint smell of bacon wafted in with him, making my stomach churn. "Thought you might need these."

"Thanks, Uncle D."

I took the pills and chased them down with the orange juice. My mouth felt like sandpaper. Drinking had seemed like a good idea last night, but now I wished someone had cut me off earlier.

"I'm sorry you had to come pick me up last night."

"Hey, don't worry about it." He crossed his arms. "I'm just glad I got there before you hurt yourself or someone else."

"I wouldn't drive drunk," I assured him. "I know better than that."

"No one knows what they'll do when they're that wasted.

And talking is cheaper than booze. Besides, everyone already knows you and Charlie broke up."

"It was only a matter of time before she got pulled back to New York. Now she can be with her family without guilt. They need her."

"Her family needs her, huh?" Uncle David asked, but I could tell by the tone of his voice he didn't agree. "And that's what got you so hammered last night?"

"I'm fine." I rubbed my temples in an attempt to chase away the remnants of my headache.

David raised an eyebrow. "Fine isn't sucking down scotch like water. You obviously need to talk to someone before you drown your liver."

Uncle David wasn't my first choice of confidante, but it was either him or my father and I definitely didn't need another Evers lecture on true love.

"You know," David said finally, "you got just like this the last time she left."

The room suddenly seemed uncomfortably hot. I threw off the blankets. "No, I didn't. We hated each other."

I'd never hated her but that didn't mean I was ready to admit that to him.

"I'm going to put something out there. It might be crazy. But is it possible that you *didn't* hate her? That you were actually in love with Charlie in high school?"

My first instinct was to deny it, but then images of the last month flashed through my mind. Fixing her house while getting my fix of her sweet smiles. Then I thought of how I'd left her without a proper goodbye. A pang of guilt twisted in my gut.

"Maybe," I conceded finally.

"Is it possible that you are in love with her now?"

I glared at him.

He smiled triumphantly. "Hah. I knew it."

I ran a frustrated hand through my hair. "It feels just like it did last time. Like I'm chasing her but can't catch her. No matter how fast I run."

He sighed. "Things are different now. You're not kids anymore."

"Maybe not. But this place hasn't changed. Neither have I."

"What hasn't changed is that you still aren't telling her what's important."

"Like that worked last time."

"You're right, you haven't changed. You're still a dumbass. She was a kid last time. She didn't have control of her own life then."

"I didn't say it was her fault. I don't blame her for leaving. She wanted something better."

"Did she? Because the way I remember it is that you didn't give her a reason to stay because you were too chicken shit to confess how you felt then. You just beat up her boyfriend with no explanation."

"Kenny Baker wasn't fit to touch her."

"And you are?"

Images of Kenny's bruised face flashed through my mind, that piece of crap smirking as he boasted to his buddies about what he wanted to do with Charlie. I wished I could punch him all over again.

"At least I wasn't just trying to brag to my little buddies about how I screwed her on prom night!"

"All right, so you protected her from some jerk," Uncle David conceded. "But did you ever tell her why? Did you ever let her know how much she meant to you?"

I swallowed hard, feeling the weight of his words press

down on me. I hadn't told her, not really. Blurting it out before walking away didn't really count. I'd been too scared to put myself out there, to risk losing her forever. But hadn't I lost her anyway by not fighting for her?

"No," I admitted quietly. "Not really. But I do love her."

David regarded me with stony eyes. "I know that. You know that. Guess who doesn't? Charlie. *So tell her.*"

Annoyed to have been so easily outwitted, I flopped back down on the bed. What he was saying made sense if you were on the outside looking in. If it wasn't your heart that would be shattered if you told a woman that she was your reason for living and she didn't care.

After all, my heat of the moment confession to Charlie hadn't exactly been met with enthusiasm. Yes, some of that was because we were in the middle of an argument. But I'd basically admitted that I'd loved her since we were kids and she hadn't said anything. Just stared at me in horror.

"I'm not just busting your balls for no reason, Rix. Anybody with eyes can see that girl is into you."

I took a deep breath, trying to steady myself. "I'm just trying to do the right thing for Charlie. She always puts her family first, and I don't blame her. I thought it would be easier if she could leave with nothing tying her down."

"I understand what you're trying to do but families grow all the time. How do you think you arrived in this world?"

"Seriously?" I rolled my eyes. "I don't need a birds and bees talk."

"Are you sure about that?" He grinned, but his eyes remained serious. "Because it seems like you've forgotten that people leaving their families to form new ones is how the world turns. The problem here is that you never actually asked Charlie to stay. You just made the decision for her."

His words stung, but I couldn't deny the truth in them. I

had been too afraid to face the possibility of losing her, so I'd pushed her away instead. My hands clenched into fists as I tried to find the right words.

"What if I do that and it doesn't work? What if she doesn't want to stay?"

"Then at least you'll know you tried," David replied firmly. "Show her how much she means to you, Rix. Give her a reason to stay."

———

Nothing was the same with Charlie gone. All the things we'd said and done swirled around my brain as I attempted to continue my usual routine.

Shifts at the hardware store.

Spending time with my family.

Painting.

However, as I went about my usual routine it was obvious there wasn't anything usual about it. There was a gaping Charlie-sized hole where all my happiness used to be. A hole so big I was pretty sure everyone around me could see right through it.

I wanted her dancing around making pancakes and singing off-key when she thought no one could hear. I even missed her million and one lists for everything and all the times she pointed her "attack" dog at me.

God I even missed that little gremlin.

I missed all the things that brought Charlie-flavored joy into my life and if I didn't get my head out of my ass she was never going to come back. Instinctively I knew this time was different. We weren't kids who'd fucked up a good thing because we were young and immature. If we didn't learn to speak the same language and figure this thing out then we were both going to suffer. This was the kind of hurt that not even time could heal.

However, David's words rang through my mind. If I wanted her then I needed to give her a reason to stay. So far I hadn't done such a great job at that. Instead I specialized in running away, leaving before I could get left. This wasn't the time to be a coward. If I wanted Charlie to see the big, beautiful, messy life I envisioned, then I needed to show her.

I needed to paint it like a picture.

The idea slammed into me with all the subtlety of a truck. I hung my head. Instead of drinking like a fish and rage painting, I could have been working on something for Charlie. Something that could show her how I felt.

I wasn't good with grand gestures. Never had been. I was a hands-on kind of guy. I might not be able to give her poetry and diamonds, but I could give her the one thing she really wanted. While Charlie was gone, I would finish the renovation and get the other bedrooms ready.

I sighed. I was going to need some backup if I wanted to get this done quickly.

HENDRIX

You want to install kitchen cabinets with me this weekend?

VAN

Why would I want to do that?

HENDRIX

You wouldn't but you owe me this. You owe me.

VAN

I let you live with me.

HENDRIX

And charged me rent.

VAN

Still counts.

HENDRIX

I saw your ass.

VAN

…

VAN

What kind of cabinets?

I sent him a middle finger emoji before I switched over to text Tana. It was about fifty-fifty whether she would ignore me but I was counting on her wanting to help.

HENDRIX

Is it too late to pull off the Rescue Charlie plan?

A few minutes went by before I saw the little bubbles dancing around indicating that she was typing. Then they stopped. Then they started moving again.

HENDRIX

I know I'm an ass and ten years too late. Cut me a break here.

TANABANANA

As long as you know it.

HENDRIX

She's worth it. That's all I know.

The phrase stuck in my head. She was worth it. It was alarming how different my life could be if I'd figured that out ten years ago. I'd been so focused on all the things I couldn't give her that I'd never bothered to ask about what Charlie actually needed.

Anyone else would have been pissed to have to fix up and live in a ramshackle old house, but Charlie had never seemed happier than she was puttering around that place making her plans. All she'd ever talked about were the things she wanted to do in town and the friends she would invite over. The life she wanted to live.

In Violet Ridge.

One day I'm going to live in Gran Grace's house...

And I'll never have to leave...

She'd told me what she wanted when we were kids. It had just taken me two decades to really hear her.

The men in New York might be able to offer her more money but they couldn't hope to beat the force of an Evers man on a mission. If she wanted family then I had plenty to share. If I was lucky I could give her a new last name, too.

Buoyed as the beginnings of a plan formed, I knew it wasn't going to be as easy as it seemed. I couldn't just call her out of the blue and think everything was forgiven.

And that wasn't me being dramatic. I literally couldn't call her because I was ninety percent sure she'd blocked my number when I was ignoring her.

HENDRIX

I need to borrow the gremlin.

TANABANANA

:eyeball emoji:

HENDRIX

If I'm going to New York then a pee cannon might come in handy.

TANABANANA

Finally! I wondered how long it would take
you to figure it out. Go get our girl. Bring me
back a T-shirt.

HENDRIX

How about I bring you back a sister-in-law?

thirty-three

. . .

CHARLOTTE

Over the next couple of days, Retta and I were on a mission to have the entire apartment cleaned and organized. She had focused on packing all my dishes while I'd cleaned out my office and boxed up all of my books. Billie had even come down to help, although she was more like moral support since she couldn't do much with only one hand.

We hadn't gone through any of Aaron's stuff yet. I planned to just dump it all in boxes and let him sort it out. I wasn't sure what would happen to this building since everything Christian owned was likely to be sold off at some point. But I figured if Aaron didn't come get his stuff then it would go to whoever bought the building. At this point I didn't really care.

Thursday morning, I opened my eyes to the smell of coffee. Retta was up early. I threw on a sweatshirt over my pajamas and went out to investigate. Retta stood at the stove making an omelet.

"Morning." I rubbed my eyes as I shuffled into the kitchen.

"Hey. You hungry?"

"You didn't have to cook. I should be cooking for you. I

never could have gotten this place in order so fast without your help."

"Believe me when I say, I was happy to. I love my mother, but she has been driving me crazy. Now she's trying to fix me up with some guy at her job who looks like he's about two decades past retirement."

I poured myself a cup of coffee. "You're not the sugar daddy type."

"Hell no." She waved the spatula around. She made quite a sight in her mismatched pajamas which consisted of striped lounge pants and a top that was clearly part of a Christmas set. "I have way too big of a mouth to be anybody's trophy wife. Because I am going to tell you the truth no matter what."

"Cheers to that." I held up my mug in solidarity.

We ate in silence before Retta brought up the thing that I knew was on both of our minds. "You're going back today?"

"Yeah. I think it's time. The lawyers seem optimistic and now that Mom knows sailing off into the sunset isn't a good idea, I think it'll be okay."

Retta shook her head. "I can't believe she was just going to hop on a yacht. I kind of envy that level of audacity."

"That's one word for it. Luckily, Alan told her that was a bad move since she definitely doesn't listen to me. Plus, with the pending case against Christian, leaving the country wouldn't be the best idea anyway.

"It's just going to be hard to drive away knowing that I'm leaving Billie behind. For real this time." I swallowed hard, the bitter taste of reality hitting me.

"Charlie, it's time." Retta reached over and gave my hand a reassuring squeeze. "It's time for you to figure out what you want. You can't follow your mom and sister around forever, trying to solve their problems."

I stared into my coffee mug. Retta was right. I had spent so much time worrying about others that I had neglected my own happiness. But the thought of leaving my family behind still gnawed at me.

With Retta's words echoing in my mind, we began the dreaded task of cleaning out Aaron's closet. It was mainly sweaters and long-sleeved dress shirts so this was obviously his winter wardrobe. I put Retta on the front lines so that if she came across anything she thought I shouldn't see, she could trash it before I was traumatized. I didn't really want to find out Aaron kept a secret stash of his ex's nudes or something.

Retta pulled a pile of sweaters from a shelf and handed them back to me. "He's lucky you aren't the vindictive type. Somebody else would have sold all this on eBay. This is *cashmere.*"

"Honestly, I just feel bad leaving a mess for whoever has to deal with these apartments."

She gave me a look. "You have to stop being so nice. Haven't we talked about this?"

As we continued our purging, she handed back a few books. I tossed them on top of the clothes in one of the boxes. A flash of light caught my eye. There was an earring sitting on the shirt in the box. I picked it up.

"Whose earring is this?"

Retta turned around. "Where did that come from?"

"I guess it was in one of these shirt pockets. But it's definitely not mine."

She winced. "I should have been checking the pockets. I'm losing my touch."

I laughed. "It really doesn't matter. He is so far in the past it's not even funny."

Retta's eyes narrowed as she studied my face. I could see the wheels turning in her head, like she was trying to figure out what to say next.

"Seriously, Retta. It's fine."

"You know what, let's speed this up. Because why are we doing this the hard way?" Retta grabbed a handful of clothes and threw them in the next box. "Everything of his goes into the burn box."

"The burn box?" I laughed. "That's a bit extreme. I think the trash is fine."

Retta pouted. "Are you sure? I always wanted to burn up some guys shit just like Angela Bassett in that movie."

As I watched her drop the next armful of clothes into the box, I couldn't help but feel a sense of closure.

"Aaron was never right for me. My *entire life* wasn't right for me. It was all just for show. Now since living at Gran's house, my hair's never done and I can't even remember when I last had a manicure." I looked down at my chipped nails and grinned. "And I've never felt more beautiful."

"I can tell," Retta admitted.

"Because with Rix, I didn't have to try." I shrugged. "He loved me just as I am. I need to get back to him. I need to fix things."

Retta smiled, clearly pleased. "Now, we're getting somewhere. Girl, leave all this crap behind and get back to your country hunk. I've been waiting for you to come to that conclusion since your first phone call from your Gran's house."

"Really?" I said, surprised. "I thought you were surprised my *bougie ass* was there at all!"

"Please." Retta rolled her eyes. "It was obvious from the moment you started gushing about life in the woods that you were finally where you were meant to be. And who knows, maybe when I come visit, I'll find myself a hot country boy too!"

At that, we both burst into laughter. The image of Retta with her designer outfits and perfectly manicured nails, trying to navigate life in a small town was undeniably amusing.

"Retta, those country boys wouldn't know how to handle you," I teased between giggles.

"Maybe so," she conceded, "but it would be fun to see them try, wouldn't it?"

We spent the next hour figuring out which boxes would fit into my car and which ones I needed to have shipped. Retta volunteered to stay and wait for the carrier to pick everything up so I could get on the road.

"Okay, I think that's it. I will handle everything. You just take that cute tush back to your handyman. Let him put his hands all over you."

I gave her a look. "How long did it take you to come up with that one?"

She laughed and pulled me into a hug. "Here's to new beginnings."

"Retta." I suddenly couldn't speak, my throat thick with emotion. "Thank you for everything."

Her eyes softened as she looked at me. "Go. Spend time with Billie before you have to get on the road."

After one last hug, I got on the elevator. I had talked with my mom and Billie yesterday so they knew I was coming. I was excited to spend time with them. But I was also excited to get home.

I had a date with a country boy.

He just didn't know it yet.

———

After spending a teary hour with Billie, I left right after lunch time. It had been harder than expected to tell Billie that I was now planning to figure out a way to help Mom keep her in New York. Mainly because I could see how relieved she was, which only drove home how long I'd missed the clues that she didn't want to move.

I rode down to the lobby and then walked over to the concierge desk. Any mail or packages coming after today would need to be forwarded, something I knew they could take care of for me. After explaining what I needed, I filled out a form with my new address.

My favorite doorman, Angel, was on duty. I waved and he gave a formal bow in return which made me laugh. All my memories of this place weren't horrible. It was nice that I could now remember the good things. I walked back to the elevators so I could ride down to the parking garage.

"Miss Monroe?"

I turned. "Angel? Is everything okay?"

"I'm not sure. There was a gentleman here asking for you. He isn't on the approved visitors list. We called up for you but no one answered."

"What was his name?"

"Rick."

My mouth went dry. "Rix? Hendrix?"

He pointed to the front door. "He's still out there. He's been there for about half an hour."

I hurried over to the front doors and stepped out onto the sidewalk.

Even though I was expecting to see him, it was still a shock when he turned around because he looked so out of place. His hair whipped around his face since it was still a little too long and his ripped T-shirt and jeans wouldn't have looked strange if we weren't in front of a ritzy building on the Upper East Side. But there was just something about Hendrix Evers that marked him as not from the city. He looked so earthy and real. Like he should be in a forest hauling lumber not in the middle of a concrete jungle.

"What are you doing here?"

He shifted a knapsack on his shoulder and it growled. The bag *growled*.

"Would you settle down in there?" Rix muttered. "No wonder we couldn't get past that stuffy doorman."

The bag shifted again and Meatball pushed his head out of the top. He snuffled in my direction.

"Meatball!" I leaned over and kissed the top of his little head.

"I figured if I was going to come and beg for another chance that I needed to bring out the big guns," Hendrix admitted.

My eyes flew up to meet his. "Is that what you're doing? Begging for another chance?"

He took a deep breath. "Charlie, I know your mom and your sister need you. I understand that completely because I need you too. Nothing has been the same since you left Violet Ridge. That shouldn't be a surprise since nothing was the same the last time you left either."

"I'm sorry I left without talking to you. Everything just happened so fast. You were mad at me and I didn't know what to do about that. Every time I think I'm settled, something happens to ruin it and I was scared it was a sign we weren't meant to be."

He slid his hand around my neck in the way that always made me melt.

"All it means is that we need to learn to talk to each other instead of making assumptions. I found out that you might be leaving and it hit me hard. Even harder than it did the first time you left. I was a kid then and I didn't know how to handle it, but I'm a man now. I'm not going to let you go without a fight."

It was almost impossible to see him with tears in my eyes but I didn't let that stop me from throwing myself in his arms.

He staggered back under the force of my weight and Meatball let out an annoyed grunt.

"I don't want you to let me go," I whispered.

"I love you, Charlotte Monroe. I'm just sorry I didn't figure it out sooner. If you need to be here in New York then I guess we'll have to figure out how to survive in the Big Apple."

"We?"

"Apparently me and Meatball come as a package deal. He's decided he likes me after all. Either that or he likes all the food I drop on the floor."

Laughing, I patted Meatball on the head again. "I knew it. No loyalty at all."

"He misses you almost as much as I do."

I leaned my forehead against his and suddenly everything seemed right again. "I love you, too. Were you really going to move to New York?"

He shrugged. "I'm going where you are. I'm all in."

His words made me feel warm all over but as usual my fears got the best of me. "Are we moving too fast?"

"We're not kids anymore and we don't have to follow anybody's rules but our own. I want it all with you. Forever."

"Forever Evers?" I whispered.

His chuckle made the warmth settle right in the center of my chest. "Forever Evers. That's what I want."

"That's what I want, too. More than anything."

He looked behind me. "So this is home?"

I looked back at the building where I'd spent the past ten years. Even though I'd experienced a lot of milestones there, it had never felt like home.

"No. It was just a place I stayed for a while. Violet Ridge is home. It's where I've always wanted to be."

That was when I noticed the bag in his other hand. "What's that?"

For the first time, he looked uncertain. "I made something for you. But it's stupid." He opened the bag and lifted out a miniature house made from wood.

My mouth fell open. "It looks like Gran's house!"

"I was trying to show you the addition I wanted to build on the back. But I messed up on the porch and the roof is all wrong."

I kissed him quiet. "Always the critic. It's perfect."

He tried to put it back in the bag. "It was supposed to be to scale. But, it's fine. I'll make you another one."

"No. It's mine. You can't take it back. I love it. You made me a *house*."

He pulled me into another kiss. "I'll make you a home if you let me. That's all I want, Charlie. To come home to you."

epilogue

. . .

HENDRIX

Charlie bustled by with an armful of clean laundry. Ten minutes later, she appeared in the living room with a bottle of Windex and a rag.

"Didn't you already clean the windows?"

She rubbed manically at a spot. "There's so much dust in here."

"Baby, it's fine."

My voice trailed off as she left the room, trailing the scent of chemicals behind her. I shook my head but went back to work tightening the hinges on the kitchen cabinets. When I'd opened the cabinet this morning it had been so loose it almost hit me in the face. I figured I'd better tighten them all before Charlie got wind of it. She was nervous enough about her mom and sister visiting.

I heard Charlie singing softly to Meatball so I knew I had about fifteen minutes to work on my surprise. My toolbox was already upstairs in the small bedroom Charlie had originally used when she first moved here. She'd finally cleaned out her grandmother's room. That had been a long emotional day. But after carefully packing away the last mementos she wanted to keep, we'd moved in the king size bed we'd bought and changed the furniture around. Now she planned to put Billie into her old room.

Now painted a soft buttery lemon shade, Charlie's old room was decorated with filmy white lace curtains at the windows and a fluffy down comforter on the bed. My surprise was under the window, waiting to be assembled.

I knelt down and got to work, so I would be able to drill everything in place pretty quickly. Charlie (and Meatball) were used to noise at this point but I figured I'd have less than five minutes of privacy left once I turned the drill on.

True enough, about five minutes later I heard footsteps on the stairs.

"Don't come in yet," I called out.

The footsteps paused. "What are you doing?"

"It's a surprise."

I heard a soft little stomp and laughed. Charlie still wasn't great with surprises. Knowing that she was out there losing it made me work fast.

"I'm just putting the finishing touches on. Okay, now you can come in."

The door flew open and Charlie looked around curiously. Then her eyes settled on me and she grinned. I moved out of the way so she could get a better view.

"Oh, Rix. You built a window seat?" Her whole face softened as she took it in, walking closer to run her hand over the seat cushion. I'd gone with a yellow gingham print to match the color scheme in the room and it made the space look bright and airy.

"I figured when Billie gets here she might want a place to relax or read a book."

Charlie wrapped her arms around my middle. "This is perfect. Thank you."

We stood like that for a minute just taking in the finished room. Charlie had agonized over every little detail down to the type of lace on the curtains.

"I know you're worried about this visit since everything isn't done yet. But it doesn't matter if it's not perfect."

"It's not that. It's just that coming here when I was a kid was so amazing because of Gran Grace. I wish Billie could have that, too."

"She will. It'll be amazing because she gets to spend time with her sister."

"And don't forget Meatball. I think she's most excited about getting to spend time with him. The only reason she's not here already is because she wanted to finish out her summer camp. No more parkour luckily."

I laughed thinking of the spunky little girl who had immediately captured my heart the first time we'd spoken. Even though we'd only met through video calls, I felt like I knew her already. She reminded me a lot of her incredibly spunky, determined, older sister.

Charlie moved back suddenly and then pulled her phone from her pocket.

"Mom? Is everything okay?"

I waited anxiously, watching her face for signs of trouble. Every time her mom called with updates about the custody case Charlie was so tense afterward. She was working hard on separating herself, but I knew it would take time before she didn't feel the instinct to rush out and save them.

"So it's over? Just like that."

After a few more questions, Charlie hung up looking dazed.

"What happened? What's over?"

She sat on the edge of the bed. "The Delacourts dropped the lawsuit."

I whooped. Meatball came rushing in at the noise and added his contribution by barking madly.

"That's great news! So you don't have to worry about that anymore. I wonder what made them drop it. Did the lawyers threaten them with something?"

Charlie smiled sheepishly. "No, I threatened with something. I called them directly and said if they pursued this, I would be forced to file for custody of Billie myself. I told them I was getting married soon to my childhood sweetheart and since I'd been with Billie her whole life, the courts were probably far more likely to grant custody to me."

I let my mouth fall open in mock surprise. "*Charlotte Monroe*. You lied?"

Her shoulders shook with her laughter. "I figured it was worth a shot. I was hoping they really did just want to keep Billie close and wouldn't like the idea of me adopting her and moving her to Virginia. At least my Mom plans to stay in New York now."

"Diabolical. I like it." I smirked. "Also, getting married to your childhood sweetheart? Way to rewrite history."

She pinched my stomach. "I had to say something. Childhood nemesis who tormented me constantly probably wouldn't have had the same effect."

"Childhood sweetheart is actually accurate. I was sweet on you, even if I didn't know how to show it. I was talking about the married part."

Her cheeks flushed. "Well, I had to improvise. Courts aren't impressed by people shacking up."

"Well, that part will be accurate too. One day. Because I plan to marry the hell out of you, Charlotte Monroe."

"Is that right?" She raised her eyebrows.

"Yeah. You plan on giving me a hard time about it?" I looked down at her, loving the way her eyes sparkled while she was giving me hell.

"You bet I am."

epilogue

. . .

CHARLOTTE

Shrieks of laughter ricocheted around the yard. I skirted to the side as Billie ran by screaming with Meatball hot on her heels. The bowl of fruit salad in my hands teetered precariously.

"I've got it." Rix plucked the bowl from my hands and walked over to the table we'd set up for the food.

He'd rigged an umbrella to provide shade but I'd waited until right before everyone was supposed to arrive to bring the food out. We were hosting our first party as a couple and I wanted everything to be perfect.

It was silly to be nervous as if I hadn't known the Evers my whole life but this was different. After Rix had declared he planned to *marry the hell out of me*, he had launched a full-scale campaign to convert me to all the benefits of being an Evers. We'd attended Beck's baseball games together; Tana had been happy to babysit Meatball so we could go on date nights; and we hadn't missed a Sunday dinner yet.

The man really did know the way to my heart.

After placing the bowl squarely in the middle of the shade,

Rix moved a few other things over. He gestured to the table. "Does it look okay?"

"Yeah. The table looks great."

"Then why do you have that look on your face? What are you thinking?"

I turned to walk back to the house. He ran up beside me and slung an arm around my shoulders.

"Do you ever get that weird feeling like you've seen something before? Or like you've already lived this life?"

"Déjà vu?"

"Yes. That's it. This feels so familiar." I glanced over at him curiously. "If we knew each other in another life, I wonder if you still drove me as crazy as you do now?"

"Probably. Maybe we were slinging insults across a saloon in the Wild West or doing the Charleston in a prohibition era jazz club."

"If we were in the Wild West then I probably would have shot you."

He cracked up. "I believe it. Dad would say it's because we've been together before. Soul mates who found each other again. Actually he said something weird one time about how we were fated because of our names. Which didn't really make a lot of sense."

I stopped walking as I thought about it. "Oh wow. He's right. Our names match. We're both named after music legends."

He looked confused. "Charlotte?"

"Gran had a thing for jazz singers. My mom is named after Lena Horne. When it was her turn, Mom carried on the tradition but with our middle names. My sister is Elise Billie for Billie Holiday. And I'm Charlotte Ella after Ella Fitzgerald."

He stared. "He was right. I almost don't want to tell him that. He'll be insufferable."

Just then my mom walked out into the backyard. "Do you need any help?"

I waved her over and gave her the job of arranging some of the flowers Rix had brought home into bouquets for the table. She'd always had a knack with flowers and it would give her something to do. I could tell she was a little nervous about seeing everyone all at once again, too.

Things had been better after our talk. It had been a hard conversation but I think she finally got where I was coming from, and after some reflection I felt like I understood her better, too. With hindsight it was easier to see how stifled she'd felt growing up here and how she'd thought she was giving us a better life.

Now that she wasn't trapped in this town, she seemed better able to appreciate it. Ever since they'd arrived, she'd been just as excited as Billie to meet my friends and get involved in my new life.

Rix pulled me into his arms from behind and rested his head on top of mine. "You look happy."

"I am happy. I have everything I ever wanted."

As my eyes wandered over the newly fenced in yard, the scent of honeysuckle tickled my nose. Billie and Meatball ran by again.

As I watched them play, I gasped. "This is my dream."

I closed my eyes, remembering. Immediately I was swept with an overwhelming feeling of *home*.

"The dream that I used to have all the time. Living in this house with the smell of honeysuckle on the air and my kids running around the yard. I just realized this is it. This is the dream."

He turned and watched Billie collapse in a heap before

Meatball climbed into her lap. They were both filthy and probably smelled like wet grass but they were having the time of their lives.

"Our kids, huh?"

We both laughed.

"Not exactly what I expected but I'll take it," I said.

Tana's head poked over the top of the newly installed fence. "Is this a private party or can anybody join?"

Rix chuckled. "What's the password? We don't want just any riffraff off the street coming in."

She pushed open the gate and the entire Evers family trailed behind her. In a matter of minutes there was music playing, Mrs. Evers had set up another table for the food she'd brought along and Van was playing a game of cornhole with his father. Beck and Campbell tossed a ball back and forth before joining Billie where she was trying to teach Meatball to play fetch.

"Where did all this come from?" I asked, looking over at Rix in astonishment.

He just shook his head. "You know how my family rolls. They're basically a traveling circus."

"That's because we're awesome," Tana sang playfully before pulling me into a hug.

When Billie saw who had just arrived, she jumped up with a whoop. "Aunt Tana!"

"Billie Bug!" She leaned down to hug her. "Don't let my brothers bother you. They aren't used to being civilized."

Billie looked over her shoulder. "Don't worry. I can handle them."

Tana smiled. "I bet you can. I've been outnumbered for years. We can use a little more girl power around here."

"I was supposed to move here," Billie said. "But now we're

staying in New York. But I can bring *all* the girl power in the summer."

I hugged her close, thrilled that the custody situation was settled. Now that the Delacourts were assured Billie wouldn't be leaving the country, they'd actually been making more of an effort to see her. It turned out all they wanted was the chance to spend more time with their only grandchild, hardly an unreasonable request.

They wouldn't win grandparents of the year any time soon, but I could admit to being a little biased. After Gran Grace, I had pretty high standards.

"We're counting on it," Tana said. "Your sister and I used to run wild all over this place every summer. We have *so much* to teach you."

I laughed thinking of all the times we'd dragged Rix and Carter into our schemes. Now Violet Ridge would have a whole new generation learning her secrets. When I met Tana's eyes, I could tell she was thinking the same thing.

She bumped my arm. "I'm really glad the Rescue Charlie plan worked after all."

"Did your friends rescue you?" Billie asked looking between Tana and Rix in confusion.

I thought about it. About everything that had led us to this moment, all the losses, all the pain but mainly, all the joy. There were hundreds of memories wrapped up in this house and these people, and we would hopefully make hundreds more.

I sure hoped Gran was somewhere watching all of this. Because this was exactly what she'd wanted for me.

"My friends did rescue me." I squeezed Billie's hand. "But in the end, I think I really rescued myself."

———

Thank you so much for reading *You Ruin Everything*!

Want more? Join my newsletter at mmalonebooks.com to get your free bonus scene *Dinner with The Evers*!

---

my cock-a-doodle-doo won't crow.

It's a tragedy. The only woman who makes him stand up is my co-worker. My *rival*. To impress the client I'm suddenly fake-engaged to a woman who hates me AND would gladly put my balls in her purse. But in the end, it's still a competition. May the best man win. **Start reading BEG ME now!** Or turn the page for a special excerpt.

more romantic comedy

MY ROOSTER WON'T CROW.

I can't believe it either. It's a tragedy.

Years of perfect performance and now this traitor decides to get picky. And the only woman who makes little Milo stand up and *c-ck a doodle doo* is my co-worker, Mya Taylor, a.k.a. my competition for the biggest ad account this side of the Atlantic.

Our client wants a wedding expert so I'm suddenly fake-engaged to a woman who hates me AND would gladly put my balls in her purse. But when I find out she's never taken a trip to O-town, we make a little wager.

Not only will I win the client, but I'll prove to her that

multiples are NOT a myth. We work together all day and fight between the sheets all night. But at the end of the day, it's still a competition.

May the best man win.

BEG ME is a frenemies to lovers, completely inappropriate romantic comedy. Side effects may include clutching your pearls and laughing until you almost choke. Download BEG ME now at minxmalone.com/begme

No plastic cows were harmed during the creation of the book. OKAY, there was that one time. But other than that, none.

———

mya

I can do this. I can do anything I put my mind to.

I am strong.

I am brave.

I repeat the words softly, hoping repetition really is the key For the past week, the atmosphere at Mirage has been focused on one thing and one thing only.

The Vegas meeting.

We've all been working longer hours, doing research or Lavin Couture's last five collections and preparing example dossiers of our work on other fashion brands.

It's been exciting, and I'm thrilled to have this opportunity I will not allow something like a slight fear of flying to ruin thi for me, so I buckle my seatbelt and close my eyes all the way through takeoff. There's a slight bump as the wheels come up, and I let out a small squeak.

Oh, screw being brave.

My fist clenches in a death grip around the plastic cow that is the only thing standing between me and a complete nervous breakdown in the middle of this airplane.

Not that these are bad accommodations for a first-time trip to the loony bin. I've never been on a private plane before, but I can't imagine anything more luxurious than this. The seats are covered in dove-gray leather and the carpet on the floor is plusher than what's in my apartment. Gleaming gold accents adorn the armrests and the trim overhead.

Andre Lavin has the same impeccable taste in personal aviation as he does in everything else.

Unfortunately, it's all wasted on me. It's my first time flying like a rock star, and I'm two seconds away from curling up in the fetal position in the middle of the aisle.

A toothy flight attendant leans down to offer me a drink, but honestly, I'm afraid to even pry my lips apart to turn it down. So I give a tense nod, and she continues on her merry way down the aisle, offering drinks to everyone as if we aren't all in danger of plunging thousands of feet to a fiery death. I squeeze my eyes shut and start counting.

Breathe, Mya.

"Nervous flyer, huh?"

My eyes pop open at the deep baritone in my ear. Milo has switched seats with Wallace and is now entirely too close for comfort. The last thing I need is my competition seeing my weakness.

"What makes you say that?" I'm going for nonchalant, but my voice sounds an octave higher than usual.

Milo inclines his head toward my lap. "The death grip you have on Miss Moo there."

It takes some effort, but I manage to loosen my fingers so I can show him. "This is Chelsea, the stress cow. Lots of people use them."

His eyes dance with amusement. "I don't see anyone else squeezing the life out of a plastic farm animal, do you?"

I sit up straighter, ready to let him have it, but just then the plane hits a pocket of turbulence. My stomach feels like it's now in my esophagus.

"OH MY FUCKING GOD! THIS PLANE IS GOING DOWN."

This comes out way louder than I would have hoped. Milo chuckles under his breath as everyone turns around to stare at us. After a few moments, they finally turn around, but James raises his eyebrows as if to say, *Are you okay?*

I wave and force a smile so he won't worry. When he finally looks away, the breath I've been holding releases in a gasp.

"I'll be lucky if I still have a job by the time this trip is over," I mutter under my breath. Obviously not quietly enough, because Milo laughs again.

"Imagine that. Spent your entire life on the straight and narrow and it all ends on a private plane sitting next to the devil himself."

When I glare at him, he shrugs in that nonchalant and completely hot way that totally does *not* get my panties wet.

"Just saying. I'm a big fan of irony. It just proves what I've always known."

"And what is that, oh wise one?"

"That the universe fucks us all in the end."

Dirty words coming from his mouth should not be so arousing. Especially when he's completely right about me. Not that I'll ever tell him that.

"Well, the joke is on you. You're assuming I've spent my entire life on the straight and narrow. I could have been a real bitch in my past. Maybe this flight from hell is my karma for deeds done wrong."

"Maybe," he concedes with that infuriating smirk that means he actually believes the total opposite.

"You think you know so much about me. You think I'm just this boring workaholic who goes home at night and curls up with a million cats. Admit it."

His eyes focus on me then, like two electric blue lasers. "No, I don't think that at all. But it sounds like someone else has made you believe that's true."

My last argument with William rolls through my head like a movie on repeat. Our relationship was never perfect, not even when things were new and interesting. But I'm not the kind of woman who looks for perfection anyway. I don't care about socks left on the bathroom floor or who took the trash out last. All I've ever wanted is someone who gets me.

Milo is watching me again, this time with something that looks suspiciously like pity in his eyes. He's intuitive; I'll give him that. But damn him for using that on me.

"I heard about your breakup. Sorry. That sucks."

I look out the window at the clouds passing by. Normally I don't do this. Looking at clouds from this angle just reminds me of where I am, in a tin can hurtling through the sky. But contemplating the likelihood of total engine failure is preferable right now to Milo Hamilton looking at me with pity.

"Thank you, but I'm fine. All I want is to focus on why we're flying to Las Vegas in the first place. To impress this client and snag the hottest ad account in the country right now."

Milo nods. "I'm not sure if James even went home last night. He was in the office early doing research."

I'm not surprised by that at all. Andre Lavin is the

preferred designer of all of Hollywood's leading men. Although he's known for menswear, after designing both the bridal tuxedo and the wedding dress for Hollywood's reigning power couple, he was rumored to be launching an exclusive bridal line. This account could catapult the Mirage Agency into the upper echelon of advertising overnight.

If James is looking for a partner, whoever locks down this account is on the fast track.

"Let me guess, so were you?"

His tight smile confirms it. Milo hates to lose, and no doubt he was in the office almost as long as James. But he might as well get ready because I'm going to be the one to lock this account down.

"I wanted to talk to you about something," Milo leans closer. "What did you mean when you said I stole an account from you?"

My blood freezes in my veins. Had I said that? My thoughts race back to that day when he'd first told me about the partnership. Clearly I hadn't been thinking straight. I'd just been so excited.

Over the past few years, I've worked on some extraordinary campaigns. I put my heart and soul into each one, and I know I've done great work for Mirage. But so far, most of the accounts have been mid-level, and doing great work on them isn't enough to show James that I have what it takes to be promoted. I've been waiting for the type of project that would really let me show off what I can do.

This is it. Lavin Bridal is what I've been waiting for.

So that day in Milo's office, my head had been swimming with visions of the future. That's the only explanation I have for why I'd tell my nemesis that he'd ever gotten a leg up on me.

"I'm not sure what you mean. You must have misunderstood."

Milo narrows his eyes, and a beat passes in tense silence. Then he smiles, showing both rows of teeth.

Like a barracuda.

"Okay, if you want to play it that way, fine. But I don't poach accounts, and when I convince Andre Lavin to sign on the dotted line, I want it known that I did it fair and square."

"When? Hah. You really think you're going to win a bridal account? The king of one-night stands is suddenly an expert on weddings?"

I shouldn't have said that. Not only because it makes it sound like I'm keeping track of his personal life outside of the office but because it opens the door for him to bring up my own failures. Namely, being dumped six months before my own wedding. He could argue that my personal life makes me a bad candidate to pitch for this account, too.

He looks like he's thinking about taking the bait, but surprisingly his face softens. "I think that we're both willing to do whatever it takes to win this client. No matter which one of us gets to the finish line first, in the end Mirage benefits."

I look to the front of the plane where Kevin sits next to James. He's a nice guy but a bit of a suck up. He brings in clients at half the rate Milo or I do, but for some reason, James still promoted him to be a team lead.

"What if Kevin is the one to convince them to sign?"

Milo follows my gaze up front. "Seriously?"

"Okay, I admit that's unlikely."

"Look, for the next twenty-four hours, let's call a truce. We can go back to being sworn enemies when we're back in the office, but right now, we need to work together to win this. Let's lock down the account, and then we can duke it out later as to who is going to take lead."

As much as I hate to admit it, it's a fair plan. This account is a boon for the entire company, and working together, we have a better chance of convincing the Lavin team that we're the right fit.

"Agreed."

"So, truce?" He holds out his hand and we shake quickly.

The plane hits another bout of turbulence, and I squeeze the hell out of his hand. "Truce," I manage to say finally.

He carefully extricates his fingers from my death grip. "Seriously, it's all going to work out. As long as we don't encounter any other problems, we've got this in the bag."

———

By the time we land in Vegas four hours later, I'm a quivering mess. Chelsea has been mangled between my fingers so often the plastic looks permanently deformed, and poor Wallace, who had the misfortune of sitting in front of me, heard every four-letter word in the English language.

But Milo has been strangely quiet the whole time. After his truce declaration, he put on his headphones and closed his eyes for the rest of the flight. Watching him sleep so peacefully while my heart was in my throat was extremely irritating.

It was also fascinating to watch him when he wasn't sneering at me or trying to steal my clients. When he's asleep he almost looks... nice. Like the guy I thought he was before I found out how far he'd go to win.

Milo gets his phone out as soon as we leave the plane.

"Calling your girlfriend?" I applaud myself for keeping the disdain out of my voice when I ask.

Truce, remember?

"My mom," he replies, deadpan. "She's not a fan of planes either, so I always like to let her know when I've landed safely."

"Oh. Well, that's actually sweet."

"Considering how much she likes poetry, you'd think she'd

be a bit more open to adventure. How does it go? 'For in that sleep of death what dreams may come.'"

"Is that... Shakespeare?"

He eyes me. "Why do you sound so surprised? My mother named me after John Milton. My younger brother is named Tennyson, for fuck's sake."

I pantomime zipping my lips. "I didn't say I was surprised."

But I can't deny that I'm shocked. Then I remember this is Milo. He's probably memorized sonnets to help him hit on women. "Wait, your brother is named Tennyson? Why don't I remember that?"

I met his mom and brother at last year's company Christmas party. His mom is beautiful, a discovery that's not shocking considering what Milo looks like. His younger brother is a quieter, gruffer version of Milo. He introduced himself and then didn't speak again for the rest of the night.

Milo grins. "He hates his name as much as I hate mine. He goes by Ten. Most people hear it wrong and assume it's Tom. He doesn't correct them."

Mr. Lavin arranged for a car service to pick us up, which takes us directly to the hotel. I squirm in my seat with excitement. I've always wanted to see the Bellagio. It's a beautiful hotel and makes me feel like a character in a Hollywood heist movie. James heads straight to the front desk to get the keys to the block of rooms he reserved for us, so I take the opportunity to look around.

It's too bad we're only here for a night. I'd love to have a chance to explore more, maybe even catch a show.

"Okay, here are your keys. Most of us are on the tenth floor, but Milo you're on the twelfth. Everyone, please be on your best behavior. The Lavin team is also staying at this hotel, and you never know who might see you. Keep that in mind."

Everyone breaks off and heads for the elevators. Most of us

just brought carryon bags, but Kelly, the junior associate from Kevin's team, has a huge rolling suitcase more suited to a month's vacation.

James follows my eyes and then shakes his head. "You two, I need to have a word."

Milo and I exchange glances before following him as he walks off to the side of the concierge desk. I wish I could have gotten a chance to talk to James alone before we go upstairs to get ready for dinner. I have a few ideas for the Lavin account that I wanted to run by him.

But I squash my competitive side as I remember that tonight is about securing the account more than anything.

This isn't the time to crush my competition. Milo and I have agreed to a truce, and I intend to honor it. We're going to be charming at dinner tonight and show the Lavin team all the reasons why Mirage is a perfect fit for a luxury brand. Milo's words on the plane come back.

As long as we don't encounter any other problems, we've got this in the bag.

James finally finds a space next to a rack of luggage that's private enough. He glances around before speaking.

"We have a problem."

To his credit, Milo keeps a straight face. But inside he has to be thinking the same thing I am. What now? How could there be a problem when we've just arrived? Luckily, James doesn't keep us in suspense too long. His words come out in a nervous jumble, like he's in too much of a panic to take breaths between sentences.

"Elizabeth is here. My Elizabeth," he continues as if either of us didn't know who he was talking about. "She found out about the Lavin deal somehow, and her company is talking to Lavin, too. Tonight. One of the associates she took with her when she left still talks to Anya. Apparently, they're pitching the Lavin team over drinks right before they meet with us. We might lose the job before we even get the chance to meet."

I put my hands up to catch his attention because he looks like he's on the verge of hyperventilating. "Take a breath. Let's take a step back and look at the whole situation. Andre Lavin sent his plane for us. He wouldn't have gone to all that trouble and expense if he wasn't going to listen to our pitch as well."

James's face is bright red, but he's listening to me intently. After a brief pause, he nods briskly. "That's true. He wouldn't have done that."

"So that means that no matter what Elizabeth says to him at drinks, we still have a shot at making him forget about it at dinner. And we will. Milo and I are already working on something that's going to blow him away."

"You are? Of course, you are. That's why you were talking on the plane ride." James closes his eyes, and finally, his color starts to return to normal. Or at least not one shade away from a tomato.

"I should have known you two were prepared. Anya's message didn't come through until we landed, so I think I just panicked for a moment."

Milo claps him on the shoulder and then steers him toward the elevators. "Everything is going to be fine. Why don't we go to our rooms and take a load off before the meeting? We don't want to be jetlagged and cranky later."

"Good idea." James nods and pulls his small suitcase behind him. "Are you guys coming?"

Milo hesitates. "No, you go ahead. I want to talk to the concierge. I think I forgot my toothbrush."

He gives me a look that I immediately interpret as, *We need to talk.*

"Yeah, I think I'm going to check out the gift shop before I go up," I add.

We stand together and watch as our boss gets on the first elevator going up. At least he doesn't look nearly as crazed as he did at first. Before the elevator doors close, he waves.

Then Milo turns to me. The affable smile he wore for James's benefit is gone.

"What the fuck are we going to do?"

———

milo

Mya and I stand in the lobby in shock for a few minutes. Finally, she blinks and then blows out a long breath.

"No pressure, huh?"

The tension breaks and we both laugh. Jesus, as if the stakes aren't high enough already, we have to add in our boss's feud with his ex-wife. Juggling this many balls something is bound to break.

The thought gives me renewed determination to impress the Lavin team tonight. James is a good guy, if a little intense. I wasn't here when the whole thing with his wife went down, but I've seen enough of the aftermath to know how important this is.

We cannot let James down.

"I can't believe Elizabeth is here," Mya remarks as we walk toward the gift shop in the hotel.

"What's the deal with her? I wasn't around when she left, and I definitely don't want to ask James."

She shakes her head. "It happened a few months after I was hired, so this was about three years ago. Elizabeth and James started Mirage together, but then after a decade of running the business as a team, she left him for one of their clients, Gareth Whittington."

I wince. "The guy who puts on all those wild slumber parties in Hollywood?"

"That's the one. The porn king himself. James wasn't excited about taking him on as a client in the first place, but Elizabeth convinced him it was a good idea. It was a big account for us, but James was worried about all the moral implications of working with a borderline legal brand. I mean, you've heard about some of the stuff that happens at those parties, right?" Her face conveys her disgust.

Oh yeah, I've heard about them. In fact, I've attended one, not that I'll admit that to Mya. Besides, it wasn't my scene. Everyone there was either drunk, or high, and while I have nothing against wild times, I would like to at least remember what I did and who I did it with.

"Um, yeah, I've heard they can get pretty insane."

She scoffs. "Not just insane. Violent. There have been multiple court cases already about underage girls who've been drugged and abused at those parties. He was in the news just last week because some actor overdosed and no one around him even noticed until it was too late."

Oh shit.

"Okay, I didn't know all that," I admit.

"Anyway, the guy is bad news. But it turns out James shouldn't have been as worried about our image because it was his *marriage* that actually took a hit. Three months after we took on Gareth as a client, Elizabeth filed for divorce. She left and formed her own company, taking half the Mirage client list with her. She even had the balls to send him an invitation to her wedding to that guy. James still hasn't gotten over it."

I feel an instant kinship with James. We may not know each other that well, but we're part of the same brotherhood, men who once bought into the idea of true love and got kicked in the teeth. We should have membership cards.

"So, if she's the one who left, why is she so determined to get back at James?"

None of this is making sense to me. I mean, I get the *Elizabeth is a cheating bitch* part, because... obviously. Fucking a client behind your husband's back and then trying to tank the business you built together is a dick move.

What I don't get is what she wants *now*.

Mya sighs. "Because apparently part of the reason why they broke up was because he didn't like her ideas. She wanted to take the firm one direction, and he wanted to go another. I'm sure this is her way of proving to him that he was wrong."

We've reached the gift shop now, and I step back so Mya can enter before me. She has her small duffel bag thrown over her shoulder and looks like a college co-ed in her black yoga pants and long T-shirt. She makes a beeline for the right wall where all the toiletries are.

"Didn't you say you needed a toothbrush?"

I shake my head. "I just said that so James would go up without us."

"Right. Well, I actually did forget mine." She grabs a blue toothbrush and then a package of over-the-counter sleeping pills. Then after a moment of hesitation, she grabs a package of potato chips and a candy bar.

When she sees me watching, a shy smile covers her lips. "For later. Once we nail this presentation to Mr. Lavin, I'm going to need to veg out for the rest of the night. I don't travel well."

"You don't say," I drawl before grabbing a bag of chips and a package of gum for myself. "But seriously, what's the plan for tonight? Elizabeth is obviously on a mission to stick it to James, so she's going to be fighting dirty. We need to be ready."

She looks worried, and for some reason, I hate to see that look on her face.

"Hey, don't worry. I don't think Mr. Lavin is looking for concrete plans yet. After all, he's kept everything so hush-hush about this deal that we don't even know for sure that it's a bridal line."

Mya nods. "True. But I'm getting a bad feeling about this. Like maybe Elizabeth knows something we don't."

Despite my determination to stay positive, I'm pretty sure she's right.

———

I dress carefully for dinner.

Not that I don't put a lot of thought and attention into what I wear with every client, because I do, but this is Andre Lavin. The man doesn't just set trends, he starts fashion movements.

We're going to this dinner to convince him that Mirage is the best choice for his company's advertising and brand management, but make no mistake, he'll be checking us out as people, too. My hand hovers over a maroon tie before coming back to the lighter one I'm holding.

The interior of his plane was gray, so it's probably not a completely wild guess to assume he likes neutrals. Now that I think of it, most of his runway looks are monochromatic as well.

Hmmm.

Making a quick decision, I grab the gray tie. It's better to be on the conservative side until I've met him in person. My suit is already hanging in the closet, pressed and ready to go.

When I reach the lobby, the first person I see is Mya. My mouth drops open slightly. She turns, and it's like one of those scenes in a movie where time slows and birds start singing and shit.

Her dress is one of those magical drapes that probably looks like a bag when it's on the hanger, but on her body, it wraps each curve lovingly. Most of the other women roaming the lobby are wearing skirts so short you can tell whether they wear G-strings or bikinis, but Mya's dress is long enough to completely cover her knees.

Something about how she's so demurely covered up but yet rocking such obvious curves is a total turn on.

No, not a turn on. We are not turned on by a coworker.

My dick is not taking orders from my brain, as usual, so I button my jacket to give myself a little coverage. Not that it helps much, but anything is better than greeting a client with an extra arm extended for a shake.

"You're late," is the first thing out of her mouth as I approach. But I don't miss how her eyes roam up and down, taking in the custom-fitted suit and the bulge trying to bust through the seams of my pants to greet her. Her cheeks are slightly pink by the time she meets my eyes again.

If we weren't about to meet with a major potential-client, I would tease her about checking out my package, but this isn't the time to get Mya riled up. I need her on her game tonight, so I just tap my watch.

"Five minutes early, beautiful." The compliment slips out before I can question the wisdom of it, but Mya visibly blooms under the attention.

"But the Lavin Team is already here, which means we are late."

Since I've already thrown professionalism out the window, I gesture for her to spin around for me. After a slight pause she turns, giving me another glimpse of the round globes of her ass in the clinging material.

"You really are stunning, you know that?"

It comes out more intense than I meant for it to, but there's no help for it now. She's a vision and she should know it.

Mya bites her lip. "You don't think it's too short, do you?"

My eyebrows lift. "Short? It's not even showing kneecap. Half the chicks in here are flashing their Brazilians in plain view."

That gets a soft huff of laughter and the pinch in her forehead relaxes slightly. "Oh good. I didn't think so, but Will always said... well, never mind. I just like my skirts a little on the longer side."

Translation, the dipshit she was once engaged to made her feel bad about showing off her gorgeous body.

Insecure assholes are always worried about losing the woman they're with. Which should be a clue that they don't deserve the lady in question.

Before I can tell Mya exactly that, James appears at her elbow. "Mr. Lavin and his team are already seated. Luckily, Kevin and the others were early enough to greet them."

There's a subtle warning in his voice. We should have been here early and been the first ones to greet the client. Mya catches my eye and I can see that she's having the same thought.

There's no way we're letting Kevin worm his way in on this account.

Time to get our game faces on.

As we approach the table, everyone stands, and the introductions are made all around. Maybe it's because I'm watching Mr. Lavin so closely that I see how his eyes follow Mya after she shakes his hand and then walks around the table to greet the other members of his team. She knows all of their names, as do I. Then she takes a seat right next to me.

Before I can even sit down, James is already ordering a scotch from the waitress. Then I see why.

Elizabeth is sitting two tables away.

She raises her glass of wine in our direction. I turn to see

James give a begrudging wave. I'm not sure if anyone else has noticed her yet, but she's already accomplished her goal.

There's no way James can focus completely on the client tonight with his ex-wife sitting right in his line of vision.

"Thank you all for traveling to meet with me. I've had this week scheduled with potential investors for months, so it's been helpful that you could come to me while I'm already in the States."

"When do you go back to Italy?" Wallace asks. "I follow you on Instagram. You guys, his page is *lit*. Fast cars, beautiful clothes. You're living the dream, man." He sighs before digging into his salad course enthusiastically.

Andre just laughs. "Thank you. This is our goal, to be as the kids say, *fire*. Why is all of the American slang centered around temperature, I wonder? It used to be that things were *cool*, now they're *hot, fire, bomb* or *lit*. Fascinating. I have an entire team of people who study the social media trends."

James looks like he has no idea what is happening. But I strongly suspect that Wallace in his own unique, bumbling way has just broken the ice for us.

Well, if he's broken the ice, I might as well jump in first.

"Mirage employs a lot of talented young designers. It's why our ad campaigns are so on trend. We combine years of experience in understanding what makes people buy with the fresh perspective of different generations."

Mya grins over at me. "Wallace is on Milo's team. He's been with us for almost a year now and graduated from Columbia with honors. He's also an amateur photographer and is pretty popular on Instagram, too."

I glance over at her. *He is?* How does she know all that?

Maybe there is something to paying attention in those bullshit icebreaker sessions at work after all.

Wallace looks shocked, too. "My account has nowhere near

the numbers some of my friends have, but I just passed ten thousand.”

Mr. Lavin actually looks impressed. “That’s quite an accomplishment, especially for a hobbyist.” He clears his throat. “I’m happy to meet with you all in person after hearing about you from Mr. Lawson.”

James gives him a tight smile. “I’m extremely proud of my team.”

“It shows,” Andre replies.

Dinner proceeds with the typical pleasantries. Wallace looks a little confused, but I can only pray the kid can hold his tongue.

With these types of clients, you never rush right into business. You need to woo them, almost like a woman you’re trying to convince to come back to your place after dinner. She’s not just going to come with you if you ask within the first ten minutes. She needs you to show her that you’re worth her time.

Are you going to savor her the same way you do the ten-inch porterhouse on your plate?

Or will you rush through the act like a kid scarfing down an ice cream cone?

I can’t imagine a man like Andre Lavin scarfing anything. He needs to see that we’re not only the best team to take over his marketing but also that we’re people he can work with.

We need him to *like* us.

As the waitress is clearing the entrees, Andre looks around the table with satisfaction. “Perhaps it is old-fashioned, but I care to meet with any agencies that work on our marketing directly. It’s important that the people crafting our image understand what we’re about here at Lavin Couture.”

Everyone instantly ceases their side conversations and pays

attention. Now we're getting to the good stuff. The reason we're all here.

"What is your vision for the company, Mr. Lavin?" Mya asks. "I've read the official mission statement, but I would love to hear it from you."

"Please, call me Andre."

The way he's looking at her makes it clear he just wants to hear her say his name.

My hand sitting on top of the table curls into a fist. It shouldn't bother me. He's just a client, throwing a little charm at the pretty ad executive. I've seen it plenty of times, and I've had my fair share of clients, male and female, attempt to flirt with me.

None of those made me want to growl in frustration. Or made me worry that Mya might actually want to flirt back.

"It's much more than just the clothes," Andre begins after a brief pause. "Our brand creates the garments that become part of people's memories. And for our newest venture, we're looking for a partner that understands the importance of family, friendship, love."

The woman sitting next to him sniffs. *Cristiane Laveque.* From my research on the Lavin team, I know that she's a top designer for Lavin Couture.

"Apologies, but this is not a strength of American companies, we have found. So few understand *l'amore.*" She shakes her head ruefully as if the vulgar ways of the American market are just too much.

Mentally, I'm rolling my eyes, but this could be a real obstacle to winning their business. If they think that we're not cultured enough, it will be difficult to change that opinion. Granted, Mirage does plenty of "American" commercials and brands, but it's not like we're all racecars and beer. We have plenty of upper-echelon brands in the jewelry, hotel and entertainment industries.

"I believe Mirage can handle anything. We have such a diverse workforce that all of our clients find someone they can relate to. We also have more women in leadership roles than many of our competitors."

Maybe that'll calm her fears that we don't get *l'amore*. Mya in particular handles a lot of brands that cater to women, including a high-profile lingerie line.

Andre sits back in his chair and seems to be considering her words. "I must admit we've been approached by other firms that are run by people who are married. They understand what brides want."

James sits up straighter. "So, it is a bridal line?"

Andre laughs lightly. "Yes, the rumors are true. Lavin Couture will introduce a new line called Lavin Bridal next year. It will be a separate division of the company which is why I'm meeting with investors. I didn't want word to get out until it was all finalized."

James looks like he's going to be sick. This is why Elizabeth has been so smug. She must have heard the Lavin group wanted someone who has been through the process of planning a wedding. Just another way for her to rub her recent marriage in James's face.

"I'm sure all the women on our team have mentally planned their dream wedding, even if they aren't married." I send a panicked glance at Mya.

This would be a really good fucking time for her to pipe in with some story of how she's been dreaming of her wedding dress since she was a little girl.

Unfortunately, Andre seems to be following my line of thought because he turns directly to Mya, too. "If you were planning a wedding, for example," he says, "wouldn't you want a wedding planner who was married?"

Mya pauses with her water glass halfway to her mouth. "Well, yes. I suppose I would."

James just blinks. Wallace pauses mid-chew with a piece of iceberg lettuce hanging from his lip. The whole table seems stunned into silence. She didn't mean to say that, and everyone can see it on her face. But in a rare, caught-off-guard moment, Mya has done the unforgivable.

She's been honest.

An awkward silence descends over the table. James takes another gulp from his scotch. Across from me, members of the Lavin team exchange significant glances before taking an interest in their plates.

Worst of all, Andre Lavin just looks amused.

Meanwhile, Mya looks devastated.

You know how sometimes you can look back and identify the precise moment you fucked up? Well, later tonight I'm sure I'll be remembering the exact second I pushed us all off the cliff together.

"I agree," I state loudly.

James chokes slightly, and Wallace pounds him on the back. I ignore his panicked look and keep my eyes on Mr. Lavin.

"I agree with Mya," I repeat in case anyone at the table missed it the first time I pushed my career in front of a bus. "Having a married wedding planner would be great. Although I'd be more concerned about the people actually doing the work. That's really what sets Mirage apart."

By now, everyone is staring at me, especially James, probably wondering where the hell I'm going with this.

Mya, however, is watching me with a small, tremulous

smile on her face. Like she can't believe that I'm backing her up right now. And damn if that smile isn't what does me in.

Because I don't just bet on distracting Mr. Lavin, I double down and take it all the way to the bank.

"Mirage is really the best fit for anything to do with weddings. After all, it's the only agency I know with two team leads that are in love and engaged to be married." I turn to Mya and whisper, "Just go with it."

Then I tilt my head slightly and brush my lips over hers.

———

Find out more at www.mmalonebooks.com/begme

BEATRICE

Thinking about trying a dating app? My advice- *don't*. Seriously, save yourself.

If I wasn't on a dating app, I never would have been hiding in the bathroom of an Italian restaurant to avoid the most aggressive of Crypto Bros. And I never would have called the one person who *always* bails me out. August Gordon.

Once upon a time he was the adorkable guy who helped me with my biology homework. Now he is six-foot one with eyes like a dream. Now he's the guy who kissed me on the forehead before saying something that made Crypto Bro look scared for his life.

Nope. This is not happening.

I am not falling for my best friend. Because things between us have always been easy. Uncomplicated.

But if there's one thing I'm good at, it's complicating things.

Excerpt of BANG © M. Malone

I can't let him come outside with me. I already told him I called an Uber so I don't want him to see Auggie waiting for me.

And I *definitely* don't want Auggie to see him.

It's not like we haven't talked about dating before but something about Auggie actually seeing me on a date feels weird. Luca seemed good-looking on his profile, but standing next to August, I'm pretty sure he'll look like a pale imitation of what a man should be.

Actually seeing Auggie is pretty much a guarantee to kill any date, even if the guy isn't glued to his phone.

"You should go ahead," I continue. "It was nice meeting you, Luca."

But his grip only tightens, his voice holding a trace of annoyance as he says, "You're not going to let me see you home Bea? You already spent half the time in the bathroom and now you're leaving early? That's just rude."

I pull back, trying to yank my arm free. "What?"

His aggression is startling, an unwelcome shift from the apathetic facade he displayed earlier. I figured he'd be a little disappointed but not this upset. Then again, nothing about this date has been what I imagined it would be.

"You're one of those women who just use men. You just wanted a free dinner and now you're trying to ditch me," he snaps.

His words echo in my head. Yes, I was trying to ditch him but not for the reasons he thought.

"Um, I paid for my half of dinner. So..."

I wasn't going to message him again anyway but after this sudden show of aggression, I no longer feel even slightly bad about that decision. Now I just need to get away. But before can respond, or turn to walk away, I see a familiar figure come through the door of the restaurant.

August.

He takes in my stance next to the booth and Luca's hand on my arm with a darkening scowl. Luca follows my gaze to see what I'm looking at and he glances at me uncertainly as August heads our way.

"You're going to want to let go of her arm now," Auggie growls.

"Who are you?" Luca asks.

Instead of answering, Auggie steps closer until he's right up in Luca's face. The move breaks his hold on my arm, thankfully and I rub the spot which is already getting sore. Auggie sweeps his arm around, folding me close against his back and out of Luca's sight.

"Don't look at her," Auggie barks when Luca tries to look around him at me. "Talk to me."

"I don't even know you," Luca mutters.

"Exactly. And you don't know her either. From this moment on, you have permanent amnesia when it comes to her. Got it?"

"Wait a minute. You can't just–"

Auggie turns around, completely ignoring my blustering date behind him. His lips against my forehead shock me out of the trance I've been in since he showed up.

"Go wait for me right outside, okay?" Auggie says in a low voice.

"Okay," I mumble, not entirely sure what's going on but happy to get away.

Auggie watches me as I walk to the door of the restaurant. Once I push through, he turns back to Luca. There is a large party coming in at the same time as I'm leaving so I step aside to let them through.

Once it's clear, I step back up to the window to look back in. The guys are still talking but all I can see are their profiles. Auggie seems to tower over Luca, and with every word the other man seems to shrink. As Auggie continues to speak, Luca's shoulders hunch, his earlier bravado crumbling under August's intensity.

Finally August steps away and when he turns, his face is completely blank. Our eyes meet through the window and the air buzzes with something electric. Caught, I quickly step back and stare aimlessly at the cars going by. My heart is racing for some reason I can't identify.

What was that? I wouldn't have believed it if I hadn't seen it myself. My aggressive date had been completely shut down by whatever Auggie said.

And I am completely turned on.

Join the fun at patreon.com/minxmalone

also by m. malone

the mirage agency
(Office Romance / Romantic comedy)

Beg Me : My rooster is on strike. Yeah, I can't believe it either. But he'll only crow for one woman. Spoiler Alert *she hates me*

Ask Me : Am I arrogant? Maybe. Do women still want me? Abso-F'ing-lutely. Then I meet the one woman who isn't impressed.

Want Me : No strings attached. Sounds good, right? Except if I'm not her boyfriend ... the position is open for someone else.

Need Me : Crazy sh*t every day keeps relationships away. Except there's one guy who just *keeps* showing up. And if I'm not careful, I might get used to needing someone.

blue-collar billionaires

Inheriting billions from the father they never knew sounds like a pretty sweet deal. Until they find out what he really wants in exchange.

Tank : Fake Dating the billionaire's son should have been easy. He's a bad boy and not my type. But he's also loyal and kind with an unexpected soft spot for rescue cats. Suddenly all I want is for this "fake" love to be real.

Finn : When she left me, I had nothing. Now I have it all: money, cars and most importantly, power. She's struggling to save her business, and I'm in the perfect position to save it. For a price.

Gabe : She thinks I'm arrogant and cocky as hell. She's right. A reformed con artist and a perfect little princess don't belong together. But I still can't leave her alone.

Zack : She's my brother's ex. Off limits. But she needs a nude model for her show so I'm taking one for the team. Turns out she needs more than just my picture...

Luke : My online BFF is the only hacker better than I am. Then I'm asked to consult on a hacking case for the FBI and the hauntingly beautiful suspect seems to know a lot about me. Things I've only told one other person...

Blue-Collar Christmas : Emma has a plan to bring the high-rolling billionaire Marshall brothers back to their roots with the perfect blue-collar Christmas. But it turns out the "perfect" Christmas has a price tag no one expected...

bad business

(The Kingsleys)

Bad King: My parents just put a gold diggers target on my back. But if all they want is a wedding, I'll find the fiancee of their nightmares. *Who Wants to Marry a Billionaire? Must be completely inappropriate.*

Bad Blood : I'd do anything for my best friend's little sister. Until she asks for the one thing I can't give. One night. No rules. ***RITA® Award Winner!***

the alexanders

One More Day : "Good girl" Ridley has always attracted bad guys. Now she's on the run and has nowhere to hide. So when Jackson Alexander mistakes her for her twin, she decides to do something she knows is wrong. *She lies.*

The Things I Do for You : Nick Alexander finally has what the woman of his dreams needs. He'll give Raina a baby if she gives him what he wants. *Her.*

All I Want: All Kaylee wants is for Elliott Alexander to notice she's alive. When her car skids out of control on Christmas Eve, she's forced to reach out to the only man she trusts to save her. **(VIP List only)**

All I Need is You : When the man she loves leaves town after their steamy kiss, Kaylee Wilhelm is done. But when she's targeted by a stalker, Eli is the only one who can protect her.

Just One Thing : Bennett Alexander is a bona fide genius but he still can't figure out how to "get the girl". So he hires a dating tutor. What could go wrong? Other than falling for his teacher, of course.

One More Chance : Now that Ridley is expecting, everything is different. All she needs is for Jackson to pretend that he finds her as sexy as he used to, even if it's not true. But with a little advice from her meddlesome twin, she has a plan to seduce her own husband.

the simmons

Birthday Cake : Ever since Mara walked into her brother's dorm room freshman year and came face to face with a shirtless Trent, she's known he was *The One*. She finally has a plan to get him exactly where she wants him. *In her bed.*

He's the Man : Matt Simmons is over Army doctors poking him until he sees his old babysitter, now a physical therapist, is h-o-t. Suddenly he's seeing the benefits of therapy.

Say You Will : Mara Simmons has always known Trent Townsend is *The One*. But when she suspects his frequent business trips have *nothing* to do with business, she sets in motion a chain of events bigger than she can imagine and discovers that the man she loves just might be a stranger.

Join my VIP list for FREE books

newsletter.mmalonebooks.com

about the author

M. Malone is a RITA® Award winner and a NYT & USA Today Bestselling author of completely inappropriate romantic comedy. She lives with her husband and their two sons in the picturesque mountains of Northern Virginia even though she is afraid of insects, birds, butterflies and other humans.

She also holds a Master's degree in Business from a prestigious college that would no doubt be scandalized at how she's using her expensive education.

mmalonebooks.com

9 781938 789922